DEATH
prefers
BLONDES

caleb roehrig

Feiwel and Friends
New York

For my parents, Amy and Charlie Roehrig,
for a lifetime of support.

You've always been my biggest fans, and the feeling
is entirely mutual.

A Feiwel and Friends Book
An imprint of Macmillan Publishing Group, LLC
175 Fifth Avenue, New York, NY 10010

Our books may be purchased in bulk for promotional, educational,
or business use. Please contact your local bookseller or the Macmillan
Corporate and Premium Sales Department at (800) 221-7945 ext. 5442 or
by email at MacmillanSpecialMarkets@macmillan.com.

Library of Congress Control Number: 2018944940

ISBN 978-1-250-15582-5 (hardcover) /
ISBN 978-1-250-15581-8 (ebook)

Book design by Rich Deas
Feiwel and Friends logo designed by Filomena Tuosto

First edition, 2019

1 3 5 7 9 10 8 6 4 2

fiercereads.com

'Tis now the very witching time of night,

When churchyards yawn and hell itself
    breathes out

Contagion to this world: now could I drink
    hot blood,

And do such bitter business as the day

Would quake to look on . . .

Hamlet (act 3, scene 2)

PROLOGUE

Somewhere over the Atlantic Ocean

FORTY-THOUSAND FEET ABOVE THE EARTH, THE Boeing 777 shuddered violently on a delicate membrane of thin air, and the girl in 5A steadied her drink. With a sudden wobble, the aircraft dipped, drawing a sharp gasp from the man seated beside her, and he cast an instinctive glance out the window in their row. There was nothing to see—just a dizzying, sightless plunge through frozen darkness—and she wanted to apologize. The anger that swelled inside her was hot as the earth's core, its pull just as powerful, and it wouldn't surprise her if it was strong enough to drag two hundred and thirty-three tons of metal, plastic, and improbable human lives clean out of the atmosphere.

With an electronic *ding*, a voice came over the intercom. "Attention, passengers, due to some unexpected turbulence, the captain has turned on the fasten seat belt sign. For your safety and the safety of others, please return to your seats and keep your seat belts fastened until the sign has been turned off."

The man in 5B turned to her with a weak smile. "I hate this part. It always feels like the end, you know?"

She forced a smile—but it was always the end for someone, wasn't it? And as they hurtled westward, the nose of the plane carving through the air like a bullet, the end drew closer and closer. For her, maybe. For someone else, definitely. In only a few hours, they'd be landing; in only a few hours, she would set things in motion.

Soon, but still not soon enough.

There were scores to be settled, accounts left unpaid, and the empty ledger demanded its pounds of flesh. The plane shook again and the darkness inside of her stirred and rose, the inky airlessness of the night sky outside calling to it, like to like. Cold and comfortable, it whispered into her pounding blood—tasks and targets, friends and foes, a list of actions leading to a last, inexorable confrontation.

Leading to the end.

She turned to the window this time, but saw only her reflection looking back, pale and startling in the overhead light. How long had it been since she'd last recognized herself? How many weeks had passed while she was lost and lonely, sinking like a chain through fathoms of hurt and grief and self-recrimination? But now something vibrated in the darkness that spilled through her veins, something familiar and furious, and one heartbeat at a time it lifted her up.

She'd found herself again, at last, and she was coming for those who had wronged her with deadly trouble to share. The plane stumbled and dipped again, but she smiled.

Hell itself couldn't stop her now.

Act One:
OUTRAGEOUS FORTUNE

AS IT TURNED OUT, A PISSED-OFF DRAG QUEEN

with a grappling hook was a force to be reckoned with. Crouched low between an SUV and a hybrid sedan on the fourth floor of a downtown Los Angeles parking garage, her blond hair tucked away beneath a platinum wig, Margo Manning stared up at her best friend with a growing sense of concern. Axel Moreau (also known as Liesl Von Tramp) towered above her, his knuckles white around the stock of a crossbow onto which the dangerously sharp tool was mounted, his extravagantly beautiful face drawn into a furious scowl.

"Well, where the fuck is he?" Axel snapped, voice barely in check. His heavily made-up eyes were focused out over the structure's railing, aimed across the alleyway at the upper windows of the facing building; but his tone was accusatory—and Margo knew that both his question, and the venom with which it was posed, were directed at her.

Fact was, he'd made no effort to hide his anger that night. Fact was, he'd told her to her face not twelve hours earlier that if anything went wrong with this job—and he was sure it would—he'd never forgive her. But in the past, no matter what personal issues he had, with Margo or anyone else, Axel had always been able to pull it together when the time came. When he wanted to, he could focus like a laser, even under the worst of pressure; it was why Margo had always known she could count on him. Now, watching his cool facade come apart at the seams, his fingers flexing anxiously on the expensive piece of gear clutched in his hands, she began to wonder if she'd made a huge mistake.

"Can you handle this, Liesl?" Margo asked with a military crispness. Their team had a rule: From the moment they suited up, it was drag names only until the end of the night—even Margo, the only one who wasn't *technically* a drag queen. Along with the makeup that dramatically altered their appearance, the contrasting and brightly colored wigs that concealed their hair and drew eyes away from physical characteristics that were harder to disguise, and the nylon bodysuits that hugged artificially padded curves, it was one more way to reduce the risk that one of them might be identified. "Because if you're having trouble keeping your shit together, then you can trade places with Dior and take some time to calm down."

"Don't tell me to calm down!" Axel spun on the chunky rubber heel of one boot, dark eyes flashing below the fringe of his neon-red wig. Even through the layers of foundation, powder, and rouge on his face, she could see his color starting to rise. "We've got no idea what's happening in there! He's *late*. We should have heard from him by now—he should be in place!" Axel shook his head, the crystals glued to his cheekbones glittering in the slanted light cast through the cold, concrete garage from the electrified city outside. "I told you, Margo. I *told* you something bad would happen. Joaquin's never done anything like this before! If he's been caught, he won't have any idea—"

"*Anita* will be fine," Margo stated, pointedly correcting Axel's careless use of a real name. "We're only five minutes off schedule, and there are a million possible reasons for that kind of delay."

"And one of them is that he's been caught." Axel pursed his lips, staring daggers into her. When he spoke again, his voice was unsteady. "One of them is that you sent my little brother into the lions' den, alone, on his very first job, and he's already been caught because he has *no fucking clue* how to do this." Tossing a hand up, he let it slap down against his side, eyes glistening. "How could you, Margo? How could you talk him into this behind my back? He's only fifteen!"

Margo wanted to point out that she and Axel had been "only fifteen" when they first started down this particular road together two years earlier—two bored kids breaking into Malibu mansions when they knew the owners were vacationing in Saint-Tropez or Saint Thomas, making off with cash and useless trinkets to hock at pawn shops in deteriorating neighborhoods; but now was not the time to indulge in argument. Rising to her feet, she looked her best friend in the eye and spoke as calmly as possible. "I didn't talk Quino into anything; he asked to be a part of the team—he practically begged." The boy opened his mouth, but she silenced him with a warning gesture. "Listen to me: I made him prove himself just like everybody else. He knows how to fight. He ran the obstacle course and didn't falter once, and even beat my time at it. He beat *your* time, Axel." Placing her hands on his shoulders, she met his eyes. "He's good—better than good. I know he can do this. And I hope you know me well enough to trust that I'd never put someone in play if they weren't ready."

"You should have told me," Axel insisted stonily, his false eyelashes casting spidery shadows across his cheeks. Margo hated those things; they were cumbersome and hampered peripheral vision, creating variables she couldn't control—but the boys had been appalled at her attempt to ban them. Davon had been ready to go on strike over the matter, rising up to his full six foot five in stiletto pumps, declaring, *"If you want to take my lashes, honey, you're gonna have to cut off my fucking head to get them."*

"You and I can fight about this later." Margo stepped back, her words cold steel. "But right now, we've got work to do. This job called for five people. We needed to add someone anyway, and I gave *Anita* the same shot I'd give anyone. She has the skills, the guts, and—most important—I trust the bitch." Reaching down, she yanked the crossbow out of Axel's hands and hoisted it up, angry streetlight gilding the metal grappling hook a sulfurous gold. "You want to protect your brother? Then pull on your big-girl pants, do the job I know you're capable of, and we'll all be safe in bed two hours from now."

With that, she shoved the contraption against Axel's padded chest. They continued to glare at each other for a long moment; but, finally, the boy put his hands back on the stock and foregrip, adjusted his hold, and turned to look out over the railing of the parking garage once more. Four stories below stretched the fragmented pavement of a wide alley, strewn with trash and reeking of urine, while directly across from them stood the three-tiered Beaux-Arts building that housed the Los Angeles Museum of Fine Art. It was just after four in the morning, the quietest hour that downtown LA had to offer, but light spilled over every inch of stone, brick, and concrete in sight nonetheless; even the sky overhead was scummed with an orange glow, a lingering haze drifting in the night sky and reflecting back the city's endless wakefulness.

Somewhere inside the museum, provided he hadn't already been discovered by LAMFA's twenty-four-hour private security team, was Joaquin Moreau—also known as Anita Stiffwon—Axel's little brother. And five minutes ago, he was supposed to have given them a signal that he was in position, that the coast was clear, and that the break-in Margo had spent weeks planning could finally commence.

At the time, recruiting Joaquin had seemed like a brilliant idea. Already Margo had been forced to turn down two different well-paid jobs, because no matter how many different scenarios she ran in her head, she couldn't come up with a strategy that wouldn't expose their four-person team to unnecessary risk. She, Axel, Davon, and Leif had earned a reputation—one she greatly enjoyed having, even if she couldn't brag about it—and she refused to get cocky, take bad risks just because the prestige would be all the greater if she managed to pull it off. They needed to add someone new to their ranks . . . but an elite group of anonymous teenage thieves can't exactly put out an ad online.

Enter Joaquin Moreau. Like his brother, he was a trained acrobat; like his brother, he was someone Margo had already known for years; and, like his brother, he was never going to take no for an answer. Axel had limped home too many times with ruined makeup, inexplicable injuries, and even less explainable cash, for his nocturnal activities to remain a mystery forever. Quino wasn't stupid—another point in his favor—and from the minute he realized what was going on under his very nose, he had demanded to join the team.

Margo knew Axel would be angry about it, which was why she did it behind his back—and she at least had the decency to feel sort of guilty about it. But she'd assumed the guy would get over himself when he took some time to breathe, when he saw what his brother could do and how much sense the new lineup made. But now, with each second that passed, each moment with no sign from Joaquin, the silence stretched tighter and tighter between Margo and her best friend, like a cord looped around both their necks. If anything *had* gone wrong . . .

The comm crackled to life in Margo's ear so suddenly she

almost gasped, a hushed and intent voice—Joaquin's voice—reporting over the airwaves, "*Set.*"

"That's it," Margo said, making a show of double-checking the straps on her harness as an excuse to hide the relief on her face. "It's go time."

Axel set his lips into a thin line, but dropped to one knee, grappling hook up, and turned to watch over the railing for his own signal. At the same time, thirty feet behind them up the parking ramp, the side door of an unmarked panel van slid open, and another black-clad figure emerged. Tall and lithe, with vibrant purple locks skimming his shoulders, Leif Dalby sprang toward them through the shadows as graceful as a cat.

"Electra Shoxx, reporting for duty." Leif gave a mock salute when he reached them, flashing an easy grin, the only one of them who never seemed ruffled. Axel refused to acknowledge him, serving up the same cold shoulder he'd given all of them since first learning of Joaquin's participation, but Margo offered the newcomer a welcoming nod.

"Ready?" She tugged at the straps of her harness a third time, and Leif mimicked her motions, testing out his own.

"I'm always ready," he answered cockily, his delicate, almost elfin features shimmering with powder in the amber light. He'd drawn his cheekbones in a high arch, his mouth a cupid's bow, and his eyes smoldered like a femme fatale's from the silent era. He was insultingly pretty.

Margo cast a glance back at the parked van, the side door slowly gliding shut again. All she could see of the driver was a single gloved hand resting against the dashboard, but she waved anyway, and two fingers forked her a peace sign in response. Davon Stokes (drag name: Dior Galore) was their resident gearhead and wheelwoman, and if their luck held, he'd remain in the van throughout, engine ready for their getaway.

Out across the alley, the offices on LAMFA's third floor were dark, a row of windows that gleamed like squares of black stone above a shallow ledge supported by decorative corbels. As Margo, Leif, and Axel watched, something flared suddenly in the shadowy room directly opposite and roughly ten feet below their position— a red-gold ember throbbing and expanding, gradually turning a bright, dazzling white; and then an angry, orange furrow began to crawl across the glass, a molten snail trail appearing inch by inch as Joaquin Moreau used a super-heated wand to cut through the pane.

Most of the museum's exhibits were housed on the first and second floors, and the windows were barred, the glass wired to trigger an alarm if it were shattered; but one side of the third floor was exclusively administrative space, and high enough off the ground that bars had been deemed an unnecessary expense. These potential entry points, low-risk though they were, had still been armed with motion sensors; a burglar would have to first scale the building to the third floor without getting caught, and then somehow climb in through a window that couldn't be opened.

The solution, Margo had eventually determined, was to simply cut the glass clean from the frame—and preferably with as little noise as possible.

"You did at least teach him how to use that thing safely, right?" Axel asked through his teeth, as the glowing track of molten glass crept unevenly forward.

Margo and Leif cut each other a glance, and she huffed, "I'm not even going to dignify that with an answer."

The wand was not a tool to play around with. None of the tools they used were to be played around with. The grappling hook in Axel's hands, for instance, could cause damage, death, or grievous bodily harm in limitless ways, and Margo had made every member of the team—herself included—practice with it for hours to ensure safe handling. Every job was hazardous, and ugly surprises were everywhere; and as the team's leader, Margo's chief responsibility was to eliminate or minimize as many dangers as she could.

Eventually, the wand completed its sluggish journey, and the wide square of shining glass melted into the shadows of the empty office. A few seconds later, Margo's comm activated again, Joaquin's hushed voice coming through with the next signal. "*Clear.*"

Her skin prickled, adrenaline brightening her blood in a sudden rush, and anticipation flooded the air. This was the moment she lived for: this addictive, heart-pounding instant when the night rested on a fulcrum, success or ruination waiting at the slightest tip of the scales. The feeling ran through her like a current—ran through all three of them, all five. She could sense it sizzling around them like a force field. This was it.

All business now, Axel aimed the crossbow out over the railing of the garage, staring down the telescopic sight at the exposed window. They all knew how to operate the device, how to use it without maiming themselves—but Axel had an uncanny sense for the weight of the hook, the path along which it would fall when he fired at the target. Margo had meant it when she said she'd swap him with Davon, but she'd been hoping she wouldn't have to. No one could drive like Dior Galore, and no one could aim like Liesl Von Tramp; she needed both queens right where they were.

Axel took his time lining up the shot, his hands steady as a surgeon's, and then he released a breath and squeezed the trigger. With a *snap*, the grappling hook was cast into space, its sharpened teeth flashing hungrily, pulling fifty feet of lightweight cable behind it. The shot was off, though, Margo could already see—the eager metal claws flying too high, too far to the right—and her stomach dipped. Then she watched in awe as the device arced and pulled, obeying the wind and its own weight, curving back toward the target and then plunging straight through the center of the missing window. Axel had been right again.

The comm crackled. *"I've got it."*

"Good work," Margo breathed out, but her best friend ignored the praise. All business, he rested the crossbow against the wall, gathered their end of the cable in his hands, and began taking up the slack.

Within seconds the line was stretched taut as a bowstring between the parking garage and the empty office on the museum's third floor. Pulling hard on the cable to check its integrity, Axel secured their end of it around the SUV's trailer hitch in an elaborate knot.

Finding an SUV in a Los Angeles car park was like looking for hay in a haystack; finding one with a trailer hitch presented more of a challenge; finding an SUV with a trailer hitch, left overnight in a middle spot on the east-facing side of the fourth floor of the structure across from LAMFA, was an impossible order. This one they'd been lucky enough to find on the south ramp of the seventh floor, and it had been a matter of minutes for Davon to work past the locks, hack the ignition, and move it to the necessary location.

With the cable anchored, Margo rose to her feet, buckling the straps of a heavy-duty nylon satchel across her back. Moving to the railing, she eased her hips onto the edge of the wall, casting a glance along the alley and out to the street. It was quiet; the drunks were indoors, the roadway free of cars, and the windows were dark in the buildings that surrounded the museum.

Checking her harness one last time, Margo clipped it onto the cable, and turned to face the boys. "You guys know the drill."

"See you on the other side," Leif responded, eyes bright as he readied his own clip.

Axel didn't answer right away. His eyes were dark, his glossy lips pulled into a hard knot, like he'd trapped something he was afraid to let out. Finally, in a stiff voice, he declared, "If anything goes wrong, I'm not leaving without my brother."

Margo opened her mouth to speak, and then snapped it shut again. If something went wrong, their rule was to scatter—immediately—and to start lining up their alibis. But this was the other half of her mistake: ignoring what she knew of her best friend's character and letting herself hope he would simply accept Joaquin's presence. Every choice Axel made was to protect his family, and deep down she'd known this would be a problem. What scared her wasn't that she'd misjudged the situation, or even that she'd failed to listen to her own intuition, but that she'd accepted this risk out of the hubristic certainty that the moment to enact their emergency protocol would never come; that they were just too good.

A chill breeze gusted up the alley, tossing the white tresses of Margo's wig, and she fought the urge to shiver. Her eyes on Axel's, she stated, "We'll make sure nothing goes wrong, then."

Turning around, she swung her legs over the railing, four floors up, and dropped into thin air.

2

A SUDDEN PUFF OF WIND RUSHED THROUGH THE
gutted window of the third-floor office, lifting a few errant papers
scattered on the desk. Crouched in a corner of the room, ears tuned
to the possibility of sounds from the hallway outside, Joaquin
Morcau watched across the alley as Margo shared some final words
with his older brother. He couldn't see Axel's face from his position,
and he was pretty sure he didn't want to. Given the way they'd left
things earlier in the afternoon, "not seeing each other's faces" felt
like a pretty good long-term strategy. Maybe a permanent one.

Expelling a breath, he consciously pushed the conflict from his
mind, rolling his shoulders and working a few more kinks out of
his neck.

He'd been testing the limits of his flexibility since he was five
years old, his mother walking him through splits and backflips
and boneless contortions that defied human physiology, his joints
bending like wire with the slightest discipline. All he'd needed for
motivation were the jaw-dropping videos she would play for him
of her glory days with the Cirque du Soleil; her face painted like
a woodland goddess, her body an impossible coil wrapped in

glittering scales or vivid feathers, Jacinta Flores was magnificent. Joaquin idolized her, wanted to *be* her, and the smile she gave him every time he mastered a new trick felt like sunshine.

He'd terrified a new nanny once during a game of hide-and-seek, folding his body up so compactly that he'd disappeared into an empty drawer in the kitchen. The poor woman had searched the house for nearly an hour, growing increasingly frantic, until she'd finally called Joaquin's mom in a state of abject fear at having lost her employer's son.

"Check the drawers," Jacinta had suggested automatically, "and if you find Quino, tell him that the next time he tricks someone into playing hide-and-seek, he better hope he stays lost."

One hour stuffed in a drawer had been boring, but compared to how he'd spent the past twelve, he remembered it like a vacation. Reflexively, his shoulders rolled again.

Across the way and one story up, he watched as Margo swung her legs over the railing and hurtled into space. Feet raised and head back, her body was sleek and straight, flying like a bullet along the tense cable. The grappling hook pulled hard against the metal pipe where Joaquin had anchored it, but it held, and within seconds, the girl's boots were thumping against the stone ledge outside.

Hoisting herself up, Margo unclipped her harness and climbed through the window, taking care not to jar the sash and set off the motion sensors. Leaping to the floor, she hurried into the shadows beside Joaquin, her eyes gleaming with excitement. Squeezing his arm gently, she murmured, "Nice work, Anita."

Joaquin couldn't keep the smug pride out of his voice. "Thanks, Miss Anthropy."

Margo's honorary drag name was an awkward mouthful. Everyone hated it, but the more they tried to talk her out of it, the more stubbornly Margo insisted it was perfect. And, in the sense that she liked it so much because it annoyed everyone who had to deal with it, it *was* sort of perfect.

"Any trouble?" Margo gave him a serious look, inquiring about the delay.

"I met a rat with a grudge and had to take a detour." Hastily, Joaquin added, "I don't want to talk about it. Otherwise, everything went like clockwork." On the other side of the alley, Leif Dalby levered himself up onto the wall, his athletic body long and sinuous in the golden streetlight. Self-consciously, Joaquin reached up and ran gloved fingers through the shiny, acid-green waves of his hairpiece. "Do I look okay? Is my wig straight?"

Margo hesitated just long enough that Joaquin knew she was going to lie, and then offered him a chipper, "You look fine!"

"*Fine?*"

"I'm serious, you look amazing." She waved a hand, trying for damage control, but it was far too late.

"Obviously, I do *not* look amazing, or you'd have said, 'You look amazing,' and you wouldn't have said it like you were trying to cheer up someone in an electric chair," Joaquin sputtered. "'*You look fine*' means 'even Bigfoot wouldn't fuck you!'"

"I hear Bigfoot has pretty low standards. You might be surprised."

"Not. Funny."

"Okay! You've got a little bit of lipstick on your teeth." She pointed at her own mouth in a helpful demonstration. "And your contouring is sorta . . . Kabuki-ish."

"*Kabuki-ish?*" The grappling hook pulled again as Leif jumped from the parking garage, flying their way along the makeshift zip line. Joaquin fumbled in the bag he had slung across his back, producing a soiled cosmetic sponge, which he thrust at Margo with an urgent, "Quick! Blend me!"

"Relax, you drama queen," Margo said kindly. "No one is going to judge you."

And then Leif was unhooking his harness and stealing quietly over the windowsill, crouching down and reporting his success over the comms. Joaquin swiped blindly at his face with the sponge a few times, hoping he wasn't just making the problem worse, and straightened up. Outside, the cable drooped as it was uncoupled from the SUV's trailer hitch, allowing Leif to free the hook from the metal pipe and throw it back out into the night. It glittered menacingly as it flew across the alley again and began a herky-jerky return to the fourth floor while Axel reeled it in.

Joaquin tossed his wig nonchalantly and tried to look composed as Leif crept over to them. Eyes bright, the violet-haired boy flashed them an exuberant grin that showed every one of his perfect teeth. "Everything's all right? No trouble?"

"Nothing I couldn't handle," Joaquin answered, trying to sound cool.

"Your brother was convinced they had you in the basement, hooked up to a car battery."

Joaquin huffed out an exasperated sigh. Axel couldn't give him credit for anything. When he was six, and kids were picking on him at school—for the way he walked, the way he talked, the way he always wanted to play a girl superhero during make-believe—it was a relief to have his older brother looking out for him, fearless and protective, ready to swing on anyone. But at some point Axel's protectiveness went from being the thing that gave Joaquin his freedom to a burden the boy constantly had to fight his way out from under.

Plucking irritably at his gloves, Joaquin asked, "How pissed is he?"

Leif's tone was diplomatic. "It's hard to say, since he's not speaking to any of us."

Joaquin was winding up an even more aggrieved sigh, when Margo interjected, "He'll get over it." She said it firmly, but they all knew this was unlikely. Axel was the kind of guy who would only agree to forgive and forget if you died first.

After a moment of silence, Joaquin realized that Leif was scrutinizing his face, and heat rushed to his cheeks. Holding up a hand, he said, "Listen. I had to put this face on while sealed up in a wall with nothing but a penlight and a hand mirror!"

The other boy blinked in surprise. "Huh?"

"My makeup." Joaquin shut his eyes, cheeks burning even hotter. "I know it's bad, but these were extreme circumstances. I'm usually better than this, I swear!"

"Your face looks fine," Leif replied, seeming genuinely bewildered by the outburst; and even though he'd used the same word Margo had—*fine*—it sounded like an actual compliment, rather than a genteel southern insult. Narrowing his eyes, Joaquin cut the girl a suspicious glance. She was biting her lips and trying not to look him in the eye, and he decided then and there that he was going to kill her. Oblivious, Leif added, "I was just . . . I guess I never noticed how much you look like your mom."

"Oh. Uh, yeah." Joaquin self-consciously fingered the strands of his wig again. "You can really see it when I'm in makeup. Axel takes more after Dad."

An awkward pause followed—the same one that seemed to come on the heels of any mention of his dad these days—and Joaquin deflated just a little, silently cursing his father for ruining yet another moment in his life. The outward ripple of Basil Moreau's selfishness was as destructive as it was endless. Scrambling to fill the uncomfortable silence, Leif coughed. "Wait. '*Sealed up in a wall*'? Miss Anthropy here told us you were hiding out in a wing that was under renovation."

Both boys turned their eyes on Margo, and she tossed her hands out defensively. "Technically he *was* hiding in a wing that's under renovation!"

Technically, Joaquin had been crouched in a wall cavity behind a maintenance access panel in said wing, where a new air filtration system was due to be installed the next week. At four o'clock that afternoon, dressed in nondescript street clothes, the boy had entered the museum through the main entrance, a hat pulled low over his forehead, a pair of costume glasses perched on his nose; a fortuitously convenient distraction in the form of two live rats appearing suddenly and mysteriously in the Grand Hall had provided him the cover he needed to slip past the guards and safety cordons, and into the bowels of LAMFA.

The maintenance panel had been easy to open, thanks to a mechanized lockpick Margo had produced from her seemingly bottomless bag of tricks, but it was the next step that posed the real challenge. Twelve hours in a dark and nearly airless space, essentially the two-bedroom equivalent of a gym locker, had been the true test of Joaquin's commitment to being part of the team—a trial by fire he'd endured without complaint. At the appointed hour, he'd emerged from the wall and, aided by rubberized pads strapped to his elbows and knees, slithered up an air vent to the third floor.

With a pointed look at the display on her watch, Margo announced, "Okay, enough wasted time. Let's lock this thing down." As a group, the three of them moved to the door of the office, pausing to listen at the jamb for noise in the corridor outside. Quietly, Margo said, "Remember: Once the main power goes out, there's only thirty seconds to disable the backup, or we're screwed."

Leif saluted. "We got it."

"And stay off the comms unless absolutely necessary," she added.

"Right."

"And remember to head for the extraction point the second your job's done."

"And put on a sweater, and feed the dog, and call Grandma," Leif continued for her, twirling his wrists. "Stop freaking out, girl. We know the drill."

Margo nodded. "Then it's go time."

ORDINARILY, THE LOS ANGELES MUSEUM OF FINE ART HAD three watchmen on duty overnight, one positioned behind a bank of monitors in a room on the ground floor, with the others making semiregular sweeps of the building's many substantial galleries. Two weeks earlier, however, LAMFA had unveiled an important new exhibit of rococo paintings—rarely circulated canvases from eighteenth-century masters like Watteau, Boucher, and Fragonard— that were on loan from the French government. The collection was priceless, and a strengthening of security measures had been named as a prime condition in permitting the prestigious works to be presented. For that reason, two additional guards had been added to the graveyard shift, and new fail-safes had been introduced to the alarms.

On top of new guards and scarier alarms, the army of wall-mounted cameras that watched over every corner of the museum's exhibition spaces had also been updated. Enough prying eyes to make Big Brother jealous, these produced a regular feed, and left a miserably scant number of blind spots to exploit. One vulnerable area, however, was the third-floor administrative corridor, with its dusty potted plants and managerial offices, and another was LAMFA's extensive ventilation system.

With so much canvas, wood, and gesso on display, the museum required a continuously moving supply of clean, dry air. Thus, a vast network of ducts spread throughout the building like veins, metal tunnels connecting every room and every floor, with entrance and exit points as regular as subway stops.

And, lucky enough, one of those stops happened to be at the end of the administrative corridor itself.

Leif shivered a little—with adrenaline, rather than nerves—as he and Joaquin came to a stop beneath a wide, rectangular hole in the wall, some ten feet up off the ground. It was an air vent, but the grate had been removed and now lay discarded on the floor. The hallway was dimly lit, the bright red glow of an emergency exit sign beating down on them from the door to a back stairway, casting an illusion of warmth.

Joaquin nodded at the hole, his lips shiny and his wig a strange grayish-brown in the ruddy light. "This is where I came in. It should be a straight shot down from here for both of us. More or less."

"I've got the grid memorized," Leif murmured, unhooking his pack and fishing out the rubber knee and elbow pads he'd need for the descent. His eyes skimmed furtively over Joaquin—taking in the boy's elegant neck and long fingers, the slim waist and sinewy limbs—and he fumbled a little with the straps in his hands.

They'd met each other a year ago, the first and only time Leif had been to the Moreaus' home—shortly before everything went to hell—and hadn't seen each other since. Axel still talked about Joaquin like a nosy, tagalong kid, a nuisance frozen in amber, and so Leif was a little startled by *this*. This *guy*, practically his own age, lithe and confident and apparently just as capable as Margo had promised.

A little wave of guilt washed over him. Right after he'd hooked himself up to the zip line, just as he was about to throw himself ten feet down and thirty feet across into the bosom of an art heist already in progress, Axel had made Leif promise to protect Joaquin.

"Swear you'll make sure nothing happens to him," Axel demanded.

"And you should swear on your life, because I will untie this fucking cable when you're halfway across and drop your skinny ass straight down into that alley if you don't."

He already felt like kind of a shitty friend for not joining Axel's protest when the news that Quino had been recruited to the squad was first made known; but as Leif looked up and down at the boy beside him, he felt disloyal and weird in a whole new way. Hormones were a son of a bitch.

Pads in place, Leif got to his feet, eager to lose himself in the mission and find his mental equilibrium again. "Okay. Once I get down to the basement, I'll signal you on the comms. Until then, we're radio silent."

"Sounds good to me." Joaquin tossed a few ferociously ugly green tresses out of his face and took a step back, gesturing at Leif with his right hand. "Gimme a boost."

"What? No." Leif shook his head. "I'm going in first. *You* give *me* a boost."

The other boy folded his arms across his chest. "I've already climbed up those ducts once, and I know what we're dealing with. I should be the one in front."

"We'll get to your position first, which means I'll have to wait behind you while you let yourself out. Plus, I have experience, and your brother will kill me if anything goes wrong." Leif ticked the points off on his fingers. "Not to mention the fact that I'm taller than you are, and if you go first and I lose my grip or something I could fall on top of you."

"Maybe I'd like having you on top of me," Joaquin rejoined immediately, and for just a moment, Leif was speechless. His eyes widened, his mouth dropped open, and the green-haired boy took full advantage of his surprise.

Leaping almost three feet into the air, Joaquin kicked off the wall opposite the vent, launching himself back across the narrow corridor and the rest of the way up to the shadowy opening. His boots gleamed with the red burn of the exit sign as he kicked a leg up, folding his body into the duct with impossible agility. Glancing back over his shoulder to where Leif continued to stare in amazement, the boy winked and then dropped out of sight.

3

A SMILE COULD BE JUST AS USEFUL AS A grappling hook if you knew how to wield it right. Other natural resources Margo had learned to weaponize included: doe eyes, short skirts, the male libido, and her well-known last name. They weren't all as fun as firing a metal claw thirty feet through the air or slicing a hole in a pane of glass without a sound—but, employed properly, they could be three times as effective.

Two weeks earlier, out of pseudo-drag and in her regular, daytime persona, Margo had waltzed right through the front door of the museum, there to attend the aggressively hyped reception for the high-profile rococo exhibit. The invitation had been just one of many that came like clockwork addressed to her father, this one being exclusively for LAMFA's top-level donors.

Come join us for an evening of hors d'oeuvres, wine, and fine art, the embossed cardstock had implored, *as we celebrate the grand opening of PASSIONS TO ELEVATE THE SOUL, our temporary exhibition of rarely seen works by the French masters of the 18th Century.*

It had been a stultifying evening, one boring and self-congratulatory speech leading into another, lists of names read aloud and glasses raised to people Margo didn't know and didn't want to. Finally, the guests were released to mingle, drink, and admire brushstrokes—and, with a sigh of unmitigated relief, she'd made a beeline for a young man with an official LAMFA ID badge, whose eyes had not left her boobs for the entire presentation.

She'd tossed her hair, batted her eyes, flattered his muscles, and generally played the Dumb Blonde to the hilt. Then she'd slipped her arm through his and nonchalantly mentioned that her father *might* be thinking of lending a few masterpieces from his private collection to LAMFA—but how could he be certain the museum would keep them safe?

What followed had been the only truly interesting lecture she'd heard all evening, as the young man offered up a bounty of precise details regarding the museum's security protocols. Two days later, when she'd gone downtown to bring her favorite corrupt city employee a bagged lunch composed of hundred-dollar bills sandwiched between other hundred-dollar bills, she'd walked out with blueprints and schematics of the Beaux-Arts building—a complete overview, right down to the ductwork and wiring.

Now as she stood at the head of the administrative corridor, staring intently at the backside of the door that would let her out into a glossy, gilt-edged, camera-filled maze of art, she hoped that all her information was accurate—that all her precautionary efforts had this job as close to a slam dunk as possible. She hoped that they hadn't been seen, and that no drunk would make the mistake of wandering up the alley to take a tinkle and play Good Samaritan by reporting the damaged window to the police.

Breathing softly, waiting for her comm to activate, standing as still as one of the statues that waited in the gloomy chambers ahead, Margo went over the plan again and again. She'd been precise; she'd been careful.

But there were always ugly surprises.

INCHING STRAIGHT DOWN A METAL CHUTE FOR ALMOST thirty feet proved to be about as easy as inching thirty feet straight up it in the first place. Joaquin had been so determined to prove himself, so proud of his daring exit line—*maybe I'd like having you on top of me.* He'd had a crush on Leif Dalby since the first time he saw him, with his freckles and flirtatious grin, and he'd been so determined to impress the guy that he hadn't really stopped to consider that maybe going first was a mistake. Twelve hours trapped in a wall followed by a three-story climb up a glorified chimney had taken its toll; a subtle burn was beginning to develop in his shoulders and thighs as he maneuvered down the ventilation duct.

It didn't help that Leif really *was* practically on top of him, his large and booted feet mere inches above Joaquin's boot-averse skull. It didn't help either that, in spite of the conditioned air flowing around them, sweat was starting to roll from beneath the itchy, synthetic cap of his wig.

When he finally reached his destination, a wide metal grate set into a wall on the first floor, offering a view into a cramped and dismally appointed room, Joaquin was practically delirious with relief. From his pouch, he produced a small, battery-operated device—another tool from Margo's spectacular arsenal—that used powerful magnets to turn screws from the inside, rotating their threads and forcing them out.

Within seconds Joaquin freed three corners of the grate, allowing the vent to swing open, and he gulped in a blessed mouthful of musty-smelling air. Scrambling up, he eased through the opening and dropped quietly to the floor. Behind him, Leif continued down the shaft, offering a silent and abbreviated wave before he vanished.

Dusting himself off, Joaquin looked around, on high alert. Raw wood shelves bore a bounty of cleaning supplies beside the dented cover of a sizable fuse box; a sink set into the floor gave off the sickly reek of mildew; and an array of ancient-looking pipes, crusted with lime deposit, rose up through the floor. It was a custodial closet, a hidden corner of LAMFA's sprawling empire, which happened to share a wall with the central guardroom.

Cords snaked through holes in the ceiling, over thirty of them, twisting together in groups of five and six before disappearing through the wall to feed the bank of monitors that allowed the watchmen to see the entire museum at a glance. Swallowing uncomfortably, Joaquin eyed the jumble of brightly colored cables, trying not to feel overwhelmed. Each one of the lines brought in the relays from multiple cameras, representing a hundred or more views throughout the museum, on alternating four- and five-second intervals.

Digging into his pouch, Joaquin pulled out yet another useful device: a portable monitor attached to an auxiliary cord, which ended in a clip fitted with sharp metal teeth. When snapped around any one of the cables, the clip would slice through the rubber casing and complete a circuit with the wire underneath, splitting the video feed and siphoning it to his private screen.

All he needed to do was isolate the input from the third floor, figure out where all the cameras were, determine the exact order in which the relays alternated, note which feeds would be up on separate monitors at the same time, negotiate a safe passage, and commit the information to memory. And he had to do it before Leif got into position in the basement. No sweat.

Drawing a shaky breath, he fitted the clip around one of the many snaking cords and drove its teeth home.

THE MUSEUM'S BACKUP POWER GENERATOR WAS UNMISTAK-able, a fifteen-foot-wide metal enclosure housing a diesel-powered riot of tubes and wires—a slumbering, steampunk dragon just waiting for its wake-up call. Margo's source at the reception hadn't offered any details about make and model, merely boasting that, "In the *highly unlikely* event of a power outage," the museum had a secondary system that would automatically come online within thirty seconds; so Leif had studied countless schematics from different manufacturers, wanting to make sure he'd be ready, no matter what.

In the highly unlikely event of a power outage: The generator would kick in, and any alarm that had been tripped in the interim would start screaming immediately. If the generator did not kick in—which was Leif's objective—the alarms would stay silent and the video feeds blank. But the guards would still call for backup, and police response times were somewhat breathtaking in the service of well-funded museums.

Caged fluorescents hung from the ceiling, but Leif had left them dark; they'd be going out soon enough anyway, and there was no time like the present to get used to navigating without them. Even if the musty basement was spooky as hell in the dark. Even if the surprisingly fierce beam of his little LED flashlight had a way of sending massive, distorted shadows dancing across the walls like demons, freshly risen from hell and hungry for souls.

Sweeping the light around, Leif watched as black shapes jumped and melted like smoke, the emptiness that greeted him somehow sinister. Water dripped somewhere, and the sound of his own breathing threw quiet echoes around the room.

His voice embarrassingly thin, he activated his comm. "I'm in place."

RACHMANINOFF WAS A PISS-POOR SUBSTITUTE FOR CIGA-rettes, but smoking was another one of Margo's "variables"—the euphemistic term she used when she meant "shit I hate"—and so Davon Stokes hadn't touched tobacco in over nine months. Usually the withdrawal was surprisingly okay; but there was nothing "usual" about the nights that they pulled these jobs, and on each occasion, he found his fingers restless and his blood itching for relief. Whatever, it was fine. He'd been meaning to quit anyway, and giving up his one real vice had been worth the leverage he'd needed to take a stand on the eyelash thing.

The Eyelash Thing. What did it say about his life that he'd once *Norma Rae*-ed for false eyelashes?

Checking the time, he took a breath, flexed his hands, and tried to focus on the classical music coming from the van's cheap speakers. In his side-view mirror, up the parking ramp and half swallowed by darkness, the front end of a second SUV gritted golden teeth under yellow safety lights. He didn't mind being on the outside for this job. Not exactly. He was going to take home his full cut of the haul whether he put his ass on the line or kept his ass in the car. But the waiting was unbearable.

The waiting, and Axel's constant stream of wounded outrage beside him in the passenger seat. "I just can't believe she would do something like this. After all the years we've been friends, all the things we've gone through, I can't believe she would let Quino just . . . *do this* without even telling me! And you *know* she knew she was being shady, or she wouldn't have tried to hide it!"

Davon's fingers twitched, his lungs burned, and he turned up the Rachmaninoff just a little bit. Staring a hole into the side-view mirror, examining the golden mouth of the SUV up the ramp, he wondered who would leave such an expensive car overnight in a downtown parking garage. It didn't belong there.

"OKAY, MISS A." JOAQUIN'S VOICE ERUPTED IN MARGO'S EAR, puncturing the silence of the empty corridor so suddenly it made

her jump. "*The third floor is clear. When I give the signal, you'll have six seconds to make it through the Dutch masters, four seconds for sixteenth-century Venice, eight seconds for the Spanish Counter-Reformation, and then six seconds for French Renaissance sculpture.*" There was a momentary silence, and then he added, "*That's the long gallery.*"

"Twenty-four seconds, total." Margo cracked her knuckles. "How much elbow room?"

"*For the gallery? None.*" The answer was definitive. "*Sorry—it's just too exposed. Parts of it are visible on three different cameras.*"

"Got it." Margo put her fingers on the handle of the door in front of her, tried to feel the building's energy—imagined that the museum could sense her, too. "It's fine. I can do forty yards in six seconds." She made the claim with as much confidence as she could muster, determined to believe. "Just . . . you know, make sure you cut the power right on the sixth, okay?"

"*Confirmed,*" Joaquin responded. "*And . . . you know. Break a leg, or whatever the hell you're supposed to say for stuff like this.*" There was another moment of tense silence, and then, "*Okay. Now.*"

She stepped out of the dusty corridor and into a high-ceilinged chamber drowned in shadows, narrow windows letting in a sepia glow from outside that colored the air a tarnished bronze. Paintings encumbered the walls above an elaborate wainscoting, and through a wide opening Margo could just see into the next room before it was swallowed up in darkness. Floor-level bulbs burned through the gloom ahead, a handful of sickly golden pinpoints marking out the sides of each passage.

Two weeks earlier, this space had been crowded with the heat and chatter of high-end donors, all red-faced with drink and self-importance, name-dropping Frans Hals and Johannes Vermeer as if they were personal friends. The artifice of it made Margo choke, and she'd barely paid the works any attention; now, alone and embraced by silence, she found herself awed. Animated faces peered out at her from oiled canvases, intelligent eyes and luminous skin offset by folds of luxuriously rendered fabric.

Behind her, the door to the administrative corridor slipped home, the latch snapping into place like a hammer striking stone, and Margo's breath caught.

Six seconds.

Turning on her heel, she darted across the room. She tried to move as quietly as possible, but each salon flowed into the next, and the empty spaces gathered sound and tossed it about until her heartbeat was a kettle drum in her ears.

As she passed into the next exhibit hall—Veronese, Bassano, and Titian welcoming her to sixteenth-century Venice—an updraft of cold air lifted the shimmering ends of Margo's pale wig. To her right, an opening spilled downward, a flight of wide, marble steps that plunged to the second floor through a cavernous, echoing space. The ceiling of the museum climbed high above the staircase, its carved and gold-painted roundels like craters on a distant moon.

She stumbled into the Spanish Counter-Reformation in the nick of time, four seconds exactly, her pulse rising. Here, lugubrious canvases by El Greco and Velázquez contrasted with ochre walls suggestive of sun-drenched stone. Margo slowed, eased her breathing; adrenaline could burn a hole through your energy faster than a 10k—and the sculpture gallery was next.

The noises reached her, heavy steps and murmured voices lifting to bounce against the vast ceiling, a second before her comm coughed to life in her ear.

"*Guards,*" Joaquin squawked, voice pitched high. "*Two of them. Climbing the stairs to the third floor.*" Instinctively, Margo looked back, rising onto the balls of her feet as Joaquin asked, "*Miss Anthropy, do you copy?*"

Unable to speak, she clicked her comm once to signify that she understood.

"Are we calling off the job?"

Margo clicked twice, decisively: *No.* This was an unfortunate complication, but not a deal breaker. She'd tangled with security personnel before. The guards were behind her anyway, and with luck, they'd return to the ground floor when the power went off. If they didn't . . . well, adrenaline fueled fight just as well as flight.

"Okay." Joaquin didn't sound thrilled. *"Three seconds until you can enter the sculpture gallery. The micro-charge is already in place, and I'll stand by."*

Margo stood in the wide doorway, looking down the length of the next room. Roman gods and Christian saints shared a checkerboard marble floor with the busts of lesser nobles, a straight shot nearly a hundred and twenty feet long to the entrance of the new rococo display. To the left, massive windows of darkened glass were draped with heavy, brocade curtains; opposite them, a stone railing with carved balusters was the only barrier preventing a dizzying fall to the second floor.

"Go! Now!"

Margo took off. She tried to be stealthy, but time was not on her side. She rushed past a pale cupid and a mournful Madonna, ornate chandeliers dripping with crystals overhead and the air swimming with the guards' voices as they came closer.

"—that civil war they got going on in Malawi."

"The hell are you talking about?"

"Man, don't you ever watch the news?"

Up ahead, yellow lights beckoned at the entrance to the rococo room, walls taking shape in the shifting darkness. She could make it, she knew it—and, in her ear, Joaquin was counting down, *"Four . . . three . . . two . . ."*

The guards' conversation stopped abruptly, one of them asking, "Did you hear something?"

Fifteen feet from the doorway, Margo could finally see the actual writing on the actual wall—PASSIONS TO ELEVATE THE SOUL.

"... *one ... zero.*"

And then everything went dark.

4

AMONG THE MANY THINGS THAT JOAQUIN
Moreau had never done before, detonating a localized EMP was
one of the most exciting. Roughly the size of a pack of cigarettes, the
micro-charge was designed to release a high-intensity burst of dis-
ruptive, electromagnetic energy that would fry the circuits of any
electrical equipment within its blast radius—and he had placed the
device squarely inside of LAMFA's central fuse box.

His stopwatch running to track Margo's remaining time, the
portable monitor connected to the input from the camera aimed
at the two guards mounting the main staircase, Joaquin had kept
his thumb on the micro-charge's trigger while anxious perspiration
rolled down his neck. He was sweating so much he was afraid
his whole, awkwardly made-up face was melting clean off, like in
Raiders of the Lost Ark.

And then the moment came, and he pressed the button. He
wasn't sure what he'd been expecting—a ripple of blue light, the
crackle of lightning, maybe an actual explosion—but the EMP
emitted only the quick snap of a dry spark . . . and then the lights
had gone out, and there was silence. Real silence. The kind of silence
you notice only because you'd thought it was quiet before.

The fluorescents dimmed and died, the portable monitor flickered and went blank—and in the sudden darkness, the faint hum of machinery that lay underneath everything faded like an exhaled breath. The circuit breakers, incapacitated by the pulse, were now useless. There would be no toggling of fuses to fix this power outage; the museum's state-of-the-art alarm system had just been neutralized.

Switching on his LED flashlight, Joaquin swiftly recovered the spent EMP—per the team's rule to leave none of their tech behind—and then rushed for the door. There was no time for a laborious escape through the ductwork; within seconds one of the guards would be heading for the custodial closet to see about bringing the power back online.

Stepping into the hallway, the darkness was so total it was like he'd been pulled into deep space. Fumbling a pair of sunglasses out of his pack, he slipped them on and pressed a small button set into the frames, activating optoelectronic screens that had been constructed to look like ordinary tinted lenses. With a flicker, the corridor materialized around him in a palette of sickly greens, night vision technology combining near-infrared radiation with amplified visible light to bring the immediate area into focus.

Turning left, Joaquin darted for a corner at the end of the hall, ducking around it just as the guardroom door banged open behind him and the skittering beam of a flashlight ricocheted through the air like a gunshot. Nerves streaked across Joaquin's shoulders and down his spine, just as he spotted what he was looking for—the doorway to a back staircase, appearing in green outlines dead ahead.

A man's angry voice resounded: "I mean the power is out—*all* of it! Monitors, lights, alarms—" The custodial closet door slammed, the voice faded, and Joaquin hurtled up the hard, granite steps for the second floor.

At the top would be a short passageway to the back of the

Grand Hall—followed by a quick, if exposed, sprint to the main stairway and the Venetian exhibit on the third floor. This was the riskiest part of the strategy: the reckless race for the exit. But with an escape, speed is more important than stealth, and the quickest way out is the quickest way out.

He pictured it in his head as he ran—his boots pounding the moonlit steps to sixteenth-century Venice, the shouts behind him when he inevitably caught the attention of the guards—and so he was taken completely by surprise when he crested the back stairs, barreled into the passageway to the Grand Hall, and nearly ran straight into something blocking his way.

His rubber soles squeaked an alarm as he drew up short, the hulking, broad-shouldered figure of a man in a dark uniform spinning toward him in the narrow hallway, six feet away. Eyes burning like headlights in the monochrome field of the boy's night vision lenses, the guard clutched a long, deadly-looking nightstick in one upraised fist.

"*Who the fuck is there?*" he demanded.

Distracted by the raised weapon, Joaquin didn't notice what the man was holding in his other hand—until the beam of a flashlight blazed to life, exploding across his photosensitive lenses in a dazzling, painful supernova, blinding him.

ROCKETING ACROSS THE THRESHOLD TO THE ROCOCO ROOM, her blood warm from the sprint across the gallery, Margo switched on her night vision glasses and fit them into place. At the reception, she'd spent nearly thirty minutes at this exhibit alone—studying the paintings, gauging distances, mentally rehearsing. Mainly portraits and coy vignettes, the canvases were surprisingly small for their incredible value.

There were three works by François Boucher, scenes inspired by Greco-Roman mythology—Venus surrounded by winged infants,

Apollo embracing Daphne as she transformed into a tree, the muse Erato whispering inspiration to a peasant boy as he wooed a shepherdess. It was this final one that Margo approached first, running her fingers down the sides of its ornately carved frame.

A little force was all it took to release the painting from its wall mounts, and two quick swipes from a pocketknife severed the lead lines that connected it to the now-deactivated alarm system—but when Margo pulled it down, she realized something was wrong. The write-up on the exhibit had provided the dimensions of each work, and the docent at the reception had explained the framing materials in exhaustive detail; she'd done her homework, crunched the numbers, and calculated how much the Boucher ought to weigh. It was off.

Heat prickled under her arms, the guards barking tensely through their radios, still too close for comfort. With agitated fingers, she turned the painting around and slid her knife through the paper backing, peeling it away. Her heart sank when she saw a black plastic tube glued to the inside of the frame, a tiny light blinking smugly at her from one end. A security device, maybe a remote alarm, probably placed there by the French government—and no doubt equipped with GPS. Despair gusted through her and left behind the bitter residue of self-disgust. She should have expected this.

Gripping the device, Margo gave it a firm tug, but it was hopeless; whatever glue the French had used, breaking its bonds was going to be a little ugly. Briefly, she considered prying the thing loose with the edge of her knife, but this was definitely not the time—there was no way she could afford the curiosity that kind of noise would arouse at the moment. It would have to be done later.

Heat climbing inside her catsuit, Margo freed three more of the smaller artworks from their moorings, cursing their client under her breath. All they needed was the Boucher, but stealing just one painting would be as good as leaving a calling card; and because the client wanted the shepherdess in the frame, she needed to take others that way, too, to disguise their intent. She'd planned on three pieces, but not on the additional weight of their heavy tracking devices; it was going to throw off her balance.

Determined to make all the effort worthwhile, Margo gripped her pocketknife and sliced each of the two Fragonards clean from their frames—with only a few pangs of guilt—rolling both together and tucking them into a metal-reinforced tube. Stashing everything into her satchel, she hoisted the burden onto her back and clicked her comm a few times to signal that she had the goods and was heading for the extraction point.

The piercing shriek of a radio split the hollow silence of the sculpture gallery, frighteningly close, a half-second before a man's voice shouted, "*Intruder on the third floor!*"

Margo swiveled toward the doorway and froze. She wasn't surprised that they had found her—and she wasn't even surprised that they were running toward her at top speed through the graceful, twining statues of the Renaissance display. What made her blood run cold was the fact that, unlike what she'd known to expect from LAMFA's regular watchmen, these guards were holding guns.

"You know what the problem is? The *problem* is that she gets away with everything, because nobody's ever had the balls to say no to her! So now she just does whatever she wants, and when she fucks up, it's all, 'Oh, that's just Margo! Free pass!' Well, not this time. Not this damn time. Not when it's my baby brother's ass on the line!"

Axel was still going, amazingly, and Davon's head had begun to throb with the effort it took to not start screaming. His body was ravenous for nicotine, his electric-blue wig felt three sizes too small for his skull, and he'd probably ground his back teeth into talcum powder by now. There were a million things he wanted to say to the boy ranting and raving beside him, but he'd learned a long time ago that Axel would see any kind of engagement as an invitation to argue. It was best to just let him bitch until he ran out of steam.

Only he wasn't running out of steam. Axel had more steam than a fucking old-timey locomotive, and his negative energy was polluting the air with equal efficiency. The radio had moved on to Beethoven, and now the sprightly chords of Symphony no. 6 lanced through Davon's eardrums and threatened to draw blood. He squeezed the steering wheel until he was sure something would crack—the plastic or his bones—and stared bullets into his side-view mirror at the fancy, golden-mouthed SUV parked up the ramp.

It was an Escalade, the Cadillac insignia too damn ugly to miss, with a boxy front end making it look like a shipping container with wheels. Wheels, a four hundred and twenty horsepower engine, and a hideous, laughing golden mouth.

Who the fuck parked a personally detailed Escalade overnight in a shitty downtown parking structure?

"And, to be honest, I cannot believe you and Leif let her get away with this. For real, that fucking hurts. I mean, I'm not even going to *ask* if you knew about it and didn't tell me, because I don't know if our friendship would survive, but *did you?* I think I have— hey, where the hell are you going?"

Shoving open the door, Davon jumped out of the van, sucking in air that smelled like gasoline, piss, and decay. It was almost a relief. Axel was still squawking, and Beethoven's merry chords were tooting the fuck away, but Davon blanked it out. Flexing his fists, spoiling for a fight, he strode up the darkened parking ramp in the direction of the mysterious Cadillac.

It didn't belong there.

DAZZLED BY THE GLARE OF THE FLASHLIGHT, HIS VISION A kaleidoscope of bright, pulsing spots, Joaquin sensed rather than saw the guard lurch forward, swinging the heavy nightstick in a lethal arc. Reflexively, the boy arched his back, nearly parallel to the floor, and felt the breeze against his face as the weapon shot by.

Lunging upward before the man could swing again, Joaquin reached out sightlessly, his hand finding one meaty forearm; rolling under it, the boy spun inward and drove his elbow into a wall of solid muscle that passed for a stomach. Rewarded with a grunt, he bunched together the fingers of his left hand to form a point and, aiming for his right palm, drove it as hard as he could into the guard's wrist.

The man emitted a guttural shriek, dropping the nightstick to the floor, and Joaquin ducked free. Grabbing the weapon and rolling to safety, the bright spots in his vision were finally beginning to recede, but the flashlight's beam burned like wildfire every time it hit his high-tech lenses. Swiping them off his face, he blinked into the mottled darkness—just as the man darted forward again, arm aloft.

Joaquin thrust the nightstick upward just as the flashlight came down, plastic meeting wood with a sharp *crack*. The bulb flickered, and the force of the blow sent pain vibrating through his weary shoulder. The guard swung again, the device moving with such power the air whistled—and this time, although he narrowly managed to block it again, the impact knocked the stick clean from Joaquin's grip and sent it to the floor.

Skittering backward, pain still humming up his arm, the boy struggled to regroup. His eyes adjusted at last, and he could see his opponent now behind the glare of the flash. The man was huge, built like a grizzly bear, with a solid foot in height and at least a hundred pounds of muscle on Joaquin.

But the boy had other advantages.

Gritting his teeth with determination, he jumped forward into a walkover, followed by a double aerial and then a front handspring. In constant motion, his feet scything the air, he drove the man backward. Coming out of the handspring, he made a three-point landing and hammered an ox-jaw blow to the tender muscle of his opponent's groin. The guard staggered back with an agonized oath, awkwardly lashing out with his booted foot, but the boy had already rolled out of range.

Leaping up, Joaquin kicked off one wall and ricocheted to the other, launching himself up again, almost to the ceiling; and then he came down hard, delivering a savage elbow strike across the guard's face with all his strength and body weight combined.

He dropped to the floor at the guy's feet, arm throbbing from the blow, strands of his wig sticking to the sweaty makeup on his face. The guard stumbled back a foot or two, but then shook his head and, impossibly, seemed to recover. For the first time, Joaquin felt a ripple of panic up his spine. With a vicious, bloodied grin, the towering man moved back in, throwing a club-fisted punch that the boy dodged too slowly.

The huge fist caught him behind the ear, and the hallway erupted into bright, ringing fireworks as Joaquin toppled to the ground. His head spun and the corridor tilted dangerously, and before he could scrabble upright again, a massive hand closed around his neck and started to squeeze.

Pressure mounted behind his eyes, blood thundering in his ears, and Joaquin thrashed in vain as he was lifted off the ground and into the air. Pinning the boy against his chest with a cast-iron arm, the guard bore down, crushing Joaquin's lungs and squeezing his neck tighter at the same time.

His legs kicked helplessly, and he clawed at the hand wrapped like a tourniquet around his neck, but it was useless. Joaquin couldn't breathe and he couldn't reach his comm to signal for help, and every move burned precious oxygen he'd never get back. His chest burning, his tongue swelling in his mouth, white pinpoints swarmed before his eyes as his vision began to fade.

5

DISMANTLING THE GENERATOR WAS A BREEZE.
Just after the lights went down, a digital display sprang to life on the machine—a battery-powered countdown, ticking off the thirty seconds left until electricity would be restored to the building.

His glasses already in place, Leif turned on the night vision and made short work of the generator, disconnecting the cords and cables, uncoupling the fuel source and power output, and finally jimmying open the control panel and dragging his pocketknife through a nest of wires underneath. At five seconds to go, the digital display blipped out for good. Maybe it was overkill, but the harder he made it for the museum to undo his damage, the better his team's chances were of getting away clean.

Job complete, Leif snapped the knife closed and tucked it into the belt at his waist, turning for the stairs. Cast in the stark and ethereal green luminescence of his lens filters, everything looked like a lost reel from some crappy found-footage horror movie. He couldn't wait to get out of there. Soon they'd be sending people down to check on the generator, and he'd just as soon be gone, anyway.

Vaulting the steps two at a time, he encountered no one as he passed the first floor, hearing only the muffled shouting of a distressed guard behind closed doors; but as he came to the second-floor hallway, the unmistakable sounds of a struggle reached his ears. It was wordless, just the heavy puff of hard breathing and the scrape of bodies pressed close, but a spike of adrenaline sent Leif bursting around the corner at top speed.

A guard about the size of a yeti blocked the passage, all trunk-like legs and a menacing scowl, lit freakishly from beneath by a dropped flashlight; and caught like a helpless house cat in his massive arms, wriggling and gasping for air, was Joaquin Moreau. The boy's eyes were huge and panicked when they locked onto Leif's, the veins in his temples bulging as thick as fingers, and it was clear there was no time to waste.

Leif didn't even slow down. Diving into a front roundoff, he did two handsprings and then hurtled into the air at the guard, twisting his body to the side and knifing out his legs. At the last second, Joaquin let his body go completely limp; deadweight in the guard's arms, he slipped several crucial inches into gravity's embrace. In almost the same instant, Leif's boot flashed past, slamming into the enormous man's jaw.

The guard's head snapped back and his arms went loose, his body reeling and collapsing to the ground; Leif tucked his feet, completing a tight roll, and landed in a crouch beside Joaquin. The boy in the green wig was sprawled across the tiled floor, breathing hard and struggling to regain his composure.

"Are you okay?" Leif asked gently, cursing himself for how patronizing he sounded. Joaquin had gone to a lot of trouble to prove himself, and probably wouldn't appreciate being talked down to.

Fortunately, the guy didn't seem to notice. Gulping a couple of deep breaths, Joaquin offered a shaky nod. When he spoke, his voice was rough. "I'm okay. Thanks."

The guard was still facedown on the floor a few feet away, evidently out cold, and Leif stood up again. Offering his hand, he said, "Then let's go."

Taking the assist, Joaquin scrambled to his feet, and they hurried past the guard, breaking into a run the second they hit the Grand Hall.

They got there just in time to hear the gunshots.

HURLING THE SATCHEL OF PRICELESS ARTWORKS TO THE floor, Margo broke out in a dead sprint. With no fire escape, no back staircase to the second floor, and no entrance to the administrative corridor, there was only one way out of the rococo room: back through the sculpture gallery. She had one choice, and one chance.

When the guards saw her coming, running full tilt and unbuckling her zip line harness, the one in front stumbled to a confused halt. "*Stop!*"

Margo picked up speed instead, ripping the harness off and gathering one end in her fist. With ten feet to spare, the first guard drew his firearm. Planting his feet shoulder-width apart, he jerked out the weapon and squeezed the trigger.

The bullet hit nothing but air; the report was deafening and harmless as Margo hurled herself to the ground. Her knees bent and her back pressed to the floor, momentum sent her across the slick marble tile like a hockey puck, her nylon bodysuit putting up minimal resistance as she shot straight between the first guard's feet. The second man was taken by complete surprise, utterly unprepared when she slid into view, legs already scissoring up.

One boot caught him in the thigh, the other in the groin, and she brought him off his feet. Unable to get his hands in front of him in time, he went down like a condemned building, slamming fast and hard onto the unforgiving stone; a groan huffed weakly from the back of his throat, and then he went still. Margo kept moving, though, rolling up onto one knee and spinning to face the first guard. The man was already turning, firearm outthrust, and she swung hard with the zip line harness.

The thick straps tangled around the guard's wrist, and Margo yanked him off-balance just as he pulled the trigger a second time. This bullet slammed into the floor, while the recoil and lack of control cost the man his weapon. Flying from his grip, the gun bounced and skidded into the dense shadows that swarmed the statuary.

Spinning again, still on one knee, Margo slammed her boot into the man's stomach. He stumbled back, winded and gasping, and she kipped up to her feet. For a moment, they squared off; the guard had other weapons at his disposal, and her next move would depend on which he chose to attack with. He eyed her warily, backing up another step, and then his face creased in shock. "You're . . . you're just a *kid*."

"I'm kind of a problem child," Margo admitted, panting. The man immediately grabbed for the Taser on his belt, fumbling with the holster snaps, and she darted forward. The second the weapon was in the clear, she took hold of his wrist, bracing it and stepping to the inside of his arm—her back to his front—hammering her elbow into his ribs. He responded by wrapping his free arm around her chest, pulling her against him, trying to immobilize her.

Kicking her right leg up, hyperextending her hip joint, Margo allowed the weight of the limb to do the work; it swung past her face, her calf brushing her ear, her shin touching her shoulder, and her boot slamming into the forehead of the man behind her.

Dazed, he lost his hold—on her and on the weapon—and she easily snatched the Taser out of his grasp. Spinning, she took two steps back and fired, the electrified prongs popping quietly as they streaked the short distance and plunged through the man's uniform right above his name tag: GERARD.

Gerard the guard? Margo made a face as the man went stiff, eyes rolling back, a shudder passing through his frame. When the charge was spent, he slumped dramatically to the floor. Margo nudged him a little with her boot, just in case he was playing possum. A smell like singed hair rose up, and she decided he wasn't.

She had rebuckled her harness and retrieved the bag with the stolen paintings when Leif and Joaquin appeared in the upper gallery. Both boys were disheveled, but their eyes were bright. Leif gestured at the two prone bodies. "We heard a gun. You had trouble?"

With a sly smile, she hitched a shoulder. "Nothing I couldn't handle. You?"

A look passed between the two boys that she'd have loved to interrogate, but all Leif said was, "Same."

"Good to know." The guard she'd brought down first, the one who'd face-planted firmly on the marble floor, was starting to move again; quickly, Margo took the pistol from his belt, emptied the clip, and tossed the works over the stone railing and down into the Grand Hall. The other gun was still somewhere nearby, hidden in the statuary, but there was no time to hunt for it. "Let's get the hell out of here."

Together, the three of them retraced the steps she'd taken earlier—Spain, Venice, Holland—and they were just easing open the door back into the administrative corridor when the bright chirp of a walkie-talkie rang out under the vast ceiling. One of the guards was up, his unsteady voice carrying through the empty space.

"... multiple intruders ... two, maybe three ... didn't get a good look ..."

"*Go*," Margo whispered, ushering the two boys ahead of her

into the pitch-black hallway and back to the office where they'd first entered the building.

A cool, damp breeze brought in the scent of urban life through the gaping hole of the window, and Margo sucked in a lungful. When the door was firmly shut behind them, she snatched off her glasses and activated her comm. "We're in place. Commence extraction."

"*Are you* all *in place?*" It was Axel, his tone a challenge.

"*Yes*, damn it!" Margo glared out the window at the concrete tiers of the parking garage across the way, suddenly wishing her fancy glasses had been equipped with a death laser as well as the night vision tech. "Fire the fucking thing already, Liesl!"

A moment later, there was a *snap*, and once again the grappling hook was hurtling out of the shadows and through the air above the alley. This time, however, it was rising up from a point on the second floor of the structure, its glittering fangs revolving slowly as it neared the window. When it cleared the emptied pane, it first struck the ceiling, then fell to the desk and rolled onto the floor, where Margo snatched it up. Anchoring it on the metal pipe below the window, she reported back through the comm, and watched as the cable was pulled taut from the other end.

"Okay, guys, time to get lost," she urged, unable to dull the razor edge of anxiety in her voice. The guard would realize immediately that they hadn't escaped by the central staircase, and the administrative hallway, with its emergency exit, was the only other way out; if he was looking for them, if he was close enough to have heard the grappling hook . . .

Axel broke in on her fretful train of thought. "*All set.*"

Margo signaled to Joaquin, who hooked his harness to the cable, climbed onto the sill, and jumped. His body shot across the alley, sleek as a torpedo, and Margo breathed a sigh of relief.

One down. No matter how much mayhem they faced on a job, the getaway was always the most stressful part. Nothing counted if they didn't stick the dismount.

Then, as Joaquin heaved himself up over the railing of the parking garage, a heavy crash sounded from the far end of the administrative corridor—the door being flung open.

Their time was up.

"*Go, go, go,*" Margo hissed at Leif, shoving him toward the cable, but the boy resisted.

"I'll hold him off." With the delicate point of his chin, he gestured to the door leading into the hallway. "You should go first."

Margo stiffened. "I'm always the last one out. That's the rule."

"Yeah, but you've got the stuff," Leif returned, urgency heating his voice. Knobs rattled and more doors banged open along the corridor, the guard getting closer, checking offices. "If the paintings don't get out, what was the point to any of this?"

He was right. Grimly, Margo yanked the satchel off her shoulders and shoved it into the boy's arms. "The framed canvases have trackers implanted; you'll see them as soon as you take off the backing. The second you get across—and I mean *the very second*—you rip those things out. Do whatever you have to, just don't damage the merchandise!"

"Got it." Leif nodded shortly, slinging the bag onto his back and tightening the straps. Then he hooked himself up to the zip line, and with a last look of misgiving, dropped out of sight. His clip made a sizzling noise at it skimmed the length of the cable, but the thump of Margo's heart nearly drowned it out.

Or maybe that thump was the sound of the guard tossing open the door of the adjoining office.

Scrambling into the window, she clipped herself to the zip line and maneuvered onto the stone ledge. Across, Leif was dragging himself onto the lip of the second-floor wall, each instant passing like an eternity. Unbalanced by the satchel, his leg slipped, and he had to try again. Margo's mouth felt as dry as a bag of flour, her skin raging hot under the nylon.

Behind her, the doorknob jiggled, a key scraping the metal tumblers of the lock before snapping it open. Her body went electric with nerves. Leif cleared the railing, the door behind her flew open—and Margo dove off the ledge and into the air.

Ten feet down and thirty feet across, the plunge took seconds that felt like years, wind streaming over her as the guard rushed to the window. Her feet hit the wall a moment before the first bullet did the same, ripping loose a chunk of concrete the size of a golf ball, and her pulse thundered in her ears. More gunshots came in rapid succession, one missing her by an inch as she dragged herself over the railing, diving into the safety of the garage.

Moments later, a beat-up panel van with a missing license plate careened down the exit ramp of the parking structure, crashing through the barrier gate and fishtailing onto the street. Sirens wailed in the distance as the unmarked vehicle slewed across lanes, rocketing past the museum and picking up speed, tires screaming to protest a hard left onto Spring Street. The only witnesses still on the sidewalks at that hour were people with no interest in getting involved with the cops, and they found convenient shadows to melt into as the high-pitched croon of police cruisers drew closer.

The fleeing auto jumped the curb for an illegal right onto Third, and then skidded left when it hit Main. The cops were gaining, though, sirens coming from more directions, and the ungainly van lost speed and ground with every corner. Flashing lights blazed in its rearview as the driver blew through a red at First, and a phalanx of cruisers streamed into the intersection at Temple, forming a hasty and impromptu blockade.

At the foot of the imposing tower of City Hall, the van

swerved and skidded to a stop, all out of escape routes. And there it waited, exhaust pipe huffing a trail of vapor into the night air. The police first shouted instructions through a megaphone for the driver to exit the vehicle, and when these passed with no response, a group of five officers approached the target on foot—guns raised, body armor strapped in place.

Four officers took tactical positions around the van, while the fifth—an eighteen-year veteran named Emilio Ramirez—cautiously approached the driver's door. Wrenching it open, he thrust his gun into the cab . . . and then recoiled at the fetid stench that billowed out—alcohol, soiled clothing, and unwashed flesh. An old man with grimy skin hunkered over the wheel, eyes huge and unfocused, his mouth shaped into something like a grin.

"She paid me," the man slurred, his breath stinking of cheap whiskey and rotting teeth. "Paid me and she said, '*drive, drive, drive!*'"

He giggled and coughed wetly into his lap, and then Ramirez hauled him out from behind the wheel. On the other side of the van, an officer yanked open the side door and jumped back, eyes as big as the Hollywood Bowl. "*Shit*. We've got possible explosives back here—we're gonna need the bomb squad!"

A perimeter was established. The driver was cuffed and escorted outside of the potential blast radius, where Ramirez and his lieutenant bombarded the clearly intoxicated man with questions about what they'd found in the back of the van—four black, plastic cylinders, each with a tiny, blinking light at one end. The suspect was uncooperative, and possibly non compos mentis. No matter what they asked, or how they phrased their demands, he just kept repeating the same story over and over: *She paid me, she told me to drive, she told me, she said, "This is for you, and all you have to do is drive."*

"Who paid you?" Ramirez demanded. "Who told you to drive?"

"An Amazon." The old man's eyes were wide and dreamy, fixed on City Hall. "She had brown skin and blue hair and diamonds on her eyelids, and she was as tall as that building right there. And she said, '*This is yours, and all you have to do is drive . . .*'"

6

SHORTLY AFTER THE UNMARKED VAN BLITZED through the parking gate, a luxury Cadillac with tinted windows and a grille of shining, golden metal followed it almost soundlessly down the ramp, turning the opposite direction and zooming discreetly away. It diligently obeyed all traffic laws, even pulling to the curb when three police cars roared past with their sirens howling, lights pulsing against the night.

Heading north, the SUV maintained an even speed until it left downtown, skirting the edges of Elysian Park before angling eastward. The streets were silent, the sky turning indigo behind its field of stars—and if you weren't inside the vehicle to listen to Margo's furious tirade, you'd think it was the beginning of a peaceful morning.

"An *Escalade*?" She practically screeched, stuffing her platinum wig into a netted bag and then cramming it into her duffel like a pair of old socks. With effort, Davon stifled the urge to share a piece of unsolicited—yet clearly necessary—advice on the care of one's hairpieces. "Are you freaking *kidding me*, Davon?"

"It worked, didn't it?" He nudged the gas, the vehicle's speed edging up at a feather touch of the pedal. He wasn't going to let her ruin this for him. "Feel how well this baby handles? And look: we're almost there!"

"We had a plan in place. What was wrong with the Subaru?" Margo demanded. She began wiping off her makeup with a towelette, her skin flushed pink underneath.

"See now, you just answered your own question," Davon countered. The other boys were wisely staying out of the argument, assiduously removing their own wigs, makeup, and padding, looking like students terrified of being called on to answer a question about material they hadn't studied. "That Subaru was twelve years old, and it looked like somebody had used it as a damn piñata."

"The fact that it looked like a piece of junk was the *point*." Margo unpinned her hair, strawberry blond locks tumbling past her shoulders. "You made a last-minute decision to steal a frigging Cadillac for our getaway car! Why didn't you just hijack a fucking blimp? We could've spray-painted 'PAY ATTENTION TO ME!' all over the side and saved some time."

"Hijacking a blimp is way harder than boosting a Caddy," Davon riposted, and regretted it the second the quip was out of his mouth. With a sigh of contrition, he said, "Margo, honey, trust me. The cops don't pull over folks in Escalades—unless they're asking for it, or the Escalade has been reported stolen. And whoever left this gorgeous ride in that parking garage is not paying that close attention to their things."

Margo's expression was still dour as she massaged her scalp with her fingers. "That's not even—"

"—the point, I know," Davon finished for her.

"Changing the plan without consulting or telling anybody introduces—"

"—variables that can't be predicted, I *know*." Davon clicked on her seat warmer, hoping it'd relax her a little. *Kill with kindness,* his mother always said, *and if that doesn't work, use a knife.* "I was eliminating unpredictable variables, Margo. That Subaru was on its last legs, and it had zero pickup. If the cops hadn't fallen for the decoy, we'd have been just as screwed as if we'd taken the van ourselves."

Pulling her arms out of the bodysuit's sleeves, Margo was silent for a moment. "Is that true?"

"On my auntie's grave, may she please die soon." Davon didn't even feel guilty. It was *mostly* true. He wasn't absolutely sure a twelve-year-old Subaru could outrun the cops—not as sure as he was about the Caddy—and that variable sure sounded unpredictable to him. "You told me I could make the calls when it came to anything automotive, I'll remind you, and this thing is pretty automotive."

Margo was still scowling, but her shoulders didn't look quite so tense as she shoved her bodysuit down to her ankles. She was wearing a sports bra and, on top of it, a *second* bra—this one padded, so that her silhouette would still match her teammates'. She stuck her feet into a pair of jeans before she spoke. "Don't do it again. I don't like surprises."

"Neither do I." Axel's snotty remark was loud enough for everyone to hear, but it was enthusiastically ignored.

"I promise this was a one-time thing," Davon stated, crossing his fingers. Like hell he'd pass up a Cadillac if there were ever another chance at one. And anyway, it wasn't like Margo could fire him.

Chain-link fencing appeared at the side of the road, a seemingly endless length of it erupting out of hardscrabble weeds, and Davon slowed the Escalade. Beyond the wiry lattice, swamped in darkness, the crumbling remains of a long-abandoned mall sprawled like a lost island in a sea of fissured, concrete pavement. At regular intervals, scratched and dented KEEP OUT signs were lashed up with twists of metal—but at equal intervals, sections of the enclosure had been ripped open so people could crawl through.

Turning up a weedy, disused drive, Davon brought the Escalade to a stop before a wide gate across the entrance to the parking lot, secured with a chain and industrial-sized padlock. Leaving the engine running, he hopped out and stepped quickly to the barrier. Within seconds, he had it open, and the Cadillac glided through.

Fact was, he probably could have picked that lock in his sleep, but he hadn't needed to; Margo had taken the fun out of everything—like usual—earlier in the day with a pair of bolt cutters and a brand-new padlock to which she held the key. *It eliminates one more variable*, she'd started to explain, and then Davon had begun bleeding from the ears.

The Cadillac's engine was so quiet it barely made a sound as they drove across the decaying lot toward the gloomy, forsaken hulk of the old mall; but even so, figures materialized beneath the shadowy overhang of what had once been an entrance to the food court as the car drew near, swaying like zombies, their eyes glinting in the moonlight.

Turning the wheel, Davon guided the SUV around the looming end of the complex, to its desolate backside. Fragments of glass littered the pavement, twinkling in the moonlight like earthbound stars, and more bodies shuffled around, passing joints, food, and bottles of beer from hand to hand. Parked beneath a burned-out security light, well concealed from the road, were a gunmetal-gray Dodge Challenger and a matte black Zero DSR electric motorcycle. Five men gathered by the vehicles, talking and smoking, each one maintaining a casual grip on a baseball bat or a nasty-looking length of pipe.

As the Escalade eased to a halt, the men straightened up; and when Davon climbed out, the largest of the five sauntered up to him, a metal bat clutched in one meaty fist. He flashed a grin that was missing a few teeth, taking in the bright blue wig, sparkly eye makeup, and exaggerated curves. With a gesture to the SUV, the man spoke in a gruff voice. "Nice wheels."

"Nothing but the best for Dior Galore," Davon purred, pulling off a glove to examine his long, glossy fingernails. He towered over the guy with the bat, looking down from an advantage of at least eight inches in his high heels—another thing Margo had passed an edict against, believe it or not. They were *drag queens*, for fuck's sake, and she didn't want them to wear heels.

"*You can't run from armed guards in four-inch heels, Davon*," she'd claimed, preposterously. "*What if you twist an ankle?*" In response, he'd shown her clips of French figure skater Surya Bonaly doing backflips on the ice in the 1988 Olympics, landing flawlessly on a single blade. Margo had folded her arms across her chest. "You *aren't Surya Bonaly.*"

It was maybe the rudest thing she'd ever said to him.

Never mind that he performed in four-inch heels three nights a week, doing leaps, death drops, *and* fucking backflips; it was still out of the question. But he'd spent every part of tonight sitting behind the wheel, and he got to make the call on all things automotive, so on went the good shoes—and Margo could kiss his sweet, padded ass if she didn't like it.

"We watched the Dodge and the bike just like we agreed, Miss Galore, and nothin' happened to 'em. You can check 'em out." The man gestured to his buddies, who were paying keen attention. Davon moved over to the Zero and then the Challenger, running his hands along the side panels and making a show of looking for possible damage, while the guy continued, "Couple of the tweakers thought they could try somethin', but we shut 'em down. Nobody else even dared after that."

"You boys did a great job." Hours earlier, the first time they'd pulled into this parking lot, Davon searched among the dazed and day-drunk mall-walkers to find the most trustworthy of the bunch.

These five had been the winners. With an approving nod, the boy in the blue wig produced a wad of paper money and handed it over. "Here's what I promised you for standing guard—and here's a little something extra." With a flick of the wrist, Davon tossed over the keys to the Escalade as well, giving the vehicle one last wistful smile. "Don't spend it all in one place."

Whooping and jostling one another, already arguing over who got to drive it first, the men charged for the Cadillac as Margo, Axel, Leif, and Joaquin made their way over to Davon. Pale blond hair sticking out all over in adorable disarray, Leif looked even more surprised at the unexpected bonus than the men did. "You're seriously just *giving* them the Escalade? After all that?"

"What the hell else am I gonna do with it?" Davon sighed, lifting his hands in a philosophical shrug. Within a few hours, the luxury SUV would be stripped to the axles, leaving one less thread by which to track them down. As the Cadillac lurched out of park and jolted forward, swerving through a carpet of broken glass and narrowly missing a metal trash barrel, he just hoped the five men didn't get themselves killed. "Anyway. Job well done, blah blah blah. I don't know about you all, but I need a drink and some beauty sleep."

Two helmets dangled from the handlebars of the Zero, and before Davon was even finished speaking, Axel had grabbed both and hurled one at Joaquin. The younger boy barely got his hands on it in time, shooting an injured look back at his brother. Slinging his leg over the seat of the bike, Axel snapped coldly, "Get on. We're going home."

"No." Margo snatched the helmet from Joaquin, jamming it over her own head and snapping the visor open. "I'm riding with you, Axel. You and I need to talk."

"*No*, I'm taking my brother." Axel glared at her, his dark eyes hard enough to punch holes through steel; but in a battle of wills, they were equally matched.

"Quino, you're riding with Leif and Davon," Margo decreed over her shoulder as she marched to the Zero, and to Davon she added perfunctorily, "If that's cool with you?"

"Oh sure." Davon knew way better than to stick his head into this particular nest of fire ants. "I'm in no hurry. I can drink and sleep any time."

Truth be told, he was happy to have an excuse to stay out just a little bit later, to avoid what most likely awaited him at home—and Margo knew it.

"This is stupid," Axel insisted hotly as the girl jumped onto the bike behind him, zipping up her leather jacket and wrapping her arms around his waist. "Joaquin and I live together, remember? We're going to the exact same place!"

"And I live five minutes from the two of you, so Davon would have to drive all the way to our neck of the woods anyway." She waved at the other boys, shooing them toward the Challenger. "Now, put your helmet on, take some deep breaths, and let's go."

His face darkening like a storm cloud, Axel did as he was told, if only because a protracted argument with Margo generally resulted in no winner at all. The Zero sparked to life and surged forward, making a graceful curve before speeding into the darkness and disappearing beyond the mall.

Joaquin looked relieved, running a hand through the dark, sweaty hair that tumbled across his forehead. Still, he grunted, "He's gonna kill me, isn't he?"

"Nah, you're good," Davon promised, unlocking the Challenger and climbing behind the wheel. "Those two are going to murder each other long before they make it back home."

Firing up the engine, he let the two boys pile in, and then he cruised off after Axel and Margo, waving to the homeless men doing donuts in the Escalade. Moonlight flashed on the burgundy polish of his acrylic nails, and Haydn's fourth violin concerto swelled from the speakers of the car, silvery ribbons of sound threading through the moist, cool air that filled the night.

Sometimes life was good, and sometimes it was crap, and sometimes it was both at once.

HIS THIGHS HUGGING THE ZERO, THE ELECTRIC lights of the city blazing across the black leather of his riding gloves, Axel checked his mirrors and squeezed a little more speed out of the engine. They'd gone the long way around, taking surface streets, sticking judiciously to the speed limit. Four police cruisers streamed by as they passed the copper-green tower rising up above the Wiltern Theatre, and the boy kept his head down.

Even if he did want to jiggle the motorcycle until Margo lost her grip and went flying off through the window of a passing truck.

The minute she'd said they needed to talk, he'd forgotten every single word of the diatribe he'd been reciting for Davon all night long, and he was grateful for the helmets and noise that forestalled yet another one-sided conversation. He spent the ride trying to re-organize his thoughts, but it was impossible to rehearse his side of the argument without succumbing to a murderous rage over the fact that her arms were wrapped around him.

They'd done this so many times, these dusky tours of the city—not always a getaway, but always an escape—getting lost in order to find themselves. He'd text Margo one line (*I'm losing it*), and she'd write back immediately (*meet at the gate in 10*); she'd have a bottle of wine from her dad's cellar or a flask of scotch, a bag of fire-works, graphic novels, or junk food, and they'd just go until they found somewhere to stop and make the world vanish.

He wasn't even sure he could safely articulate how betrayed he felt that she had recruited his little brother for this. Quino wasn't like them—and he didn't have to be. Axel thought Margo had understood that. He'd thought she was one of the few people in the world who had any idea how shitty his life had actually become.

The sun was rising, rust-orange light inflaming the horizon as the Zero finally neared the I-10, and a drumbeat of anxiety throbbed in Axel's gut. He hated coming home at dawn, hated the questions he always expected but was never asked. He hated that instead of making him feel young and alive, staying out all night just made him feel tired and sad. His heart sank slowly as they hummed through Santa Monica and onto the Pacific Coast Highway, wind-ing north between palm trees and beachfront homes, while white-caps rose and fell as the ocean drove hard against the beach.

Ruddy fingerprints bruised the sky above them when he steered the bike up into the twisting canyons of Malibu, coming to a stop in front of a grand, wrought-iron gate. Bang in the center of it was an ornate and deliberately recognizable insignia: a bold letter *M*, set within a circle and bisected by a lightning bolt. Axel didn't bother to turn off the Zero; he just waited for Margo to dismount and go.

She didn't. And after ten minutes of sitting there while she messed around on her cell phone, he couldn't take it anymore. Jerking off his helmet, he spun around with a glare. "I cannot believe you told Quino he could be a part of this!"

"I know you're upset," she began in a maddeningly docile tone, as if he were being unreasonable.

"Of course I'm upset! You sent my kid brother to rob a museum!" Was she *delusional*? "They had *guns*, Margo. They were shooting actual bullets at him!"

"They were shooting bullets at *me*," she corrected coolly, "and I wasn't any happier about it than you are. But none of us would've faced any bullets at all if you'd fired the hook when I told you the first time."

"Don't you dare try to turn this around on me." Axel shook his head in disbelief. "I cannot believe you won't even apologize for—"

"Axel," Margo interrupted sharply, gray eyes blazing, suddenly all business from the top down. "If you want to chew me out, relax—you're about to get your chance. But first it's my turn." She ripped off her gloves, lips pressed into a flat line. "I don't care how pissed you are at me, you don't refuse to perform when the clock is ticking. You put all of us in danger, you risked the whole job, and you did it just to have the last word in an argument. Do it again, and you're out."

Axel nodded along sarcastically. "That's a great speech, Margo, and I'd feel super guilty right now if we weren't talking about the fact that you put my brother in play and didn't tell me until you knew it was too late for me to do anything but lockstep." A gull swooped overhead, wheeling out to sea. "You manipulated me. You took my choices away so you could get what you want, and that's fucked up."

"Okay." Margo nodded carefully, running her fingers over the stitching on the seat. "I hear what you're saying, and you're right about that much. I did it because I wanted you to give Quino a chance, and I knew you wouldn't unless I forced your hand. Maybe it wasn't the most honorable move." She met his eye. "But look at what he did, Axel. Out of all of us, he had the hardest job, and he nailed it. He's *good*, and we wouldn't have pulled it off—"

"Don't do that!" Axel fumed, thrusting an accusing finger at her. "Don't ends-justify-the-means me!" And, just like that, tears pricked hotly at the corners of his eyes, and he struggled to keep his throat from closing. "How could you, Margo? Joaquin isn't . . .

he's not a part of this, and I don't want him to be. He should be at home, asleep. He should be having a normal life."

"But he doesn't, Axel," she said softly, and her face took on that hideously mournful look she got whenever she was about to invoke his father's bullshit. "And it's not something you can give him, anyway. It's not your responsibility to—"

"Don't tell me about my responsibilities."

And then there it was: "You're not your dad."

"I *know* I'm not my dad, okay?" He snarled. "As far as I'm concerned, Basil Moreau is dead. That bastard died a fucking year and a half ago, and it would be awesome if people would just stop saying his name around me already." His pulse throbbed in his neck, and he felt deranged. "He has fucked up *literally everything* he's ever touched, and until tonight, I was praying that didn't include my baby brother."

A year and a half. It was hard to believe it had been that long since the feds had come rolling up, an armada of shiny black cars appearing without warning in front of their Spanish-style villa, to arrest Axel's financier father on a shockingly long list of criminal acts. Securities fraud, mail fraud, wire fraud, tax fraud, and money laundering had been the juiciest; but as the investigation exploded open in the national media, plenty of lesser charges had poured out as well. The victims of Basil's breathtaking scam could have doubled as a Who's Who of their close-knit Malibu community, and the Moreaus had become pariahs overnight.

Their front gate was vandalized repeatedly, garbage and feces thrown into their yard, and for weeks they didn't feel safe leaving the house at all. School was no better. Axel and Joaquin were harassed in the halls, their lockers defaced, and their teachers—wary of the politics afoot—saw nothing. Through it all, the only person to stay by Axel's side, the only friend not to turn on him, was Margo. It was a debt he couldn't possibly repay.

When it first happened, it had felt like an extinction-level event; but time marched on, and somehow they were still here, still stepping around a jagged crater in the middle of their lives a year and a half later. Nothing would ever again be the way it once was, and age had numbed their wounds rather than healed them. Basil Moreau was alive and well in a federal penitentiary, while his family died for his sins every single day.

"Axel." Margo made a move as if to touch him, but he inched back subtly, and she got the message, turning her gaze to the ocean. "Part of why I didn't tell you Quino was joining us is because he asked me not to. He knew you'd find a way to shut him down, and he wanted this. He *wants* this." She faced him again, eyes searching. "You need to talk to him. He didn't come to me because he thinks stealing shit is 'cool.' He's not trying to compete with you, or impress you, or spite you. He made a case to me, and it was a good one, and I thought he'd earned a chance. Maybe he's earned one from you, too."

Axel shook his head again, trying to make it all go away. He didn't want to hear Margo's advice, and so he decided not to. Putting his helmet back on, he flipped up his visor. "I should get home and check on my mom. Apparently she's been alone all night long."

With an unhappy sigh, Margo climbed off the Zero, the oversized satchel still strapped to her back and the small duffel hanging from one shoulder. Axel kicked speed into the bike immediately, sending up loose stones behind him, drowning out Margo's parting words. "Please, just think about it!"

And then he was buzzing his way higher up the canyon, back toward home.

Or what was left of it.

HER CONCERN FOR AXEL MOREAU WAS NOT ALL THAT weighed heavy on Margo's shoulders as she punched her code into the keypad and watched the gate swing open, the thunderbolt *M* making way for her to enter. The satchel was like an anvil on her back as she trudged up the short drive, curving through a spiky privacy hedge, the exhilaration of the daring theft finally wearing off.

Before her rose a vast, two-story mansion, a "luxury modern" construction of metal, stucco, and plate glass. The thunderbolt *M* repeated itself at the bottom of a reflecting pool in the forecourt, and recessed lights glowed outside the front door, letting her know that someone had wanted her to feel welcome when she returned.

Even before deactivating the alarm, Margo dropped her bags to the floor of the austere foyer. The safest place for them would be her bedroom, but she needed something to eat and a moment to breathe first. Crossing into a spacious living room, where glass doors looked out onto a shimmering infinity pool and the ocean stretching behind it, she felt as light as if she were zip-lining again. The ocean was lighting up, lavender and gold kissing the coastline, and for a moment Margo absorbed the tranquil view of dark green hills tumbling to the sea.

In the kitchen, where black stone counters and stainless steel appliances ringed a central island, she made a beeline for the refrigerator. Ripping open a plastic tub of sesame noodles, she forked every last glistening ounce into her mouth as fast as she could, still cold. It wasn't until her lips were greasy and her stomach full that she finally noticed what rested on the counter in front of her.

A plain rocks glass lined with an amber residue that smelled of smoke, it weighed down a brief note: *Found in his room. THIRD TIME THIS WEEK!* It was unsigned, but Margo knew immediately who'd written it. Only one person would bother. Frustrated and weary, she put the glass in the dishwasher, retrieved her bags from the foyer, and headed upstairs.

Her private suite occupied one end of the second-floor hallway on the west side of the house; at the other end was her father's. Once upon a time, so long ago her memories of it were now hazy and soft around the edges, he'd shared the room with her mother; but following the couple's divorce when Margo was five, a vengeful and acrimonious split that fueled millions of gossip magazines from coast to coast, Mrs. Manning had left not just Malibu but the entire continent of North America. Now living in Europe, the woman made it clear she would gladly move to Jupiter if it meant getting that much farther away from her hated ex-husband. For his part, Harland Manning never remarried, and for twelve years he and his daughter had occupied the mansion alone together.

When she reached the top of the steps, Margo froze at the sight of a telltale electric glow beneath the ornately carved door to the master bedroom. *Her dad's light was still on?* A million possibilities galloped through her head, most of them bad—but before she could act, a querulous voice called, "Margo? Is that you?"

Caught, she blinked, unsure if she was relieved or afraid. "D-dad?"

"Are you just getting home?" The voice was weak, muffled by the door, but still radiated outrage and disappointment.

"Just a minute!" Margo hustled the bags into her room, scrubbed off the last vestiges of her drag makeup, and returned to her father's door. Heart beating with a familiar and reflexive fear, she knocked and then let herself inside.

Propped up against a padded headboard, dead center in a massive, four-poster bed, sat Harland Manning. Light from a bedside lamp played sideways across his face, casting dramatic shadows over his sunken cheeks, and heavy curtains blacked out the windows. The effect was powerful, her father in a spotlight as though onstage, the theatrics making up for the strength he no longer possessed.

"You're up early," she began, in as neutral a tone as she could.

"I might say the same of you," her father snapped, his voice tremulous but full of disdain. "I'd ask where you've been, but I'm certain I won't like the answer."

"I was out with Axel." Margo hated how thin her voice sounded, how defensive; it was astounding how much of her spirit the man was capable of ripping out with just a few words and a cruel tone.

"I don't understand why you insist on consorting with that family." Harland made a dismissive gesture. "Do you have any idea how it reflects on you, rubbing elbows with the son of the most notorious criminal in America? How it reflects on me?" He shook his head. "Or maybe that's the point. Maybe this is just one more way for you to show your contempt for everything I stand for."

"Not everything is about you," Margo retorted, feeling just a little bit of herself return. There was silence as Harland calculated how much energy he had for a fight, and seemed to come up short. With an aggrieved sigh, he subsided into the cushions behind him, withering just a little more right before her eyes. Clearing her throat, Margo ventured, "Irina left a note. She says you've been drinking again."

"That meddling Russian spy!" His face colored a little. "I ought to fire her."

"I'd just hire her back again." This was an old argument as well.

"You might remind her that I still sign the checks, and that she's being paid to mind both the house and her own damn business." Harland glowered. "I'll not tolerate her snooping about or tattling to my teenage daughter!"

"She's worried about you." Margo pulled on the cuff of her jacket, shifted her weight. She wanted to say she was worried, too, but had no vocabulary for it; that kind of sentiment had been extinct in the Manning household for years. "Your doctors said you shouldn't—"

"I am fully aware of what my useless doctors have said about alcohol, Margo," Harland growled, his discolored gums hideous in the sideways light. "All the times I've been poked and prodded, all the expensive tests they've run, all the things they've told me to do or don't do, eat or don't eat—" He ran out of air, wheezing. When he spoke again, his voice was thinner, but no less heated. "None of it has helped. It hasn't changed a thing. Teetotaling isn't going to *save* me, and it isn't Irina's business or anybody else's how I choose to spend what time I've got left."

"Don't talk like that." Margo felt hot, then cold. Harland had been deteriorating for months, this strange, unnamable illness descending like a curtain—symptoms shifting, multiplying, defying every diagnosis—but this was the first time he'd sounded anything but inconvenienced by it; now he sounded almost *resigned*, and it shook her to the core. "Your body needs to heal," she stammered, parroting back more of what she'd heard the doctors say, "and alcohol compromises your immune system! You should be resting, so—"

"*I cannot rest!*" He finally barked, his tone savage, and her jaw snapped shut. "I cannot sleep, Margo, because I am in too much pain, and I cannot abide the slow torture of any more dietary exclusions! First it was alcohol, then meat, then sodium, dairy, sugar—none of it is helping." He shook his head again, his face an unhealthy purple. "I'm miserable enough. My immune system is already compromised, and whiskey is the only thing left that does what I expect it to. The only thing in my life not hell-bent on disappointing me."

This last he said with a cutting look at his daughter, and Margo came unmoored. He was lashing out, angry and scared—for the first time in her living memory, her father was *scared*—but he also meant this. Even as he accepted that his time might finally be running out, he still used some of it to wound her. Stiffly, she turned and left the room without another word, pulling the door shut behind her.

She couldn't remember when things had gotten so bad between them. Once upon a time, Bring Your Daughter to Work Day had been practically sacred; and Harland had readily indulged her with the very best instructors in skydiving, gymnastics, judo—whatever caught her fancy—carving space in his busy schedule for competitions and ceremonies. While other teenagers in her rarified zip code were signing endorsement deals and recording vanity albums, Margo was pursuing competitive archery, and she was certain her father was proud of her for it.

The problem was that he'd never actually said so. The medals, trophies, and certificates had piled up, and Harland had shrugged them all off with a grunt, the message being that excellence was the bare minimum requirement for a Manning. At some point he stopped noticing the times she clocked doing sprints or laps, stopped noticing the grades she brought home.

But he noticed the first time she got drunk at a party. And he noticed when tabloids started documenting her dating life. She'd never imagined herself becoming that particular cliché—the poor little rich kid acting out for attention—but it had been as easy to slip into as a pair of designer shoes. The first time she and Axel broke into someone's home, it had been half for the thrill of it, and half a private *fuck you* to her perfectionist father.

She'd come home, later every night, to a passive-aggressive newsstand arranged on her bed—an assortment of the day's most unflattering headlines. Margo, waving around a martini glass at a party; Margo, bleary-eyed on the beach at dawn with an older man; Margo, darting into a car to escape a brawl she'd started at a club she should never have been let into in the first place. The gossip columnists even had a nickname for her.

MAD MARGO'S MAIN MAN: MARRIED?!

BOOZY BAD GIRL—IS 'MAD MARGO' HEADED FOR REHAB?

SEXTING SCANDAL FOR MAD MARGO: DADDY'S DISAPPOINTED!

Most of them were plainly false, others half-true at best, but they were all anyone saw when they looked at her anymore. To some, she was a spoiled brat, the epitome of everything wrong with the indolent rich; and to others, she was an icon, a carefree, trend-setting party girl who had everything but limits. Sometimes it seemed like if there was anyone who didn't know exactly who Margo Manning was, it was Margo herself.

No new headlines awaited her when she got to her room—just her bed and the harsh, molten light of the morning that poured through her open windows. Utterly drained, Margo crawled between her sheets, put her head beneath her pillow, and for the first time since her parents' divorce, cried herself to sleep.

8

JUST BEYOND A FLIMSY SECURITY FENCE, THE
scrubby hillside plunged dizzyingly into a gorge of sharp rocks and
parched foliage, and Margo allowed herself a moment to take in the
view. One week after the LAMFA job, the winter sun uncomfortably bright at 8 a.m., she found herself at the top of Griffith Park—
in a wig. It wasn't the platinum one that she wore as Miss Anthropy,
but a dun-brown shag, lank and loose so it would hang in her face; in
her hand, she clutched a large, white carrier bag.

The three distinctive domes of the observatory loomed ahead
of her, the whitewashed spindle of the Astronomers Monument
poking at the clear blue sky. The parking lot was almost empty, but
a family strolled past on the opposite side of the lawn, and Margo
pushed a pair of large sunglasses up her nose and hurried onward.

The walkways overlooking the bluff were deserted, the city
spreading out in every direction below, and Margo squinted into
the distance out of habit. A cluster of buildings poked up like birthday candles in the center of downtown, and from this angle she
could just make out the one that bore the distinctive thunderbolt
M of the Manning logo. She took a breath when she reached the

observation terrace, where telescopes angled out at the sprawl; a solitary man stood there, waiting, his face a mask of tension.

"Good morning, Monsieur Genet," Margo murmured as she leaned over the wall a respectful distance away, setting the carrier bag down beside her.

"Were you followed?" The demand, lifted straight out of a cut-rate spy flick, sounded almost charming in his lilting French accent.

"No one followed me; no one noticed me when I arrived," she assured him. "And if you want to keep it that way, maybe stop staring at me like I'm Godzilla."

He darted his glance away, wiping his upper lip. "I'm sorry, I . . . I'm not comfortable with this." His patrician features were colorless, his crimson necktie dripping from his throat like blood. "Why must this exchange be so public?"

"Would you rather I'd come to your hotel room?" she asked dryly. There wasn't a valet, bellhop, or desk clerk in the city who wouldn't get gossip magazine–sized dollar signs in their eyes if "Mad Margo" waltzed in to visit a guest. Wig or no wig, these were people trained to recognize public figures. "Trust me, this is better and safer for both of us. Here, we're just two tourists seeing the sights."

"I'm not comfortable with *you*, if I may be blunt." He made a dignified show of shooting his cuffs. "This is . . . a lot of money, and my contact told me the job would be handled by a professional. I was not expecting a, a—"

"A girl?"

"A *socialite*." He hissed it like a bad word. "I am aware of your reputation, Mademoiselle. I believe the entire planet may be aware of your reputation. I did not agree to pay three-hundred thousand dollars so some . . . teenage floozy could play cops-and-robbers!"

Margo allowed him a moment to collect himself before she said, "Pick up the bag."

"Excuse me?"

"Pick. Up. The bag." Her eyes still on the city's glittering horizon, she nudged the carrier bag a few inches in his direction with her foot.

Warily, Guy Genet did as instructed. Inside he found a heavy, rectangular object, swaddled in pale tissue—and, with trembling fingers, peeled back the layers until he saw what he was holding. Letting out a moan somewhere between relieved and orgasmic, he slumped against the wall. "I cannot . . . is this real? Is this really it?"

"*Courtship of the Shepherd Girl*, by François Boucher, circa 1742," Margo recited helpfully. "You asked, and I delivered." She peeled off the gloves she'd been wearing, her sweaty hands grateful for the air. "And nobody says 'floozy' anymore. You're in America. We say 'thot' now."

"Forgive me, I . . ." Genet shook his head and then produced an actual lace-edged handkerchief to swab his face. "I never believed this moment would come. I never thought I would actually hold it in my hands . . ."

"You've been after this thing for a while?"

"A decade, at least. We have petitioned the government, sued in court, appealed to international bodies . . . to no avail." He gave her a look brimming with self-importance. "I am the thirteenth Duke of La Valette."

Margo knew this detail—the job had been arranged by an intermediary, the client's name withheld until after the painting had been acquired, but she'd had time to research Guy Genet since then. She didn't particularly like everything she'd learned, and felt no obligation to pet his ego. "I thought France didn't have dukes anymore."

Genet sniffed disdainfully. "France may have turned her back on la noblesse, but *we* have not forgotten our legacy. In 1738, my ancestor Jean Armand de La Valette—the third duke—took for his bride the young Élisabeth de Lévis, a notoriously beautiful young woman." He caressed the carrier bag in a way that was decidedly creepy. "Even the great François Boucher was charmed by her. She was the model for the shepherdess in this painting—and it is entirely evident from her diary entries that Boucher intended her to have the canvas as a wedding present when it was completed."

"I'm guessing the French government has a quibble?"

The color returned to Genet's face. "They say there is no proof that Boucher ever followed through, no proof that the duchess ever had the work in her possession, no proof that the girl in the painting even *is* Élisabeth de Lévis!" His tone curdled with disgust. "The diary entries are detailed and clear, and yet the government has the temerity to suggest that they are a fantasy, or—even more insultingly—forged!"

"Bummer," Margo offered. She was aware from her research that Genet had refused to submit the diary for formal analysis, but she didn't know if that's because it *was* forged, or if the man had clung to this dream too long to risk a definitive, bad ending.

"But it is in La Valette hands again; this time for good." Reverentially, he reached back into the bag and teased the wrapping open so he could take another look.

"All's well that ends well," she said, but a frown was spreading across the man's face.

"The backing is torn." His expression was neutral, but something in his tone made Margo's spine prickle.

"There was a tracking device planted in the frame. It had to be removed, or your shepherdess wouldn't have made it six blocks from the museum."

He was elbow-deep in the bag now. "There seems to be some splintering to the wood, as well."

"The tracker was glued down. It had to be pried out on the fly." It had been quick and brutal work, Axel and Leif forcing the cylinders out with their pocketknives.

"The terms I stated for the deal were perfectly plain. I said no damage must come to the *Shepherd Girl* or the deal was forfeit." He sounded very pleased with himself.

"The painting is in pristine condition," Margo enunciated, her face hot, "and the splintering is minimal. There's no structural damage to the frame, and you won't even be able to see it when it's on the wall!"

"Nevertheless, there *is* damage—a violation of our arrangement." He glanced at his ostentatiously expensive watch. "I have an appointment and don't wish to draw this out, so I'm willing to be magnanimous. I'll pay you . . . let's say a hundred thousand? And we can put this matter to rest."

"You'll pay three hundred like we agreed." Margo struggled to keep her voice down. "Or 'this matter' will get ugly."

"Oh?" Genet sneered. "And what do you propose to do? The painting is in my hands now, so as for leverage, we are at something of an impasse. You cannot expose me without exposing yourself. I'm afraid you're not in any position to make demands."

Margo was silent for a moment, breathing slowly so she wouldn't jump the guy and kick him clear down the hillside into Griffith Park. "So the painting is only worth a hundred thousand to you now. Okay." She ran her tongue along the inside of her cheek. "How about your marriage? What's the price on that?"

"Excuse me?" His eyebrows went up.

"I'm assuming Madame Genet doesn't know about Éloïse Lombard, the sixteen-year-old student at the Lycée Molière that you've been exchanging naughty emails with for the past three months?" Margo pulled out her phone and made a show of scrolling through her image gallery, drawing up a choice screenshot. "My French is rudimentary, but did you really compare her butt to a bowl of ice cream? I mean, points for creativity, but--"

"*How did you*—" he cut himself off with a strangled gulp, his face turning red; then, he spluttered implausibly, "I have no idea what sort of vulgar trick you're playing, but I have done no such thing!"

"Really?" Margo scrolled through a few more screenshots. "Because there are some pictures in here, too, my friend, and they don't leave much to the imagination." Helpfully, she showed him one. "You might want to have *un docteur* take a look at this mole on your thigh, Guy. It looks a little iffy."

Genet's face went from red to purple to white again, and his grip trembled around the handles of the carrier bag. "You little bitch," he whispered. "How could you possibly . . ."

"If there's one thing teenagers know how to do, it's homework," she answered coldly. "And you might want to make your password harder to guess than 'LaValette.'"

Genet's tone was angered and unsteady. "So this is, what? Blackmail? Extortion?"

"I prefer to think of it as business insurance." Margo closed the photo gallery. "You can call it whatever the fuck you want, so long as you pay me what we agreed."

Muttering a string of remarks in French that Margo doubted were quite as flattering as what he'd said to Éloïse Lombard, Genet produced his phone and, with shaking fingers, made a call. At last, he faced her again, his lips white as bone. "It is done."

Margo waited until she received a notification that three-hundred-thousand US dollars had indeed been transferred to her offshore banking account, then gave the man a tight nod. "I'd say it was a pleasure doing business with you," she stated, tucking the cell back into her pocket, "but you're an asshole."

"My wife . . . she won't find out about those messages?"

"Not from me." Margo headed for the stairs up to the walkway skirting the observatory, Guy Genet staring after her, his jaw trembling with fury. Over her shoulder, she remarked, "Enjoy your painting."

On the north side of Griffith Park, craggy hillsides and fragrant pines spilled into the San Fernando Valley—an asphalt jungle of wide boulevards, midcentury architecture, and ugly temperatures. Shortly after leaving Genet to stew in his own au jus, Margo found herself walking down Victory Boulevard in the heart of Van Nuys, the satchel once again dragging at her shoulders.

She stopped at a tiny storefront business sandwiched between a donation center and a run-down nail salon, peeling letters above the door spelling out BRIGHT EYES TRAVEL. A bell jingled as she pushed her way inside, the air smelling of smoke and burned coffee, faded travel posters covering the walls. There were a few plastic chairs against the wall, a dead plant hanging from the ceiling, and a girl with stringy hair behind the counter.

Thumbing through a magazine, not bothering to look up, the girl announced, "Computers are down."

"I was told my itinerary was already printed out," Margo returned.

At that, the girl's eyes snapped up from the magazine. Leaning forward to press a button on the underside of the counter, she said, "Go on back."

An electronic buzz sounded as the door to the rear office unlocked; beyond it, Margo encountered a second door, where she had to wave to a camera and wait for yet another buzz. When it came, she stepped through and into a crowded and dimly lit storeroom with concrete floors and exposed bulbs, the walls hidden behind shelves that sagged with an astonishing collection of stolen goods.

Near the back of the room, behind a broad desk that looked like it had been used as a scratching post by a mountain lion, sat a rangy man in a wide-brimmed homburg. Burn scars shaped one side of his face, the skin shiny and textured, and the tough tissue resisted his grin when Margo walked through the door. "Well, well. Look who's here."

"Good morning, Vojak," she said, resting the heavy satchel on the floor.

"It's funny, I was just talking about you."

"Let me guess." Margo brightened. "Another satisfied customer?"

Vojak tipped his head to the side. "According to Monsieur Genet, you have quite the way with words."

"He tried to pull shit, and I was nice enough to explain why that wasn't such a good idea," she replied serenely. "I did him a favor, really."

"Yeah, he sure sounded grateful on the phone." Vojak leaned back, another smile tugging up one side of his mouth. "I *think* he expected me to include his comments in your performance review."

"Well, damn. There goes my promotion." Margo perched on the edge of the desk. "He paid up, though, and unless he has more long-dead ancestors immortalized on canvas somewhere, I wasn't counting on repeat business." Respectfully, she added, "Thanks for hooking me up with the job, even if that Guy guy was a prick. I transferred your cut into your preferred account already."

"I know, that's why I decided to let you come in." He gestured to the satchel. "What have we got here?"

"You'll never believe it," Margo said, hoisting it onto the desk. "I went to the museum, and these paintings just followed me home!"

"It's because you've got a kind face." Vojak lifted out the canvases, fitting a jeweler's loupe into his eye so he could examine their brushstrokes.

Margo stayed silent until he'd gone through each of the pieces in turn, and then asked, "So, what do you think? Can you find new living arrangements for a couple of Fragonards, a Wattcau, and two . . . third-guy-whose-name-I-can't-pronounce?"

"Possibly. Probably." Vojak peered up at her with a smile. "We'll have to see."

Margo tolerated this gamesmanship with admirable self-control. News reports had been cagy, but enough information had been released to ascertain what had been taken from LAMFA; Vojak, one of the most prolific and connected fences in the LA area, had probably been feeling out potential buyers for days, anticipating this haul—maybe he'd even initiated a preliminary auction.

Trafficking stolen art wasn't like moving black market electronics, or even cars; the paintings would be expensive, and the buyer would never be able to display them or brag about the acquisition. Only a handful of collectors were wealthy enough and fixated enough to want that kind of bad deal—and Vojak was the man most likely to find them.

The fact was, though, that Margo knew very little about her fence that wasn't available on the surface. He ran his operation out of the back of a dummy travel agency; he had facial scarring and walked with a cane; and he was quite the snappy dresser. *Vojak*, a word that meant "soldier" in a few Slavic languages, was almost certainly not his real name, and five different sources had given her five different accounts of his background.

"By the way," the man said, moving the paintings to a stand-up rack behind the desk, "I've got a couple of buyers interested in the items your team 'liberated' from the Chinese consulate last month. I've been offered fifty for the Scythian doodads, thirty for the coin collection, and six hundred for those diamonds."

Margo almost fell off the desk. "S-six hundred *thousand*?"

"Guessed it on the first try!" Vojak spread his hands. "Get the little lady a prize."

"I . . ." She searched for words. "They were so teeny, though!"

"Size can be deceiving. You should go after jewelry more often, you know. It's lighter, easier to sell, and stones can be recut and reset like that." He snapped his fingers. "I can't believe that you, of all people, don't know how much diamonds are worth."

"I . . ." Margo's voice stalled out again. Another cliché she'd lived up to without realizing it was "rich kid who doesn't appreciate the value of things." The jewelry she owned had either been gifted to her or purchased through a private buyer on a parent's account. She'd never paid much attention to prices.

"You know, if you'd snagged a couple of hard drives or blank passports while you were in that embassy, we could be talking about numbers in the seven figures," the fence pointed out smoothly, but Margo was shaking her head before he even finished.

"No thanks. You know my disclaimer: I'm a thief, not a spy." She drew a hard line at government secrets and identity papers; the implications were too broad, and too serious. Depriving the French government of a Boucher was one thing, but enabling a national security breach was another. "I'll think about the jewelry thing, though. In the meantime, say yes to the doodads and diamonds, but hold out on the coins. They're worth more than thirty grand, and with six-hundred coming in, we can afford to wait and see if the offer goes up."

"You're the boss," Vojak said, as Margo took the satchel and headed for the door.

"Don't forget it!" she sang back. Then, halfway into the vestibule between the two locking doors, she turned around again. "And, Vojak? No more thirteenth dukes."

9

ON THE LONG DRIVE BACK FROM VAN NUYS TO
Malibu, traffic jamming the freeways as east-siders fled west and
west-siders crawled east, Margo called Axel from the car. They'd
barely spoken since the break-in, and the distance between them was
starting to throb like a toothache. When he answered the phone,
she began talking immediately.

"I'm going to be putting some money in your account. And,
Axel? It's a *lot* of money."

When she relayed the numbers, the boy actually gasped out
loud. "Shut the front door—are you serious?"

"That was my reaction, too!" Margo squealed. "I mean, apparently we need to be looking for bags of diamonds way more often."

"Margo, babe, I don't know who you think you're talking to,
but I am always on the lookout for a bag of diamonds."

They giggled together, and she felt a rush of warm relief. She
and Axel didn't fight often, and when they did, it made her feel
like a piece of herself was missing. Afraid to let the moment escape,
she asked, "How's your mom?"

"Okay." He sounded cautious, afraid of invoking a jinx.

"Today's a better day. She spent some time on the deck, and she's sleeping now."

"That's good." She nodded to herself. "If you need anything—"

"I need a favor," he said, almost at the same time.

"Name it." She crossed her fingers, hoping against manual labor.

"You have to go to a party with me." His voice was small. "It's tomorrow night, at Astrology on Cahuenga."

"Astrology?" Even though he couldn't see her, Margo grimaced. "That place is the literal worst, Axel. Everything is sticky, the people are gross . . . it's where all the teenage floozies hang out!"

"Listen, you owe me," he began argumentatively, but then stopped short. "Did you say 'floozies'?"

"I'll owe you anything else, okay? I'll take you drag shopping. I'll buy you a pair of Louboutins, if they make them in your size." She thought for a second. "I'll *commission* a pair of Louboutins in your size! Just please don't make me go?"

"I can't . . ." he trailed off uncomfortably, and mumbled, "I won't get in without you."

"Because you're underage? Please. Astrology has lower standards than that. You don't need a hot chick to talk your way past the bouncers."

Mumbling even quieter, his tone miserable, Axel revealed, "Ryan's hosting a thing there. And . . . I'm not exactly invited."

"Oh." Ryan Labay, the son of an actress and a record executive, was one of the more popular guys at Somerville Prep—their tiny private school near Zuma Beach. He listened to the best music, threw the best parties, and had the best abs in the senior class. Once upon a time, he had also been one of Axel's best friends.

But then came Basil's infamous arrest, which made the Moreau name a social disease that no Malibu resident wanted to catch— and the Labays had been among the crooked financier's many victims. Axel still kept hoping he could live down his father's reputation, still get back a little bit of what had been taken from him, and Margo didn't know how to tell him it was pointless.

"There's a list, so just call him and tell him you want to come, and that you're bringing a plus one." Axel rushed on, "Or maybe you don't even have to bother! If you just showed up, it's not like they wouldn't let you in."

"Okay, Axel," Margo said, trying not to sound as depressed as she felt. "I'll get you into Ryan's party."

Hanging up, she hoped she wasn't making a terrible mistake for both of them.

When Margo got home, the salty breeze from the ocean cooling the canyon, she found two cars parked in the forecourt—a beat-up sedan and an even more beat-up SUV—only one of which she recognized. Letting herself in through the garage, the bright, lemony scent of cleaning spray greeted her immediately, and she called out, "Irina?"

"Margo?" The voice came from the kitchen, where she encountered a stout woman with a suspicious frown and hair that was magenta from a bold henna rinse. "What are you doing home? It is school day, no?"

"I had . . . stuff to do?" Margo anticipated a lecture, but the stern-faced woman merely tossed up her hands and muttered in Russian. Narrowing her eyes, the girl remarked, "You know, I'm getting a little tired of people cursing me out in languages I don't speak today."

"You think this is curse? This is nichto. My grandmother would give you curse, God rest her horrible soul." The woman snatched up a rag and started wiping down the countertop so ferociously, Margo half expected the black stone to turn white.

"Irina, is everything okay?"

The Mannings' housekeeper sighed, her motions slowing.

"Your father is not feeling well. I think . . . I think he gets worse."
Shortly, she added, "We exchanged ideas."

"I can imagine how that went. Did he fire you?"

"He tried. I tell him no." Irina shrugged dismissively. "And don't
change the subject. What do you mean, 'stuff to do'? You had school
to do!"

Wordlessly, Margo reached into her purse and drew out an
envelope that bulged with paper currency, and placed it on the
counter before Irina. The woman's dark, intelligent eyes darted
quickly around the room, and then she swiped the money up and
stuffed it into a pocket of her apron. Softly the girl said, "That's
forty-eight thousand, and I've got more coming."

"Spasibo," the housekeeper murmured, looking nervous. She
gave the girl a little smile, and then resumed cleaning.

Years ago, in another life, Irina Zhukova had been a nurse in a
suburb of Moscow, married to a writer and activist who was critical of the current regime. When the woman had treated patients
of a chemical explosion the government was attempting to cover up,
she smuggled copies of the charts to her husband, who subsequently
published them. Two weeks later, he was dead—killed in a staged
home invasion—and Irina, fearing for her own life, fled the country. Her name smeared by planted stories back home, she'd been
forced to abandon her medical career and seek whatever employ-
ment she could find; but that didn't mean she'd given up helping
the sick and the desperate.

"Is the clinic doing well?" Margo asked softly.

"We do okay." Irina bobbed her head, patting the new lump in
her apron. "This will help. Always we need more medicine, more
supplies, more everything."

A year and a half earlier, when a romantic evening with her first
serious boyfriend had ended in a broken condom and a lot of panic,
Margo turned to Irina for help. Freshly sixteen, she didn't dare tell

her perpetually disappointed father—and, already a public figure, the girl was terrified of being photographed buying a home pregnancy test.

The housekeeper hadn't even blinked. Bundling Margo into her aging sedan, she'd whisked the girl all the way from Malibu to one of the worst neighborhoods in the city, where, in the belly of a gutted tax preparation office, an unlicensed health center had sprung up. The small front room was packed with weary and frightened patients, mostly women, and the sudden revelation of the place took Margo's breath away; shut out by the system and with nowhere else to turn, some people waited for days to get an appointment.

It had been humbling. With access to more money than she'd ever need, Margo was stealing out of sheer boredom, while hundreds of people depended on one illicit field hospital for basic care. That afternoon, skipping to the front of the line to receive a brief exam and some emergency contraceptives, she brooded over a sudden wellspring of guilt.

From that day forward, Margo contributed her entire cut from every heist to the health center—money that couldn't be declared to an organization that couldn't exist—helping the women who ran it to pay for everything from bandages to bribes. Unable to donate any portion of her considerable allowance, thanks to Harland's scrupulous management of her expenses, it never felt like enough.

"Irina, whose car is that in the courtyard?" Margo asked after a moment. The dented SUV had been driving her nuts, because she couldn't profile the owner. The auto was a newer model, and not a cheap one, but it looked like it had been rolled down a ravine a few times. While on fire.

"Your father has visitor," the housekeeper answered unhelpfully. "A gentleman."

"Who? What gentleman?"

"You're so curious, go upstairs! See for yourself." The woman scowled, but with a glimmer of something in her eye Margo couldn't quite identify. "I am told that my job is to mind my own business! So here I am, minding business."

Attacking the stovetop with the rag, Irina muttered more Russian profanities under her breath, and Margo followed her curiosity upstairs. There, she found the gentleman visitor slouched in a decorative chair outside her father's bedroom door, thumbs flying over the screen of a smartphone. Dressed in a black polo shirt and pressed khakis, she was surprised to find that he was young—maybe only a few years older than she was.

Margo cleared her throat and the guy looked up, his face breaking into an unexpected grin that showed startlingly perfect teeth. He had close-cropped dark hair, a cleft chin, and warm brown eyes. Before she could speak, he headed her off. "Well, if it isn't Margo Manning."

"Do I know you?" she inquired coolly, because it was always best to be cool around gorgeous boys.

"Ouch!" The guy made an exaggerated show of flinching, hands over his heart. "It's been a while, but I thought for sure you'd remember. Do you forget all the guys you've seen naked?"

Margo's eyebrow arched so high it almost scratched the ceiling. *"Excuse me?"*

The guy shot up from the chair with a panicked expression. "Oh shit, sorry—that really didn't come out the way it sounded in my head! You were, like, five years old at the time." Margo crossed her arms over her chest and narrowed her eyes, and the boy's face turned hot pink. "I'm just digging this hole deeper, aren't I?"

"When you reach six feet, I'll start piling in the dirt."

"We used to know each other," he blurted. "I'm Dallas. Dallas Yang?"

It took Margo a beat to recover, the name Dallas Yang hurtling out of the past and towing a surprisingly long train of memories. They were hazy, from around the time her parents had divorced—a page of history she'd put effort into forgetting—but they were good ones. Deciding to make him work just a little harder, though, she shook her head resolutely. "No. I'm sorry, but I remember Dallas Yang. He's a scrawny, seven-year-old showoff who can't shut up about Harry Potter. You're nothing like him."

"Double ouch." Dallas rubbed the back of his head with a sheepish look, and Margo couldn't help noticing just how rigorously his biceps and shoulders tested the integrity of his polo shirt. "Is that really the impression I left? I thought I had way more game than that."

"All guys overestimate their game."

"Hey, you'd be surprised how often my Harry Potter trivia works." He gave her a rakish, lopsided smile that had her thinking, *No, I probably wouldn't be surprised at all*.

Until she'd passed the bar herself, Dallas's mother, Liliana Perez, had worked as a paralegal for Winchester Martin—Harland's longtime personal attorney. Practically family, Win was a frequent guest at the mansion; and, as Liliana had become practically family to him, she and her husband and their scrawny, showoff son had been around often as well.

Margo had been fascinated by Dallas when she was a kid. Two years older, he was brash and outgoing, seemingly fearless. She remembered a stick-wielding, gap-toothed whirlwind careening around their expansive lawns, screaming at the top of his lungs. And now? Now he was at least six foot two, with broad shoulders, a lantern jaw, and a pouty bottom lip with a slight cleft in it, like a ripe plum, begging to be tasted—

"Earth to Margo—everything okay?" Dallas was looking at her funny. "Your eyes kinda glazed over for a minute."

"Sorry, yeah, I'm good," she said, trying to shake off the sudden warm feeling in her stomach. "What brings you to Malibu after, like, a decade?"

"We moved out to Pasadena a while back, to be closer to mom's office. I'm here because I'm actually interning for Win now, and"—he gestured to a briefcase resting against the wall—"I have some stuff for your dad to sign. Only, your terrifying Russian guard dog downstairs told me that if I woke him up, she'd bury me in cement. And I'm not sure it was a figure of speech."

"I thought Win was scaling back his practice?" Having recently turned seventy, the Mannings' attorney was gearing up for retirement—if Harland would allow it.

"He is. He did." Dallas shrugged. "No more assistant, no more paralegal—just me, answering phones, filing stuff, and getting paperwork signed. He kind of took me on as a favor to Mom."

"Just, like, as a job? Or are you going to be a lawyer?"

"The second one. I'm at UCLA, following in Mom's footsteps!" He gave her that smile again, and she was proud of herself for not feeling woozy. "I was actually in Switzerland for the summer, doing a program on international law. My parents are a little pissed at me, though, because I spent more time jumping out of airplanes than sitting in class."

"Jumping out of—sorry, you're going to have to back up."

His expression became utterly serious. "Switzerland is basically the extreme sports capital of Europe. Skydiving, snowkiting, hang gliding . . . it's amazing!"

"I don't know what 'snowkiting' is, but it sounds pretty extreme," Margo offered. "So. Dallas Yang is going to be a lawyer. I remember you wanting to be an explorer or a robot."

"Turns out robot jobs are easy to find, but the pay sucks." He stretched his arms out, the fabric of his shirt riding up enough to show a couple inches of bare skin, and Margo clenched her teeth together to keep her tongue from scrolling out. "I'd ask what you've been up to lately, but you're famous enough these days that I guess I don't have to."

She smiled a little, automatically, but felt suddenly defensive. Millions of people followed her life in magazines and on the internet, a sensationalized mix of highs and lows—Margo Manning at fashion week; Margo Manning on the beach; *MAD MARGO HEADED FOR REHAB?*—and she was pretty sure she'd given up caring about the opinions of relative strangers. So why did his casual remark bother her so much?

"Who needs social media when you've got the paparazzi?" she volleyed back to cover her disappointment, and they both laughed awkwardly.

"So, um, I hope this isn't a sensitive question," Dallas began, "but what's the matter with your dad? All Win said was that he hasn't been feeling well, but your housekeeper made it sound like he should be in an iron lung or something."

"We don't really know." She experienced the usual stab of hopelessness whenever she admitted those words out loud. "At first we thought it was a digestive thing, then a blood infection, and then they started looking into autoimmune disorders, but . . . no conclusive results."

"Some buddies of mine were interns at this hospital in Geneva with a whole unit on rare illnesses. Maybe—"

"He's seen all the specialists," Margo declared flatly. "He's consulted *everyone*. Nobody knows what this thing is. Nobody knows how to treat it."

There was a thick silence, and then voices rose from the first floor—Irina's blunt accent hammering against a quiet and smooth male voice. Footsteps pounded the stairs, and then a tall, gaunt man in a pricey suit emerged into the hallway. Seeing the two teenagers, he gave a wolfish smile. "Margo! What a pleasant surprise."

"Mr. Brand, hi." Margo greeted the man unenthusiastically, but he moved forward anyway, taking the girl by the arms and leaning in to kiss her cheek. Instinctively, she stepped back, putting her hands out to stop him, something hard and heavy in the man's coat pocket bouncing off her wrist.

Brand ignored the rebuff. "How nice that you're home. I thought you'd be in school."

"Half day," Margo mumbled. "Dallas, I don't know if you remember Addison Brand—he's the executive vice president at Manning. Mr. Brand, this is Dallas Yang. His mother, Liliana, used to work with Win Martin."

Brand acknowledged the boy without apparent interest. "Good afternoon, Mr. . . . Yang, was it? I thought Liliana's name was something Mexican."

"Cuban," Dallas corrected, his polite smile hardening in place. "She kept her last name after marrying my dad."

"How nice. Well, you young people enjoy your day. I'm here for Harland."

As he headed for the bedroom, Dallas called out, "Mr. Manning is asleep. I don't think we're supposed to disturb him."

"He'll want to see me," Brand replied, his tone the verbal equivalent of an eye roll, and shoved open the door without knocking.

Dallas turned an apologetic grimace on Margo. "I'm sorry. If he's really going to wake your dad up, I might as well get these papers signed. But it was nice to see you again. Maybe we can catch up sometime?"

"Sure," Margo answered as he grabbed the briefcase and headed for the bedroom, but her mind was on the object she'd felt in Addison Brand's suit pocket—the weight, the shape, the flash of silver she'd caught when he turned; it was a hip flask, and she knew she'd just figured out where her father was getting his whiskey from.

10

THE MOREAUS' HOME WAS GUARDED BY AN

iron gate, the scalloped edges of its Spanish-style roof just visible past a tall screen of manzanita. The brick gateposts were painted a sloppy black, and the pavement of the driveway was badly scarred, multiple acts of vandalism requiring the cheapest solutions. Margo had helped Axel with the cleanup a few times, lungs burning as she scrubbed away ugly epithets with caustic chemicals.

The villa itself was beginning to look haunted, a year and a half's worth of unhindered decay casting a long shadow. Paint peeled from the walls, weeds emerged between pavers in the flagstone walk, and the pool—which cost too much to drain and too much to clean—had been covered indefinitely, the water growing murky and rank in the permanent darkness.

That evening, Margo parked her car in the forecourt beside a long-dry fountain, and let herself inside, where a barren foyer opened onto an equally barren atrium. Beyond it, past a grandly soaring arch, lay the living room. Through tall windows backed by moonlight, Margo could just make out the few sticks of furniture that remained. With stone flooring, delicate ironwork, and hand-carved molding, it was a home with amazing bones—from which the flesh had long since been stripped clean.

"Is that Margo?" A thin but musical voice echoed in the cavernous dark, and a moment later a lamp sprang to life in the living room, illuminating the familiar figure of Jacinta Flores. Reclining on a small sofa, half hidden by a thick blanket, she looked Victorian and delicate in the sea of shadows. "It's so good to see you! How are you, mija?"

"I'm good," Margo said reflexively.

"And your father?"

"About the same."

"I'm sorry to hear that." Jacinta's voice softened and drifted through the empty rooms. "Why don't you come here and take a seat, let me keep you company while you wait for Axel. He's still getting ready, that show pony."

Obligingly, Margo settled on one of the two chairs that faced the couch. But for the seating arrangement, the lamp on the floor, and a modest television, the living room was empty. Most of the house was empty. By degrees, the villa had been plundered—first by the feds, who seized whatever was in their warrant, and then by Axel, who sold everything else to keep the lights on.

"I'm glad you two are going out tonight." Jacinta smiled warmly, but her eyes were shadowed, her face puffy from her medications. "Axel . . . he just worries so much. He has his shows, and he has you, and sometimes I'm afraid that's all that keeps him going." It was a struggle to process this, a compliment wrapped around a gut punch that made Margo feel twice as guilty for the fight they'd had. Jacinta's eyelids fluttered and drooped, and the woman took a deep breath, shaking herself awake. "I'm sorry, mija, it's these new pills. They help with the pain, but they make me so drowsy."

"It's okay, I understand."

"I wish it could be different—well." Jacinta gestured listlessly at the vacant living room, featureless walls looming in the darkness. "I wish everything could be different. We don't get to pick our cards, I guess."

"No," Margo said quietly. "We don't, do we?"

Long before Harland had taken ill, long before Basil had been arrested, Jacinta had begun to experience recurring phantom pains. At the time, it hadn't seemed a mystery; a few aches and pains were to be expected from a long acrobatic career and two complicated pregnancies. But then the pain got worse, metastasizing, new symptoms sprouting: fatigue, headaches, insomnia, muscle spasms. Doctors couldn't settle on a single diagnosis, trying different medications and different therapies as Jacinta steadily deteriorated.

And then Basil was arrested. His assets seized and his accounts frozen, it left Jacinta, Axel, and Joaquin with little income and no insurance. In a matter of months, medical bills and lawyer fees ate what was left of their savings, and then moved on to consume the art, the furniture, Jacinta's car. And still they needed more—more bills to pay, Axel and Joaquin's tuition at Somerville Prep coming due. The villa, miraculously in Jacinta's name rather than Basil's, could still be sold . . . but it was a safety net they could only fall into once.

The best solution, or so it seemed at the time, was for Margo and Axel to turn their hobby of petty break-ins into a career of high-stakes crime.

"Hey. You ready to go?"

Margo turned to see Axel framed by the high arched doorway. Dressed in a leather jacket and skinny jeans, his hair painstakingly styled, he looked more nervous about Ryan Labay's party than he ever had about committing a B&E or facing down an armed guard. Getting to her feet, Margo answered, "As I'll ever be."

"You two have fun," Jacinta called as they headed for the door. "If I'm asleep when you get home, don't wake me."

"We won't, Mom," Axel called. "Love you."

The echo of the front door banging shut was the loneliest sound in the world.

HOLLYWOOD IS A STUDY IN CONTRASTS: GLAMOROUS AND trashy, full of petty crime and pettier people, and overrun by trendy bars—an invasive species in LA's ecology. With the proper zoning permits, the dingiest block in town could suddenly become home to the hottest and most exclusive club; and then, when the shininess wore off, the city's hive-minded pleasure-seekers would abandon it for an even dingier block.

Astrology, a lounge on Cahuenga Boulevard north of Sunset, had been a particularly blistering hot spot in LA's social scene when it first opened two years earlier; but its temperature had plummeted since and, with it, the quality of the clientele. Now it was the sort of place that happily suspended disbelief when teenagers from Malibu came by with passable fake IDs—and thousands in cash to spend on bottle service in a private room.

Axel decided to wait until they were passing Vine, way too close to their destination for Margo to seriously consider turning the car around, to tell her what he'd been holding back. "So, uh, I think maybe I forgot to mention it, but this is a birthday party."

"A birthday?" Margo made a noise in her throat. "You should've said something! Are we supposed to have a gift? We're gonna look like assholes." And then it clicked. "Wait—I thought Ryan's birthday was in the summer?"

"It is." Axel shifted uncomfortably, inching his fingers closer to the door handle so he could jump out if she started hitting him. "It's, uh . . . he's *hosting* the party, but it's not for him. It's for . . . Valentina."

"Valentina? *Valentina?*" Margo turned a shocked, baleful look in his direction, eyes like laser cannons. "You tricked me into going to *Valentina's birthday party*? We *hate* her!"

"We can stay on the other side of the room," Axel promised. "There'll be a ton of people there. We probably won't even have to talk to her."

"We'll still have to *see* her. We'll have to share oxygen." Margo glowered over the steering wheel. "Air molecules that she exhales from her lungs may go into my lungs, Axel. If that happens, I'm going to kill you."

Axel tried not to smile, but it was hard to resist. Valentina, the daughter of a Russian billionaire who'd made a fortune in mining rare metals, was one of the richest kids at their school. She lived in an actual reconstructed castle, shipped brick by brick from England to a sprawling property in Topanga Canyon, and her father owned additional homes in St. Petersburg, Paris, and Dubai. For a little while, she and Margo had been a Thing—arguing at school but hooking up together at parties, their chemistry volatile and irresistible; but when Basil was arrested, and the Somerville Prep kids picked sides, Margo had chosen Axel while Valentina chose . . . well, everybody else. Being his best friend had cost Margo a lot, a heavy truth that gave their occasional disagreements the weight of a small planet.

Pulling up in front of Astrology, they handed the car keys to a valet at the curb, and then started down a narrow alleyway leading to the club's private entrance. They were dressed alike, Axel realized: leather jackets, white shirts, fitted jeans—Margo in high, black heels to his dark boots. It looked like a uniform, like they belonged together, and somehow it made him feel stronger. A rush of gratitude swept through him, so strongly that tears heated his eyes.

Crashing this party was maybe a bad decision. He'd been

popular at Somerville, way back when, and he knew he had more pride than common sense. The previous summer, Quino had practically begged Jacinta to let him go to a public school in the fall, but Axel had paid their tuition with his ill-gotten gains, and that had been the end of the discussion. They were still the targets of a lot of misdirected rage, but Somerville was the best private school in the county, and Axel refused to let Basil take one more thing of value away from them.

It was a daily struggle, though. The furious energy of those early days had subsided, and for most of the past year he'd simply been ignored at school. Like the dry fountains at the villa, he'd become a sad symbol that people were too polite to notice.

But Axel *wanted* them to notice; he wanted all of them to realize that they weren't Basil Moreau's only victims. He would show them, if they would just give him the chance, that he hated his father twice as much as any of them ever possibly could.

The bouncer at Astrology's back door was tall, beefy, and bored, scarcely glancing at their expensive fake IDs before waving them through to the private room. Inside, music thudded and murals shimmered under blue lights, the bar's theme expressed in paintings inspired by the zodiac. With a wide banquette of pale leather and roughly ten square feet of open dance floor, the air smelled strongly of spilled beer and cleaning solvent.

As soon as his eyes adjusted, the crowd of Somerville faces swimming into clarity, Axel decided this had *definitely* been a bad idea. A few gazes turned his way, then a few cold frowns, and then a few backs. Others simply pretended not to notice him, like usual.

"We don't have to stay," Margo ventured, reading the room loud and clear. "As long as we keep it low-key and you let my chest do the talking, I bet we can get drinks at the main bar."

"No." Axel tried to sound confident. "We're here. Let's at least say hi to Ryan, and . . . and then we can do whatever."

They found him at one end of the banquette, right beneath a painting of Taurus; long-limbed and dark-haired, his body toned from pitiless hours in the gym, the boy had one arm slung over the cushions—and the other wrapped around Valentina Petrenko. The girl was laughing uproariously at something he'd just said, slowly stirring a clear drink, her platinum hair as shiny as the conspicuous emerald necklace draped in her décolletage.

"Fuck." Margo's shoulders drooped, and she turned to Axel. "If we do this, I don't owe you anymore."

She didn't wait for an answer, just marched forward, plastering a friendly smile across her face that looked like it hurt. "Hey, guys, nice party! Thanks for the invite—my fake ID needed the exercise."

"What about your other fake parts?" Valentina asked sweetly.

Margo turned a look on her that would have sliced a redwood log in half, but kept the smile firmly in place. "Valentina, I love your necklace! It really brings out your boobs."

"Margo, thanks for coming out," Ryan said, but his eyes were on Axel, his face flushed from alcohol and his mood unreadable. "Moreau, what's up?"

"Hey." Axel tipped his chin. "Um, happy birthday, Valentina."

"Real cool of you to come all the way out for V's big day." Ryan's face was still expressionless, but something about the moment felt off, his voice a little too loud. "I thought we forgot to invite you."

"It's—I, I guess." Axel's face started to heat, his nerves screaming *abandon ship*. He'd hoped that a party outside of Malibu—somewhere far away from the ugly rut of everyday life—would give him a chance to make the Somerville kids see him in a different light; but Ryan was staring at him blankly, eyes somehow hot and cold at the same time. "We just wanted to say hi, and that we hope Valentina has a fun party."

"Oh yeah?" Ryan achieved an expression at last, his brows going up. "A fun party, really? But you didn't bring her a present!"

"Oh, I . . . I—" Axel froze, put on the spot. "It was kinda last minute—"

"Or maybe you wanted to buy her a drink? To celebrate her birthday?" The boy's voice was getting even louder. "I mean, it's the least you could do, right?"

"Sure." Axel nodded mechanically, his underarms boiling. Suddenly he just wanted to turn and walk away—to run out the door and not stop till he hit the beach. "Yeah, sure, no problem."

"Or maybe you want to buy everybody a drink." Ryan grinned, his face redder. "Make up for how your dad fucked us all the fuck over." There was nothing to say to this, so Axel dropped his gaze to the floor, while Ryan bellowed to the room, "Hey, everybody: Bottle service is on Moreau tonight! He's gonna use the money his dad fuckin' stole from us to buy a few drinks! Ain't that fuckin' cool?"

People stared, people muttered, Valentina whispered to the girl next to her and giggled. Axel was trying to figure out if he'd still be able to afford food until the payoff for the diamonds came in, when Margo spoke up. "Something funny, Petrenko? Maybe you'd like to share with the rest of the class."

"It's nothing." Valentina gave an insolent shrug of one slim shoulder, her glossy mouth in an unfriendly smirk. "I was just saying how sweet it is that you two dressed the same. Like the X-Men! You're like . . . Superthief and Wonder Whore!"

"First of all, those names aren't even remotely creative," Margo said impatiently, "and second of all, Superman and Wonder Woman aren't even X-Men. They're not even characters from the same superhero universe!"

"But you don't deny being a whore."

"Save the slut-shaming, V. I'm not embarrassed of my sex life."

Valentina cupped a hand to her ear. "I'm sorry, Margo, I couldn't understand you with all those dicks in your mouth."

Ryan had called attention to their corner, but Margo was

drawing an audience as she returned, brightly, "I'm sorry, I just realized I never wished you a happy birthday. I'd ask how old you are, but I think it'd be more fun to cut you in half and count the rings."

Struggling to her feet, Valentina stood an inch taller than Margo in her precarious heels. "Maybe we should count *your* STDs!"

"Fine." Margo gave a smile that showed all her teeth. "Let's start with the ones I got from fucking your dad."

It was at that point that Valentina hurled her drink in Margo's face, and Margo tackled Valentina over the back of the banquette. Moments later, two very large men scooped both girls off the floor, and Margo and Axel found themselves being escorted very roughly back outside. They'd been standing at the curb together in silence for a moment, waiting for the valet to bring the car around, when Axel finally started to giggle.

"'Cut you in half and count the rings'?" He repeated, his eyes crinkling. "'Start with the ones I got from *fucking your dad*'? Did you really say that?"

Margo started to giggle, too. "Valentina brings out the best in me, I guess."

They grinned at each other stupidly for a moment, and then Axel reached out and took her hand. "Thanks."

"For what?"

"You know what you did."

Margo shook her head. "I have no idea what you mean."

"No one's going to remember what Ryan said to me." Axel gave her a little smile. "No one's even going to remember I was there."

Margo didn't say anything for a moment. "It was worth it." She shot him a sly look, tossing her hair over her shoulder. "While I was busy mashing Valentina's face into the floor? I figured out what our next job is going to be."

11

AT THE TURN OF THE TWENTIETH CENTURY,
Bunker Hill was the most exclusive neighborhood in Los Angeles, a
rise just west of City Hall that bristled with the mansions of railroad
tycoons and oil barons; fifty years later, the posh district had subsided into slum-like conditions, the stately buildings rotting on
their foundations; and by the seventies, the entire community was
gone—stamped out completely to make way for an aggressive program of urban renewal.

Where ostentatiously gabled homes once stood, skyscrapers
now reached for the heavens—dizzying columns of darkened glass
that fed a vain city its own reflection. It was into the underground
garage for one of these, a fifty-five story tower bearing a distinctive
thunderbolt *M* insignia, that Margo steered her car the next
Thursday afternoon. A backpack over her shoulders and her face
scrubbed clean of makeup, she practiced an innocent expression as
she took an elevator up to the lobby.

"Miss Manning!" A stocky guard in a dark uniform saw her
coming as she crossed the cavernous entryway, his voice booming off polished stone the color of honey. Marble gleamed
underfoot, on the squared-off support pillars, and reflected in

the floor-to-ceiling windows that fronted the street. "Nice to see you again. To what do we owe the pleasure?"

"Hi, Lloyd. My dad sent me with some things for Dr. Khan." She angled her shoulders helpfully, showing him the backpack.

"No problem. Let me just call down and let them know you're here." Lloyd backed to the desk, picking up a phone. "Dr. Khan expecting you?"

Margo made a face. "Maybe?"

He inquired after Harland while he dialed, and she offered an awkward response, saved when someone picked up the line and Lloyd turned his attention to the receiver. "I've got Margo Manning up here with a delivery for Dr. Khan." He listened for a moment. "Okay, you got it." Hanging up, he smiled again. "I'll just log you in, and you're all set!"

The elevators to the rest of the building were in a deep alcove off the lobby, and when Margo boarded one, Lloyd leaned through the doors to swipe his key card over the scanner mounted on the wall panel. He even punched the button for the sub-basement level where the lab was located—as if Margo could have gotten into the secured underground parking facility in the first place if she didn't already have her father's master key card. But she smiled and said thank you as the doors slid shut, and then flexed her jaw when the elevator plunged, her eardrums popping.

When the car slowed and the doors opened again, she faced a sterile waiting room, colorless and drab with a few stiff chairs against the wall. There was a young man seated at a reception desk, and behind him a sturdy gray door bearing an emphatic sign that read AUTHORIZED PERSONNEL ONLY BEYOND THIS POINT.

"Hi there," the receptionist said, adjusting his glasses and giving her what he clearly thought was an irresistible smile. "Dr. Khan will be out soon, if you'd like to take a seat?"

He wasn't even finished speaking, however, when the gray

door creaked open and Dr. Nadiya Khan herself appeared. Disarmingly petite, her black hair cut sleekly just beneath her chin, the woman's dark brown eyes radiated intelligence. With a perfunctory smile and a soft accent, she said, "Margo, it's so nice to see you again."

"Stuff from my dad," Margo explained. "Do you have a minute? He said you might want to make some notes or something for him to look over."

"I can spare some time." She held the door open. "We'll go to my office."

They walked along a corridor, passing windows looking into a sanitized room full of arcane circuitry and robotic arms, and stepped into a wide area filled with workstations. Technicians sat before massive computer screens, typing in figures, checking results; if any one floor could be called the heart of the Manning Corporation, it was this one.

Specializing in the development and application of microtechnology, Manning had designed parts and systems that were used in everything from cell phones and onboard navigational interfaces to infrared satellites and surgical equipment. What was not as widely known—not even by all of the company's employees—was that they were also a major government contractor, outfitting the US intelligence community's operatives with top secret, next-generation gear. Their particular expertise had resulted in the creation of items such as earrings equipped with parabolic microphones; covert surveillance devices so innocuous in appearance that they could be planted right in front of a target without arousing suspicion; and even optoelectronic lenses with night vision capability crafted to look like ordinary sunglasses.

Dr. Khan led Margo to the door of a private office with a placard that spelled out NADIYA KHAN, CHIEF SCIENTIST. The space inside was filled with books, binders, and samples of Manning's most enigmatic innovations—and once the door clicked shut behind them, it was also soundproof.

"How did it go?" The scientist asked softly as she took a seat behind her desk.

Margo smirked. "I didn't get arrested, did I?"

"Don't joke about that, Margo, please." Dr. Khan rubbed her temples and grimaced. "You must know, that is a very real fear of mine."

"We were careful," the girl promised soberly. "We're always careful." As if to demonstrate, with delicate motions she opened her bag and began removing its contents. "The op went exactly according to plan. The wand and reverse screwdriver thingy worked like a charm, and the little EMP was a lifesaver. I already wired your cut to your account, and the transfer ought to have cleared by now."

"It did; thank you," Dr. Khan mumbled as Margo set the wand, screwdriver, and pocket-sized EMP on the desk. "Did you have any trouble?"

"With the tech? No." Margo eyed the scientist carefully. "Is everything okay? Did something . . . happen?"

"We got five more out yesterday," the woman finally said, her eyes on the EMP.

"Five? That's great!"

Dr. Khan merely shook her head. "It was supposed to have been eight. Three didn't make the window, and I don't know how soon we'll be able to try again—or if they'll still be alive when we do."

"I'm sorry." Margo studied the woman's face, pulled between grief and self-reproach. "But five more people get to live; five more people have a future again. That's something, right? Without what you're doing, that number would be zero."

"Maybe so." Dr. Khan finally spared Margo a weak smile. "It just gets to me sometimes. The people I communicate with—for them, it's all numbers and euphemisms. 'Eight packages for pickup,' 'five successful deliveries.' Like they're trying to forget that they're talking about human lives." She shrugged lethargically. "Perhaps that way is easier."

For years, Nadiya Khan had been working with an underground organization to smuggle refugees, many of them children, out of her war-torn homeland in the Middle East; couriers ferried false papers and communiqués in and out of extremist-held territories, agents in the field guided escapees to safe houses, and collaborators provided shelter or cover. All of it was deadly work, and the amount of untraceable money needed to keep it going was incalculable. Fourteen months earlier, when the scientist had caught her boss's wealthy teenage daughter trying to slip the working prototype of a digital safecracker into her purse during a tour of the lab, she thought she'd found her golden goose.

She'd been right.

"Okay, I didn't want to say anything until the deal was finalized, but you're going to make me cry, so you leave me no choice." Margo straightened in her chair. "We hit kind of an unexpected jackpot, and as soon as my fence seals the deal—which could be any minute now—I'll be putting sixty-thousand dollars into your account."

"*Sixty-th*—" Dr. Khan sat up this time, eyes bulging. "Are you serious?"

"As a diamond heist." Margo waited until a genuine smile broke across the scientist's features, and then pushed a scrap of paper across the desk. "Now that I've got you in a good mood, here's a short list of stuff I'm going to need to hit our next target."

As she read through the items, Dr. Khan made a face. "We have some of these things in the vault already, and a few of them I can jury-rig from existing parts, but the others . . ." She glanced up at Margo, eyes doubtful. "I've got a pretty healthy discretionary budget, and your father allows me a lot of freedom to explore new tech and requisition prototypes, but . . . a fingerprint duplicator is going to raise some eyebrows."

"Really? Seems like the CIA or whoever could get a lot of use out of something like that."

"They could. They probably have a few already," Nadiya answered smoothly, "because they haven't asked us for any." The scientist sat back, tucking a hand beneath her chin. "Margo, ever since your father stopped coming into the office, oversight of the lab has changed. Harland would let me commit murder down here, so long as I produced results; I built those heat-neutralizing bodysuits for you, if you'll recall, and he found a way to sell the designs to the government. But since he's been gone, Addison Brand has assumed many of his responsibilities, and he's taken a significant interest in research and development. He wants an explanation for every expense—and even though I don't technically answer to him, his questions are difficult to ignore without drawing scrutiny neither of us need."

"So don't ignore them," Margo returned. "Just tell him . . . I don't know, call the thing a miniaturized 3-D printer, or whatever—there's got to be a million applications for something like that."

Dr. Khan nodded, but with a cryptic frown. "My concern is not that he'd try to stop me from making the device." If she had more to say on the subject, she stopped herself. Gesturing to the wand, screwdriver, and EMP, she murmured, "I appreciate your bringing these items back so quickly."

"I always do," Margo chirped, which was mostly true. The sunglasses and comms were more or less on permanent loan from the lab's vault, as the team used them so frequently and—due to severely restricted access—the odds anyone would notice them missing were slim to none. "Thank you for letting us use them in the first place."

Dr. Khan met Margo's eyes with a very serious look. "Thank me by not getting caught."

12

THE PISTOL-SHAPED ENCLAVE OF WEST HOLLY-
wood, less than two square miles of homes, heartache, and glittering
nightlife in the middle of LA, was mobbed that Friday evening.
Tourists flocked to its famous Sunset Strip, while locals overflowed
the watering holes on Santa Monica Boulevard—including the
Ruby Lounge, a gay bar that hosted a wild, twice-monthly drag
show called Tuck/Marry/Kill. Ruby's was always packed, but that
evening, one dressing room in the back remained conveniently
empty.

"As you all know," Margo began, leaning against a dusty
countertop, her back to a row of vanity mirrors, "Valentina Petrenko
is a sleaze and a cankerous asshole."

Leif leaned into Joaquin, smelling of soap, the hair behind his
ears just a little damp from a recent shower. A smile in his voice, he
whispered covertly, "I keep forgetting that you fancy Malibu types
are friends with Valentina Petrenko."

"*Please*, we are enemies." Joaquin smiled a little, too. The last
to arrive, Leif had chosen the seat right next to him, flashing him a
furtive grin that made it feel like there was some kind of private joke
between them.

"What you may *not* know," Margo continued brusquely, "is that her father, Arkady Petrenko, is an avid collector of art and antiquities. He gets most of it from auctions or private buyers, but I happen to know that he'll buy from the black market, too, if he wants a piece bad enough. Name something obscure and valuable, and he's got a pile of it in his actual fucking castle: tapestries, rare books, religious artifacts . . ." She paused, looking around the room. "Royal jewels."

"I feel like that's my cue or something," Davon remarked drolly, sweeping the wild blond curls of a wig over his shoulder. He and Axel, both regular performers in Tuck/Marry/Kill as Dior Galore and Liesl Von Tramp, were in full drag—heels high, waists snatched, their faces beat to the gods.

For Joaquin, drag was a hobby, a game of dress-up in wearable art; for Axel and Davon, it *was* art. A consuming, transformative, fulfilling art that demanded everything and gave back more. The only time Joaquin ever saw his brother smile anymore—really smile, the way you do when it's for yourself and nobody else—was when he was onstage.

"Axel!" Margo barked the boy's name out like a headmaster from some BBC boarding school drama. "Describe what Valentina was wearing to her birthday party."

"Um." Axel squirmed, his taffeta frock rustling. "A really tight bandage dress that should've stayed back in 2011 where it belonged, and an emerald necklace so fucking big it could've anchored the Queen Mary."

"That necklace," Margo announced, sweeping an iPad up from the countertop to display a black-and-white portrait of a cheerless woman in lace, "once belonged to a Russian princess named Xenia Zavadovskaya." Atop the princess's head, a complicated tiara perched on a coil of dark, wavy hair, and across her collarbone spread an array of gemstones the size of poker chips. "Her family fled the

Bolsheviks for Western Europe in 1917, where they quickly sold or bartered her emeralds. Sometime between then and now, the jewels found their way into Petrenko's hands. It's hard to estimate how much they're worth today, but if I had to guess, I'd say a shitload."

She swiped up another portrait, this one of a frail woman with a diadem of dark, shining stones, with matching starbursts at her ears and around her throat. "Countess Yekaterina Golovkina. She was killed in the revolution. I don't know where her earrings and necklace ended up, but I saw this same *ruby crown* on Valentina's head at her sweet sixteen sophomore year. And there are a lot more examples.

"Long story short: With the Communist uprising, a lot of blue-bloods headed for the hills, taking with them only what they could carry. And since jewels are lightweight and useful as currency, they were popular." Margo looked around the room again. "It's anybody's guess how many pieces that once belonged to Russian nobles still survive a hundred years later, but Petrenko has made a lifelong quest out of obtaining as many of them as he can—and by any means possible."

"So that's the target, then?" Leif asked. "Petrenko's jewelry collection?"

"That's the target." Margo swiped to another picture on the iPad, this one an aerial photo of the Petrenko home in Topanga Canyon, lifted from a profile in *People* magazine. "I've been inside Valentina's actual fucking castle before, and the whole place is one big exhibition gallery. But because of their value, and because they weren't all procured through legal channels, Arkady can't display his prize pieces openly." On the screen, she zoomed in to a rear corner of the imposing residence. "For that reason, he converted this turret into a special showroom for his most precious items, all of which are displayed in bulletproof cases fitted with biometric locks. That's where the jewels are."

Tentatively, Joaquin raised his hand, his cheeks already warm as he prepared to ask a question. At school, everyone just waited for him to fuck up, sneering at his humiliation every time he was called on in class—and it was no less intimidating to be a newcomer to this group, where they threw around official-sounding jargon they'd spent most of a year learning together. "Um, what's a bio-whatsit lock?"

"Biometric," Leif answered, and Joaquin was relieved to see his smile was friendly. "It means the lock includes a mechanism that measures a physiological trait—like a fingerprint or a retinal pattern—so it can only be opened by specific people."

"Okay. Sure." Joaquin nodded, although he'd only followed about half of that. When Leif addressed him, their knees had brushed together. And now they were *still* together. They were still touching, and it was like a marching band had come crashing into the room, stomping in a big, obvious circle around the point where their legs touched, and heat swept back up Joaquin's neck and into his face.

"Before anyone asks, I'm already exploring a solution for those locks," Margo went on, impossibly oblivious to the touching knees, "and we should know soon if it's workable."

"I don't mean to sound negative, girl," Davon remarked, "but how are we supposed to storm an 'actual fucking castle,' anyway? I mean, my broadsword is in the shop, and this place looks a little . . . fortified."

"Yeah. About that." Margo shut off the iPad, studying the blank screen. "Before we put this to a vote, there's two things you guys need to know: First, Arkady Petrenko is kind of a security nut. He's got powerful friends, but also some powerful enemies, and two attempts have been made on his life back in Russia—part of the reason he lives in the US full-time now. The goons who pulled me off Valentina at Astrology? They were her personal bodyguard detail. To put it bluntly, his castle is protected like he's expecting trouble, and he has an armed patrol guarding the place twenty-four-seven."

"Swell," Axel said, sarcasm dripping from his voice. "What's the second thing? He can shoot laser beams from his eyes? He has a nuclear arsenal?"

"The second thing you need to know is that this haul, if we can pull it off, could be the biggest any of us will ever see. In a lifetime." She met their eyes one by one, her excitement palpable. "The resale value of precious stones is outrageous, and if we have the settings melted down ... we could be looking at a payoff of millions of dollars—*apiece*." The four boys stared, not sure whether they'd heard correctly, and so she drove the point home. "Guys: Each one of us could walk away from this heist a millionaire. It could be the last time any of us have to do this again. So ... by a show of hands, who's in?"

Hers was already up, but Joaquin's followed it immediately, then Davon's and, after a brief hesitation, Leif's. Only one voter abstained.

Margo's brow furrowed. "Axel?"

"I'm sorry, Margo," Joaquin's brother began, "but I don't like it. We're supposed to break into a fucking fortress belonging to a paranoid whack-job, steal some necklaces from a hypersecure vault, and then sneak them out under the noses of a pack of gun-toting private bodyguards?" He shook his head, wig bouncing. "It's too risky. And you only want to do it to settle a personal score, anyway."

Margo took a step back as if she'd been slapped. "Excuse me? There's no love lost between me and Valentina, but if I was that petty, I've got about fifty videos on my phone of her doing scandalous shit that I could post online anytime." A mic test sounded from the front of the club, but you could've heard a pin drop in the dressing room. "I'm proposing this because the payoff is ridiculous, and some of us"—she skewered him with a pointed look—"need the money."

From the side, Joaquin watched his brother's mouth clamp down into a tight line. Mutinously, Axel inquired, "Think you can pull this job off without a grappling hook?"

"There's more than one way to skin a cat." Margo's voice was as hot as Axel's was cold.

Davon rotated in his seat to stare at the queen beside him, his face screwed into a question. "Girl, do you need to go outside and take a moment?"

"It's a bad idea," Axel shot back, his words clipped. "We don't need this kind of risk."

"Oh, *this* is a bad risk?" Davon blinked extravagantly. "Because last month, when we broke into a foreign consulate, fucking with international laws and throwing hands with military dudes toting assault rifles, you were down with it!" There was an unkind silence, and he continued, "Did you miss the part about 'millions of dollars'? Because—"

"I'm willing to think about it," Axel interrupted, eyes on Margo, "and maybe I'll change my mind. On one condition." He licked his lips. "Quino is out. He stays home."

"What the hell, Axel?" Joaquin was on his feet before he even knew what he was doing, his chair juddering across the floor behind him.

Axel stood up, too, but ignored the outburst. Eyes still on Margo, he said flatly, "It's him or me. And I think you know the right call to make."

Pivoting on his heel, taffeta skirt swirling, he flounced for the door. He only made it a few steps before Joaquin caught up with him, his skin prickling with rage. "What is your fucking problem? What gives you the right—"

"Will you keep your voice down?" Axel hissed irritably. "This is where I work."

"*I don't give a shit.*" Joaquin was so angry his tongue felt forked. "You've been avoiding me at home, and now you're trying to stuff me in the fridge, and I'm sick of it!"

The older boy grabbed him roughly by the upper arm, dragging him first through a narrow hallway, and then out a rear door into an alley behind the club. Once they were in the open night air, jaundiced light splashing down from a bulb that dangled on a cable overhead, Axel snapped, "You want to know why I'm 'stuffing you in the fridge'? It's because of *this*. This . . . *temper tantrum*. You're obviously not mature enough to handle—"

"Fuck you, you shithead!" Joaquin's whole body was trembling, anger burning his veins like a dose of battery acid. "You don't get to treat me like a little kid and then call me immature when it pisses me off—and you don't get to decide what I can handle!"

"You shouldn't even be here, Quino." Axel radiated disappointment. "You should never have been part of this thing to begin with."

"Well, I am! And you don't get to decide that, either."

"You should be home with Mami," Axel pressed on self-righteously. "Did you even think about the fact that she's alone right now? That she's got nobody? What if you get your head blown off trying to sneak into Valentina's castle? What's that gonna do to her?"

Joaquin was humiliated to feel tears spring to his eyes, the sudden rush of emotions so strong he couldn't contain them all. He could barely speak, his voice a broken whisper as he shook his head. "You are so fucking selfish, Axel. You never think about anybody but yourself. Do you have any idea what it's like to live with that?"

"Excuse me?" His brother actually stumbled back a step, his mouth flapping silently for a second before he could speak again. "For a year and a half I have been the only one trying to hold our family together. The only one! *Everything* I've done has been for you and Mami; I don't even get to take a *breath* anymore unless you two get oxygen from it also!"

"Is that what you're doing?" Joaquin waved at his brother's wig, his makeup, his dress. "Is this you *breathing* for me, Axel? Is this you holding us together?"

"How dare you!" The older boy's lip curled. "You know what this means to me. Forgive me if I do one damn thing for myself twice a month! This is literally the only break that I get from worrying about the two of you, taking care of the two of you—"

"And when do *I* get a break?" Joaquin shouted, his throat raw. "When is it *my* turn to do something for *my*self?" He spun around like he was going to storm away, made it two steps, and then turned back. "You know, if you want to sit this job out, maybe you should! You can be the one to stay at home with Mami, trying to figure out what you'll say if your brother doesn't come back. *You* can sit and stare at the pool we can't swim in, or look at a blank computer screen because we can't afford the internet anymore, or play shitty games on your shitty phone because you don't have any friends to text with, because *everybody you know fucking hates you!*"

His chest was heaving, and his face was wet, but he refused to wipe his eyes. "At least you have this, Axel. At least you get to have this one thing that's just yours. What about me? You won't even let me pick where I go to school."

"Quino . . ." Axel blinked, his eyes huge in the stark light. "This sort of stuff, these jobs . . . they aren't a game. It's dangerous, and it's illegal, and it's not something we do because it's fun; it's something we do because we have no other choice."

"Breaking into LAMFA was the first time I've felt alive, the first time I haven't felt like a zombie since Dad went to prison," Joaquin finally confessed, tired of stepping around the subject—tired of "Dad" being a dirty word, tired of hopscotching over Axel's feelings. "I don't care if you like that or not. You want me to help

Mami? Then get out of my way. You've been getting twenty percent as your part of the cut, and we still have to spin the wheel on which bills we're gonna pay. Together, our cut goes up to thirty-six. That's almost double, in case you need help with the math." He tossed his hands up pleadingly. "She's my mom, too. They're my bills, too! My life is fucked up, and you can't save me from it, so you might as well let me be happy—even if what makes me happy isn't want you want for me."

There was a moment of awkward, unbearable silence, Axel just staring at him, eyes zooming in and out of focus. He wasn't going to give up, Joaquin realized; he was just looking for a new way back in to the argument. The door to the club swung open again and Davon cleared his throat. "I was sent to get you for the sound check, but it probably won't be necessary. The whole neighborhood can hear the both of you, loud and clear."

"Go back inside and start *breathing*, Axel," Joaquin snapped bitterly. "You're having fun for three now."

Turning on his heel, he stalked away down the alley, headed for the sidewalk, the blaze of streetlight blurring in his eyes.

WHEN THE ANGRY CLATTER OF RETURNING FOOTSTEPS sounded in the corridor, marching back into the bar, Margo instinctively faced the open doorway. Axel appeared a moment later, framed in shadows and lit by a failing golden bulb, and her heart gave a twist as their eyes connected. It had been impossible not to hear the argument, and there were a hundred things she wanted to say; but their earlier confrontation stood like a wall between them, and it was impossible to maneuver around. No matter how much she wanted to lecture, to console, or play peacemaker, he'd challenged her authority and she couldn't afford to bend. Deliberately, she turned away to pack up her things, and when she looked back again, he was gone.

13

SANTA MONICA BOULEVARD WAS A NEON
gallery, bass-heavy music thudding so loud Leif could feel the
vibration in his lungs when he passed the packed clubs and bars.
Tipsy boys in tight-fitting shirts laughed and shouted, crowding
the outdoor seating areas, eyes bright and gestures broad. A few of
them whistled at Leif as he walked by, and his cheeks turned a little
pink—but he smiled back at the cute ones, his heart racing.

He'd never fit in anywhere before, had never felt understood
until he discovered West Hollywood. Back home there was nothing like this. After fifteen years of trying to fake it, to speak a language that didn't belong in his mouth, he'd finally found this
magical community that was fluent in his native tongue. He was
an ugly duckling who'd joined his fellow swans at last—flamboyant,
proud, occasionally slutty swans—and it had changed everything.
He hadn't even realized how hopeless he'd felt about life until he
got here and realized he didn't feel hopeless anymore.

He walked all the way into Beverly Hills before he finally caught
the bus, enduring a lurching ride down the boulevard and into Santa
Monica, texting with his roommate. Some of the other students at
the academy were going out, and no one could decide what to wear.

Another benefit of life in LA: He could finally dress however he wanted—from ripped jeans and crop tops to angel wings and body glitter, nobody batted an eye.

At Lincoln Boulevard, he disembarked, zipping up his jacket against the cool air rolling in from the ocean, and hurried the rest of the way home. *Home.* The Marechal Academy of Ballet occupied a complex of studios and classrooms on Ocean Park, along with a theater, a clinic, and two dormitories for the room-and-board students. He'd worked his ass off to get accepted there, and even in his second year, he still sometimes had trouble believing it was real.

Hurrying up the front steps of the boys' dorm, he threw open the door and nearly collided with a tall woman in a gray cardigan and flowing black slacks. Recognizing him, she smiled. "Mr. Dalby! What a coincidence."

"Dean Mountjoy?" Leif stepped back, surprised, a million anxious thoughts swirling up like silt billowing from a riverbed. "What are you . . . ?"

"Doing in the boys' dormitory at eleven o'clock on a Saturday?" Abigail Mountjoy, dean of students, concluded wryly. "Nothing salacious, I promise. I had to pick up some paperwork from my office, and while I was on campus I . . . actually, I was dropping off something for you." Her tone softened when she said it, and Leif felt his pulse go a little haywire. "Do you have a moment?"

"Um . . ." He wanted to say no, to make some excuse, but his words failed him and Dean Mountjoy took his frozen, blank-eyed stare as a yes.

"Per our conversation at the beginning of September, I've been doing periodic check-ins with your instructors, and all of them have made glowing reports about your work since what happened over the summer term."

Her tone was encouraging, but it felt like a warning nonetheless. Leif split his tuition with his parents, but the cost was so high that the first year had wiped his savings out completely. He'd spent most of the summer working three jobs, putting in hours before and after classes during the week, and both days on weekends; he'd been fatigued and stressed, constantly at the breaking point, and his dancing had noticeably suffered. Dean Mountjoy had adopted this same delicate tone when informing him that he was "no longer performing at a level that met the school's standards," and that she needed to see more focus and commitment from him if he wished to maintain his spot.

The worst of it was that the summer term wasn't even part of the normal curriculum; he'd signed up for it because it gave him a reason not to have to go back home. But his three jobs barely afforded him enough to cover the five-week special course, and he'd begun to seriously panic about where he'd get the funds for the coming year. Thank God for the guest instructor from São Paolo, who had convinced him to take an elective class on capoeira, the Afro-Brazilian martial art discipline that joined dance and acrobatics. Thank God he'd turned out to have a natural aptitude for it.

And thank God, too, for that class's public demonstration on the Third Street Promenade, where he'd lost himself in the physical symphony of constant, fluid motion—the rocking feints and spinning kicks, the clever transitions and impromptu attacks. They'd performed for nearly an hour, and when it was over and he was flushed and sweaty, he'd finally examined the gathered crowd and seen a startlingly recognizable girl watching him from the periphery.

He'd met Margo Manning just in the nick of time.

"I've . . . found a better job," Leif stated diplomatically.

"I'm glad to hear that." Dean Mountjoy continued to smile like someone was paying her to do it. "We like it best if our students have no outside distractions, of course, but scholarships are hard to come by." There was a stilted pause as the woman cleared her throat. "On that note, Mr. Dalby, it was brought to my attention that your tuition payments for the current term are . . . behind schedule."

Leif blinked. "But that's . . . I brought a check to the bursar's office two weeks ago!"

"Yes," the dean said gently, "but it was only for half the amount due."

"Right." Leif's chest began to itch with heat. "I pay half and my parents pay half—they send their checks directly to the office. That's how we've done it since I started."

"Well, maybe there's been a mix-up." The dean seemed to sense how agitated he was becoming. "Maybe your parents forgot to mail it, or they wrote the address wrong. Whatever the case, it's best that it's sorted out quickly, before it becomes a . . . problem."

She said some other things that he didn't hear over the roar of his blood in his ears, and then, with a friendly pat on his numb shoulder, she left him alone. As soon as she was gone, Leif pulled out his phone again, fingers damp and clumsy. He dreaded these calls, because they always went as badly as he feared, but this one couldn't be avoided. After the second ring, his mother answered with her standard greeting.

"Praise the Lord." Mrs. Dalby had said this so many times it sounded joyless and mechanical—an accurate barometer of her religious rigor. "I was wondering how long it might take for you to call your poor mother."

Leif ignored the jab at his guilt; it was his least vulnerable spot these days. "Mama, Dean Mountjoy just . . . My tuition payment was due last week, and the dean says your half hasn't arrived yet." There was silence on the line, and as it stretched out, a bead of sweat slipped down Leif's rib cage under his shirt. "Mama?"

"That's right," Mrs. Dalby finally said, full of confidence.

"*That's right?*" It was not the reply he'd been expecting. "What do you mean, '*that's right*'? Did you forget? Because there isn't much of a grace period—"

"Your daddy and I have been speaking with Pastor James," Mrs. Dalby interrupted, just as confidently, "and I have been having long conversations with Lord Jesus. Leif, it's time for you to come back home."

"What?" He rolled his eyes irritably, in spite of his nerves. "Mama, no. I can't just come home in the middle of a semester. I was cast in the spring production of *La Sylphide*, and I have an important role. It's a huge honor, and I need—"

"I'm not talking about a visit." Mrs. Dalby's tone was imperious. "Leif, this is no good. I have never been comfortable with you off by yourself in that city of wickedness! You did not come home this summer, and you almost never call . . . I can feel you slipping away. I can feel you moving away from the light of Lord Jesus, and it has me heartsick."

The pressure in Leif's body changed so quickly that his head spun, and he slumped against the building for support. "Mama . . ." Only he didn't know what to say. Anything he told her that was even remotely honest would only make things worse. "Mama, you're being silly. I'm not 'slipping away,' I'm just—"

"Backtalk!" she snapped furiously. "You most certainly did not learn backtalk in my home, but one year in that den of iniquity—"

"It's an *academy*, Mama," Leif retorted, anger and fear making him unstable. "It is a prestigious school, with some of the most gifted dancers in the country. It's a privilege to be accepted here—people fight to be accepted here—and when I graduate, I'm all but guaranteed to land a job with an important ballet company!"

"I do not believe that's your path." This reply, firm and self-assured, stunned him into silence. "We've had our doubts, as you know, about this pursuit of yours, and the kind of men who go in for it." The inference was as familiar as it was unmistakable, and

Leif's stomach went cold. "It's not natural, and your eternal soul comes before any school—no matter how prideful or prestigious."

"*All* kinds of men go in for ballet, Mama," he said frantically, although he hated the words, no matter how true they were. He *was* one of "those kinds of men"—he was already what his mother feared ballet would turn him into—but to say so would be apocalyptic. He was still a minor, and there was a lot his parents could do that he'd be powerless to stop.

"And that city!" She wasn't even listening. "All sorts of devilry thrives there; all manner of ungodly lifestyles!" Again, it was crystal clear which particular lifestyle she had in mind, and sweat now rolled freely down Leif's back; they'd been down this road before, but it had been a while since the argument came up with such clarity. "Pastor James says I ought to be worried about you falling into . . . *that way*, and I need you to reassure me, Leif. Are you experiencing sinful urges?"

A panicked laugh bubbled up his throat. Of course it was Pastor James; his mother rarely saw what she didn't want to, and his father barely even looked at him, but Pastor James had always eyed Leif with cold distaste. "You have nothing to worry about, Mama," he babbled, reaching out for whatever might stop this line of questioning. "God wouldn't have given me this gift if He didn't mean for me to use it. He doesn't make mistakes."

"But men do." Mrs. Dalby sighed ominously. "Especially in a city with all manner of temptations laid out, and no parents to stand watch."

Leif had grown up in a town of two thousand people; there had been less than two hundred students in his entire high school, and all of them had known one another. His freshman year, one of the junior boys had been caught looking at "sinful pictures of men," and had been sent "away."

Eager to sink her fingers into the scandal, Mrs. Dalby had made a casserole and taken Leif with her to see the boy's anguished parents, and had spent the afternoon praying loudly for Lord Jesus to save their lost lamb. Leif had sat in a corner, burning all over and trying to disappear, filled with the desire to go upstairs and see the boy's bedroom—to be in his space, even for just a minute, so as not to feel so horribly alone.

"Mama, there's sin everywhere." He struggled to regain his footing. How was it that he could run from armed guards and do handsprings into a man's face without losing his cool, but talking to his own mother undid him completely? "But there's only one Marechal Academy, and the instructors are really strict about our behavior. *You* may not believe that this is my calling, but I do. I know that this is where I belong." He bowed his head and said a quick prayer; he didn't believe in the same version of God his parents did, but maybe there was a kinder one. "I need you to trust me."

His mother was silent for so long he was afraid she'd hung up on him, but at last she spoke. "I'm sorry, son, but I don't agree with this. My mind is made up. If this is the path you insist on taking, you take it alone; your father and I will not be spending any more of our money on this dancing school of yours."

"That's fine," Leif blurted impulsively, before he considered what he was saying, "because I've applied for a scholarship, and if I get it, I won't need any more support." Unable to help himself, he added, "If God blesses me with this scholarship, Mama, you can't deny that He wants me here."

His mother insisted that they pray together—long exhortations that Leif would see the light, that he wouldn't fall into wickedness—and by the time she hung up, he felt ill. He couldn't abandon the thing he loved, the thing he'd worked so hard for, or go back home and pretend to be someone he wasn't. His parents would see through his act eventually, and then it would be his turn to be sent "away." His hopes of freedom now depended on paying Marechal's exorbitant tuition without any help.

The Petrenko job couldn't happen soon enough.

14

WHEN THE LIGHTS WENT OUT AFTER THE FINAL

number, the crowd was on its feet, cheering and catcalling the queens. As they took their bows, Axel winked and blew kisses to the cutest boys in the audience. "*Liesl is a flirt,*" he'd explained reasonably, but Davon had given him a skeptical look. "*Uh-huh. How come your name isn't Liesl Von Flirt, then?*"

They all stayed in character until they got to the main dressing room, and then Axel collapsed into his makeup chair, peeling off the long, dark wig he wore for the closing act, and massaging his scalp. Davon sat down beside him, face shiny with sweat, and they grinned at each other in the mirror.

"Good turnout tonight," Axel commented, still riding his post-performance high.

"Girl, we *slayed* our number together." Davon grabbed a handful of makeup wipes and began deconstructing his face. "And that boy was drop-dead."

Just before the big finale, Liesl and Dior performed a duet of Brandy and Monica's "The Boy is Mine," pretending to fight over a guy from the audience. It always brought the house down, and gave them an excuse to fondle the best biceps in the club. Pulling off his earrings, Axel reached for the zipper of his dress. "He was watching me during the curtain call, so, sorry 'bout it, sis, but the boy is mine!"

"In your dreams." Davon laughed throatily as he transferred his wig to a dummy head on the counter. There was a knock at the door, and a man leaned into the room.

"You ladies decent?" It was Roman, the manager, a scruffy thirty-something with tattoos snaking up both arms. He was met with a chorus of welcomes, and pushed his way inside, setting a frosty cocktail glass in front of Axel. "The, uh . . . gentleman from the duet sends this with his compliments."

Giving Davon a smug look, Axel took a sip and felt his muscles begin to loosen. He got paid in cash, and as long as he didn't order drinks for himself, no one at Ruby's had a reason to check his ID; and even if Roman knew he wasn't twenty-one, the guy was happy to look the other way for his performers. "I told you he was checking me out."

"Yeah, yeah." Davon rolled his eyes.

Roman rested a hand on the back of Davon's chair. "You guys were great tonight. Georgia would've been proud. How's she doing?"

"Hanging in there." Davon kept his tone light, but there was no mistaking the sudden tension in the air. Teasing off his false lashes, the boy began scrubbing the makeup from his face, hiding his expression.

"You tell her we're thinking about her," Roman continued, his gaze following the curve of Davon's neck, the swell of the muscles in his upper arms. "The show's not the same without Georgia Vermont."

"I'm sure she'd say the exact same thing." Davon managed a laugh with the quip, but there was no humor in his eyes. Standing up from his chair, he offered his back to the club manager, a hasty change of subject. "Unzip me, okay?"

Roman complied, and Davon shrugged out of the dress, quickly loosening his corset and setting it on the counter. Bare-chested, he made a show of sucking in a deep breath, muscles flexing across his flat stomach, and gave the man a relieved smile. "Thanks, baby. I was about to pass out."

He sat back down again, and for a moment Roman just stared and shuffled his feet, flustered. Finally, the man nodded. "No problem. Congratulations on the show."

As soon as he left the room, Axel nudged the highball across the counter and Davon snatched it up, swallowing half of the drink in one gulp.

"I THINK YOU AND ROMAN WOULD BE CUTE TOGETHER," Axel argued as the Challenger cruised up PCH, salty air rushing through the open windows. Davon leveled him a murderous look, and Axel turned his palms to the sky. "What? I mean it. You're eighteen now—it's not like there's anything wrong with it."

"The man is twice my age."

"That's never bothered you before," Axel pointed out with an innocent smile.

"For a hookup, maybe, but we see Roman all the time! Can you imagine? What if he's weird in bed?" Davon pursed his lips, nodding at his own suggestion. "He gives off a total weird-in-bed vibe, like he'd be into feet or diapers or something."

"What's wrong with feet?"

"I'm gonna do us both a favor and pretend you never said that." Davon shuddered delicately. "And anyway, I don't shit where I eat."

"Anymore."

"Anymore," the boy echoed, and they shared a look. They were silent for a bit as Davon steered the Dodge up the canyon road, winding past a couple of private gates—including Margo's. Finally, he sighed. "You know I have to bring it up."

"No. You don't." Axel's mood deflated, his hands tightening on the seat belt.

"Quino is coming after Petrenko's shit with us whether you're part of the team or not, Ax. Cutting off your nose won't change that, and at least if you stay on board you can watch his back. You know, since you're so worried."

"Davon, seriously, fucking stop." Axel shook his head. "How I deal with my brother is none of your business."

The other boy's eyebrows rose in a high arch and he made a noise in the back of his throat. "Oh, excuse *me*, Miss Thing. Only, I wasn't telling you how to handle your brother—from what I heard being shouted all up and down that alley, you've already been told; I was just offering some free advice, and wondering if you wanted to discuss that piping-hot bullshit you served up in the meeting tonight."

"Oh great, here we go."

"Yeah, here we go." Davon stopped the Challenger at the gate in front of the Moreau home, the bars dented by people who couldn't get close enough to damage Basil himself. "You hear 'millions of dollars' and you say, 'No thanks.' Okay, fine—makes no sense, but okay." He punched the code into the keypad and the iron palings rattled as they slid aside. "But then you accuse Margo, your best friend, of pushing a personal agenda, when you're only taking a stand in the first place so *you* can push a personal agenda."

"Davon." Axel's jaw was tight. "I told you to drop it. I don't want to talk about this."

Davon eased up the drive, coming to a halt in the courtyard, where the dusty fountain rose up in the dark like a monument to a forgotten god. "I'm not talking about it," he said ludicrously. "I'm just giving you a quick recap in case you forgot what happened."

In spite of himself, Axel started to laugh. "You are a real piece of work."

"Thank you."

Axel was silent for a moment, staring up at the villa. Lamps illuminated the front door, but all the windows were dark. "Do you think he booby-trapped the entrance? Maybe I'll walk inside and a bucket of knives will fall on me?"

"If you're asking about your brother," Davon mused dryly, "I'm guessing he's at Margo's tonight. I'm not gonna tell you that you need to think about what he said to you—because that would be talking about it, and I'm not doing that."

Axel gave a distant nod, still staring at the black windows fronting the mansion. The place was like Pompeii: suspended in time and full of ghosts. "None of this would be happening if it weren't for Dad. None of it. It's like . . ." He trailed off. "Every day I discover some new thing he managed to ruin. And while we're getting spat on at the grocery store and fighting just to keep our heads above water, he's chilling at a minimum-security fucking federal resort." His tone was so acidic he was surprised it didn't burn the dashboard. "He eats better than we do, he gets to see a doctor whenever he has an ouchie, and the other inmates kiss his ass."

"Do you ever visit him?"

"Are you kidding?"

"Nope." Davon watched him in the shadows that filled the Challenger. "I mean, you're mad as hell, and you've got every right to be. Maybe he needs to hear it. You obviously have a lot to say to him. It might do some good to let it out."

Axel shifted, rubbing his mouth. "Nothing I could tell him would make me feel half as good as pretending he doesn't exist."

"Okay." Davon backed off easily enough. "I've probably reached my limit for meddling, anyway. Even my radiant charms won't save my ass forever."

Axel laughed again in spite of himself. "Your *radiant charms*? You conceited bitch."

"It's not conceited if it's true." Davon grinned, eyes shining. He really was gorgeous, in or out of drag, and it was easy to see why Roman couldn't leave him alone.

"Do I need to remind you that Mr. Drop-Dead bought *me* that drink tonight?"

"Because you were rubbing your ass all over him during the show!"

"I told you a million times: Liesl is a flirt!"

"Liesl is a *ho*," Davon insisted, and then they both burst into giggles, smiling stupidly at each other. "We really did nail it tonight, though."

"Of course we did." The air in the car was feeling warmer, and Axel knew he needed to get out before they did something foolish—again. "Nailing is one of the few things we never had trouble with."

Davon shook his head, expelling a breath. "That's my cue to leave, isn't it?"

"Probably." But neither of them moved. "I shouldn't invite you in. That would be a bad idea."

"Your mom is home," Davon agreed. "And we tried the dating thing once. It really didn't work. If you asked me inside, I'd just say no."

"Luckily," Axel noted, unlatching his seat belt, "your car has a lot of room."

They lunged forward over the center console, mouths tangling, breath hot as their hands sought familiar territory beneath each other's clothes. As he wrestled Axel's pants open, Davon grunted breathlessly, "This isn't a thing, okay? We're not gonna be friends with benefits. This is just a one off."

"Like last time," Axel agreed, lifting his hips to shove his jeans and underwear down to his knees. "And the time before that."

Davon climbed into his lap. "Just like that. Smart-ass."

15

HIS FATHER HAD BEEN A MECHANIC, AND SO
by the time he was twelve, Davon Stokes already knew how to take an engine block apart and put it back together—blindfolded. What he *couldn't* do, what he was dying to master, was a smoky eye.

He bought a tube of lipstick with his allowance, cheap and waxy and candy red; and late at night he'd touch the color to his lips, make a dress out of his blanket, and work the room like a catwalk. The internet was a wellspring of how-to videos, showing the finer points of contouring and blending, making your eyes pop, and he was dying to try. One day, when he was sure he was alone in the house, he finally snuck into his parents' bedroom and stood at his mother's vanity.

Time passed as he struggled to pick the right colors, to execute the tricks he'd seen online, but it was way harder than it looked. He was so lost in concentration, trying to balance the soft, dark shadow against the pale-gold highlight, that he didn't realize someone was behind him until the floor creaked. He spun around and froze, his father standing there, large as life and twice as frightening. Davon felt like he'd fallen out of a plane, the disaster total and irreversible, his face thick and hot with layers of incriminating cosmetics.

They stared at each other for a long moment, something twisting at his father's expression like a cat under a blanket, until the man spoke and Davon realized he'd been trying to suppress a laugh. "I think this is more your mother's territory than mine."

He'd disappeared, and a minute later, Davon's mother had swept into the room. Taking a seat beside him at the mirror, she grabbed for a handful of tissues. "Your eyes are all crooked, baby," she'd said with a smile, swabbing at his face. "Let's start you over."

Her version of the smoky eye wasn't quite as dramatic as what he'd wanted, but way better than what he'd accomplished by himself. The next day, she'd bought him some makeup of his own, so he didn't have to use hers—and his father had come home from work with shin guards and a padded helmet. "Life can be kinda hard on kids that are different," he'd said, "but if you know how to throw a punch, being different is easier."

And so, the day after his first makeup lesson, he'd started learning how to fight. His dad's words had proved pretty true, and Davon was aware of how lucky he was.

Until the day all his luck ran out.

Debussy was playing on the radio as Davon pulled off the freeway into Boyle Heights, just east of downtown. It wasn't the worst of all neighborhoods in LA, but there was a greater than average chance the Challenger would mysteriously disappear if left on the street overnight, and so he paid an exorbitant monthly fee to keep it in a secured garage. It ate up money he didn't have, but the Dodge was the one thing of any real value that he owned, and he'd put too much work into it to take the risk.

Hauling his wig, makeup case, and three garment bags, he started walking—sticking to well-lit areas, since a guy alone at night with a bunch of shit in his arms was all but guaranteed to be mugged—and soon he was home: an ugly, single-story duplex of grungy stucco and peeling shingles squeezed cheek-by-jowl between more of the same.

The metal gate gave out a telltale shriek when he pushed through into the scrubby yard, and he hadn't made it five feet up the walk before an angular figure emerged from the front unit, leaning against a sagging overhang. "Hey, Black Beauty. Welcome home."

The raspy, taunting voice made Davon's skin crawl, and the muscles in his shoulders tightened. Five words, and all of the night's good feelings scattered like ashes in the wind. Warningly, he growled, "It's late, and I'm too tired for your bullshit, Peck."

Peck came down from his stoop, though, and got directly in Davon's way, leering up at the boy with a gap-toothed, unfriendly grin. "Aw, now, that ain't being very neighborly." Short and spare, he was probably in his late twenties or early thirties, but reckless living had aged him like beef jerky, his filthy tank top hanging off bony shoulders. "I spent all day looking after Georgia. Least you could do is say thank you."

"No, Peck. The least I can do is ignore your ass." Davon's fingers tightened around the hooks of the garment hangers, metal digging into his flesh; it hurt, but it was centering. He was so sick of Peck's bridge-troll act, this confrontation every night, the scrawny little shit demanding a token of submission to his imagined power. "Why don't you go to bed and let me do the same?"

"Afraid I can't," Peck said unpleasantly, grabbing Davon's arm as the boy tried to shove past, the skeletal fingers at least as sharp as the metal coat hangers.

Carefully and slowly, Davon stated, "I think it would be a good idea for you to keep your fucking hands off me."

Peck exaggerated his compliance, not in the least bit scared. Davon could have force-fed him his own ass if he wanted, a truth of which they were both aware; but other factors were at play, and they made Peck untouchable. His bloodshot eyes glittering in the moonlight, the hatchet-faced miscreant lit a cigarette and blew smoke in Davon's face. "Georgia owes me money. Which means *you* owe me money."

"I don't owe you shit," Davon snarled, losing the tenuous grip he had remaining on his temper. "Are you fucking kidding right now? You think you can come to me for money?" He tossed the garment bags and makeup case to the ground—although not the wig; not everybody was as careless with their hairpieces as Margo—and squared his shoulders. "You know, why don't you try to take it from me? I could use a good laugh."

"I sold her fifteen pills, and she told me you had the green." Peck gritted his discolored teeth, his narrow features stretched with menace. "That's a full grand, and I ain't fixing to be patient about it."

"You didn't sell them, then," Davon corrected him. "You gave them to her on credit, dumbfuck, and if you're too stupid to recognize a bad risk, it's not my problem."

"She owes me, you little cocksucker." The cords in the guy's neck stood out like the rigging on a sailboat, and he jabbed a finger into Davon's chest. "I know you got money. Maybe you can hide it from her, but I know you got it just the same—and if you think she's in a bad way now, you should see what'll happen if you don't deliver."

Anger poured through Davon like rocket fuel, his vision going red and hazy as he fought against the countdown to blastoff. "I ought to beat your sorry ass right now."

"I think it would be a good idea for you to keep your fucking hands off me." Amusement danced in Peck's beady eyes as he parroted back Davon's own words. "My buddies can be here in eight minutes. Remember?"

Eight minutes. That was exactly how long it had taken the last time, when three guys with baseball bats had turned up to put Davon in the ER after he had punched out two of Peck's rotting teeth. It was still a tempting thought; the satisfaction of pounding the shit out of his drug-dealing neighbor was almost worth another trip to the hospital, and Davon was getting better and better at fighting armed dudes bare-handed.

But there was Georgia. And Davon couldn't protect them both. Fuming, but without a word, he scooped up his things and shoved past Peck, storming for the door to the rear unit. Behind him, his neighbor chuckled mirthlessly.

As Davon struggled with the key in the lock, his hands unsteadied by rage, Peck called out, "I want that money by tomorrow. Or my friends are coming over anyway."

The apartment smelled of cigarettes, cheap perfume, and spilled chardonnay when Davon finally managed to get inside, and on the TV a woman with shiny hair read a news report about the ongoing civil war in Malawi. The air was thick as soup, a plastic oscillating fan stirring it around like a wooden spoon, but it was heavenly anyway. Getting away from Peck always felt like breaking the surface after a deep-sea dive. The relief didn't last long, though; the weight of the cheerless apartment pressed down, heavy as the lid on a coffin.

The plaster walls were cracked from past earthquakes, the paint discolored by a dozen years of smoke from candles lit "for the romantic effect," and the roach problem was best ignored. And then there was Davon's roommate. Flopped sideways across the ancient sofa cushions, snoring loudly and decked out in a marabou-trimmed peignoir, was Georgia Vermont—his drag mother and unofficial guardian.

On her legal documents, she was Stanley Darga; but, in or out of drag, nobody had ever called her anything but Georgia. The founder of Tuck/Marry/Kill, she'd been the first to see Davon's potential, the one who helped him elevate Dior Galore from an experiment to a star, and she'd saved him when he needed saving the most.

He'd been fourteen the night his father didn't make it back from the auto body center—the night the police turned up instead, with an incredible story of a stray bullet that had traveled three blocks to sever Mr. Stokes's femoral artery while he was walking home. Davon's mother Renata had collapsed, undone by the tragedy, keening and wailing herself into nonexistence; that first wave of grief hit so hard it scooped her out entirely, taking everything back to the sea as it retreated, leaving her body a hollow shell.

At first, Davon couldn't understand what had happened. His father was gone, and his mother was there but blank, a computer with a wiped hard drive. She could be induced to eat, and guided to stand or sit, but was otherwise unresponsive. His Aunt Marceline, afflicted with a particular strain of hard religion, declared it her duty to take care of Renata—but that duty did not extend to her effeminate nephew, whose habits were too perverse to find a place under her roof.

Davon passed his fifteenth birthday on the street.

And then: Georgia. Resourceful enough to survive, Davon grabbed his happiness in fragments outside of clubs after drag shows had just let out, watching the queens like a hunter in a blind, studying the way they moved and dressed. He learned that there were men willing to pay for an hour or an evening of his company, and he took that money to buy food and build his drag armory; he acquired better wigs, better makeup, dressed to the hilt, and plagued the queens of Tuck/Marry/Kill until they finally noticed him.

They read him for his flat hair and cheap clothes, but the attention was progress; and when Georgia grabbed his chin and tilted it to the light, he knew his moment had arrived. Her words fuzzy with alcohol, the queen had declared, "Your contouring is shit, and

I've seen sexier dresses on the sister-wives of a cult leader, but your eyes are amazing. Where do you live, kid?"

The answer was *anywhere*, and Georgia had offered him a bed for the night. He'd expected the usual strings, but she'd given him a blanket, a pillow, and a hot meal—and some privacy. One night turned into a week, which turned into a month, which turned into the new normal; Georgia took him on as a drag daughter, put him in Tuck/Marry/Kill, and even helped him find part-time work with a mechanic in the neighborhood. And, in the beginning, it had been easy to overlook her casual indulgences with pills and wine.

"Georgia?" Davon hunkered down next to the couch, giving the drag queen's cheeks a gentle slap. "Come on, Mama, you need to wake up." It was weird, calling a fifty-year-old white man in a crooked wig "Mama"; but somehow it wasn't weird at all—which . . . was also sort of weird. "It's late and I'm tired, and you're in my bed."

"D? Izzat you?" Georgia's eyes slid open on different schedules, glazed and dreamy.

"Yes, it's me. How much have you had?"

"Dunno." Georgia let out a sigh that turned into a snort, and her eyes slid shut again. "Didn't have anything. You know I stopped."

Davon would've been furious at the lie if it wasn't so inexpressibly sad. "Peck said he gave you some more pills today."

"Peck's a dickshitter," Georgia slurred crossly. "A shitterdick. A ship-shitter. *Fuck*, what's that word?"

"An asshole."

Georgia waved a heavy, bejeweled hand in the air as if to say, *Just so*. "You can't trust a thing that lowlife says, D. You know that."

"I hate the slimy little bastard like a hemorrhoid, but he doesn't kid about people owing him money." Davon paused for just a second. "And, fact is, Georgia . . . you've been telling more lies to me lately than Peck has."

Georgia's eyes opened again and she made an ugly face, heaving herself into a sitting position. "Fuck *izzat* supposed to mean? Who dare you think you are?"

"'*I didn't have anything*,'" Davon repeated back to her. "Mama, you're stoned as fuck right now, and you spilled white wine all over the coffee table."

"What?" Georgia's eyes widened in an almost comical expression of alarm, and she peered around him at the mess. "Ahhh, shit. Shit shit shit."

"Yeah, shit shit shit. How much have you had?" He asked again, and this time she inched an index finger into the air. Davon's eyes narrowed. "One? You had one pill. Come on, Georgia."

"S'true. These ones are different than the others. Better."

"Stronger, you mean."

"Same thing." She slumped forward, eyes drifting closed, and then jerked upright again. "Anyway, you know I need it, on account of my hip."

"Right, sure." Davon nodded wearily. In Georgia's defense, thirty-five years of performing in heels had done a number on some of her joints. But still. "The last doctor you saw said he didn't think more painkillers were a good idea."

"Screw that shit-for-brains." Georgia swatted his memory out of the air. "The hell did he know, anyway? I'm the one walkin' on this motherfucker, not him. I'm the one's gotta live with it. I'm the one . . ."

She trailed off, and Davon sighed as patiently as he knew how. "You're the one, all right. Come on—let's get you to bed."

He stood to help her off the sofa, and Georgia seemed to become aware of her surroundings for the first time. Gazing up at him, concern flickered in her hazy eyes. "Wait, what time is it? It's Saturday, right? We got a show!"

"Show's over, Mama." He held out his hand for her. "It went great, and everyone asked about you. You're a celebrity."

"Of course I'm a celebrity!" Georgia practically shouted. "I founded that fucking act! What do you mean, 'It's over'? Where was I?"

"Here, I'm guessing. You never showed up at the club, and you didn't answer your phone. As usual."

"That's *my* act!" Georgia struggled to her feet, swaying dangerously on the heels she shouldn't have been wearing "on account of her hip." "You shoulda waited for me! Somebody shoulda come get me! How could you . . . how could—"

"Look at yourself, Georgia!" Davon finally snapped. "Look how fucked up you are—you're missing an eyelash, your wig's on *sideways*, and you can barely keep your eyes open!" The apartment was smaller than ever, the newscaster shouting about child soldiers and rebel compounds, and it was all too much. "You're in no shape to perform. You haven't been for months."

At that, his drag mother burst into tears—loud, racking sobs—and immediately Davon felt like shit. Sobbing into her hands, Georgia blubbered, "I'm sorry . . . I'm so sorry . . . I'm trying." She hiccupped. "You got no idea how hard I'm trying, Davon."

"I do. I do know." He put his arm around her shoulders, on the verge of tears himself.

"You don't know how hard it is! You don't know what I'm dealing with!"

"You're right. I don't." It was true. Of the many battles Davon had faced, addiction wasn't one of them; he had no idea what it felt like to look Georgia's demons in the eye. "But you can't go on like this, Mama." His voice hitched, and it took him a moment to collect himself. "I'm afraid of what's gonna happen to you if you don't stop."

"I'm afraid, too," Georgia admitted brokenly, her voice a rough whisper. "I'm so afraid sometimes."

Limp and woozy, she let Davon lead her down the short

hallway to the bedroom at the back of the apartment, where he tucked her in. Removing her wig, he placed it on a stand, then gently wiped off as much of her makeup as he could manage.

Loosely, already half asleep, Georgia mumbled, "Thank you, Davon. You're good to me. Better than I deserve."

"That's not true," he said, turning out the light to hide his anguished expression in the dark. "You were there for me when I had nothing, and now I'm here for you."

"I love you, you know." Georgia's voice moved like a feather, floating down. "Like my own kid. I had nothing back then, too. We were there for each other."

It took a long time before Davon was capable of speaking, and when he did, he could only muster a hoarse whisper. "We've got to get you clean, Mama. And we've got to get you away from Peck." There was no answer, because Georgia had already lost consciousness. "I can't lose you, too."

16

THE METRO STATION AT HOLLYWOOD AND WESTERN
was damp and cave-like the following Wednesday night, warm
air lifting from the underground tunnels and pushing through
the tiled platforms and ticketing vestibule. Dressed in her lank
brown wig and a pair of thick cheater frames, and carrying several
large shopping bags, Margo's shirt was already stuck to her back
by the time the red line train to Union Station rumbled in on
the rails.

Choosing an empty seat at the back of the last car, she arranged
her bags beside her, opened up a book, and tried to radiate hostil-
ity. She was in what Axel called "day drag"—her contouring was
strong, but not theatrical, and her color palette bold but limited.
The red line served a few major tourist destinations between North
Hollywood and downtown, and although it was fairly empty on a
weeknight, she couldn't afford to be recognized by some starstruck
visitor from out of town.

At Vermont and Sunset, a petite woman with a large gray shopping tote boarded Margo's car. Stopping right in front of the girl,
she cleared her throat. "Excuse me, but is this seat taken?"

Grunting, Margo shifted her bags to the floor, and Dr. Nadiya Khan sat down beside her. She placed her tote at her feet, crossed her legs, and then surreptitiously nudged it across the floor. Murmuring behind her hand, Margo asked, "Is this everything?"

"Most of what you asked for. The trackers, fog canisters, rebreathers, and picklocks were simple—and I even managed the print duplicator."

"Are you serious?" Margo resisted the urge to throw herself at the woman in a bear hug, but only just. "You're my hero right now."

Nadiya smiled faintly. "Don't get too excited. I couldn't get the gas you wanted—our lab doesn't make it, and I had no way to justify the request. Your father has a strict policy against the design or manufacture of anything resembling offensive weaponry. But I have a feeling you won't have much trouble getting your hands on the substance you need."

"I've got some idea where to look," Margo answered thoughtfully, eyes trained on her fingernails. Any decent-sized animal hospital should have what she was looking for, and the security at those places rarely presented a challenge. "Thank you for all this."

"You know what I say," Dr. Khan returned, rising to her feet as the PA system announced the next stop. "Thank me by not getting caught."

The train pulled to a stop and Nadiya got off, while Margo surreptitiously tucked the woman's heavy gray tote into one of her own shopping bags. Two stops later, the girl switched trains and headed back the way she'd come, returning to Hollywood and Western and climbing the steep, filthy steps into a hideous plaza that matched the station below.

Almost the second she was in the open again, her phone buzzed in her pocket, and Margo had to shuffle her bags around so she could free it. "Hello?"

"Hey. Um, it's me."

"Axel?" Obviously it was Axel—it said so on the display; but they hadn't spoken since Saturday, and Margo had spent most of her time since then planning what she would wear to disrupt his funeral someday. "Are you . . . what is it?"

"I'm calling to say I'm sorry," he mumbled in a rush, like he needed to get the words out before she hung up. "I'm still not happy about Quino being involved, but . . . he's right. It's not my place to decide what he gets to do. Especially when I'm already doing it." There was a pause, and then he continued, quiet and uncertain. "I just worry about him, you know?"

Margo softened her voice. "I do."

"I'm angry all the time," Axel finally admitted, "and I guess I forget who I'm supposed to be angry at. I'm sorry for being an ass."

"It's okay. Everybody's allowed one good meltdown every now and then."

"Yeah, but I wanted to save mine for something more fun." They both chuckled a little, a laying down of arms, and then Axel said, "Joaquin's gonna do this whether I like it or not, and me staying home out of spite will only make the odds worse." He swallowed audibly. "So . . . I guess what I'm saying is, if it's cool, I'd like to be part of the job after all."

"Of course it's cool, you idiot! I'm just glad I didn't have to embarrass myself by begging you to reconsider. But while you're still feeling guilty, I could use a favor . . ."

"This time I owe you," Axel acknowledged. "What is it?"

"Break into a veterinary clinic with me tonight?"

* * *

ASIDE FROM THE UNWANTED ATTENTIONS OF AN AGITATED German shepherd, whose kennel was not nearly as secure as it should've been, the break-in at the Glassell Park Animal Hospital went off without a hitch; and on Friday evening, the team reconvened at a lonely stretch of disused service road near Inglewood Oil Field to talk strategy and study their equipment.

By Saturday night, they were ready to move.

Act Two:
SLINGS AND ARROWS

17

IN OCTOBER OF 1922—TWO WEEKS BEFORE
archaeologist Howard Carter uncovered the steps leading to Tut-
ankhamun's tomb—the legendary showman Sid Grauman launched
his spectacular Egyptian Theatre with the first-ever Hollywood
premiere. Adorned by hieroglyphs, sphinxes, and gaudy detailing
in fake gold and lapis, the eye-catching cinema brought its theme
to life with everything but subtlety.

A century later, the Egyptian Theatre still stood on Hollywood
Boulevard, and still hosted the occasional movie premiere. One
such event took place that Saturday night, and spotlights swept
the air outside the building's main entrance. Pausing only long
enough to bathe in media flashbulbs, the attendees arrived in style
and entered on a red carpet. Among them was a young socialite
named Valentina Petrenko.

Three blocks away in a valet parking lot, Joaquin crouched next
to Leif behind one of the city's ubiquitous black SUVs, and watched
Davon crawl through a sea of vehicles. At school on Friday, Margo
had stuck a GPS transponder inside the wheel well of Valentina's
prize BMW, and the three boys had followed the signal all the way

to where the gleaming white convertible now sat in the midst of a carefully calculated gridlock.

"Think he'll be able to get inside?" Joaquin asked, smoothing out his acid-green wig. Axel had actually helped him do his makeup that evening; they hadn't really talked much, but it had been a significant gesture.

Leif smirked. He'd done his "silent screen" look again—Garbo eyebrows, heart-shaped lips, violet wig in precise finger waves. "Dior Galore can get into anything."

Joaquin watched as Davon eased up behind the BMW, shrugging off his pack. "Think we'll fit?"

"It'll be tight, but we'll make it work."

"That's what he said," Joaquin returned, and immediately his face swam with heat. *What was wrong with him?* Only Leif appeared delighted by the ribald quip.

"That's what *who* said?" The boy asked playfully, nudging Joaquin with his elbow.

"Wouldn't you like to know." He nudged back.

"Maybe I would." Leif gave him a sly, flirtatious smile—and even though the exchange was totally corny, pressure built immediately in Joaquin's groin, and the tape between his legs started to pull. Tucking was the most awkward part of drag—strapping down his most sensitive parts with strips of sports adhesive—and Leif's suggestive tone was inciting his dick to stage a full revolt against its imprisonment.

The problem was, he couldn't tell if they were actually flirting, or if Leif was just *being Leif.* The boy was so beautiful, he was probably used to flirting—and their first encounter at the villa had been a disaster. Struggling to make a good impression, Joaquin had been humiliated when Axel introduced him as his "baby brother," and then scolded him out of the room like a toddler trying to stay up past his bedtime.

Davon's hand emerged from the sea of chrome and metal, flashing the signal they'd been waiting for, and both boys crept out from their hiding place. The trunk of the BMW was open, and aside from a tire iron and a refillable water bottle, it was empty. Definitely big enough for one . . . but for two?

"Okay." Joaquin took a stilted breath. "This is going to be . . . intimate."

"I call big spoon!" Quickly, Leif folded himself into the cramped space, curling onto his side to leave room for Joaquin. Peering up with guileless blue eyes, he asked, "Are you coming or what?"

Swallowing hard, Joaquin climbed into the trunk after him. He was used to close confines, of course—but not sharing them. And certainly not sharing them with someone like Leif. His back was squeezed up tight to Leif's front, the boy's hips pressing kind of noticeably against his ass, and he swallowed again.

Davon nestled two utility packs into the narrow bit of remaining space, and lowered the trunk lid, immersing them in darkness; and then, immediately, Leif slung his arm around Joaquin. Like they were cuddling. And then Leif tucked his nose into the nape of Joaquin's neck, and goose bumps swept up the younger boy's back and across his shoulders. Making a strange noise, Leif murmured, "Okay, are you wearing cologne, or is that just a really good body wash?"

"Body wash," Joaquin squeaked, scarcely able to breathe.

"I like it." The boy's breath was warm against his skin, lips tickling the rim of Joaquin's ear.

He was going to need much stronger tape.

Leaving the way he'd come, Davon climbed back into the van he'd boosted for the night's work. It was a decade-old Nissan belonging to a flower delivery service, but all identifying characteristics had been painted over in a quick but thorough afternoon, and the plates had been swapped. The police weren't going to stress out over this particular auto theft, and as long as he drove carefully, it was unlikely he'd encounter any problems.

With Mendelssohn playing on the radio, he guided the van down mostly residential avenues all the way from Hollywood to Malibu—a feat requiring the patience of a saint—where he picked up Margo and Axel; from there, the trio made the meandering climb to the summit of Topanga Canyon, one thousand feet above sea level. Just off the coiling switchback that marked the crest, where the road descended into the Valley, a short driveway led to the parking area of a scenic overlook.

The viewpoint was technically closed after sunset, and Davon tried not to feel too guilty about breaking the law as he guided the vehicle all the way to the back of the lot, swinging into a space that was partially screened by trees before killing the engine. They had a contingency plan in the event that the van was discovered, but patrol cars only made occasional sweeps, so the risk of a tow was minimal.

"What's the story on Valentina's Beemer?" Margo asked when they were all huddled together under the vault of the night sky. Behind her, the Valley spread out for miles, a sea of winking lights that touched the foothills of the distant Santa Susanas; while to the right, beyond the boundary of the parking lot, there loomed a tumult of wild brush and spindly trees, choked with darkness.

Davon checked his receiver, the signal from Margo's tracking device still submitting loud and clear. "Miss Petrenko is headed home, right on schedule. T minus . . . maybe forty-five minutes?"

"Let's be in place when she gets there, okay?" Pulling up the hood of her black nylon catsuit, Margo tucked her platinum wig out of sight, and then slipped on her night vision glasses. When

Davon activated his own, the Valley flared up like high noon, while the sedge and manzanita cloaking the hillside glowed an otherworldly green. Margo looked from one of them to the other. "We ready?"

"We're ready," Axel promised, tightening the straps on his pack. Whatever bad blood had been between the two of them before, it had been exorcised. That familiar energy surged between them all, a shared heartbeat, and Davon grinned.

"Then damn the torpedoes," Margo said, and the three of them slipped into the underbrush, the Nissan's engine ticking a countdown behind them as it cooled.

"OKAY, NOW YOU'RE JUST FUCKING WITH ME." LEIF STRUGGLED to suppress his laughter as the BMW accelerated around a tight bend in the road. It was hot as hell in the trunk, and after hours of telling stories and knock-knock jokes, he and Joaquin had gotten slap-happy. Leif had proposed a game of truth or dare, but since there was no way to execute much in the way of dares, they were now just playing . . . truth. "There's no way your favorite childhood movie was *Spice World*."

"It was, I'm serious!" Joaquin giggled. "I found it on TV when I was, like, eight, and laughed my ass off. I had no idea what was going on in it. I thought they were superheroes!"

"That explains a lot, actually." Grinning, Leif slipped his hand down a little and tickled Joaquin's stomach. About an hour earlier, he'd figured out that the boy was extremely ticklish, and that he made this kind of adorable squeaking noise when you got one of his sensitive spots—which seemed to be pretty much everywhere.

"Stop it!" Joaquin gasped out between fits of his silent, squeaky laugh. "Stop, you ass!" Finally, giggling, Leif relented. "Anyway, I answered your stupid question, so it's my turn now. Truth or truth?"

"I believe I shall go with truth."

Joaquin hesitated for just a second. "What did you think the first time you saw me?"

"What did I think?" Leif fumbled a little. He'd been expecting something deliberately provocative. *How big is your dick?* or *How often do you jerk off?* The sort of questions he'd be asking if Joaquin were anybody else—if he were not, for some reason, inexplicably insecure about pushing those particular limits.

For a moment, Leif flashed back to that afternoon at the villa, when Margo had invited him to Malibu to meet Axel and Davon. He remembered the crumbling fountains, the dusty hallways, and the pool filled with murky, toad-green water. And he remembered a boy lying out in the sun when they reached the back deck, with golden brown skin and long, dark eyelashes.

He remembered trying to be unobtrusive while the two brothers argued about who had a right to use the deck and who was being immature, and then peeking at Joaquin as he stormed away because Leif kind of wanted to see what his butt looked like.

"I thought . . ." Leif licked his lips, grateful Joaquin couldn't see his face. "I thought your butt was cute."

"Wait—what?"

Breezily, Leif continued, "Okay, my turn! Truth or truth?"

"Wait—no, wait!" Joaquin squirmed a little in the dark, like he was trying to turn around. "You were looking at my ass?"

"You already asked a question," Leif said primly. "Two is cheating."

He started tickling him again, and the stuffy trunk filled with the sound of Joaquin's squeaking laughter and desperate protests—until, all of a sudden, the car began to slow and both boys went silent immediately. The BMW made a turn, pebbles crunching beneath its tires, and then began a steep climb. One turn later, the vehicle stopped, and Leif heard muffled voices outside.

The BMW jumped forward again, the grade quickly leveling out as they made a wide sweep before gradually coming back to a stop. The purr of the engine died, the vibration that had lulled them for nearly two hours vanishing. There came the mechanized rumbling of garage mechanics, a shifting of weight, and the rocking *thump* of a car door slamming shut, and then the faint sound of footsteps—and then nothing.

The nothing extended, the vehicle remaining quiet, suspended in time; Leif took soft, shallow breaths, straining his ears against the silence, and they waited. Three minutes became five, eight, ten, and finally Joaquin pulled the trunk release. The faint *thunk* sounded like a tree falling through a six-story greenhouse as the lid eased up a few inches, revealing the gloomy bounds of what they knew to be a darkened four-car garage.

A four-car garage that was connected directly to the castle by a breezeway, which Valentina was routinely careless about securing.

Leif and Joaquin slipped out of the BMW's trunk. Slinging their packs over their shoulders, they crept to the inner door, and into the brightly lit corridor that would lead them to the heart of Arkady Petrenko's heavily fortified compound.

THE RUGGED HILLSIDES THAT DROPPED INTO TOPANGA Canyon were crisscrossed with old horse trails, many of which had been gradually consumed by a gluttonous Mother Nature. Margo would find a section that went for ten or fifteen feet before dead-ending in a clot of milkweed or sagebrush, and then pick her way through the undergrowth for a while until stumbling onto the next remnant of cleared pathway.

It made the going slow, but she knew her bearings, having thoroughly studied the route while strategizing the infiltration of Castle Petrenko. The mining magnate's property was astonishing in size, the acreage encompassing tennis courts, a guest cottage, a band shell, and a paddock for Valentina's prize Clydesdale, Krasavitsa. There were only three ways in or out, and since the team didn't have a helicopter, it left them with the front gate—a steel-reinforced barrier manned twenty-four-seven by armed guards—or the rear one.

The still-usable portion of the horse trail wended along the back side of the canyon in a closed loop. It was accessible from Petrenko's estate by a single point in the perimeter wall that enclosed the grounds, where a radio-controlled iron gate also stood under guard at all times. Nonetheless, it was the most advantageous point of attack, and when Margo at last led the boys out of the dense chaparral, she signaled to them to proceed with caution.

A ribbon of pale earth snaking over the hillside, the trail sloped up to the right, where it curved behind a screen of bushes and disappeared. At the top of the ridge, just visible through the trees, Margo could make out the angular crenellations of Petrenko's outer wall. Adrenaline beginning to flow, she started up the slope with the boys behind her.

THREE STORIES OF OCHRE STONE AND COUNTLESS WINDOWS, Petrenko's home was a slice of Elizabethan England in the middle of Southern California. No expense had been spared in outfitting the castle with the latest in modern conveniences—and, with thick carpeting and damask drapes, ornate balusters and carved panel ceilings, the place was designed to impress inside and out.

It was late enough that Arkady and his wife, Olga, would be in bed—at least, according to his usual bedtime as recounted to a reporter from *Time* magazine the previous year—but Joaquin still crept as silently as possible, following Leif out of the breezeway and into a dimly lit vestibule at the back of the estate. Even if her parents were asleep, Valentina was awake—and in addition to home security personnel, each member of the Petrenko family had a full-time bodyguard.

All was quiet, though, as the two boys eased along a claustrophobic hallway and down a short flight of stairs to the basement—where, along with the kitchen, pantry, and laundry facilities, sat the main guardroom. Located at the back of a dead-end hallway, it was the nerve center of Petrenko's security system, connected to nearly every alarm and camera on the property—except, unfortunately, for the turret display room and front gate.

When the boys reached the head of the corridor, a ceiling-mounted surveillance camera blinked a bright red warning from its opposite end, and they ducked back out of sight. From a zippered pouch in his utility kit, Leif produced a small metal fob with a telescoping antenna—a directional signal jammer courtesy of Margo's tech wizard, capable of disrupting radio and video output for brief intervals.

From his own pack, Joaquin withdrew a metal gas canister and a coiled length of narrow-gauge surgical tubing. Looping the rubber hose around his shoulder, he nodded to indicate that he was ready. Then, reaching out from their hiding spot, Leif angled the fob upward and activated the switch.

A shrill whine sounded, and Joaquin leaped into action, sprinting down the hallway. Ducking under the camera, he slipped into its blind spot just as Leif deactivated the jammer. Only two seconds had passed, but Joaquin waited on tenterhooks for several long moments to see if the guard inside the room would investigate the brief glitch. The boy was already fitting the surgical tubing tightly around the nozzle of the gas canister, but the heavy metal object would make a convenient weapon if necessary.

But the moments passed, and all Joaquin heard from inside the room was the faint murmur of a television set—no sounds of alarm.

Dropping to the ground, he squeezed the open end of the flexible rubber hose through the crack beneath the door, and then cranked open the canister's valve.

Odorless, colorless, and fast-acting, the anesthetic gas that Margo and Axel had stolen from the animal hospital was concentrated enough to put the average adult human under within minutes; unsure of the room's dimensions, Joaquin waited awhile before twisting the valve shut again. Then, cautiously, he rapped at the door.

There was no answer. Slipping a rebreathing mask out of his pack—a respirator, equipped with a fifteen-minute supply of clean oxygen—Joaquin secured it in place; next came a mechanized picklock, which had the door open in less than a minute; and then the boy kicked his way into the room, fists up, in case the guard was still awake and this was about to be a fight.

Inside, an elaborate console spread beneath a bank of monitors that offered a black-and-white perspective on every corner of Petrenko's personal fiefdom. The lone guard sagged limply in his ergonomic swivel chair, down for the count, a full mug of coffee steaming in front of him. Stepping back, Joaquin removed his mask just long enough to report into his comm. "Guardroom secure."

"Thanks," Leif said a few minutes later, as they were trussing the guard with zip ties. "I've got it from here, if you want to head upstairs." With a nod, Joaquin gathered up his things. Just as he made to stand, though, the other boy put a hand on his arm. "I'll do my best to watch your back, but . . . be careful?"

If it had come from anyone else, Joaquin would have been annoyed; but coming from Leif—he felt something warm spread through his chest. "I promise."

Slipping out the door again, he waved once to the camera before heading back for the stairs leading up into the house.

* * *

THE TRAIL ROSE SHARPLY, LEVELING OFF WHERE IT MET THE Petrenkos' back gate, but the skulking trio stopped short of that final slope—well out of any potential sight lines. The night was alive with the chirr of crickets and the rustle of what Axel sincerely hoped were neither rattlesnakes nor coyotes—because while Margo and Davon waited patiently on the cleared pathway, *he* was crawling through the brush like prey.

The edge of the trailhead was bordered by mountain lilac and Indian paintbrush, clustered on the steep incline, and they provided excellent cover for Axel to position himself directly across from the gate. He could see lights on the property through the bars, could hear faint music from the guard post. The air smelled of resin and earth, and he *really, really* hoped that rustling sound wasn't a snake.

It would serve him right to get bitten to death by some legless reptile after all his sanctimonious lectures to Quino about the dangers of security guards and cops with a thing against million-dollar jewel thieves, no matter how noble their reasons. Sliding his pack off his shoulders, readying himself for when the signal came, he tried not to think about what his little brother was doing just then. The kid had possibly the riskiest job of them all, and if he got caught . . .

Axel wasn't going to think about it.

"Freeze."

Leif's voice, crackling through the comm, brought Joaquin to a stumbling halt. At the top of the steps, he'd ducked into a sewing room decorated in gaudy shades of pink, and from there into a self-consciously masculine smoking room, the walls hung with hunting scenes and antique rifles. Here, moonlight slashed through the windows, making crystal decanters of amber liquid glow, while Joaquin stood paralyzed beside an antique globe.

"Two big guys are headed for the smoking room from the salon. Go back."

Joaquin hesitated. His destination was the drawing room, just ahead through a connecting door; he could see it. But the sharp hiss of approaching whispers in the salon made the hair on his neck rise, and he pivoted, darting back into the sewing room's rosy embrace. Plastering himself to the wall, he waited, breathing through his mouth.

"Shit. They're looking around. I don't know if they heard you, or if—wait."

His heart thumping hard, Joaquin swallowed, eyeing the door to the rear passage and breezeway—but that was a dead end. Of course, the castle was nothing *but* dead ends; what made this part of the plan so dangerous was that there was literally no way out for him. Not yet. Holding his breath, he focused on the quiet conversation in the other room.

"Okay, wait. They're just . . . they're going for the bar cart." Leif's words were drenched in cool relief. *"They're bumming a drink of the boss's whiskey. I think you're safe."*

Joaquin stood frozen for a handful of endless minutes, listening to the world's longest story about the world's most boring bar fight, every muscle tensed *just in case*—until the heavy footsteps at long last sounded again, this time receding.

"They're heading back into the salon," Leif announced, and Joaquin exhaled again, the back of his neck slick with sweat. *"Give it one more minute . . . okay, the coast is clear. Move that cute little butt."*

Joaquin almost tripped as he hurried back through the smoking room, suddenly feeling Leif's eyes on him—suddenly very aware of his ass. Wherever the cameras were mounted, he hoped they couldn't see the stupid grin on his face.

The drawing room was appointed with raw silk wallpaper, pastoral landscapes, and a fireplace big enough to stable a pony. Fresh wood was stacked in the grate, but the hearth and firebox—subject to meticulous, routine cleanings—were both pristine. Crawling in on his knees, Joaquin reached up to open the damper and clear the flue.

Designed long before the days of central heating, almost every room in the castle had a fireplace for warmth. Now in LA, they were mostly ornamental—a touch of continental class—but in an interview with *Vanity Fair* when the reconstruction had first been completed, Petrenko bragged about preserving their functionality. Most were built back-to-back, arranged overtop each other floor by floor, so that the smoke from all eighty fireplaces vented out through only fourteen chimneys.

And the same chimney that served the drawing room, also two floors up, served Arkady Petrenko's bedroom.

Joaquin shrugged off his pack—it was going to be a tight fit—and tied it to a length of cord. Securing the other end to his belt, he snapped on his night vision glasses and slithered up into the narrow column of brick and mortar.

THROUGH THE GRAINY FEED ON THE MONITORS, JOAQUIN'S pack looked like a fat nylon spider, dangling beneath him as he inched up the chimney and out of sight. The next minutes were critical, and Leif tried not to think about how there were no cameras inside Petrenko's bedroom—that he wouldn't be able to help if anything went wrong.

The guard at his feet was still unconscious, and Leif continued to suck clean oxygen through his rebreather, eyes turning to the feed from the grounds. He had a clear view of the rear gate, and could see the guards lurking there, but no sign yet of Axel or Davon.

Removing his mask just long enough to activate his comm, he advised, "Hold tight for a minute, guys. Anita Stiffwon is on her way up to the nosebleed section now."

"*Standing by*," Margo's reply came, crisp and professional as always, and Leif idly wondered what it would take to disturb her sangfroid.

He wondered if Axel was even half as collected just then, knowing what Joaquin was about to attempt all alone.

CROUCHED IN THE BRUSH, HANDS CLAMMY INSIDE HIS GLOVES, Axel was about two seconds away from pissing himself. That rustling sound was *definitely* a fucking rattlesnake.

THE CHIMNEY WAS REMARKABLY CLEAN, WITH ONLY TRACES of soot, and Joaquin wondered if they were ever used at all. Hand- and footholds were easy to find on the rough brick around him, and the ascent to the third floor went even faster than he expected.

Once he was in position, feet braced against the walls, he peered down the angled channel that guided smoke from Petrenko's private fireplace into the chimney column. Reeling up his pack, he drew out the surgical tubing, still fitted tightly onto the canister's nozzle; then, scarcely daring to breathe, he reached down and very slowly eased the damper open just enough to feed the hose through and into the room below.

They had no idea what the actual dimensions of the master suite were—how many modifications might have been made since the *Vanity Fair* piece had been written, how many windows might be open to the night air—and so Joaquin simply cranked the valve all the way open and flooded the room with anesthesia. Rebreather in place, he waited, watching the needle on the gage plummet to zero.

Only when the canister was completely empty did Joaquin ease the damper the rest of the way open, nerves buzzing like an alarm clock. He could see into the firebox, the pale stone flickering with the unmistakable glow of a television set. Newsy-sounding voices murmured quietly in Russian, and a faint snore rattled the air. Dizzy with nerves, Joaquin slid feetfirst into the Petrenkos' fireplace—rebreather in place—and entered the bedroom.

Despite molded ceilings and soaring windows, the suite was dishearteningly garish: cornices gleamed with gold leaf, personalized frescos covered the walls, and a Roman statue loomed over a velvet settee. Sprawled in a four-poster canopy bed, faces slack and colorless, were Arkady and Olga Petrenko. It was only the twinned rumble of their breathing that kept Joaquin from thinking they were dead.

The room held a fortune in goods, many that could be easily carried out, but Joaquin had no time for browsing; he was there to get two things only, and the first of them he found in plain sight on Petrenko's armoire. Then, skittering to the bedside, he pulled out Margo's fingerprint duplicator—a small device with a sensor plate to read loops and whorls, and a miniature 3-D printer with enough liquid latex to produce two exact copies.

Petrenko lay on his back, breath wheezing slowly in and out. Jumpy and anxious, revved on adrenaline, Joaquin carefully disentangled the billionaire's right hand from the sheets, and held his index finger to the sensor. This part was do-or-die—literally. The master suite was flanked by the bedrooms of the couple's personal bodyguards, and it was well-known that Arkady kept a loaded gun within reach at all times. But neither sleeper stirred as a red light slid across the duplicator's screen, reading the print, its machinery warming in the boy's hand.

Petrenko snorted loudly then, and Joaquin jolted back. The man's mouth slopped open and shut a few times, his eyelids bunching for an awful, spine-tingling moment . . . and then he sagged back into sleep with a blubbering sigh. The duplicator chose that moment to give a soft *click*, and the boy took only long enough to make sure he had two clean copies of Arkady's print—and then all but fled for the door, twisting open the numerous locks and darting out into the gloomy upper hall, his heart clenched like a fist.

18

"I'VE GOT THE PRINTS!" JOAQUIN'S VOICE, breathless with pride and disbelief, sounded over the comm; and hearing it, knowing his brother was alive and well, was enough to make Axel slump against the snake-infested hillside with gratitude to the powers that be. *"I repeat: I have the prints. Phase One is complete; go, Phase Two!"*

Davon didn't waste a second; with easy strides, he marched straight up the path for the back gate, his blue wig shining like a gas flame in the moonlight. The approach was deliberately noisy, and two guards were already waiting when he reached the trailhead, glaring suspiciously through the iron bars.

"This is private property," the guard in front snapped brusquely, his version of a greeting. "I'm gonna have to ask you to turn around."

"Private property!" Davon exclaimed, sounding impressed. "You mean the whole canyon? Or just this side of it?"

"Ma'am, this isn't a joke." The guard came closer to the gate, a hand resting on the butt of his gun, and Axel tensed. This was a delicate dance—the second guard was still too far back, lost in the shadows, and Davon needed to draw him out for the plan to work;

but if the first guard pulled his weapon, they were done before they started.

"I know it's not a joke; it's why I'm not laughing." Davon stood back from the gate, but leaned forward theatrically, making a show of peering through the bars. "Who lives here, anyway? Is it an actor? I bet it's an actor. Is it Iron Man?"

The second guard shuffled forward a bit, but not close enough, and the first guard's hand closed on the hilt of his weapon. "Ma'am, if you do not disperse now, you will be in violation of trespass laws."

"Show me," Davon said immediately.

"Huh?" The first guard screwed up his face in confusion. The second guard still hung back, and Axel huffed impatiently. *Come on, asshole. Just two more steps.*

"Show me the deed to the property where it says I'm trespassing." Davon crossed his arms over his fake breasts. "How do I know you own this part of the hillside when your wall stops over there?"

The first guard was quickly turning the same red color as Axel's wig. "Ma'am you will turn around and vacate this area *immediately*. This is your last warning!"

"Excuse you?" Davon stepped to the side, clearing Axel's line of sight. The second guard was finally approaching the bars, and Dior Galore was turning her act up to eleven. "I don't care if you *do* work for Iron Man, you don't tell me what to do! You let Mr. High-and-Mighty up there know that if *this* is how he treats his fans, his ass will be sponsoring car dealerships in Fresno!"

The second guard stepped into the light at last, just as the first guard drew his gun, shouting, "*You need to cease and desist and clear these premises immediately!*"

Axel hesitated. But only for a second. Easing up, he lifted his hands, a Taser clutched in each one; with a steady exhale, he fired. There was a *snap*, and four metal prongs flew across the clearing and hit home. It was a hell of a shot: fifteen feet, past the bushes and between the iron bars of the gate, catching both men simultaneously—and Axel absolutely allowed himself to gloat when both guards dropped, bodies locking up and then going limp.

Davon spun on his heel. "Are you brain damaged? That dude had a fucking gun on me! What if he pulled the trigger when he started seizing?"

"He never took the safety off," Axel replied smugly as he climbed onto the trailhead.

"What if that's because the safety was never on in the first place?"

"Girls, stop," Margo cooed as she trotted up the sloping path to join them. "You're both pretty." Activating her comm, she announced, "This is Miss Anthropy at the back gate, requesting entry."

"Ah yes, Miss Anthropy!" Leif's voice came back. *"You are indeed on our list tonight!"* There was a buzz and a *click*, and the iron gate slid open. *"Welcome to the party."*

Quickly, they bound and gagged the guards, locking them into separate stalls in Krasavitsa's barn. Then they gathered up any radios, cell phones, and weapons, and hurled them from the trailhead into the tangled darkness of the hillside. It wouldn't stop them from alerting their comrades or rearming themselves if they managed to get free, but it would slow them down.

Looking toward the castle, its lights sparkling from far across the vast lawns, Margo set her jaw. "Okay. This is where shit gets real. In case we're separated, just remember: the safest route is from the band shell to the hedge maze to the south wall. There's very little cover on that last stretch, so stay low and stay alert."

"Got it." Davon nodded, and Axel signaled his agreement.

"All right, then." Margo activated the comm one more time. "We're moving in."

* * *

His skin tingling all over, Joaquin's feet barely touched the floor as he darted down the stairs from the servants' corridor to the basement. Suddenly he could understand cliff divers and bungee jumpers risking their lives for nothing but the thrill of it—adrenaline was an incredible drug.

Hurrying past the corridor to the guardroom, he blew a kiss to the surveillance camera. A moment later, his comm crackled. *"What was that?"*

"A preview," Joaquin replied, feeling unbeatable, capable of anything.

"A preview of what?"

"Kisses aren't the only thing I know how to blow."

There was a moment of silence just long enough for him to worry that he'd gone too far, and then Leif crowed with laughter. *"Careful, you might have to put your money where your mouth is— so to speak."*

"Why, Electra Shoxx, was that a proposition?" There was that adrenaline rush again, everything around him a little more real than real.

"Maybe," Leif answered coyly. *"Maybe we need a Truth or Dare rematch."*

Joaquin was grinning ear to ear by the time he reached the old servants' entrance—a door just off the kitchen, designed to let "the help" come and go discreetly. Made of solid wood, it looked damn near indestructible, and was alarmed to boot. "I'm in position now, waiting to hear the secret password."

Margo's voice returned immediately. *"Open sesame."*

"Alarm disengaged," Leif announced a beat later, and Joaquin undid the dead bolts, heaving the massive door open to find Margo, Axel, and Davon waiting outside. They slipped into the kitchen, a cavernous space filled with stainless steel equipment and a huge wood-burning oven.

"How's life in the castle?" Davon asked, gazing around at the massive refrigeration units, the tub-like sinks, the hanging rack that dripped with bright copper pots and pans.

"Productive." Unable to hide his smug expression, Joaquin gave Margo and Axel each a copy of Petrenko's fingerprint; and then he handed over the other item he'd lifted from the bedroom—the man's wallet.

With a greedy smile, Margo flipped it open and fished out two identical electronic key cards. "We're in business." Turning to Davon, she said, "You know what to do. We're going to make this as quick as we can, so we'll see you soon."

Saluting, Davon vanished into the hallway, heading on soundless feet for the stairs.

To Axel and Joaquin, Margo arched a painted eyebrow. "Who wants to go try on some Czarist jewelry?"

Margo and the Moreau brothers had been inside the castle before, and together with every interview and human interest story they could find that referenced its layout, they'd sketched a floor plan for the other boys. Davon had studied the blueprint so many times he could see it on the back of his eyelids, and soon he was in the garage, where the air smelled like home—motor oil and damp concrete and fresh wax. Even with the night vision glasses painting everything that sickly, paranormal green, he shivered when he saw the four magnificent cars before him. In addition to Valentina's BMW, there was a Mercedes S-Class, a Ferrari, and a gleaming Aston Martin.

"Eeny, meeny, miny, moe," he sang to himself, "I choose . . . you."

Grinning like a lovesick schoolgirl, he crossed to the Aston Martin, already reaching for the tools in his pack.

* * *

THERE WAS ONLY ONE ENTRANCE INTO PETRENKO'S TURRET treasure chamber: an arched doorway blocked by a massive steel shutter, protected by a double-lock mechanism. It was located at the back of the castle's game room, on one corner of the ground floor, where the walls bristled with antlers mounted above framed hunting scenes. Taking up her position left of the door, Margo fixed Petrenko's print to her right glove.

"Both key cards need to be inserted simultaneously, or the alarm will go off," she reminded Axel again. The double lock consisted of two electronic card readers, spaced too far apart for one person to manage alone. "The machines are linked, so when I scan the print, both will activate. I'll do a three-count, and we go on four."

"One, two, three, insert," Axel confirmed, pasting the second latex print to one of his own gloves. The display cases in the turret room were also secured by biometric locks, but thankfully only required one person to open them.

Squaring her shoulders, Margo pressed her fake print to a scanner plate beside the card reader. It lit up, glowing first white . . . and then red.

ACCESS DENIED.

Tensing, she adjusted her glove and tried again.

ACCESS DENIED.

Fighting the urge to panic, Margo stepped back, trying to calm down while Axel watched her with worried eyes. If the fake prints weren't good enough to fool the system, then this was the end of the road; they could lift a few thousand dollars' worth of crap from some of the rooms, just to keep the effort from being a write-off, but they'd taken too many risks to be satisfied with such a paltry payoff.

Thinking quickly, she reached behind her ear, rubbing the false print against her own skin to coat the latex in natural oils; then she tried again. This time, the sensors on both sides of the door turned a bright green, and relief flooded her veins.

ACCESS GRANTED.

"One ... two ... three ..." she counted out loud, and on four, she and Axel slipped their electronic key cards into corresponding slots. A moment later, there was a *chunk* and a *whirr*, and the metal shutter slowly rose up from the floor ...

TRYING TO WATCH ALL THE SECURITY MONITORS AT ONCE was like being one of those plate-spinners on the Third Street Promenade. The steel door went up on one screen, while Davon tinkered in the garage on another; but the plate that looked most unstable, the one that kept snagging his attention, was the feed from Petrenko's study—where those same two guards were back for more of the boss's whiskey.

They'd been roaming the floors, apparently making a general sweep of the castle; and clearly they felt their time was being wasted, because they'd scarcely glanced into half the rooms before heading right back for those decanters of scotch—which were only a few rooms away from where Margo, Axel, and Joaquin were getting ready to pull off the heist meant to fix everyone's problems once and for all.

"Guys, there are two guards in the smoking room, so whatever you're going to do next, do it with the volume off," he advised uneasily, and the three of them signaled their understanding to the camera.

"Anybody got eyes on sector six?" A tinny voice squawked loudly and suddenly from the radio of the immobilized guard at Leif's feet, and the boy nearly jumped out of his catsuit. *"We've been hailing them for ten minutes with no response. Scout Master, can you see them on the camera?"*

Scout Master. That was probably the guy tied up on the floor. Leif ran his tongue across the back of his teeth, and activated the comm again. "I, uh, hate to be the bearer of bad news? But I think our countdown just started. They're trying to contact the guardroom, and it's only a matter of time before the shit hits the fan."

Davon's voice filtered into his earpiece. "*One getaway car is ready to go. I just need five more minutes for the second.*"

On the screen, Margo held up a hand, flashing five fingers and then the okay sign.

"Five minutes it is," Leif confirmed aloud, hoping they had that long.

BEYOND THE ARCHED DOORWAY, THE TURRET ROOM WAS dark. Margo had seen inside it only once, when she and Valentina were still close. The tower had been gutted to the very top, the windows bricked over—save for two decorative ones, facing opposite each other above the roofline—and the walls had been smoothed with plaster and painted a blinding white; a decorative curtain of burgundy damask fell in a grand cascade from the roof down to the marble floor, an astonishing amount of fabric; and at ground level, ranged about the open space, were cases of bulletproof glass bearing unbelievable treasures.

Margo aimed her LED into the shadows, its glare flashing against the displays. There were eight of them, and if each took one minute to empty, she and Axel could finish with time to spare. The problem, however, was a row of tiny red lights set into the baseboard bordering the entire room. Pulling the pin on Dr. Khan's fog grenade, she watched as a plume of pale vapor spilled forward into the turret . . . and a grid of pinkish beams materialized, crisscrossing the cloudy air.

Another security measure. If they broke any one of those beams . . . well, they *really* didn't want to break any of the beams.

Margo found a clear path and slid the grenade forward into the room, letting the fog billow and rise to show the full extent of the laser grid. She and Axel sent their packs in next, bowling them through the same opening; then they tucked their wigs into the nylon hoods of their catsuits, lined up in the doorway, and launched forward.

It was a nerve-racking bit of acrobatics, ducking and twisting through the matrix of beams, the cool vapor of the fog grenade swirling around them. They couldn't see the room without the night vision lenses, but the optoelectronics rendered the fog an almost impenetrable green miasma, keeping them disoriented until they reached the displays.

They worked with silent concentration in the dark. Each glass case, like the door, required a fingerprint scan and card swipe, a process that ate up valuable time; and each priceless earring, pendant, and bracelet had to be bagged carefully to keep the stones from scratching one another. By the time they'd reached the last of the displays, the grenade had emptied and the mist was beginning to settle.

And then the last scanner refused to read Margo's print. Axel was clearing out his final case, time ticking down, and she felt a stab of anxiety. Before her were the emeralds Valentina had worn to Astrology, and for no justifiable purpose, she wanted them more than any of the others. Rubbing the latex against her skin, she tried again.

ACCESS DENIED.

"Miss Anthropy!" Axel's hiss was barely audible, and Margo looked up. Portions of the laser grid were vanishing—only the stretch back to the door remained. "Forget it, we have to leave!"

"I can do it! You go, I'm right behind you."

Axel hesitated, unhappy, but after a beat he complied. Sliding his pack to the doorway, where Joaquin waited, he then ducked and spun after it to safety. Margo turned back to her display case, dry mouthed, and scrubbed the scanner clean with her sleeve before trying again. This time the sensor turned green, and the case unlocked. She scooped up the emeralds, bagged them as quickly as she could, and then whirled around.

The air before her was empty. The mist was gone, the laser grid a memory, and Joaquin and Axel stood frozen in the doorway across a dangerous gulf of vacant, shadowy space, eyes wide with dread.

"THIS IS SECTOR EIGHT TEAM LEADER. SECTOR SIX STILL ISN'T *responding, and we're going to do some reconnaissance. Sector one— can you look in on Scout Master?"*

Leif straightened up at the console, eyes dancing from screen to screen. He'd bet all of Topanga Canyon that the two drunkards in the smoking room were being asked to check on him. Sure enough, he watched as one of them spoke into his radio, and a fuzzy voice filled the small guardroom at the same time. "*Uh, yeah, roger that. We're in the middle of a sweep, but we'll drop in on Scout Master as soon as we're done."*

"And that's my cue," Leif muttered to himself, activating his comm. "Our jig is up, ladies! See you at the extraction point."

"*First one to the garage gets the Ferrari!"* Davon sang back.

Checking the feed from the game room, Leif paused. Joaquin and Axel were just . . . standing there, and there was no sign of Margo.

"DO YOU REMEMBER THE LAYOUT OF THE GRID?" AXEL asked in a frantic whisper.

"I don't know," Margo answered helplessly. She closed her eyes, trying to conjure the image to mind—but it was no use. The beams were deliberately random, and there was no chance she could remember all of them. A little seasick, she crouched to the floor, setting her pack down. She'd have to slide it across first, anyway, and if it cleared the lasers, maybe she could slither after it. "If the alarm goes off, you know what to do."

"We're not leaving you," Axel stated.

"You have to follow protocol!"

"Damn it—" he started, but she didn't wait for him to finish. With as much strength as she could, she shoved her pack toward the door.

It barely left her hand before a high-pitched siren started to scream, the alarm wailing loud enough to wake all of LA and half of San Diego. The steel shutter plummeted down, and as Margo's pack flashed across the threshold to safety, she had just enough time to shout, "*Run!*"

And then the barrier slammed home and she was trapped in the darkness.

19

THE WAILING ALARM ROUSED ARKADY AND OLGA'S
personal bodyguards, who rushed to their employers' bedroom,
shocked to find the door unsecured. Their job security was flashing before their eyes by the time they managed to rouse the couple,
Petrenko coming to disoriented and already enraged.

Screaming abuse in Russian, he stumbled down the stairs, feet
heavy and uncoordinated as he hurried for the game room. From
somewhere close, he could hear shouting and banging, but a thick
fog occluded his thoughts, making it hard to concentrate.

When he reached the steel shutter of the turret, a man from his
private security force issued a fevered report. "We think one of them
is trapped inside!"

"You *think*?" Arkady repeated ferociously. He didn't have his
wallet. *Where the fuck was his wallet?* "What do you mean '*them*'?
How many are there?"

"We're not sure," the guard admitted meekly. "Lansky and
Valdez saw two women running from the scene and gave pursuit.
They're barricaded in the dining room now!"

"Women? What the fuck—women? *And somebody get this
fucking door open!*" The billionaire roared. It took a while for his

muddled brain to come up with the code sequence necessary to override the system, but soon the steel barrier was ratcheting up, and with the punch of a button the turret flooded with brilliant white light. When they at last saw what awaited them inside, Petrenko, his bodyguard, and the uniformed grunt just stared.

The room was empty.

WHEN THE STEEL BARRIER SMASHED INTO THE FLOOR, IT missed Axel's toes by about two microns. The boy jumped back, slack-jawed with horror and disbelief, and stared at his warped reflection in the brushed metal surface. Then he started shouting. "*Margo!*"

"Axel," Joaquin hissed behind him. "I mean, *Liesl*. Stop—we have to . . ."

Only he couldn't seem to finish—and Axel was ignoring him anyway. The older boy scanned his duplicate fingerprint again and again, but without the second key card, it was pointless. He kept trying, though, unable to let himself give up. *There had to be a way.*

Leif's voice burst over the comms. "*What are you doing? Get out of there before—*"

"HEY!" The shout came from behind him, and Axel whirled, eyes reeling in his skull. Two guards were running toward them from the room next door, already fumbling for their weapons. "STOP RIGHT THERE!"

"*Go to your right!*" Leif shouted. "*Through the library!*"

Axel and Joaquin took off at a sprint, guards scrambling behind, and stampeded through a room of velvet armchairs and shelves stacked with first editions. At Leif's direction, they then cut across the salon, open to the ceiling three stories up; into the ornate entrance hall; and then the dining room—where, surrounded by silver candlesticks, lace tablecloths, and massive portraits of bewigged Europeans—they hit a dead end.

There were only two doors, and the boys heaved them both shut, bolting the locks just as the guards caught up. His heart pounding behind his ears, the men banging against the sturdy wood paneling, Axel gasped for breath. "How do we get out of here? Even if the guards can't break their way in, Petrenko will have a key!"

"*Can you smash a window?*" Leif asked uncertainly.

Axel looked out through the slender panes of glass at flashlights bobbing in the dark, more guards circling the house, pulling the net tighter. He swallowed, his throat dry. "Negative. We wouldn't make it fifty yards before we took a bullet."

There was a long, awful silence before Leif said, "*I'm sorry, but I'm out of ideas.*"

Axel stared at his brother, trying to wrap his brain around it. "We're trapped."

THE RADIO AT LEIF'S FEET WAS ALMOST AS LOUD AS THE alarm—and twice as insistent. From one end of the estate to the other, the guards all knew about the break-in; and they were still, rather stupidly, trying to coordinate their response on an open channel.

He should have abandoned the guardroom the second they started talking about sending someone to check on its occupant, but then all hell had broken loose, and Joaquin had needed his help.

And Axel. Also.

So now he'd let himself get backed into a literal corner. Urgently, a voice on the radio barked out, "*Check the house—every room—two teams to a floor! We're at the south wall now . . . we'll make sure HQ is secure and guide you from there!*"

Prying open the control panel on the console, Leif took "Scout Master's" coffee mug and dumped its contents over the exposed wiring. There was a flash of hot light, a loud *snap*, and then the monitors went dark. There would be no more all-seeing eyes tonight.

And then came the sound of footsteps thumping toward him down the dead-end hallway. His company had arrived.

The sight of the plundered display cases rendered Arkady Petrenko apoplectic. He fulminated in Russian for a good while, as the two men with him made an awkward show of searching the room. But the only conceivable place for a person to hide was behind the curtain—and there was no one there. It appeared no one had been trapped inside after all.

"Where the shit is my shit?" Petrenko demanded, his voice raw. "You say there are two in the dining room? What the fuck are they doing still breathing my air? Go in and drag them out! Cut off their fucking fingers till they say where my fucking shit is!"

He stormed out of the turret with the men behind him, and the lights went off again, the steel barrier slamming back down.

Three and a half stories above the floor, clinging to the backside of about forty feet of burgundy damask, Margo had suffered through the entire performance with her arms burning and the blood draining out of her hands. Thank God the fabric was thick and sturdy, with voluminous folds that disguised how her weight pulled at it. Thank God for the dense shadows that concealed her when the bodyguard checked behind the curtain.

Thank God Margo had been working on her upper body strength, too. Aside from a few decorative cornices, the wall behind her was smooth as glass, and she'd had to drag herself all the way up, hand over hand. Digging deep, she forced herself to climb the remaining five feet—all the way to the substantial bar from which the drapes hung. Inching to the very end of it, she was only three feet away from one of the turret's two windows. Outside, she could see the parapet that ran the perimeter of the castle.

Her first kick cracked the glass, and her second kick shattered it—which was great, because she couldn't hold on for a third try.

She did her best to clear the most dangerous shards from the frame, and then launched herself through, tumbling into the night air and slamming down onto a surface of hard stone.

Her elbow hurt, and her shoulders and her knee, and a piece of glass had sliced through her upper arm—but she was alive. The problem now was that there was nowhere to run; this stretch of the parapet, bordered on both sides by a hip-high wall, led to only one place: a locked door in the next turret along. And she no longer had her tools.

Scaling down the side of the castle did not exactly appeal, and she wasn't sure her numbed arms had the integrity to try—but as she peered over the wall to assess her chances, a third possibility presented itself.

Far below, a wide terrace of pale stone spread out, wrapping around the open-air portion of a large swimming pool. Glowing with submerged lights, it was a brilliant tourmaline blue in the darkness, casting wobbly shadows against an outbuilding that faced the main estate. Just beneath the surface, Margo recalled, a submerged opening allowed passage in and out of the pool house.

Before she could give herself a chance at second thoughts, Margo backed up as far as she could go, and ran like hell. When she reached the wall, she vaulted over it and plunged.

THERE WOULD BE NO EASY WAY OUT OF THE GUARDROOM, just the hard way—which suited Leif fine. Grabbing a fire extinguisher from a cabinet in the corner, he donned his night vision glasses, turned out the lights, and then smashed the switch off the wall.

A key rattled in the lock and the door swung open, revealing two men: a beefy guy in front, and a beardy guy just behind. The first guard squinted and then leaned in, groping for the missing light switch—and that's when Leif attacked. The coffee mug whistled as it zipped past Beefy's ear and smashed directly into Beardy's chin, drawing out a yelp of pain as the heavy ceramic shattered and knocked the man back. Beefy startled, fumbling for his weapon—but the extinguisher slammed into the side of his head a moment later, and he dropped to the floor.

Beardy recovered quickly, even managing to free his gun from its holster, but a blast from the extinguisher caught him full in the face as Leif lunged out into the hall, and the guy stumbled back again. Sightlessly, he squeezed the trigger, missing his target by a foot. A hard blow behind the guard's elbow numbed his gun hand; and a swift round kick to the temple a second later sent him to the floor beside his colleague.

Leif whistled a little as he tied their hands, and then he skipped down the hall, heading for the garage.

THE BANGING AT THE DINING ROOM DOOR HAD STOPPED, which was not, in Joaquin's estimation, a good sign. It meant they knew there was no way out, and they could be patient while somebody went and retrieved the keys.

Only there *was* a way out, and he kicked himself for not seeing it immediately.

"The fireplace," he hissed, and both boys turned to look at it.

"We're right above the kitchen." Axel shifted his jaw, crossing to the hearth.

"That wood-burning stove has to vent somewhere, right?" Beside him, Joaquin got to his knees, cranking open the damper. "This must be it!"

"We'll throw the packs down," Axel declared. "Then you go, and I'll follow."

Joaquin wanted to argue; Axel was bigger than he was—taller, broader in the shoulders, more substantially built—and it would be a tighter fit for him. He'd need more time. But arguing him down from this decision would take even longer, and so the younger boy just gave a quick nod and crawled into the firebox.

One by one, Axel handed him the bags, and Joaquin shoved them past the smoke shelf and down the chimney column; then he crawled up past the damper and into the flue.

This time, there was no careful movement, no inching progress; Joaquin tucked in his arms, pointed his toes, and dropped. It was painful, but fast, and at the bottom of the chute he plummeted into the oven—crash-landing and rolling out of its arched mouth into the kitchen. It was quiet, ambient light gleaming dimly on the stainless steel fixtures and copper cookware, and as he gathered up the packs, he listened for approaching footsteps.

It took agonizing minutes—time they didn't have—before Axel's feet kicked into view. With difficulty, the older boy wrestled clear of the chimney at last, scarlet wig askew, his face sweaty behind his makeup. The second their eyes met, relief bubbled up like champagne, and they started to giggle.

As quietly as possible, they took the bags and ran, heading for the garage.

FROM THREE STORIES UP, HITTING THE WATER WAS LIKE jumping through a pane of glass, and Margo felt the impact in every joint; a second later, she felt it again when she slammed to the bottom of the pool, her teeth clicking together and the air rushing from her lungs in a turbulent gust.

For a moment, she couldn't move, so stunned by the landing that her vision crossed and her limbs felt disconnected. Her chest hurt, her body demanding another helping of oxygen, and it took all that was left of her self-control to keep from surfacing immediately. Slowly, she pushed forward through the water with disciplined strokes, the submerged lights guiding her toward the underwater passage into the pool house.

Once on the other side, she finally burst to the surface, sucking down a great, ragged gasp of air as she dragged herself from the water with trembling arms. Collapsing on the edge, she flopped onto her back, coughing and sobbing with latent fear and the relief of survival. Light and shadow chased each other across the ceiling in rippling patterns cast up by the pool, and Margo focused on them while she pulled herself together. "*Get up*," she whispered aloud, her voice echoing softly. "Get up. Feel it later."

There was no light but for the underwater bulbs, and the effect was eerie, like she'd washed up in a lost cavern. Struggling to her feet, muscles stiff from the shock of impact, Margo rolled her neck. She was familiar with the pool house and its changing rooms that exited onto the lawns, and she also knew that she was on her own now; the water had shorted out her comm, and protocol required the team to scatter in the event of a member being compromised or captured. She needed to assume the boys had fled the second that steel door slammed down with her on the wrong side.

It was possible they'd left one of the prepped cars behind, in case she got away . . . but was it worth the risk of checking, and maybe find herself at a dead end? She needed to come up with an alternative, and she needed to do it fast; her dive from the parapet had not been stealthy, and she had to assume the splashdown would be investigated. She couldn't even risk turning on the lights in the nearly pitch-black changing room as she limped into it, calculating an escape in her head, wondering how she'd get back home without her keys or her money or her cell phone.

She didn't even hear the footfall until it was too late—until something cracked against the back of her skull, sending up a shower of white sparks behind her eyes, throwing her forward to the floor.

FOUR DRAG QUEENS GATHERED IN THE SHADOWS OF THE garage, huddled between a gunmetal-gray coupe and a cherry-red convertible, their voices pitched in urgent whispers. The conference was short and tense.

"What should we do?"

"You know the rules."

"Fuck the rules! They're stupid rules."

"If Margo were here, she'd tell us to go."

"She's *not* here. That's the whole point!"

"We can't just leave her behind, guys. It isn't right."

"Okay, so what's your proposal? We steal a gun, shoot everybody dead? Maybe smash through the turret with one of the cars?"

"That could work!"

"It couldn't. You know how thick those walls are? These princessy rides would fold up like deck chairs, and we'd die inside 'em."

"We can't just *leave*!"

"We're supposed to. Her words—her rule."

"It's a stupid rule."

"So we put it to a vote. All in favor of leaving, say aye; those opposed, say nay."

Two said aye and one said nay—and, after an agonized beat, the fourth queen cast the deciding vote.

Sixty seconds later, the garage doors were rumbling up, and the coupe surged forward with the convertible right behind it. Their tires whined as they picked up speed, hugging the curve of the drive, streaking for the steel-reinforced front gate.

A button in the Aston Martin's console sent a direct signal to the massive barrier, causing it to slide open, and the men standing guard scrambled to react. Unable to override the gate's response, they barely had time to dive clear as the two vehicles shot past, rocketing out onto Topanga Canyon Boulevard. Wheels shrieked as they made the sharp turn, and their engines roared in triumph, careening up the twisting hillside.

* * *

Luckily, Margo had just enough wits left to keep moving when she hit the ground. Rolling to the side, she heard the whistle and clang of metal smashing the floor inches to her left. A shaft of moonlight spilling through a high window caught the gleam of a pool hook as it swung and came down again, seeking her in the dark; a pale flash of white-blond hair, and a savage Russian expletive, finally revealed to Margo who her opponent was.

The hook came down a third time, even closer, and she grabbed for it; rolling onto one knee, she lashed out and felt her foot connect with Valentina's body. The other girl yelped and staggered back, dropping the metal pole—but a second later, she launched herself forward again, diving atop Margo with an enraged snarl.

Their bodies close, their breathing hot and fast, the situation was dizzyingly familiar. Margo had never been entirely clear on the nature of their relationship when they were still close—trading barbs and insults one minute and making out the next, their chemistry a volatile seesaw between hate and lust. Margo hadn't even told anyone she was bi before the first time she had Valentina's tongue down her throat.

But the Russian girl had always been more cruel than kind, the passion between them tangled up with resentment. Even with one hand working between Margo's legs, Valentina had mocked the girl for her expressions, for the noises she made. Hand-to-hand combat almost felt like a relief—an interaction less charged and more honest than sex.

They grappled on the floor, too close for anything but brute-force blows, knuckles hammering soft tissue—while Margo expended half her energy trying to stay in the shadows so she wouldn't be recognized. Finally, Valentina managed to flip the girl onto her stomach, ripping off her nylon hood, and exposing the bedraggled, platinum wig. Simultaneously, Margo arched up and twisted back, slamming her elbow into the girl's face. Valentina toppled over . . . and stopped moving.

For a moment, Margo just lay on the floor, panting for air. Her skull still throbbed from the blow with the hook, and her body felt like it had been run through a mangle. When an electronic trill split the silence, she straightened up with a jolt. *Valentina's cell phone.*

Freeing it from its charger, Margo activated the phone's flashlight and swept the room. At a glance, there was little she could use: the pool hook, some fluffy towels, Valentina's handbag—knocked over in the fight, surrendering the girl's keys, makeup, and pepper spray—and Valentina herself. Sprawled on her back in a short, terry cloth robe, her pale blond hair tangled across her face, she wasn't going to be much help, either.

Or maybe she would.

A FEW MINUTES LATER, A GUARD STANDING BY THE FOUR-car garage—staring helplessly at the two empty bays belonging to the missing vehicles—was startled by a figure rushing toward him across the east lawn. He had his gun out, safety off, before he recognized the long legs, pale hair, and terry cloth robe of his boss's daughter. She was wearing sunglasses in the dead of night, but so many strange things had already happened that he barely noted this as he called out, "Ms. Petrenko! You shouldn't be outside, it's not safe—"

"There's someone in the pool house!" The girl shrieked hysterically, pointing behind her as she sprinted for the garage. Her voice sounded odd, but the guard attributed this to stress. "I barely got out alive!"

"I'll call it in, but right now you—" the guard cut himself off. Valentina was still running right at him, closing the distance like she didn't mean to stop, and there was something strange about her face . . . "Hold it! Halt right where you are!"

He swung the pistol up, but he was too late; the girl—definitely *not* Valentina Petrenko—slammed her foot into his gun hand and sent the weapon flying into the night. He threw a hasty punch, but she feinted back and then stepped in, delivering a quick jab to his nose and then a round kick to his jaw. Lights flashed and went out, and he fell to the ground.

Moments later, Valentina's white BMW revved to life, headlamps springing on. The car leaped from the garage at a touch of the pedal, and sped down the drive for the front gate. The barrier rumbled aside, and the guards leaped for cover a second time as the vehicle zoomed past, cornering sharply and disappearing up the hill.

One by one, the outbuildings that dotted the Petrenko property lit up, guards combing every inch of the estate, desperately hunting for signs of the intruders. It would take an hour or more to confirm what already seemed obvious: the women who'd stolen their employer's priceless collection out from under their very noses were long gone.

20

PULSE RACING, MARGO SCREECHED INTO THE
outlook and killed the Beemer's engine a heartbeat before a fleet of
wailing police cruisers crested the hill, zipping around the bend
in the other direction. The coupe and convertible were already
parked in the tiny lot—and to her immense relief, the stolen delivery
van was there as well. The boys had waited.

Davon put the getaway vehicle in gear the second Margo set
foot inside it, pulling out of the lot before the side door was completely closed. Yanking off her matted wig and dark glasses, she
joined a chorus of exuberant and breathless congratulations as they
rolled down into the Valley at a respectable speed, just another car
on the road. They took the 101 to Las Virgenes, wending all the way
back down into Malibu.

By the time they were at her front gate again, Margo was back
in her regular clothes. Her body ached all over, but no pain could
overcome the high she felt from what they'd just pulled off. She
waved goodbye to the boys and started up the sloping driveway,
her limbs growing heavier the closer she got to bed.

When she reached the courtyard, however, she paused uncertainly, the bag full of priceless jewelry almost slipping from her hand. Something was wrong. Every light in the mansion was ablaze, the front rooms glowing like Christmas displays behind floor-to-ceiling windows. But Harland was never up this late, and rarely left his room . . .

She broke into a sprint, shoving through the front door and shouting, "Dad? *Dad!*"

"Margo." Dead ahead, rising up from a hideously modern sofa in the living room, were two people. The one who'd spoken was Irina, and Margo's vision went fuzzy when she took in the woman's blotchy face and swollen eyes. "Please . . . you should sit."

"Is it . . ." Margo's head spun, the floor suddenly two miles away. "What's happened? Where's Dad?"

"Your father's in the hospital." This came from the man beside Irina, and it took Margo several long seconds to process that it was Addison Brand—her father's second-in-command at Manning. "I'm sorry, but he collapsed earlier this evening."

"Collapsed? Is he—"

"We don't know anything just yet." Brand came toward her, putting his arms around her shoulders, guiding her to the sofa. The flask in his pocket clanked against Margo's hip, and she felt a burst of strangling rage that disintegrated instantly, destroyed by panic. "It's likely there won't be any news until the morning."

She looked at both of them, eyes wild. "What hospital? Where?"

"There's nothing you can do right now, myshka," Irina said morosely. She was pale and drawn, wrung out by emotion. "The doctors are with him now, and you won't be able to see him until tomorrow anyway."

"But what if he—" Margo's throat caught, and her voice wavered. "What if—?"

"Harland is a fighter." Addison Brand put something in her

hands, and with a start she realized it was a tumbler of whiskey. She didn't think she wanted it, but the man guided the glass to her lips, and she swallowed it in two stinging gulps. "I called for an ambulance the second I realized something was wrong, and they got here right away. He has a better chance of beating . . . whatever this is than anybody I know."

It was a meaningless statement, but Margo found herself nodding in agreement anyway. "He shouldn't be alone."

"He's not alone. He's with the best medical team that money can buy."

"It's late, myshka," Irina added, taking one of Margo's hands. "They would just make you sit in the lobby. I'm sorry. I know how . . . You're scared, you want to do something. But best you can do right now is rest. Be ready in the morning."

"She's right." Brand upended his flask, emptying it into Margo's glass. "If there's any news, the hospital will call. And in the meantime, Harland wouldn't want you sleeping on some bench in a waiting room."

She allowed herself to be led from the living room and up the stairs, a glass of whiskey in one hand and a bagful of stolen jewelry in the other; but even after Irina closed the door behind her, promising to stay the night so Margo wouldn't be alone, the girl could feel nothing but the intense, terrifying vacancy in the bedroom at the end of the hall.

WHEN SHE WOKE UP, IT WAS FIVE IN THE MORNING, AND SHE felt like she'd been run over more times than a speed bump. Taking a painkiller, Margo dressed, left a note for Irina in the kitchen, and slipped outside. Two phone calls was all she needed to figure out where they'd taken her father, and she had to use the Manning name as currency once she reached the hospital, but eventually she was curled up in a chair in Harland's private room. He was gray and frail, and she was almost afraid to touch him. Closing her eyes, she doubted she'd ever fall asleep again.

An hour later, she was roused awake. "Margo? What on earth are you doing here?"

"Dad?" Margo straightened up, groggy and disoriented. "You're awake."

"Yes. Thank you for the observation." The grouchy comeback dissolved into a wet cough, and Margo stilled in her chair. She'd been so consumed with the Petrenko job that she hadn't set eyes on her father in more than a week, and she was shocked by how much weaker he seemed, how gaunt and withered.

"What happened last night? Mr. Brand said you ... collapsed?"

"He was being dramatic." Harland waved off this account, but the denial lacked enthusiasm. "I experienced some pains and lost consciousness for a short while. That's all."

"That's *all*?" Margo repeated the words in disbelief. "What did they tell you? What does this mean? Did they figure out how to fix it?"

"Margo ..." Harland expelled a breath, his eyes moving away from his daughter. "Margo. They're not going to 'fix it.' It's time we both face the facts."

"Don't say that," she snapped, angered and alarmed by his complacency. "They managed to do something, right? You're awake again, and you're obviously not still in pain, so they must have figured out—"

"Pain management is not the same thing as treatment." The way he issued this declaration made it clear he'd been thinking it for a while. Blinking tiredly, he added, "Margo ... I haven't wanted to tell you this, because ... well, quite frankly, I haven't known how. I'm not good at admitting to my vulnerabilities."

He was silent for a long moment, and something cold gripped at Margo's throat. She could barely speak. "Dad? What are you saying?"

"I've not been receiving any treatments for a while. A few weeks."

Margo stared at him. "What are you talking about? That's not even true—your doctors have been out to the house!"

"And they have helped me manage my pain levels," Harland stated serenely. "And, to their credit, they also agreed with me when I said I saw no point continuing invasive procedures that take up time and money and yield no results."

"Money?" Margo was on her feet in an instant, her face burning with rage. "We've got so much money it practically rolls down the canyon when you cough, and you're just . . . you're giving up because it's *expensive*?"

"It isn't about money." Harland placated. "It's about the fact that, for all the things we've tried, I just keep . . . losing, Margo. These treatments haven't been pleasant, and when they're done, I can't even stand being inside my own skin. I'm groggy and nauseous for hours, sometimes days, and when the misery finally passes, I've got nothing to show for it. I'm just weaker, and down precious hours that I'll never have the chance to live over."

"Dad—"

"I'm not giving up. I'm admitting that I've been fighting the wrong battle from the beginning. There's no beating this thing."

"What are you trying to say?" She didn't know why she was asking the question. She knew exactly what he was saying, and she didn't want to hear it. Any of it.

"I'm saying that . . . Margo, I'm saying I'm sorry." For the first time in his entire life, Harland Manning sounded uncertain of his power position.

Margo opened her mouth and then shut it again. "You're sorry?"

"I've been hard on you, because being hard on people comes easily. I see so much potential in you, Margo, and the only means by which I've ever known how to cultivate potential is by challenging it. It's a principle that has always worked at the company; but I know now it was a mistake to apply it at home."

"Dad . . . ?" She couldn't say anything more, didn't have the voice. *He saw potential in her?* "I don't understand."

"I've spent a lot of time troubling you about your public antics—the partying, the fights—because I hoped I could shame that behavior out of you. That's time I won't get back. Time I could have spent . . ." He trailed off and blinked, and with shock Margo realized his eyes were wet. "Time I could have spent telling you how proud I am of all you've accomplished. Your grades, your athletic achievements, and . . . I've observed more than you think, Margo. I'm aware of how clever you are. I'm aware of your leadership skills."

His tone was so meaningful, a shock went through Margo like a blast of cold air. She was already flustered by his heartfelt honesty, his first wholly supportive words in as long as she could remember; but was he really implying what it sounded like? "The doctors can't possibly have tried everything. I just learned about a hospital in Geneva—"

"They've tried enough for me." Harland raised his hand, then let it fall. "I'm done wasting time. It took me almost eighteen years to figure out what was truly important to me, and I'd like to enjoy it for the time I've got left."

The room blurred, and Margo barely managed the five steps to her father's bedside, where she took hold of his hand and squeezed it, unable to speak—hardly able to breathe.

21

SHE HELD HIS HAND UNTIL HE FELL BACK TO
sleep, and for more than an hour sat perched beside his bed, considering the strange new world she lived in—a world in which she finally felt close to Harland, just as he was slipping away. When the door to the private room opened again unexpectedly, she was startled from her daze, and felt warmth break through her tangle of complicated emotions when she saw who was there. "Uncle Win!"

"Margo, my girl, you're a sight for sore eyes." Clive Winchester Martin was a white-haired and florid seventy-something with a puckish grin and a dry wit. He'd been Harland's personal attorney for longer than Margo had been alive, and was as good as family. "Lovelier every day, of course, just like your mother. I think it's awfully unfair of you to keep getting older without asking permission."

"It won't happen again," Margo promised, a genuine smile breaking across her face for the first time in hours. She stood and gave the man a hug. "You heard what happened?"

Win nodded. "Your father and I had an appointment for later this week, but when Irina called . . . well, I thought Harland would appreciate it if I changed my schedule."

"An appointment? But what—"

She was interrupted when a second visitor shoved his way into the room as well. "Okay, Win, I asked the 'cute' nurse to bring us some coffee, but I swear she—Margo?"

"Dallas." Margo blinked. The boy was wearing another pair of hip-hugging khakis, and a white button-down that showed a V of golden brown skin just below his throat. "I, um . . . it's good to see you again."

"You too." He gave a smile, fleeting and sympathetic, dimples winking.

"Ah, so the two of you have already become reacquainted," Win observed.

"She was at the house the day I went to get those documents signed for you." Dallas's face turned a little rosy. Clearing his throat, he added, "I was pretty sure I'd mentioned that."

"I am pretty sure that you didn't." Win's tone was suspiciously innocent.

"How's your dad doing?" Dallas asked, his face even rosier.

"He's . . ." Margo didn't even know how to answer. *He's great—he's accepted the inevitability of death!* "He's comfortable, I guess. He's been sleeping most of the morning."

"I hate to disturb him." Win frowned, thinking. "Perhaps we should go down to the cafeteria, and see if the cute nurse will fetch us when he wakes up? Or perhaps—"

The door flew open a third time, and another man marched in, stopping short when he saw the assembled group. "Well. Evidently, I'm late for the party."

"Mr. Brand?" Dallas's eyebrows went up.

"Good morning, Addison." Win seemed surprised. "What brings you by?"

"Checking up on Harland, of course." Tucked under his arm, Brand carried a folio emblazoned with the thunderbolt *M*, and he seemed to realize everyone was looking at it. "We were going over some figures last night when he . . . took ill, and it's somewhat urgent that the matter be addressed."

"Don't you think it's rather a poor idea for him to get back to work so soon?" Win arched a brow, gifted in the art of disdainful leading questions. "Surely he can afford to rest a day or two."

Brand responded with an unfriendly smile. "Am I to assume, then, that you brought your errand boy here on a purely social call?"

"No." Win turned sober at this, his shoulders going stiff. "No, I suppose I didn't."

"It would be nice if you allowed me to weigh in on this discussion." Harland Manning's voice rose from the bed in a disgruntled crescendo. "And nicer still if you would all just shut your traps."

"Apologies, Harland." Win turned to face the patient. "I came about the matter we were to discuss on Thursday. I thought perhaps you wouldn't wish it to wait."

"No." Margo's father peered up at his attorney with a guarded expression. "I suppose it's best if we take care of that now. You have—"

"I have everything." Win's glance flickered to the side, touching on Margo and darting away. "If you'd like to put it off until we have a little more privacy, I—"

"Will this top secret conversation impact the business?" Brand's tone was remarkably bitchy. "Because, if so, it seems like something I ought to be in on—seeing as I'm acting in your stead, and all."

"It is my *personal* business, and does not require your input or approval, Addison," Harland snapped, still capable of delivering a good smackdown, no matter how weakened his condition. "Whatever you came here for can wait a few minutes while I deal with this."

With a thoughtful air, Win said, "Actually, Addison, why don't you stay—we may need you after all. Dallas?" He gave his intern an avuncular smile. "I have a feeling Margo hasn't left this room all morning, and I bet she could use something to eat."

"I am a little hungry," Margo realized. Aside from some truly abysmal hospital coffee, the last time she'd consumed anything had been before breaking into Petrenko's place.

"Don't you . . ." Dallas shuffled his feet uncomfortably. "You don't need my signature?"

"I've got Addison now, and maybe I can talk the cute nurse into acting as a second." He gave the teenagers a smile. "You two go find a corner of this place that doesn't smell like medicated ointment."

"'THE CUTE NURSE'?" MARGO REPEATED LATER, AS SHE AND Dallas roamed the hallways, following signs to the cafeteria.

"She's, like, sixty." Dallas laughed, his brown eyes gleaming. "I swear, half my internship is just Win Martin using me to Cyrano de Bergerac the ladies."

"The *sexy* ladies," Margo corrected him. "Sexy sexagenarian ladies."

"He's one part sweet old grandpa and one part gross pervert. The other day he asked me if the plural of dominatrix was 'dominatrixes' or 'dominatrices.'"

"*Argh*, don't tell me this!" Margo cried, covering her ears. "He's practically *my* sweet old grandpa—and I just hugged him, like, ten minutes ago! Now I'm thinking about him in a rubber dog mask and a choke chain."

"Welcome to my life."

They were still laughing when they found the cafeteria at last, a space of fold-up tables and linoleum, where the air smelled only slightly of medicated ointment. Margo grabbed a croissant and some yogurt, her stomach empty but sensitive, and sat down across from

Dallas as he dug his fingers into the peel of an orange. For a moment, she just watched him—his cheekbones, his pouty bottom lip, the beauty mark beneath his right eye.

Without so much as glancing up, he intoned, "Mesmerized by my beauty?"

Caught, Margo's face warmed. "I'm just trying to match you up with that loudmouth seven-year-old I once knew."

"How's it going?"

Margo considered. "You've changed."

"Yeah, I'm sexy now." Dallas grinned at her, mashed-up orange spilling out between his teeth.

"There he is. I knew I'd see that seven-year-old sooner or later."

He sipped some coffee. "You've changed, too."

"Not that much," she protested. "I wanted to be Wonder Woman when I was five, and I still want to be Wonder Woman now."

"Ah yes! But when you were five, I thought you looked ridiculous in your Wonder Woman bathing suit. I bet I would feel differently if I could see you in it today."

"That's not me changing, that's Win rubbing off on you."

Dallas grimaced. "Please don't talk about Win rubbing things off when I'm eating." He set his orange down and wiped his fingers on a paper napkin. "But you are different. I always remembered you as this bossy kid in costume jewelry ordering me around—and then one day, there you were on the cover of *In Touch*, and it was this story about you going to Paris Fashion Week and having a whirlwind romance with some actor."

"Yeah, well. You can't believe everything you read," Margo said stiffly. The "whirlwind romance" had been little more than a publicity stunt; a rising star and a buzzworthy socialite courting the media together. "I'm a lot of things, and I've done a lot of things, but magazines only tell the parts people want to hear."

"Don't worry. I know a little bit about having your book judged by its cover." In a nasal tone, Dallas whined, "'Do you have any *baby* pictures? I *love* mixed babies!' 'Where are you from?' 'No, but where are you *frommm*?'" He let out a derisive snort. "People love to assume shit about me because of my appearance, and I can't count the number of people I've known who suddenly said something ridiculously offensive and then pointed to me, like, 'I can't be racist because one of my friends is fill-in-the-blank.'"

"Yikes." Margo made a face. Axel and Joaquin had faced similar aggressions, classmates and strangers asking them intrusive questions about their racial background, their sexuality, acting entitled to answers and angry when they weren't forthcoming.

"Anyway." Dallas forced a smile. "I already knew there was more to you than just what's in the gossip rags. The girl those magazines describe wouldn't have spent the night sleeping in a motel-grade armchair just to be close to her father."

She nibbled at a point of her croissant, and then blurted, "This morning is the closest Dad and I have been in a long time. Years. Maybe since he and Mom split up." With an apologetic smile, she added, "Sorry, I'm sure you didn't mean for this to be talk-show time."

"It's okay," he said. "How is your mom?"

"Fine. She married a banker and lives in Italy. I see her a couple times a year." She made a listless gesture. "You know, neither of my parents were ever present when I was a kid, and after they ended things, she left and Dad just . . . never showed back up. It's like he went to work and never came home. And then today, he finally said some things—" Margo broke off, her chest getting hot, and stuffed a piece of croissant in her mouth to buy time. "Well, even if he was never around, he was always *around*. What am I going to do when . . ."

"I'm very sorry," Dallas said quietly.

She chased down the lump in her throat with a gulp of coffee that tasted like the floor of a barn. "Okay, enough Poor Little Rich Girl. What's the top secret business Win is upstairs conducting with Dad, anyway? Why'd everybody want me out of the room?"

The boy's expression faltered, and he took a breath. "He's finalizing his will. I guess he hadn't updated the documents in a while, and he told Win he had some changes to make. I was supposed to be a witness, but I guess Mr. Brand is taking my place. I'm sorry. I think they didn't want to say anything because . . . well."

"Oh." Margo shifted, wiping pastry flakes off her hands, her fingers unaccountably trembling. "I should've . . . I mean, really, I should've guessed that."

"Margo—"

"No, it's okay." She stood, leaving her yogurt untouched, her stomach suddenly too small to accommodate anything else. "We should get back upstairs. I mean, if you think they're done."

They were quiet most of the way back to Harland's room, but as they got on the elevator, Dallas gave her a sheepish smile. "Since we're busy confessing things, I guess I ought to tell you that I kind of volunteered to bring those papers to your dad the other day. Win was going to pay a messenger, but I . . . might have insisted."

"That's not a very scandalous confession," Margo remarked. "I'm disappointed."

"Uh." Dallas cleared his throat. "I maybe asked because there was a chance I'd run into you." His face was a lovely shade of pink. "Whether the girl in the magazines is all real or not, I've been kinda-sorta-maybe a little bit of a fanboy. For a while."

"A *fanboy*?" Margo couldn't help it; she smiled. "Oh wow, I'm flattered. Am I going to have to sign your boobs?"

"I'm sure I can think of something more embarrassing than that."

She gave him an expectant look. "Well? Was seeing me in person again as amazing as you always dreamed?"

"Meh," he replied in a critical way. "You're a lot shorter than I—*ow!* I'm just kidding!"

When they reached Harland's room, the door was open, and Win was in the middle of an energetic story about a capsized sailboat. Margo's father looked pale but relaxed, chuckling along gamely, while Addison Brand stared grimly into space, eyes unfocused, like a grouchy teenager forced to babysit on the night of the Big Party.

"Ah, Margo and Master Yang!" Win gave the two teenagers an expansive welcome. "How did you find the cafeteria?"

"Easy," Margo riposted. "We followed the signs, and there it was."

Win hooted with laughter, as if he hadn't been the one to teach Margo that joke in the first place. "Grand, just grand! Well, Master Yang, you'll be happy to know our business here is concluded. I'm sorry you came all this way for such an anticlimactic morning."

"You're the boss. I just go where you tell me." Dallas snuck a glance at Margo. "Besides, there are worse ways to spend a few hours."

"Yes, try being stuck on your back in a room with an old goat who won't shut up," Harland interjected in a surly tone that set Win roaring again. "If we're done, does that mean I can finally get back to sleep now?"

This, at last, roused Addison Brand from his stupor. "Harland, there's still the matter that I came about. I'm not happy with the numbers for the—"

"Addison, you're never happy about anything," the older man retorted. "Whatever's bothering you, I'm sure it'll still be in your craw after I've slept for a few hours."

Chastened, Brand's mouth snapped shut with a *click*, and Margo asked, "Is there anything you need? Water, something to eat?"

"The only thing I need just now is peace and quiet," Harland insisted, his face pale. His tone softened a little as he added, "But thank you."

"I suppose that means we're dismissed," Win remarked. Herding them out of the room and into the hallway, the lawyer gave his intern a sympathetic smile. "Dallas, I still feel badly for making you come out all this way and then banishing you to the cafeteria. I can handle filing the paperwork. Why don't you take the rest of the afternoon off?"

"Are you sure?" The boy gave him a doubtful look.

"Don't look the old gift goat in the mouth," Win advised with a wink. Then, "Goodbye, Margo. I hope to see you again soon— and if I have to use my assistant's charms to make that happen, I'm not above it."

Margo laughed, rolling her eyes. "Goodbye, Uncle Win."

"Wait, I'll walk you out." Addison Brand marched to the elderly attorney's side as the man began to move off down the hallway. "I have a few questions about estate law that I've been meaning to research."

"Oh, good." Win's sarcasm was thick enough to leave a handprint in, but Brand launched into a long-winded question anyway as they disappeared around a corner.

"Well, I guess this is goodbye for us, too," Dallas said, turning to Margo. "Unless . . . you know, maybe you'll let me buy you an actual cup of coffee? One that isn't made from nine parts industrial-grade cleaning solvent, I mean."

"My, you do know the way to a girl's heart," she cooed. "And how could I possibly say no to my biggest fanboy?"

"Hey now, I said I was *a* fanboy, not your biggest. My roommate last year had a picture of you taped up over his bed."

Margo thought for a moment. "I . . . I can't tell if that's flattering or creepy."

"Trust me, it's both."

AN HOUR LATER, THEY WERE SEATED ON THE PATIO OF A HIPster café, and Margo was drinking cappuccino from a comically oversized mug. The espresso was rich and earthy, the foam smooth as silk, and caffeine buzzed in her veins like hornets after one sip. "Excuse my fucking language, but this is amazing."

"They do everything by hand here," Dallas explained. "They even roast the beans on-site. It's my secret hideout; coffee is my one serious vice, and finding this place was like hitting oil. They don't advertise, because they don't want to be overrun by the trendy crowd."

"Does that mean I have to wear a disguise when I come back?" He probably thought she was joking, but in her mind, Margo was already sorting through possible "hipster coffee maven" wigs. "What other secrets are you hiding? What else should I know about?"

"Well, let's see . . ." Dallas made a face. "Here's the big one: I don't think I want to be a lawyer."

Margo raised her brows. "Then why the internship?"

"Making my mom happy. I used to play lawyer as a kid—you know, dragging around her old briefcase and pretending to take appointments—and she's never stopped thinking it's my big calling. And maybe it is, I don't know." He tossed his arms out, shirt straining across his chest. "Honestly? I don't know what the hell to do if I grow up. The only thing I really love is . . . well, diving out of airplanes. And rafting, and rock climbing, and BASE jumping. But making a living at that stuff is almost impossible—and nothing takes the fun out of a hobby like getting paid for it, because then it's work."

"Jeez, you make it sound so depressing."

"Sorry. But that's me: a caffeine-addicted adrenaline-junkie-slash-Margo-Manning fanboy who can't decide what to do with his future. What about you?" He aimed his spoon at her with a lascivious wiggle of his eyebrows. "I showed you *my* layers; let's see yours. You're not a hundred percent the girl from the magazines, but there's gotta be some of you in there, too."

"Of course there is." Margo smiled faintly. "I mean, I like fashion and going to parties; I love feeling like a pretty princess sometimes; I love that my choices are trendy just because they're *my choices* . . . but." She gave an uncomfortable shrug. "Sometimes I hate it, too. People want to use me, and I don't always know who until it's too late. Guys think they're entitled to my body because they've seen pictures of it on the internet, or that grabbing my ass is worth the bragging rights." Margo stole a glance at Dallas's face, taking in his expression. "I broke a guy's wrist once. He sued for damages and we had to settle out of court, but I'll tell you what: *That* was worth the bragging rights."

"Okay, so you're a fashion-plate party-girl-slash-Wonder-Woman enthusiast who can take a man apart with one hand."

"I used both hands," Margo admitted modestly.

"Either way, you're a surprising and fascinating person, Margo Manning. And a little intimidating."

She busied her hands, wondering how he would react if she told him the full truth—if she would ever feel comfortable telling someone that much truth. "Ah, but you are the one with the mesmerizing beauty!"

Dallas laughed, his face turning pink again, and he picked up his cappuccino. He had large hands, the huge mug sitting comfortably in one palm as he drained the last of its contents. When he set it down, he licked foam from his top lip, and Margo averted her eyes when he glanced her way. "When you're done, would you like to maybe go for a walk?"

"A walk? How *Pride and Prejudice* of you!" Margo's blood was practically singing with caffeine. "A walk sounds lovely, Mr. Yang. Frankly, I'm pretty sure I could jog all the way to Tierra del Fuego after finishing this coffee."

"Maybe on our second date," Dallas riposted, and then his eyes went huge at the same moment Margo lifted her brows. "Wait! I didn't mean—"

"Did you say 'second date'?" Margo interrupted. "Is this . . . were you—"

"That just slipped out!" Dallas's face was almost the same burgundy shade as the decorative curtain in Arkady Petrenko's turret. "Obviously, this isn't a date—I mean, unless you wanted it to be, or whatever, but obviously you don't, and that's cool! It's totally cool. I was just thinking that, you know, I *wanted* . . . what I mean is: I was *interested* . . . but, like, I know that dudes get presumptuous with you, and I don't want . . ."

He petered out helplessly, and Margo gave him a smile. "You just used a whole lotta words to not actually say anything."

"Believe it or not, I took home two debate trophies in high school."

Margo smiled again. "A *silver-tongued*, caffeine-addicted adrenaline-junkie-slash-Margo-Manning fanboy who can't decide what to do with his future." She tucked a lock of hair behind her ear. "And, just for the record, I wouldn't be opposed to going on a date. Officially. If you asked."

"Oh." Dallas looked into her eyes and a corner of his mouth quirked up, those dimples showing themselves again. "Well then. Margo Manning, would you make me the happiest of all fanboys and do me the honor of accepting a dinner invitation?"

"I would be delighted to, Master Yang," Margo said. The air shifted and she caught his scent—citrus and clove—and she fought the urge to lunge at him, mouth first. "I was afraid you'd never ask."

"I was kind of afraid of that, too." His smile broke into a grin.

Margo followed him out of the café and onto the sidewalk once her mug was empty, watching the way his pants hugged the muscles in his thighs—wondering how his large hands would feel tangled in her hair. She was a little dizzy, and not just from the espresso, when she realized her phone was buzzing in her purse. Seeing the name on the display, she tensed. "It's Uncle Win. I wonder what—"

The answer to her unfinished question occurred to her so jarringly it stole the breath from her lungs. All of a sudden, she knew—she *knew*—and it was as if she was drifting loose from her body. She didn't want to answer it; she wanted to let it ring and ring forever, but somehow the phone ended up at her ear, and she heard her own voice say hello from a million miles off.

"Margo." Clive Winchester Martin's familiar voice was so heavy it was a miracle she managed to keep the phone aloft. "Margo, my dear, I am so sorry to tell you this." He heaved a sigh, and she almost blew away with it. "I'm so sorry. It's your father. He . . . I'm afraid he's gone. He's gone, Margo."

At last the cell phone slipped from her fingers and crashed to the pavement, and her insides came apart at the seams.

Act Three:
SEA OF TROUBLES

22

SEVEN DAYS PASSED IN AN UGLY SMEAR, TIME distorting and blistering, like a film reel caught on a projector. Minutes lasted for epochs, and then Margo would blink and find herself standing in the kitchen, having lost entire hours. The world wouldn't leave her alone; Harland had imparted detailed instructions for his final exit, but still there were calls to be made, letters to answer, guests to receive—and the only one left to do it was Margo.

The memorial service erupted from the calendar like a mountain sprouting from the earth, and she readied herself that morning, surprised each time she managed to take another step forward. Her father had not been a religious man, and so all the guests gathered on a seaside bluff behind the funeral home to pay tribute to Harland Manning. It was winter in LA, which meant cloudy skies and a brooding, gunmetal ocean, but Margo kept her sunglasses on.

One by one, people she barely knew got up to share their memories, and she was stunned by how few of them she recognized. Successively, they reminisced about Harland's business acumen and ambition; there were no wistful stories about him as a friend, a mentor, a benevolent figure. His legacy consisted of charts and graphs—and Margo.

His only living heir, she made a lonely receiving line at the end of the ceremony, fielding handshakes and pitying condolences, drawing on every scrap of her willpower to remain upright. Predictably, her mother had chosen not to attend, and Margo was too dazed to figure out if she was angry or relieved about it. Axel, however, stood beside her throughout, a hand on her elbow, weathering the scrutiny of the many attendees who were victims of Basil Moreau's scam. Unable to articulate her gratitude, she reached for his hand and squeezed it as hard as she could.

"Margo." Addison Brand appeared before her with probing eyes, and pulled her into an abrupt embrace. His cheek scraping her own, his arms uncomfortably tight, he intoned, "It's so hard to believe that he's gone. Please know that this is from the whole Manning family when I say you have our deepest sympathies."

It took Margo one long synaptic moment to realize that he meant her father's company. She was all that remained of the "Manning family" now. "Thank you, Mr. Brand."

"Please. Call me Addison." He stepped back, his long fingers still kneading her upper arms. "And if there's anything that Manning can do for you, don't hesitate to let me know."

"Creepy," Axel muttered under his breath as soon as the man had moved on.

"You'd think my *dad's funeral* would be the one time he'd avoid the urge to touch me inappropriately." Margo scowled. "I can't wait to never see him again."

Brand's place was taken by an older Black man with graying hair and a pouchy face. Clasping both of Margo's hands in his, he spoke sonorously. "Your father was a great man with a singular vision, and it was both an honor and a pleasure to be a part of his success. You should be very proud of everything he accomplished."

"I am, and thank you." Margo's reply came automatically, a reflex trained by countless repetitions in the past few days.

"I hope you know, Margo, that he saw great things for you. You were the one achievement he could never fully take credit for, and the one that he talked about the most." He gave her a kindly smile, but her jaw trembled too much to manage a response, so she merely nodded until he moved on.

Axel slipped a tissue discreetly into Margo's hand. "Who was that?"

"Reginald Castor," Margo answered when she could speak again. "He sits on Manning's board of directors. He was the second largest shareholder, after Dad."

"Does that mean he's in charge of the company, now?"

"I don't really know what's going on with the company. The board chairman is different from the CEO. Or, I mean, in theory." Margo shook her head. "Sorry. It's a lot of complex business stuff, but it really depends on what my dad did with his shares. He was founder, CEO, and chairman, so Manning's never faced this kind of leadership crisis. The shareholders will elect a new chairman—maybe Castor—and the board will appoint a new CEO." She gestured after the departed man, who had been waylaid by Brand, an obsequious expression on his face. "I'm guessing that role will be Addison's."

"Damn. And I thought tucking my dick was complicated."

Margo hid her fit of church giggles with a round of coughing, and when she had regained her composure, Nadiya Khan was at the head of the receiving line. Her expression impassive, the woman said, "I want you to know how sorry I am for your loss. I had a tremendous amount of respect for your father." After Margo had mumbled her gratitude, the scientist hesitated. "I was thinking . . . would it be all right if I stopped by the house this week to see how you're doing? When my mother passed, there were so many simple tasks that felt overwhelming, and it would be my pleasure to offer some help."

"Of course," Margo answered, but tension gathered between her shoulders in spite of Dr. Khan's friendly smile. It wasn't that she doubted the woman's sincerity, but something in her tone . . .

"Margo, my girl, my dear girl." The sickly-sweet odor of metabolized alcohol enveloped her even before Win Martin leaned in to grasp her arms. His eyes were unfocused and bloodshot, and Margo was taken aback by his gloomy and obvious drunkenness. "We've lost a noble man. Your father was a pain in the ass, but one of the finest pains in the ass I've ever known." He scrubbed his partially shaven face, his breath stinging with the smell of gin, and she was so embarrassed she almost had to look away. "I'm sorry, Margo. I . . . I don't know how else to say it. There's no justice in this, and no amount of sorry will ever equal your loss, but . . . I'm sorry just the same."

"Thank you for coming, Uncle Win," she managed, every square inch of her skin crawling with the need for this moment to end.

"All right, Win, let's give Margo some space." A woman in a dark suit swept in from the side, gently peeling the man loose and guiding him back a few steps. "It's a long line, and there'll be plenty of time to chat at the reception."

With a start, Margo recognized the woman as Liliana Perez, Dallas's mother—and as Liliana steered Win off through a battlefield of plastic folding chairs, flashing a helpless look over her shoulder, her son appeared in her wake. His expression mortified, Dallas shook his head. "Sorry about that. Win's a little . . . it's been a rough week."

"Is he okay?" Margo couldn't stop staring as Liliana shepherded her father's attorney toward the parking lot, his shoulders stooped and his steps crooked. "I mean, he didn't drive himself here, did he?"

"We drove him," Dallas promised.

"I've never seen him like this."

"Neither have I. Mom always joked that he was a party animal, but that meant, you know, a glass of dry sherry, and then trying to make a roomful of grown-ups play Twister or something. But this week . . . he's been hitting the bottle like it hit him first. I know he and your dad were close, but I wasn't prepared for this." Dallas ran a hand through his short, dark hair, his features pinched with concern. She caught his scent again, and felt a twist of painful nostalgia in her heart. "Are you . . . how are you holding up?"

"Ask me when I get here." She managed a weak smile. Tossing her hands out, she took in the entire scene—the funeral wreaths, the swags of black silk covering the lectern, the roiling whitecaps on the ocean—and shook her head. "None of this feels real. I keep expecting to wake up, for someone to tell me there's been a mistake."

"I'm sorry," Dallas said earnestly. "Really, I'm just . . . I'm so sorry, Margo. I always remembered your dad as this, like, Colossus, you know? Larger than life, dominating every room . . ." He trailed off, pulling at his tie. "Are you okay? Do you need anything?"

She cast another look around the windswept bluff, at the line of people still waiting for their chance to remind her of her loss, and shuddered. "I could use a drink."

"I'll see what I can do." He gave her a conspiratorial nod, one corner of his mouth ticking up; and then the expression passed. "Margo, I feel like I should say something. I can't imagine what you're going through, but it's got to be hell. I'm not . . ." He looked at his feet, suddenly finding his shoes fascinating. "I wanted you to know that I'm not going to hold you to what we talked about at the café. You've got so much to deal with, and the timing is just . . . well, what I'm trying to say is, I'd like to be here for you as a friend. If you need one."

Just like that, Margo started to sob. Her shoulders hitched, her chest convulsed, and she struggled to get air into her lungs as Axel rubbed her back. Finally, she squeaked out, "I think I need a hug."

Dallas wrapped his arms around her, and she felt the hard planes of his body through his tailored suit, and she breathed in the warm scent of citrus oil and clove. Dallas was right: She was in no condition to think about dating right now—but for just that moment, it was a blessing not to be alone.

NEARLY ANOTHER HOUR PASSED BEFORE THE LINE DWINDLED to its end, and Margo's head was throbbing. Irina was probably already welcoming guests to the mansion for the wake, which would start just as soon as the bereaved daughter could arrive—to no doubt be hustled through yet another gauntlet of condolences. The prospect made her want to run away to the moon, but she didn't have a choice. Win, if he was still conscious, would be reading Harland's will that afternoon.

Escorting her back to the parking lot, waving to the remaining mourners who smoked and gossiped outside the door, Axel finally murmured, "Okay, girl, I've been really patient, but it's time you spilled the tea."

"What are you talking about? What tea?"

"*What are you talking about?*" He mimicked with an exasperated eye roll. "I am talking about the five-alarm-fire of a boy who hugged you earlier, and whose hot, hot body you put your hands all over without even offering to share."

"Oh, right."

"*Oh, right*," Axel repeated her. "Does tall, dark, and do-me have a name? I want a complete dossier, with all relevant and pornographic statistics."

"Well." She couldn't help feeling a little smug. "His name is

Dallas Yang, he is an adrenaline-junkie-slash-legal-intern, I think he's a Leo, and he's already seen me naked." When her best friend tripped, his eyes popping open wide, she let out a delighted cackle and filled in the blanks. "His mom left Win's practice when I was a kid, and he kinda vanished from my life. And then one day . . . there he was at the house."

"I don't want to gross you out," Axel said evenly, "but I'm going to get carpal tunnel thinking about him."

"Stop! No!" Margo exclaimed. "I am officially grossed out!"

"That was a masturbation reference, if you didn't get—"

"I got it! Stop!"

"Because if you do it too vigorously—"

"*I'm* going to get carpal tunnel punching your face if you don't—"

"Miss Manning?" The sudden voice startled her and Margo drew up short, the grin vanishing from her face in an instant. Standing before them was a tall man in a long, dark coat; leaning against a cane, a wide-brimmed fedora pulled down over one eye, his face showed the scarring of a severe burn. "I'm afraid I missed the ceremony, but I wanted to be sure I expressed my condolences to you on the loss of your father."

"Th-thank you," Margo managed, pulling up a polite smile. She'd seen him many times before, of course, but only in the dusty shadows of his back room, where they pretended he didn't know her real name. It was Vojak—her fence.

"If you need anything." With a gloved hand, the man proffered a business card, which Margo plucked from his fingers. Touching the brim of his hat, Vojak gave a nod. "Grief is a terrible thing, Miss Manning. Please take care of yourself."

His long coat swirling in the wind that gusted over the asphalt, he turned and started walking toward a dark sedan in a corner of the lot, his cane clicking rhythmically. Axel stared after him with undisguised awe. "Damn. Talk about fucking eleganza. He was wearing spats, Margo—*spats*!"

She mumbled an agreement, but her attention was fixed on the card. The front was generic—a logo, a web address, and BRIGHT EYES TRAVEL in block letters—but something had been scrawled on the back. It was a nearby address, a house on a private road just minutes away, and under it was a single word: *NOW*.

IT TOOK A WHILE TO PERSUADE AXEL TO LET HER DRIVE BACK to the mansion alone, to convince him that she needed that time to herself to regroup after the memorial; and longer waiting for his ride-share to arrive and whisk him off, so she'd know he wouldn't be behind her when she detoured to her unexpected rendezvous.

In the business of selling stolen goods, anonymity was essential. Margo had assumed her own identity was an open secret between her and Vojak—they'd spent too much time together, face-to-well-known-face, for her to have gone unrecognized by now; but he'd courteously played the farce for over a year, never addressing her by name—until today.

Halfway back to the mansion, a private drive crested a hill, ending in an empty lot with an oblique view of the ocean. A signboard advertised a forthcoming property, but for now it was a dusty waste, hemmed in by looming cypress trees that blocked the view of neighbors. Vojak was waiting for her, leaning against his car, eyes on the gray clouds rolling in over the coast.

"I appreciate a little cloak-and-dagger as much as the next girl," Margo began in a weary tone as she climbed out of her own vehicle, "but . . . maybe you could've saved this stunt for the next girl?"

"I'm sorry." Vojak's tone was somber and almost formal. "This wasn't exactly my first choice. I've been trying to get in touch with you, but . . ."

"I've been a little out of touch," Margo finished for him. There was a moment of pregnant silence, into which she nearly screamed. "I'm assuming you didn't summon me here for my opinion on zoning laws?"

Vojak glanced at the churned earth behind them, and shook his head. "No. I've got some news, actually. I found a buyer for those wayward paintings that followed you home last month." He gave a distant grin. "A certain collector I know offered a million for the lot."

Margo's brain was still moving on a slower rotation than normal, and it took her a beat to catch up. "A million? As in . . . *a million?*"

"Some of it will be cash, and some of it will be stones, so there may be a delay while I organize a clean wire transfer for you. But yes: a million as in *a million*."

"Wow. Okay. Wow." Margo watched birds circle a line of palms beyond the brow of the hillside. Money felt so abstract all of a sudden; she'd never had less than she needed, and now she had more than she knew what to do with. But a million, even divided up, would make a huge difference to those she'd share it with. "Thank you."

"Just doing my job," Vojak remarked. There was another pause as he stared at the clouds, and Margo was afraid she was going to have to shake him until he told her what was really on his mind; but then: "A couple of guys came to visit me this week."

Instantly, Margo's hackles rose, the man's tone bringing up gooseflesh on her arms. "A couple of guys?"

"Big, thick accents, covered in bad stick-and-poke tattoos of eight-pointed stars and skulls and shit." Vojak fixed her with a look, and Margo felt the color drain from her face.

"Russian prison ink?"

"They didn't exactly present me with calling cards, but I'm

guessing they were Russian mob—or mob-connected." He fingered the toothy snarl of a silver wolf's head on his cane. "They dropped in to see if I'd heard anything about the theft of some antique Russian jewelry. Apparently, a highly organized team of young women"—Vojak fired her a glance—"stole an absolute fortune in gems from a friend of theirs, and they are really eager to find out who was behind it. *So* eager that they're going around, making offers that aren't easily refused. If you catch my drift."

"You basically handed me that drift," Margo mumbled.

"I told them I had no idea what they were talking about. No clients of mine have commissioned that kind of a job, and no one has come to me trying to move any Czarist pieces." The tip of the cane scratched a zigzag in the ground at their feet. "But they weren't exactly satisfied. They *really* want to know what happened to these particular baubles, and they're willing to apply any kind of pressure it takes to find out."

"I see." Margo swallowed dryly. Her father's death had eclipsed everything so totally that she'd forgotten to even report the Petrenko haul to her fence. And now . . . what exactly was Vojak trying to say? "They think you know who took these items?"

"It's a small world, and they know I'm one of the guys most likely to hear about it," he answered diplomatically. "But I haven't heard. And I don't think I want to—because I'm not sure I could resist the kind of pressure these dudes were describing to me. So if you know who was behind this particular job, or you ever find out, maybe do us all a favor and keep me out of the loop? If you understand what I'm saying."

"I understand." Margo's mouth felt like it was full of paste.

"I hope so," Vojak stated gravely, "because I'm trying to scare you. These guys know a few dozen ways to remove body parts and keep you alive while they're doing it, and they are definitely a 'dismember first, ask questions later' kind of crew." He pushed off the side of the vehicle and opened the door. "If you know anything? Try to forget it. I intend to do the same."

The sedan did a wide circle over the barren earth, and then trundled out of sight, disappearing down the slope back to the Pacific Coast Highway. For a long while, Margo stood by herself in the empty lot, her feet frozen and her blood thoroughly chilled.

23

BY THE TIME SHE REACHED THE MANSION, THE storm clouds had burst, and Margo's stomach was as unsettled as the storm-tossed Pacific. For Vojak to track her down in person meant the threat was very real—and she should've seen it coming. Pulling her car into the garage, she switched off the engine and pounded her hand against the steering wheel until her palm started to hurt. *She should have expected this.*

She knew about Petrenko's criminal connections, and she *knew* he'd picked up art on the black market before; she even knew a few of the Czarist pieces were among his dubious acquisitions. Vojak was one of the best, and a man with the Russian billionaire's purchasing power would surely have heard of him. In retrospect, it was a given—*obvious*—that Arkady would try to track down his things by leaning on his underworld contacts.

Vojak couldn't tell what he didn't know, though, and thank God he couldn't tell Petrenko this. But she was in a hell of a position, anyway, and even if she buried the stash sixty feet below the Staples Center, she still wouldn't be entirely out of the woods. The man wasn't stupid, and he clearly had an inkling about Margo's involvement. If Petrenko's "pressure" was extreme enough, she could still be in danger—and so could the boys.

Slamming her fist against the steering wheel again, she collapsed back, sobbing helplessly. It felt like she'd done nothing but cry for a week, her father's death leaving her constantly on the knife's edge of tears. She was exhausted and overwhelmed and, now, *furious*. How could she have been so stupid? She'd seen Axel lose his objectivity, and it had convinced her that she was seeing things with clearer eyes; but she'd been just as bad. The temptation of ending all their debts, pulling off an impossible job, had kept her from thinking far enough ahead. After all her dire warnings about variables and ugly surprises, she'd fallen face-first into a snare that had practically come with a blinking marquee.

Hands shaking, she sucked down some air and forced herself out of the car. Unbelievably, she still had several more hours of her father's death to get through before she could dive into an emotional spiral on account of this particular wrinkle.

Nobody dared to tell a grieving daughter she couldn't have alcohol after her father's funeral—and rarely did anyone have the guts to say no to Margo Manning anyway—so she indulged until the crush of earnest guests felt less threatening, and the air took on a thick, dreamy quality, mourners speaking to her as though through glass.

And then finally the guests were filtering out, empty glasses and wadded cocktail napkins left discreetly behind, the foyer echoing with murmurs of, "Call if you need anything," until only a handful of people were left.

Dallas, his tie loosened, placed a champagne flute in her hand. His eyes, a deep, chestnut brown, were wide and warm. "I thought you could use this."

Margo studied the sparkling, rose-gold wine, tiny bubbles breaking its surface, and took stock of herself. She felt languid, a rowboat moored with a loose knot. "Hmm . . . I'm afraid if I have anything else, I'll regret it."

"I, uh . . ." Dallas winced. "It's time for the reading of your dad's will. I figured a little liquid courage . . ."

Margo tightened her grip on the champagne, suddenly more sober than she'd felt in months, and followed him to her father's study. Like every other room in the mansion, it was dominated by stark lines and squared edges, a minimalist theme in muted tones. Win Martin, gray and clammy, was slouched behind Harland's desk, his expression as absent as a Halloween mask. Sinking into a boxy armchair, Margo wondered which one of them was going to have the harder time getting through this formality.

The attorney waited until everyone was present—Irina and Dr. Khan, Reginald Castor and Addison Brand and others she only vaguely recognized—while Dallas perched discreetly on a stool in the corner. It was weird seeing the study occupied; it was the room that Harland had vanished into for most of Margo's childhood, a forbidden zone where she dared not to tread, effectively abandoned since his illness.

"Well, we all know why we're here," Win began brusquely, shuffling through the papers before him. His voice was clearer than it had been at the funeral home, but he appeared miserable. "Everyone in this room has been named in the last will and testament of Harland Woodrow Manning, and it was his wish that the disposition of his estate be presented in this manner." He cleared his throat, reading, "'I, Harland W. Manning, being of sound mind and body do hereby declare this to be my last will and testament, revoking all others that came before it.'"

He proceeded through several pages of minor gifts and endowments—the LA Opera, the philharmonic orchestra,

LAMFA—before moving on to more substantial sums for personal acquaintances. When Irina was named, the woman started weeping, even before she heard the number.

"'To my daughter, Margaret Evelyn Manning,'" Win read, and Margo's heart began to pound inexplicably, "'with the exception of gifts otherwise stipulated in this document, I leave the full remainder of all my liquid assets, stocks, bonds, and other material goods, and all my tangible properties, to be managed in trust by the party identified hereunder until her eighteenth birthday.'"

There was more—Harland's longtime financial manager was appointed executor of Margo's trust; a codicil allowed her to appoint a different executor when she turned eighteen, a proviso formally ending the trust when she reached twenty-one—but she barely heard any of it. Her palms sweaty, her pulse racing like she'd just dodged a head-on collision with a truck, Margo gulped the rest of her champagne with shaking hands.

It wasn't really a surprise, but the dry, legal terms made it feel so *final*. With that brief, clinical paragraph, it hit her like a wave of freezing water that this was the last she'd ever hear from her father—this document, this inconceivably grandiose behest, formed the final page in their shared story. His words would never fill the air in this study, his judgment would never stare up at her from a row of tabloid pages, he would never get to build on the ground-shaking statements he'd made during their final conversation. The tears on her lips made the champagne taste like salt.

Win moved on, launching into matters pertaining to the company, Harland Manning literally micromanaging from beyond the grave. In a better mood, the attorney might have joked about it; but instead he kept his eyes on the page, his recitation rushed, like he couldn't wait to have it all over with.

"'As for the Manning Corporation, it shall come as no surprise that I wish to leave my company in hands that will faithfully carry forth my vision. Therefore, I hereby do appoint as Manning's next chief executive officer, and trust the board shall confirm in such capacity, my loyal chief operating officer and longtime personal friend, Addison Beaufort Brand.'" A round of murmurs circled the room, and Margo stole a glance at the man in question, his face shiny with pride. There was a pause before Win forged ahead again. "'As pertains to my holdings in Manning stock, I hereby leave the entirety of my controlling, fifty-one percent share to Addison Beaufort Brand to do with as he sees fit, and also appoint him to succeed me as chairman of the board of directors.'"

This time, the reaction was far less understated. Nadiya Khan glanced up sharply, her lips pressed into a flat line; Reginald Castor blinked, his face slack, eyes flicking between Brand and the attorney as if he hadn't heard correctly; and, most curious of all, Dallas straightened suddenly in his chair, his brow furrowing as he stared a question at the back of Win Martin's head. In fact, the only person who seemed to take the announcement in stride was Addison himself.

The remainder of the will was read hurriedly, tension rising in the room like flood waters; and when Win finished the last clause, Addison was the first to exit, grinning like a shark making off not just with the bait but the fisherman as well. Castor was on his feet next, his expression composed but his shoulders tense as he approached the desk. "I am somewhat disconcerted, Winchester. Based on certain things Harland had confided in me, I was expecting a different outcome from this reading."

"I can't help what you were expecting, Reginald." Win's tone was clipped and frosty. "And I have no idea what Harland said to you. All I can tell you is that he revised his will the day he died, and these are the results. Obviously, I am legally enjoined from discussing the details, and could only speculate as to his reasons anyway. I'm sure you understand."

As the attorney gathered the loose pages, stuffing them inelegantly into his briefcase, Reginald Castor watched him with a gimlet eye. "No. I'm afraid I don't."

Without another word, Castor made stiffly for the door of the study, sparing a brief moment to pat Margo's shoulder. Almost immediately, Dallas was standing before the desk, his handsome features pulled together in a frown. "Win, I'm confused, too. I thought that—"

"Not now, Mr. Yang," Win dismissed him irritably, snapping the locks shut on his briefcase. "It's been a long day, and I don't have time to explain points of law to you."

"It's not that." Dallas's frown deepened. "I just ... I thought ..." He struggled, frustrated, seeming to rethink his words. "I was under the impression that ..."

"I'm not paying you for your impressions," Win retorted, an edge in his voice that Margo had never heard before. "In fact, I don't believe I'm paying you at all. How about you stick to filing and answering the phones, and leave the 'impressions' to me?"

Dallas straightened, his eyes going cold. "Sure, why not."

Scooping his briefcase off the desk, Win muttered a general farewell and then hastened out of the room, avoiding Margo completely. She watched in shock as he disappeared, and then turned back to Dallas. "What the hell was that about?"

Dallas just shook his head. "I don't know. I mean, I don't understand—" He cut himself short, giving her a guilty look. "I'm sorry. There's a lot I can't say, because of legal stuff. But I'm surprised and confused, and ... okay, maybe I shouldn't even say *that*."

"Surprised and confused about what?" She asked the question reflexively, but he only shook his head again, unwilling to meet her eyes.

"Margo?" Dr. Khan was standing beside her chair, her eyes troubled, and the girl got to her feet. "I ... wanted to say again how sorry I am. I'll give you a call in a few days, to arrange that visit—and I'm afraid I won't take no for an answer."

Again, there was the palpable sense of words unspoken hanging in the air, but the woman merely squeezed Margo's hand and then left.

Irina approached next, blubbering into a knot of overworked tissues, and dragged Margo into a bosomy hug that lasted way too long. She asked repeatedly if there was anything the girl needed—but there really wasn't; no one had the power to give Margo what she truly needed just then.

When the housekeeper left, the room was empty but for Margo and Dallas. He slipped off his tie, long fingers uncoiling the knot. "How come your mom wasn't here?"

"Are you kidding?" Margo snorted a laugh. "When I called her about it, she told me she could, quote, celebrate her ex-husband's death just as easily from Italy, where the wine is better and her good cheer wouldn't scandalize his hypocritical acquaintances. Unquote."

"Yowch." Dallas's eyebrows climbed halfway to his hairline. There was a moment of silence as they looked around the room, at the empty chairs still aimed toward the desk, and he shifted his weight. "Margo . . . did your dad ever talk to you about his plans for the company? I mean, in the event that . . . well, in *this* event?"

"Not exactly." Margo couldn't stop thinking about Harland's desk—the drawers she would have to go through, the items she wouldn't want to use or throw out. It was all hers now, and the responsibility felt like a mudslide. "Dad was weird about the company. He always wanted me to take an interest, but he also wanted me to have space from it, if that makes sense?"

"What's your current stake in Manning, do you know?" He seemed to realize how brazen the question was, because his ears turned a little pink when he asked it. "Sorry, that's probably none of my business."

"No, it's fine," she assured him. "I own a handful of stock—not enough to make a difference, but more than most of the casual shareholders. I always let Dad vote for me, though. Now, I guess—" And then it finally hit her: In bequeathing his full interest in the company to his second in command, Harland had transferred the family business right out of the family. For all intents and purposes, the Manning Corporation now belonged entirely to Addison Brand. Not sure how to process this, Margo looked up at Dallas, blinking. "I don't get it. He always used to lecture me about my fuckups because of how they would affect my credibility in business. He never pressured me to take an interest in Manning, but it felt like it was just . . . assumed. I know I'm only seventeen, and I'm not even sure I *want* a corporate future, but I can't believe he shut the door like that."

What she didn't say was that, all of a sudden, she was hurt by the realization. Had Harland's disappointment over her provocative and meaningless rebellion really driven him to cut her off from the company altogether, even after his emotional confession the same morning he changed his legacy? It was another question she'd never get to ask. The nevers were stacking up quickly, weights on her chest.

"I should get going," Dallas finally said with an unhappy sigh. "Are you sure you're going to be okay with no one else here tonight?"

"It's my home." She shrugged listlessly. "*Only* mine now. I've got to get used to being alone in it, right?"

He gave her a doubtful look, but she walked him to the door and said goodbye. There was a charged moment where they tried to negotiate an appropriate farewell, and then he pulled her into a hug—and she let it linger, pretending for just a moment that nothing was so fucked up she couldn't turn it right again. And then he was gone.

Alone at last, Margo paced through empty rooms. Appliances

hummed, foliage stirred around the empty courtyard, and rain pounded divots in the surface of the infinity pool. Silence rang like an alarm in the sterile kitchen. She'd been on her own in that house hundreds of times, but it was different now. This wasn't *alone*, it was *lonely*; it had teeth.

She headed up the stairs, pivoting away from her father's closed bedroom door. It was late afternoon, sunset still an hour or two away, but she undressed mechanically. Sitting on the edge of the mattress, trying to figure out if she was going to bed or just giving up, Margo noticed the glass pushed to the back of her nightstand. It was the tumbler of whiskey that Addison Brand had given her the night her father was rushed to the hospital.

For a long moment, she just stared at the sticky amber film in the glass. Then her body started trembling, a million thoughts burrowing into her brain like termites: Her father's refusal to stop drinking in spite of his doctors' warnings, his choice to isolate her from the company, the way he'd said he was proud of her—*proud of her*—and then *died*. He'd waited until just hours before he officially shuffled off his mortal coil to say something she'd wanted to hear from him since she first learned what the word "proud" meant, and now she had no place to put all the feelings that had cracked open as a result.

For most of her life, he'd been absent, and for most of her life, she'd craved his recognition, his approval; and now that she'd gotten it at last, she was furious. How dare he say something that significant and then fucking die? How dare he put her through seventeen years of doubting herself, of *proving* herself, of hurt and devotion and mixed messages, and then vanish irrecoverably right after finally saying *I'm proud of you*?

With a shout, she hurled the glass across the room as hard as she could. Sturdily constructed, it bounced off the wall, denting the plaster but not sustaining so much as a crack, and thumped to the floor. Margo collapsed, sobbing, and when she could finally breathe again, she reached for the phone. Axel answered on the first ring.

"I can't be alone tonight," she whispered mournfully. "Can you guys come over?"

24

THE MANNINGS' LIVING ROOM WAS A CAMPSITE,
the furniture cleared away to make room for a ring of sleeping
bags, clustered before a blaze in the gas fireplace. Moonbeams
danced on the surface of the pool outside and spilled through the
hatched skylights above—and even though they were all there for
Margo, talking or consoling or just being quiet, Joaquin nursed a
small kernel of selfishness deep inside.

Never had the mansion seemed so big or so empty, and the boy
couldn't help indulging a hopeful fantasy. With all these rooms and
no one to fill them, what if Margo invited the Moreaus to live with
her? They could cut the millstone of the villa from around their
necks, free themselves of the ghosts and the mortgage, and maybe
be happy again. He could see it. But the dream was as substantial
as the flames licking at the glassed-in hearth.

Joaquin wasn't the only one thinking about the future. After a
long moment of silence passed, Davon spoke into the gold-rimmed
shadows. "What are you going to do, Margo? Can you stay in the
house?"

"Of course she can stay here," Axel snapped. "It's hers. Harland
left it to her."

"She's only seventeen." Davon—the only other person there who had experienced the death of a parent—kept his eyes on Margo. "She's still a minor."

"He's right," the girl said in a hollow voice. "I'm not an adult for another two months. Until then, my inheritance is in the care of my dad's financial manager."

"Like a regent," Leif suggested.

"Basically. It'll revert to me when I turn eighteen, but until then . . ." she cast a look out at the pool, and the electric sickle of light that hugged the coastline beyond it. "Technically, I guess my mom has custody of me now. Whether she likes it or not."

"Your mom?" Axel shot up in his sleeping bag, his face pale with alarm. "You're not going to Italy, are you?"

Axel's horror made a quick lap around the room, acquainting itself with everyone there. Without Margo, their revenue stream would dry up—which Joaquin knew was bad enough—but what would become of his brother? She was his only friend, the only thing he had beyond Tuck/Marry/Kill that kept him from breaking down. The girl seemed to sense this, because she gave him a reassuring smile. "I don't think I'm going anywhere. Maybe I'll visit for a while, but just because she's responsible for me doesn't mean she *wants* to be." She turned back to the fire. "I've got Irina and my dad's attorney in case of something serious. She'll tell me to stay."

"Okay." Axel let out a breath.

"You've got us, too," Joaquin reminded her, reviving his fantasy just a little. The other boys chimed in their agreement, and Margo's eyes filled.

"Thanks, guys." She took a deep breath, and then shook her head. "Okay, I don't know how to say this other than to just say it: I have some bad news."

In broad strokes, she recounted what she'd learned from their fence, and the mood in the room—if possible—became even darker.

His hands gripped tightly in his lap, Leif asked, "So what does this mean? We went through all of that, and now we're just . . . stuck with stolen goods that we can't move?"

Stolen goods that Russian mobsters are willing to kill for, Joaquin appended silently. The police took their time responding to calls from the villa these days, and if big, bad dudes managed to find enough breadcrumbs . . . "What are we going to do?"

"Don't panic," Margo ordered. "This is a hurdle, not a dead end. Our fence is the best guy in town, but not the only guy; and all we need is a crooked jeweler to recut the stones, and we're back in business." She made an emphatic gesture. "I've got contacts in New York, Chicago, Miami—and Milan, Marseilles, and Rio, too—and if we have to sell the rocks one at a time, I promise we'll get our money. In the meanwhile, we just made an actual million on those paintings. Divided up, you're getting about one-sixty apiece. We're okay."

There was silence as the number sank in, and Joaquin watched the tension vanish from Leif's hands while Davon muttered, "*Hallelujah.*" Axel was harder to read, though, his eyes blank; he insisted on handling all the money issues himself, keeping his brother in the dark as to just how great their debt really was.

AFTER EMPTYING TWO BOTTLES OF WINE LEFT OVER FROM the wake, they slowly dropped off to sleep, one by one. Joaquin, however, couldn't get his eyes to close—fixed as they were on Leif in the sleeping bag beside him. Two weeks had passed since the Petrenko job, but they still hadn't gone on the date they'd talked about. In fact, the subject hadn't even come up.

He'd worked two heists now, and the high he felt while in the thick of things made the rest of life sort of colorless. The confidence that had flowed through him, prompting the daring words he'd exchanged with the boy of his dreams, was absent in the harsh light of day; and maybe it was just endorphins that had compelled Leif to flirt back. Maybe the other boy never meant any of it. Maybe he'd *forgotten* about it. Maybe what happened on a heist, stayed on a heist.

A rustling from Leif's sleeping bag interrupted his thoughts. The blond boy was slithering free, rising on bare feet to head for the bathroom. He was wearing only a T-shirt and shell-pink briefs, and Joaquin quickly looked away. And then he cursed himself for not staring at least a little, because, *come on.*

Minutes later, Leif returned, and Joaquin pretended to be asleep—pretended not to be watching through one slitted eye—and then the boy was back inside his sleeping bag and rolling onto his side. Margo, Davon, and Axel filled the airy room with their even breaths, deep asleep, and Joaquin tried to mimic them. A moment later, Leif whispered, "You're not fooling anybody, you know. I saw you watching me."

"I wasn't *watching,*" Joaquin protested as quiet as he could, "I was just . . . I heard a noise!"

"And you wanted to make sure my underwear wasn't a ghost?" The boy countered, a smile in his voice.

Joaquin was pretty sure his face was glowing at least as brightly as the fire. "I like the style. I might buy a pair with my recent fortune."

A funny hissing noise came from Leif's sleeping bag, and Joaquin realized the boy was laughing. "You are ridiculous! You can just admit you were watching my sinful areas, Joaquin; it doesn't bother me." In a much sultrier tone, he added, "And if you really like these briefs, I can just take them off and give them to you . . ."

"No!" Joaquin gasped, all the blood in his body dividing its efforts between his face and his groin as Leif started doing just that. "My brother is, like, ten feet away!"

"Spoilsport." He could feel Leif's eyes on him now, and if he dared to look over, he knew he'd see the firelight dancing in them. "You know, I never got a chance to reverse the question you asked that night. What did you think the first time you saw me?"

Joaquin's breath caught. How honest should he be? This was no heist, and the adrenaline pumping through him was the ordinary, anxiety kind; but maybe, if being a jewel-thief-slash-drag-queen had taught him nothing else, it was to take chances and go for broke—knowing he was broke already and had little to lose. Swallowing, he said, "I thought you were beautiful. You were nice, and you were funny, and . . . you made me feel good about myself."

"I did?" Leif's voice was soft.

"You were the first one of Axel's friends—ever—to look at me like an actual person, and not some annoying plus-one. You smiled and said hi like you meant it. Everybody else always said, *'Aw, he's so cute!'* And it was *small and precious* cute, not *cute* cute."

"For the record," Leif drawled after a moment, "I did think you were *cute* cute." Finally, Joaquin faced the boy, heart thudding, and saw a smile lighting his face. "And also for the record? You deserve to feel good about yourself. You're impressive, Quino Moreau."

"Sure. I almost died on my first mission, and I almost peed myself on the second."

"But you went through with it, both times." Leif reached a hand out between them. "And you didn't let anyone stop you. You're smart, and funny, and you get this cute, squeaky laugh when someone tickles you." He found Joaquin's hand in the darkness and threaded their fingers together, his touch intimate and arousing. After a moment, he whispered, "I'd really like to kiss you."

"Do it, then," Joaquin answered, breathless.

Leif leaned across the gulf of space. Their lips met, and then their tongues, and Joaquin felt the boy's long, perfect fingers against his jaw—and his blood filled with a bright melody, their mouths pulling softly as starlight fell on them from above.

DR. KHAN DIDN'T EVEN WAIT A WEEK BEFORE PAYING MARGO her promised visit. The girl was already at the door when a sleek hybrid pulled into the forecourt, the scientist parking close to the house and striding up to the mansion. If possible, she looked even more grim than she had at the funeral.

"Thank you for agreeing to see me," the woman said formally, her dark gaze full of dire messages.

"Thanks for coming." It had been a week of constant phone calls, but very little human company apart from Irina, Axel, and Joaquin. Margo stood aside. "Please come in."

The woman hesitated, turning instead to gaze at the horizon. "I thought maybe it would do you some good to get out of the house for a while. To go somewhere else."

Something unpleasant crawled the length of Margo's back as she took in the woman's tightly drawn mouth and furrowed brow. "Sure, let me grab a coat."

"Somewhere else" turned out to be a deserted stretch of coastline ten minutes down the road. Nadiya parked, and they picked their way down to the pale, choppy sand, gulls making rounds overhead. Wind hurtled in from the ocean, slicing through Margo's leather jacket, and she shivered a little. Dr. Khan still hadn't said a word, staring moodily out at the crashing waves, and the girl finally spoke through chattering teeth. "Not to complain, because I do love a day at the beach, but aren't you scared of polar bears?"

"I'm sorry if I've been cryptic, Margo." The woman said at last. "A lot is happening just now, and I don't know who to tell about it. I . . . frankly, I'm not sure who I can trust."

Margo's eyebrows went up. "Okay. Well, you've definitely got my attention."

"Something is going on at Manning," Dr. Khan began again slowly. "The day before your father's memorial, Addison Brand announced an emergency meeting of the board, scheduled for the end of the month; and this week, he handed out pink slips to more than a dozen executive-level employees. He's cleaning house."

Margo frowned, the sand shifting beneath her feet. "I mean . . . yeah, that seems kind of abrupt, but I guess he's in charge now. He can hire and fire whoever he wants."

The woman shook her head emphatically. "These were dedicated employees, Margo. Some of them have been with Manning for twenty or even thirty years." She met the girl's eyes. "All of them were hired personally by your father and were loyal to him."

The salty air was cold and sticky against her skin, and Margo forced a smile. "You're making it sound so sinister, but whenever a company changes hands, the new guy always brings in his own people, right?"

"I'm making it sound sinister, because I believe that it is," Dr. Khan replied seriously. "A dozen department heads in a few days is a bloodbath, Margo, and if these employees—who worked alongside Addison for years—are not 'his people,' then who are? And how does he expect to find qualified replacements this fast, unless he's been looking for a while already?" A wave hit the shore behind her, sending up a spray of frigid seawater. "The sudden personnel changes, this emergency board meeting . . . something is coming, and I don't like it. And I'm also one of your father's handpicked loyalists, by the way. Every morning when I get to the office, I'm surprised to find my access card still works."

The sand shifted again, and Margo felt a little seasick. She couldn't imagine the company without Dr. Khan in the lab—but, then, she couldn't imagine it without her father, either. "I'm sorry, but I'm not sure why you're telling me. My dad left everything to Addison. Aside from my handful of stock, I've got no involvement with Manning anymore."

"And don't you think that's strange?" Dr. Khan stepped forward, grabbing Margo's shoulder, a spark finally glinting in her eyes. "Don't you think it's odd that he cut you out like that? He always talked about the Manning name, about his legacy—"

"His legacy is a logo on the side of a skyscraper," Margo interrupted, unable to hide the bitterness in her voice, "and on our gate, and on appliances and shipping crates—" She saw the spark fade again, Nadiya's expression wilting as she failed to get the reaction she'd hoped for. "I'm sorry. My dad gave me plenty of talks about 'legacies' and the 'Manning name' when he was disappointed in me for being a teenager in public. He didn't always approve of me."

But the declaration sounded off, because Harland's own words were ringing in her ears again: *I see so much potential in you, Margo . . . I'm aware of your leadership skills.* It didn't make sense. None of it made sense, and every part of her hurt when she faced the fact that she would never, ever be able to ask her father to explain himself.

"I'm sorry, too." Dr. Khan let out a great breath of air. "And I'm not sure why I'm telling you this, either, except that . . . I don't trust Addison, and I know my time to do something about it is running out." The woman ran her fingers through her wind-tossed hair. Then, "Did your father ever mention something called Project Pluto?"

"Pluto?" Margo shrugged. "Not that I can recall. Why?"

"I've done some snooping," the scientist admitted, looking off at the gray skies over the horizon, "and I've discovered a few strange things. One is a server I didn't know about, off-site but linked to our system, containing files I can't access." She cut her eyes to Margo. "As chief scientist, very little is off-limits to me—your father made sure of it—so an entire server I apparently don't have the clearance to get into was a surprise."

Margo twisted a ring around her finger. "You don't think my dad set this server up."

"I'm sure he didn't. Because I also learned that almost all of Addison's sizable discretionary fund is sunk into something called Project Pluto, and all files pertaining to it are hidden in this server, where I can't see them." The woman tucked her hands into her pockets. "What is Addison up to that's costing him thousands upon thousands of dollars, which he doesn't want to run through ordinary channels?"

"I don't know," the girl said helplessly.

"I'm going to lose my job, Margo." Dr. Khan set her jaw, her eyes flinty—a familiar look of determination that the girl had often admired, feared, and imitated. "But I'm not going without a fight."

25

TWO MORE DAYS PASSED BEFORE MARGO RECEIVED her next dose of human company—this time from someone she wasn't expecting. When the doorbell rang, she dragged herself from an hours-long torpor in her room and shuffled down the stairs to the foyer. Whoever it was, she was in no mood for company.

"Surprise!" Her visitor said with a bright smile, holding aloft a brown paper bag. Margo froze, a slovenly deer in the headlights.

"Dallas?" Immediately she regretted not changing her clothes. Her hair was tangled, her face greasy, and she still wore the same grungy T-shirt and boy shorts she'd had on since returning home from her ominous conversation with Dr. Khan. "What are you doing here?"

"I brought you some food!" He made a game-show-model gesture at the paper bag. He was wearing fashionably ripped jeans and a sweater that somehow made his broad shoulders look even broader. "This is the only Chinese food in LA that Eugene Yang approves of, and I had to drive all the way downtown to pick it up, so I'm going to need you to sign an affidavit swearing you'll appreciate it properly."

In spite of herself, Margo couldn't help smiling. "I know better than to question your dad's taste, so I'm happy to sign the paperwork. Besides, I've been eating Irina's leftovers for a week straight, and I'm not sure I can handle any more cabbage."

"Then, uh, don't ask what's in the spring rolls." Dallas wore a goofy smile as he pushed the bag into her hands. It was a very large bag. "You know, there happens to be enough food in there for two." He picked at something on the doorframe, not looking at her. "Way more than you could eat by yourself. And in case you're not picking up the hint, I'm very hungry."

"I'm picking it up," Margo promised, "but I'm also not exactly fit for visitors."

"What visitors?" He made a show of looking around the empty forecourt. "I see no visitors. I see only a hungry Cubano-Chinese boy with a killer smile, and maybe also some homemade pastelitos de guayaba in his car. Which you can only have if you invite me in."

He punctuated this with another goofy smile and an eyebrow wiggle, and Margo laughed. "I'm seriously gross right now, Dallas. I haven't showered in . . . well, I'm not going to tell you, because the truth is actually worse than your imagination. And to be honest, I'm in kind of a bad headspace these days."

"I get it. No pressure." He gestured with one of those beautiful hands. "But you might feel, like, five percent better with another person in the house. Just for a while. We don't even have to talk if you don't want to, but at least you'd have the option." When she didn't answer right away, he made his index fingers dance, singing, "Pastelitos de guayabaaa . . ."

"Go get the pastries, you weirdo," Margo relented with a laugh.

The Chinese food was great, and the companionship was actually welcome—and the guava pastries were unbelievable, so on the balance she figured she'd made the right call. As they were slurping ropes of lo mein from oily cartons, she asked, "You take all the girls on a culinary tour of your varied ancestry, or am I lucky?"

"A little of both. I only have a few tricks, and this is one of 'em."

"It's a good trick."

"Culture's important to my parents and . . . I don't know. I like sharing it." He kept his eyes down. Then, after a noticeable silence, he ventured, "You heard about that civil war in Malawi? Rebel forces seized control of the airport in Lilongwe, and there have been more reports of child soldiers—" He cut himself off. "Yeah, I should probably stop."

Margo widened her eyes. "And I thought it had been a while since *I* spoke normally to another human."

Dallas laughed, the sound throaty and charming, and for a fleeting moment she let go and admired his jaw, the shape of his neck. His eyes catching hers, warm and soft, he asked, "How've you been holding up?"

"Pass." Margo's tone was firm but polite. "Next question."

"Sorry. You've been hearing that a lot?"

"Every time the phone rings." She sank her chopsticks into coiled noodles. "It's nice that people are thinking of me, but it doesn't help. It just takes up energy."

"Know what's good for energy?" He held up a flaky square of puff pastry. "Pastelitos de guayabaaa!" With a snort of laughter, she accepted it, their fingers brushing together. "Tell me to shut up if I'm prying, but where's your mom? Is she seriously still in Italy while you're here, alone?"

"Yeah." Margo took a bite, the guava filling so sweet it tingled in her mouth. "We talked a few days ago. She asked how I was holding up." Hastily, she added, "You have to understand. My mom . . . I love her, but we've never been close. We haven't lived near each other for most of my life, and we don't always have a lot to say."

"That's . . ." Dallas didn't seem to know how to finish his thought.

"It's fine, trust me." Margo shrugged, unbothered. It was hard for people to understand that Angela Hopwood Manning—now Ferrara—had never been anything like the moms on TV; that she'd never really been cut out for motherhood. "Actually . . ." She cleared her throat, scared to articulate a thought that had been poking at her like a spring through a mattress. "I've been thinking about maybe surprising her with a visit. For a while."

"Oh?" He tried to sound casual, digging into a carton of rice with a preoccupied expression. "Cool, cool. Like, when would you leave?"

"I don't know," she answered gently. "I've got people here who are counting on me for stuff, but . . . soon? Probably?" Tossing a limp hand around the empty mansion, she said, "This place is too quiet—or too loud, maybe. One of the two. And everywhere I go, I see my dad; I'm seeing him more now than I ever did when he was alive. I'm tripping over his memory, Dallas, and it's just . . ." She trailed off. "I don't think it's good for me."

It was the loudest silence in the world—filled with her father's laugh, her father's complaints, her father's absence; and it was filled with other voices, too, which were getting more persistent but no more answerable every day.

I was expecting a different outcome from this reading.

Don't you think it's odd that he cut you out like that?

Did your dad ever talk to you about his plans for the company?

"Dallas, is something going on that I should know about?" She asked abruptly, hoping to catch him off-guard, and he glanced up with a mouthful of rice. "Because it seemed like a lot of people—including you—were surprised by what came out when my dad's will was read."

"I . . . honestly, Margo, I don't know how to answer that." He pushed his food aside, shifting uncomfortably. "Anything I think I know is based on something I learned in confidence; and if I broke that trust, I could be in serious shit." Dallas rubbed his mouth, fingers agitated. "And I wasn't there that last day in the hospital. I don't know what prompted the changes he made that afternoon. Only Win knows what was on your dad's mind at the very end."

Win and Addison Brand, Margo thought darkly, but there didn't seem to be much point in bringing it up. She hadn't been in the room, either, and all she had was empty speculation. Everyone seemed surprised that she'd been shut out of the company—and that Addison had been handed every rein of power. Maybe that *was* strange, but so what? She was a seventeen-year-old socialite who would never have to work a day in her life; was it really so bizarre that her father had decided to leave full control of his company to someone as committed and nakedly ambitious as Brand? After their heart-to-heart, maybe Harland had decided to free her from the weight of his expectations for good.

She shook the thoughts away, silently cursing Nadiya for lacing them with paranoid suspicions. "How is Win? I hope he's, um . . . feeling better?"

Dallas twirled a chopstick, lips tugged into a frown. "He's not. He's . . . not." The boy looked back up at her. "Honestly? He's a fucking mess. I've never seen him like this. I figured he was grieving, and eventually he'd pull out of his emotional swan dive, but it's only gotten worse. *If* he shows up for work, he comes in three hours late and three sheets to the wind. And he won't talk to me."

"That's . . ." This time it was Margo's turn to lack for words. "Maybe he needs help."

"Maybe. I talked to my mom about it, and she sighed. Like, that mom sigh that feels like a knife in your ribs? She told me that Win has a 'dark side'—whatever that means—and that she'd try to talk to him."

"That doesn't sound good." It was hard to picture Win—big, cheerful, blustering Win—with anything like a "dark side." But people could surprise you, as she well knew.

"It isn't good." Dallas pushed all his food aside, conjuring a weak smile. "And now that I've sufficiently distracted you from your grief with all this talk of civil war and alcoholic despair, it's probably time I started my long drive back to Pasadena-adjacent."

"Thank you for coming," Margo said as they walked to the door. "You were right: It actually was nice to have company, and to talk. Even about civil war and alcoholic despair."

"Next time we'll talk about rising sea levels and the resurgence of preventable diseases," he promised. "It'll be a blast."

"I can hardly wait." She opened the door, and for a moment they just stood there, a few feet apart, saying nothing.

"Will there be a next time, Margo?" he asked quietly, his face silvered by moonlight. "I meant what I said at the memorial, about wanting to be here for you as a friend, but . . . I'm starting to think I was full of shit. Because the way I'm hoping there's going to be a next time isn't . . . friendly." His fingers tugged at one of his sleeves. "And maybe that's not fair. If you're planning to leave . . ."

"I don't know what I'm planning. I don't know what I want." Margo's voice caught. Why did everything have to be so hard? "Or maybe I know exactly what I want, but I don't know if it's something I can hold on to."

"I get it." He nodded slowly. "It sucks—everything sucks—but I get it."

He moved to offer a hug, just as she leaned in to kiss his cheek; reading each other, they switched, and he planted an awkward kiss on the side of her forehead while she clumsily wrapped her arms around him. A beat passed and they began to laugh.

"Our timing is for shit," he remarked.

"Drive safe, okay?"

Margo watched him jog across the forecourt, sort of wishing she'd thrown caution to the wind. She didn't want to take a big step with Dallas that would forever be linked to the turmoil of her father's death, but she hated thinking they might never take that step at all.

His taillights flared, and his battered SUV vanished down the drive; and then she became aware of an electronic jingle echoing through the empty mansion—her burner phone, plugged carelessly into an outlet in the living room, now that she no longer had to hide it from her father.

The text message was short, a set of coordinates and single word: *NOW.*

It was Vojak.

26

IN THE YEAR THAT THEY'D BEEN DOING BUSINESS,
Vojak had only ever summoned Margo once—and this text made
the second time in as many weeks. He'd already paid her for the
paintings, and she could think of no outstanding items from previous jobs he was still trying to move. Not sure what she was heading
into, she donned dark jeans she could maneuver in, her leather
jacket, and a pair of boots.

The coordinates he'd sent led to an address on Mulholland
Drive, and Margo had plenty of time to consider what lay ahead as
she steered up into the hills. It could be another warning—one
more dire than the last, which he felt needed to be delivered in
person; or, optimistically, a surprise reveal that the dogs had been
called off, for some reason, and Margo was safe from danger.

Or it could be a trap.

Turning onto Mulholland, one hand on the steering wheel,
Margo reached down to her hip where she'd tucked her retractable
baton before leaving the house. Hope for the best, prepare for the
worst.

The location Vojak had selected was yet another property under
development—a swath of cleared land, where a home had been

razed so another could take its place. She left her car beside an exposed network of water pipes and crossed a patch of dusty earth to where the man stood, inches from the precipitous verge. Eucalyptuses towered, shaking in the breeze, and the vast, glittering bowl of the city shimmered below through a curtain of lingering heat. His face swallowed by shadow beneath the brim of his hat, the fence hailed her. "Thanks for coming on such short notice."

"To be honest, 'now' didn't exactly read like an invitation open to rain checks." Margo scanned the narrow footprint of empty land, searching for anything that didn't belong, "Do you have a boner for build sites, or is there another reason we're not meeting at your office?"

"Neighbors. A travel agency with people coming and going at all hours would demand attention sooner or later." Vojak leaned on his cane, eyes on the igneous glow of Los Angeles. There was something odd about his energy, Margo realized when she got close, and she threw another glance around. The man shifted. "How have you been hold—"

"Pass," Margo interrupted. "Next question."

"Fair enough. I won't waste your time." Vojak faced her, the silver wolf's head of his cane baring its teeth. "I have a job for you."

The words settled, and Margo shook her head. "Sorry, Vojak, but I'm not sure I'm good for that right now, you know?"

"Would numbers change your mind?" Stepping closer, his cane stabbing the dirt at her feet, the man's eyes gleamed. "Because this guy is offering five million dollars, Margo."

She went still. "Okay, I'm listening." Five million would be a life-changing number for all of them; they could toss Petrenko's jewels into the ocean, for that price. "Just to be safe, your client isn't a thirteenth duke, right? We talked about that."

"No more nobles, I promise." Vojak grinned, his teeth sharp

and white under the moon. "This is your run-of-the-mill international businessman with a fetish for high-end automobiles."

Margo frowned. "Cars?"

"Predictable, right?" The fence spread his arms in a shrug. "Young, rich, likes shiny things that go zoom."

"The shinier and zoomier the better, yeah, I know the type." She'd dated plenty of them. "Look, it's a great offer, but my team . . . we're not exactly car thieves."

"But you've boosted wheels before, right? For getaways?" Vojak parried confidently, and the back of Margo's neck prickled. Reading her expression, he laughed. "Don't get paranoid. I read the police blotter, and when the Museum of Fine Art is hit, a vagrant pulled over in a stolen van with French government gear inside, and an Escalade snatched from the same block on the same night, I connect the dots." He tilted his head. "GTA might not be your specialty, but you're capable."

"We're capable," she confirmed. It was hard to see anything around a number as big as five million, which could solve a lot of problems for a long time, but something about the situation was off. "I'm not sure why you're coming to me, though. There must be other talent, auto specialists, who'd be a better fit."

"You're selling yourself short. You've pulled off every job you've taken; you've got a reputation for tech, speed, and precision; and your team has five members now, right?"

A gust of wind swept through the clearing, rustling the giant red flag that had just gone up in Margo's mind. This was another detail she hadn't told him. They'd only pulled two jobs with five people—LAMFA and Petrenko; for reasons, the jewel theft had gone unreported, and although the art heist had made international headlines, the guards had only identified three perpetrators. Schooling her features, Margo countered, "Why?"

"The target is an actor—a name you'd recognize—up in

Trousdale Estates," Vojak went on, missing her discomfort. "Guy owns a fleet of rare sports cars in excellent condition, five of which the client wants in particular; but from what I'm told, this actor has above-average security measures on account of a stalker problem. So. You infiltrate, boost the cars, and Fast and Furious your way out! You could do this job in your sleep."

"I haven't slept since my father died," Margo answered immediately. "Look, I appreciate the offer, but I don't think it's right for us, and I'm not sure I'm up to it."

She stepped back, as if pulled by her car, and cast another nervous look around the build site. Branches swayed, cars zooming by on Mulholland behind a screen of shrubs; if someone was watching, they were well-hidden. Vojak's eyebrows came together, and he repeated, incredulously, "It's five million dollars. I know *you* don't need the money, but you've been stealing for a reason. Take it to your team; see what they say."

"I speak for my team." Suddenly, she couldn't wait to be out of there. Everything about this set-up felt staged. "Thanks for thinking of me first, though, and good luck."

She slammed the car door on his response, firing the engine and quelling the urge to peel out of the lot with the pedal to the floor. Her jaw clenched tight, Margo kept her eyes on the rearview all the way down Sepulveda to Westwood, certain she was being followed.

THE FARTHER SHE GOT FROM MULHOLLAND, HOWEVER, THE more Margo started to doubt herself. Vojak had been acting oddly, but maybe he was intoxicated by the price tag. And past police reports had made note of the distinctive white, red, blue, and purple wigs Margo and the boys wore—and Joaquin, in his acid-green shag, had been seen by a guard at LAMFA. So maybe Vojak heard about a fifth color and assumed a fifth member.

Maybe.

Her phone pierced the silence with a ring, shrill tones blaring from the car's speakers, and Margo nearly yelped. "H-hello?"

At first there was nothing but dead air, quiet stretched to the breaking point; then, just as she was about to disconnect: "Margo?"

It was a man's voice, the consonants soft and dull, and she glanced at the display. *"Uncle Win?"*

"Margo." His voice was choked with misery. "Sweet little Margo . . ."

"I'm here, Uncle Win. What's going on?" *What the hell was going on?* "Are you okay? You sound—"

"I need to see you." The words came out as one, rushed with an air of relief. "There's something . . . I need to tell you something. It's important."

"All right," she said reluctantly. He was clearly drunk, and she wasn't sure she was the best person to handle him in this condition. "What's on your mind?"

"No, no, no!" The man's irritable growl was distorted by the car's wireless sound system. "Not over the phone. I can't tell you this over the phone! You have to come here."

"Now? Tonight?" Margo gritted her teeth. She was already on Wilshire, past the 405 and headed for the coast, and the attorney lived in the Hollywood Hills near Runyon Canyon. Even with no traffic at all, the drive would take over a half hour. "It's after eleven, Uncle Win! I won't get home until the middle of the night, and I haven't been sleeping—"

"I haven't been sleeping, either, Margo," he slurred morosely. "I haven't been sleeping at all, and that's why I've got to see you. That's why it's got to be tonight. It's about your father, and . . ."

Here he trailed off, mumbling something unintelligible. Margo slowed the car, hating that her curiosity was suddenly worth more to her than a good night's rest. Hating that any excuse to avoid returning to the vast, climate-controlled emptiness of the mansion was appealing—even in the form of her plastered pseudo-uncle.

"All right, you win." She sighed. "Win wins again. I'll be at your house as soon—"

"I'm not at home. I'm at the office."

"The office?" She squinted at the display as if he could see her. "What—"

"There's something I need to show you here. Please hurry." Then, in a small, sad voice, "Please come before I lose my nerve."

CLIVE WINCHESTER MARTIN KEPT AN OFFICE IN A NARROW, three-story building on Canon Drive in Beverly Hills. It took Margo fifteen minutes to get there, and another fifteen to find a parking space several blocks away. She made the hike back past the bars and restaurants that remained open, conversation carrying to the sidewalk. LA was a city where you were never alone—unless your father had died, and you lived in his massive house all by yourself.

Sandwiched between a hair salon and an art gallery, Win's building stood out, a deco structure with Zigzag Moderne flourishes. His office was on the top floor, in the back, and Margo was just reaching for the call box when she realized the door wasn't completely shut. That same prickling sensation swept up the back of her neck as she tugged it the rest of the way open and let herself into a silent vestibule with tessellated flooring, illuminated by lonely, jaundiced bulbs.

There was an elevator, but she chose the stairs, some paranoid instinct whispering in her ear, telling her to be as quiet as possible. There was no reason for it, but a sense of uneasiness, of something being *off*, was caught on her skin like cellophane. When she stepped onto the third floor, a tiled hallway stretched out, light glowing through the pebbled glass of a door at the far end: Win's. It was so quiet that even her softest step clicked like a castanet as she made her way along the corridor, and a bead of nervous sweat rolled down her sternum.

The door opened onto a spare front area—a desk with a phone and computer, filing cabinets, a modest seating arrangement—and past it, through an open doorway, was Win's office. She could see potted plants and dark windows, the glow of a lamp . . . he hadn't reacted to the subtle *click* of the latch, or the hinges' faint squeak, though. Maybe he was passed out.

On the balls of her feet, Margo slipped inside, pulse jumping, that same voice telling her not to announce herself by calling out. She edged to the side, peering through the office door, a wide, mahogany desk piled with books and papers coming into view. And then she gasped, her heart catching fast in her throat.

Win, seated in a high-backed chair, was slumped over the desk; and even from across the room, Margo could see blood pooling on the blotter beneath him.

"*Uncle Win!*" She rushed forward, into an office full of crowded bookshelves and mismatched chairs, the close air thick with the nauseating reek of copper. Reaching his side, feeling for a pulse, her knees almost gave out when she found he was still warm. "Uncle Win? Uncle Win, are you—please talk to me!"

Heaving him upright, his body too heavy and too light at once, a distressed sob erupted from her throat when she saw the blood that drenched his white dress shirt—pouring from a wound just above his heart. "Uncle Win . . ."

His skin was gray, the muscles in his face slack, but his lips moved. "Margo . . ."

"I'm here! I'm here, Uncle Win. Just hang in there, okay? We're going to get you help!"

"Margo . . ." His eyes fluttered open, unfocused. He peered at her, past her. "Margo, please . . ."

"Don't talk. Just save your energy." Her hands shook as she fumbled with the phone on his desk, the console huge and covered with confusing buttons. "What . . . how the fuck do I use this?"

"No, Margo, he . . ." Win was still trying to talk, his breath rattling, his eyes wider, imploring. "He . . . he . . ."

"Uncle Win, tell it to the police," she whimpered, a tear slipping down her cheek, time moving too quickly. "Just . . . how do I use this? How do I get a line out?"

"*He . . . he . . .*"

"He *what*, Uncle Win?" She finally exploded, another sob bursting out. "*What?*"

His hand rose, trembling, a finger extended—pointing just over her shoulder. "*He's still here.*"

27

MARGO WHIRLED AROUND JUST IN TIME TO SEE
the closet door—half-hidden behind travel posters and a potted ficus—burst open, and a man lunge out of it. Dressed all in black, his face hidden by a ski mask, a long, deadly knife glinted in his gloved hand. He ran at her from across the room, thrusting with the blade, and she just barely got her retractable baton free in time to parry the blow.

She retreated a few crooked steps as the man spun around, slashing the knife at her face in a vicious backhand; blocking with the baton a second time, she moved in, hammering his nose with a palm strike and delivering a front kick to his breastbone with everything she had.

The man hurtled backward, crashing into an antique lectern bearing up a massive legal tome, and blinked at her through the mask. Then he charged again.

Margo's blood rose, adrenaline pricking her fingertips as she fell into a ready stance. The man feinted and then attacked. Dodging a round kick and then a spin kick, she blocked another thrust with the knife. He tried to hook her ankle and she deflected, and then he tried to hook her knee. She blocked again and lunged, swiping with the baton—once, twice, the man ducking back clumsily; but with the third blow, he caught her by surprise. Seizing her wrist, he braced her arm and spun, hurling her into Win's desk.

She crashed across a pile of paperwork, an inch from the man's spreading blood, and lost her grip on the baton. The masked man rammed an elbow into her face as she was straightening up, and white lights strobed behind her eyes as she staggered away, pain radiating from the bridge of her nose.

He spun again, a booted foot flying at her temple, and Margo lurched even farther backward—nearly tripping over a wooden stool and colliding with a bookcase—the kick missing her by inches. The man danced on the balls of his feet, passing the knife between his hands, and then pounced.

Tucking her foot beneath the stool, Margo kicked it up and snatched it from the air, meeting the knife when it plunged. Darting sideways, she blocked a thrust and a slash, metal thunking against wood. He spun—again—putting force behind a backhanded swipe with the weapon, and this time the blade sank partway into her makeshift shield. Seeing her opening at last, she slammed a foot into his gut, wrenching the stool and disarming him.

The knife clattered to the floor as the man reeled away, legs unsteady—and Margo went on the offensive. Tossing the stool aside, she advanced with a series of kicks and punches, driving him across the room until he stumbled into a locked display case full of Win's prized first editions. With everything she had left, Margo spun backward and slammed her foot into the man's jaw, driving his skull through the thick glass behind him. The pane exploded with a terrific smash, and the man dropped to the ground, out cold.

Chest heaving, Margo fell to her knees, fighting air into her lungs. It took her a moment to regroup, sweat dripping off her chin, and then she peeled up the man's ski mask with trembling fingers. His jaw was red and swollen, his nose bloodied, but he was no one she knew. Dark brows, pale skin, stubble—twenties or early thirties, but who was he to Clive Winchester Martin?

His black sweater had ridden up, revealing a thick rectangle of folded pages pinned by his waistband, puckered by heat, sweat, and combat. She was just reaching for them when she heard a distant door banging open, and then the clamor of footsteps in the hall—multiple sets.

On autopilot, obeying her instincts, Margo darted across the office, retrieving her baton. No matter who was on the way, police or more assassins, she didn't want to deal with them; but there were only two ways out of the office—the door to the hallway, or . . .

A damp breeze rushed in when Margo shoved open the window behind the desk, looking down into the service alley along the backside of the building. Three floors up, it was like the LAMFA job all over again, except without the safety of a zip line. There were no fire escapes or footholds—just a sheer drop, with a landing choice of either hard pavement or an open dumpster that could contain anything from down pillows to broken computer parts.

And then the door crashed open, men trampling inside, and Margo's decision was made for her. Rolling forward off the windowsill, her stomach lifted and her head swam when nothing reached up to greet her. There was a shout from behind, air whistling past her ears as she twisted her body and prayed she wasn't about to land on a pile of glass and metal and diseased rats.

The dumpster expelled a great *whumpf* when she crashed down, bags of cardboard, paper, and rotting food compressing beneath her weight. Her hip bounced off something hard, and a sharp object stabbed painfully into her shoulder, but she was already kicking free, already dragging herself out of the foul-smelling bin when the first of her pursuers reached the open window.

There was another shout as she tumbled to the pavement, and then a sharp *thwack* just before something smashed into the asphalt beside her; Margo's eyes widened at the sight of fragmented plastic, spreading liquid, and a feathered plume—and then she was on her feet, streaking for the mouth of the alley. Her hip ached and her chest burned, but a second later she was on the sidewalk, racing full tilt for her car.

Her composure slipped as she ran, Win's death sinking its claws back into her consciousness. A sob pulled air from her lungs and she fought it down, stumbling around a corner onto Dayton and limping for her BMW. In her mind, she kept seeing the red plume on the pavement, the shattered plastic . . . it was a tranquilizer dart. *But why?*

Twenty paces from her car, she froze, something wrong in the air; and then a man—loosely speaking—stepped in front of her from behind a parked SUV. He had to be at least six foot seven, taller than Davon in heels, with a face like the front end of a battleship. Rangy and knotted with muscle, his eyes the frigid blue of glacial ice, he exposed a mouth of sharp, broken teeth when he spoke. "Miss Manning?"

She had the retractable baton free in a second, but her hand shook, her energy at a perilous low. Using all her willpower to keep her voice steady, Margo snarled, "Step the fuck back, Lurch. I may look short to you, but that just means I'm closer to busting your kneecaps."

"It wouldn't be smart of you to try." He said it tonelessly, matter-of-fact, and a shiver ran up Margo's spine when he showed her the handgun he gripped in one massive paw.

"I've faced worse odds." He was tall, sure, but that didn't mean he could run. All she had to do was zigzag a bit and beat him to that twenty-four-hour café she'd passed. "Besides," she added casually, because it couldn't hurt to try, "your fly is open."

He looked down at his crotch and Margo spun on her heel, ready to sprint—and crashed directly into a second man she hadn't even heard approach. This one's eyes were dull and bored, and he was saying something, but she couldn't understand him. Her ears were filled with static as the metal teeth of a stun gun bit into her neck.

Her nerve endings screamed, her eyes rolled, and the night faded to black.

28

SHE HAD A DREAM THAT SHE WAS OPHELIA,
recently harvested from the brook, with flowers braided through her
hair. A cart pulled her through town, her body resting on fine cushions, people watching as she struggled to wake. When the wagon
stopped, she was lifted from her casket, and a group of veiled men
gently lowered her back into the water. This time she sank, light fading as she touched the silt, content that at least it was all over.

But somehow it wasn't over. There was a sound—the quiet
rumble of air through a vent—and a glimmer of pain snaked along
her spine and into her limbs. With regret, Margo realized she was
awake.

It took several tries to force her eyes open, and a room swam
into partial focus around her. With colossal effort she rolled onto
her side. Her surroundings were austere and angular, and a wall of
French windows offered her a view of a pool filled with black water.
Beyond it, past the spiky heads of pine and scrub, the city flickered,
a rolling pile of lights. A clock on the wall told her it was one in
the morning—but where was she?

With tremendous effort, Margo heaved her feet to the floor and
stood. The room pitched like the deck of a ship as she crossed to

the glass doors, and she braced herself against the panes. From the way Los Angeles spread below the terrace, and from the grand homes climbing the opposing ridge, she knew she was somewhere in the hills—and for just a moment, she let herself believe she was at Win's house. But it didn't last; she'd been to Win's house, and it looked nothing like this. The view was all wrong.

And Win was surely dead by now.

A groggy but methodical search of the room revealed a door, an en suite bathroom, and a walk-in closet, but nothing resembling a weapon. The French windows, though locked, would be easy enough to shatter; when she recouped some of her strength, the nightstand would do the job nicely. But then . . . what? Roll down the hillside, screaming for help? Fall into a stranger's backyard and pray she didn't break her neck or get shot?

She crossed to the door, wondering who had put her here—wondering what they wanted. Just for shits and giggles, she tried the knob, and was shocked to find she wasn't locked in. Stepping cautiously into a dark and empty hallway, she followed haunting strains of classical music to a staircase and the lights of an upper floor.

At the top of the steps, she passed slowly and quietly through a modern kitchen—empty; a dining room crowded with African art—also empty; and a vast living room where two wingback chairs faced a crackling fire in a stone hearth. Margo did a double take when she realized that, seated in one of the two chairs, was Reginald Castor.

For a long moment she just stared, thinking she might be hallucinating, but then he looked up and noticed her. Inclining his head, he gestured to the other chair. "Margo, you're awake. Please have a seat."

"Where's my baton?"

The man started in his chair. "*That's* your first question?"

"I don't like when people take my things without asking." She folded her arms.

"It will be returned to you, I promise," the man said. "You were quite agitated when you encountered James by your car, and it seemed . . . wise to disarm you until we could talk."

"I don't need a weapon to do damage, Mr. Castor," Margo answered serenely. "They're just more fun."

"No doubt." He almost smiled. "James carries his gun because it intimidates people, but he, too, prefers to work without it. Isn't that so, James?"

"Yes," came a soft voice from directly behind her, and Margo nearly jumped out of her skin. Whirling, she found herself face-to-face with the broken-toothed giant from earlier in the night. He was watching her like he hoped she'd try something. "That's so."

"Please," Castor repeated, "have a seat."

This time Margo took him up on the offer. Not just because of James, but because her head was still spinning. "What did you give me?"

"A mild sedative. Nothing harmful." A tray sat between them, bearing two glasses and a bottle of tawny liquid. He poured some for himself and took a sip. "I wanted to make sure that you didn't wake up in the car and do something foolish that might put lives at risk. It's very important that you and I have this conversation."

Margo was silent for a moment, and when Castor made to speak again, she held up a hand to silence him. "Hold on. I know a million ways I could tell you to go fuck yourself, and I'm trying to pick my favorite."

"Margo." He set his drink down. "I realize you're upset, but some very bad things are happening, and I—"

"'Very bad things'?" She cut him off with a mirthless bark of laughter. "That's one way of putting it. Those were your men up in—" Her voice caught, embarrassingly. "Up in Win's office?"

"No." His eyes never left hers. "They weren't."

"I don't . . ." Margo stared. "They were shooting tranq darts, and then you zapped me and drugged me. You want me to think that's a coincidence?"

"There were three visits to Winchester's office tonight." Castor produced a small notepad from a pocket in his blazer and began to read aloud from it. "At eleven thirty-four, a man dressed in black, approximately six feet, one-hundred-sixty pounds, bypassed the lock on the front door of Winchester's building and let himself inside. At eleven thirty-six, before my men could decide if they should involve the authorities, a blond girl—identified by sight as Margo Manning—entered the building through the same entrance."

Her stomach turned. She had been two minutes behind the man who'd killed Win, and countless what-if scenarios swarmed her thoughts, stinging like killer bees.

"At eleven forty-one," Castor went on, oblivious, "five white males, varying in height and weight, heavily tattooed, armed with dart guns and zip ties, entered the building as well." Peering at her over the top of his notepad, he added, "They were heard speaking to one another in a foreign tongue. My men said it sounded like Russian."

"Russian," Margo repeated, and all her blood slowly turned to ice.

"Does that mean something to you?"

Shaking her head, Margo nonetheless saw the dots connect before her eyes. After having his goons shake down LA's high-end fences with no results, Petrenko probably resorted to subterfuge. Someone shopped around, posing as a customer and offering money no one would be able to turn down for a job tailored to fit the team that had infiltrated the castle. Vojak wouldn't even have had to be complicit, just too smitten with the payoff to see that he was being played.

They *had* been under surveillance at the Mulholland site; and she had been followed—all the way to Beverly Hills, where she left her car and gave Petrenko's goon squad an opportunity.

And tranquilizers and zip ties meant they'd intended to take her alive.

"About two minutes after these gentlemen entered the building, you exited via the third-story windows," Castor concluded, flapping his notebook shut. "I had two men staking out your car almost from the moment you were first spotted."

"Why?" she asked, her throat dry as dust. "How do you know all this? Why were your men there at all?"

Castor steepled his fingers with a moody frown. "I've been expecting something terrible to take place for some time, Margo. I've had men outside Winchester's office every night for the past week."

"They did a hell of a lot of good," she retorted bitterly. "He's dead. While your men took notes on body weight and Slavic accents, someone was putting a knife in Win's chest."

"I'm very sorry to hear that." The man sounded sincere. "I'm sorry my fears were well founded, and I'm sorry my precautions amounted to nothing. I'm also sorry you had to be there when it happened."

"What is this about? Who would want to kill Win?"

Castor was silent for a moment, swirling his drink. "Are you aware of what's been happening at Manning these past few weeks?"

"Vaguely," Margo dodged. "I've heard things."

"Yesterday Addison Brand held an emergency board meeting, where he unveiled a prototype that he says represents the company's future." He poured booze into the second glass and nudged it toward her. "His brainchild turned out to be a tactical assault weapon—a high-capacity rifle with a carbon-fiber body. Extremely lightweight, easy to carry, easy to handle."

She blinked. "Manning doesn't do offensive technology."

"It does now," Castor returned, "under Addison Brand."

"Okay." She shook her head, palms to the sky. "Dad would have hated it, but . . . it's officially Brand's company now, and—"

"What do you know about the nation of Malawi?" He asked next, out of nowhere.

"What?" Margo squinted at him. "Is this a trick question? Because—"

"It is not." His tone was so grave she fell silent. "I'm afraid this is very important. What you need to know, what is relevant, is that Malawi is one of few nations with exploitable deposits of certain rare earth minerals—yttrium, thulium, lutetium—that Manning utilizes in its manufacture of microtechnology."

"And right now, they're at war," Margo added, proud of herself for knowing a basic fact pertinent to the conversation. Whatever this conversation was about.

"For eight months, after a military junta led by General Bomani Tembo attempted to seize power. The government forces, backing President Joseph Mabedi, prevented the coup but failed to defeat the rebellion. Tembo and his faction fled the capital and have been growing their numbers and support ever since.

"What instigated the rebellion was an attempt by Mabedi to nationalize the country's resources, which include a vast and very profitable chain of mines that produce—among other things—yttrium, thulium, and lutetium." Castor leaned forward, his brown eyes reflecting the golden flames of the fire. "Manning has had a longstanding relationship with the owners of the mines, an international consortium with similar sites in other countries, and have long been given favorable deals. Nationalization would change all that, and Mabedi planned to renegotiate all contracts with foreign entities, raising costs."

"So, a raw deal for Team Us?"

"You might say. The plan to nationalize is stalled for now, but your father had been in the process of seeking out other sources for these materials, looking for new mines to partner with, just in case. But it isn't easy. The term 'rare' is a bit of a misnomer, as the elements themselves are not especially uncommon; it's just that they don't occur in concentrations large enough for any one mine to be dependable. Except in a handful of cases." Castor held her gaze. "But Addison Brand did not want to give up. He believes the rebels can win, and if they do, the mine will remain privately held."

Margo fidgeted. "I still don't see what this has to do with Win's death."

The man nudged the crystal tumbler even closer. "You're going to want this. Trust me. You've heard about the reports of child soldiers in Malawi?"

Dallas's awkward attempt at breaking the ice came back to her. "Yes. It's horrible."

"Horrible," Castor echoed. "Worse than you can imagine. Children are abducted from their homes, held against their will, force-fed drugs until they are dependent, and then—high and addicted—sent out to kill. Often they are forced to kill their own families first." Margo stared at him, appalled, and he gave a slow nod. "Yes. It's that bad. And it is child soldiers that are currently, and quickly, beefing up the rebels' ranks."

"And Brand *knows* this?" Margo sat up. "He knows this Tembo guy is sending children out to kill and die, and he still wants to work with him?"

This time, Castor physically lifted the second tumbler off the tray and pushed it into Margo's hands. "Miss Manning . . . Addison has gone well beyond passive support. He has gone to the length of designing and building an assault rifle that is high-capacity and extremely lightweight—easy for small arms to carry, easy for small fingers to handle."

The glass trembled in Margo's grip. "You can't be serious."

"Addison has a secret and private server, which I was . . . temporarily able to access, and a number of my darkest suspicions were verified when I did so. The design and manufacture of the weapons were paid for through his discretionary funds, all hidden under—"

"Project Pluto." She whispered the words, and Castor nodded with a strange expression.

"It would be highly illegal for an American company to openly arm a foreign revolution, of course, but there are ways." He stared into the fire again. "I uncovered an encrypted communiqué on Brand's server, confirming a preliminary sale of one thousand rifles to a third party—a man notorious for his lack of scruples, who also happens to be a partner in the Malawi mining consortium."

More dots connected, and Margo went slack with disbelief, even as the name came out of her mouth. "Arkady Petrenko."

Castor inclined his head. "A very good guess. Petrenko is a partial owner of the mine. He's also part owner of two different private security firms, and it would not appear the least bit unusual—on paper anyway—for him to buy weaponry. And as far as smuggling arms into the country—"

"General Tembo's forces currently control Lilongwe's airport," Margo concluded hoarsely, and took a healthy gulp from her tumbler. *What had she stumbled into?* "I don't understand this. A thousand guns didn't materialize overnight, and my dad would never have approved this deal. I know he wouldn't. Are you telling me that Brand spent the past few months just . . . waiting for my father to die so he could arm a bunch of child soldiers and hold on to a favorable import/export contract?"

Castor shifted in his chair, the fire crackling, and finally struggled for words. "Margo, I don't know how to tell you this, but I uncovered a second communiqué—also encrypted—transmitted on the subnet to an off-shore location. It was nearly eight months old, and the recipient's identity was disguised, but it made reference to the development of a . . . a genetically targeted toxin."

"What does that mean?"

"Essentially, it means a synthetic poison, so sophisticated that it only affects individuals with specific genetic markers. It means you can put a lethal dose of it in a punch bowl at a party, knowing it will only kill one person in the room."

"What . . ." Her voice failed her, a knot in her throat. "What are you saying?"

"I believe there's a reason your father's illness was impossible to diagnose," he replied bluntly. "I'm saying that Addison Brand is an investor in Arkady Petrenko's mining consortium. I'm saying that shortly after Malawi's civil war began and your father declined to support the rebels, he fell ill while Project Pluto materialized on Addison's internal memoranda."

The room twirled, and Margo felt bile crawling up her throat. Lights flashed and she bent over, head between her knees, thinking of all the times Brand had been out to the house in the past months—of her father's strange, roller coaster ride with his illness, the hip flask in Brand's jacket, and Harland's brief recovery when he stopped drinking.

She remembered the night her father was rushed to the hospital—the night Addison Brand emptied his flask into a glass and handed it to her to finish off. Had it really been poisoned? Had he been certain it wouldn't affect her? *Had he cared?*

"Please forgive me for the way you had to find this out," Castor was saying, his voice low and soothing. "I know you must be quite shocked—"

"It can't be real," Margo gasped, her hands tingling. "It doesn't even make sense." Peering up at Castor, she shook her head. "He paid for a . . . a *genetic poison* and killed my father, built an arsenal of advanced firearms, all just to hold on to a mining contract?"

"To hold on to a fortune," the man corrected, "and to make more money than you can possibly imagine. As I said, he's heavily invested in Petrenko's mine—by far more, I've learned, than he's let on to anyone in the company—and if President Mabedi succeeds, Addison could be financially ruined. If the rebels prevail? He stays rich. His guns will bring lucrative arms contracts, and a toxin tailored to genetic specifications is . . . well, the ramifications are nearly unfathomable." For the first time, his brown skin looked gray. "How much do you suppose terrorists would pay, or genocidal regimes, for a poison that could take out an entire group of people with a shared genetic marker?"

Margo just stared. "Would he do that?"

"For money? I believe Addison Brand would do just about anything."

"You have to go to the police!" She struggled to her feet, the floor unsteady beneath her. "You have to show them what you've found!"

"But, Margo, I haven't found anything," the man protested, infuriatingly. "A memo agreeing on the sale of guns to a private security contractor? An email that mentions a fantastical poison? All I have is speculation—grounded, but unprovable—and getting involved would paint a target on my back." He shifted in his chair. "Addison already wants me removed from the board. He can't do it alone, even with all his newfound power, but he's exploring ways to get it done."

"Why? And how do you know all this?"

"Before I joined the private sector, I worked in security and counterintelligence. I know how to spot a threat, and even if things have changed a bit since my cloak-and-dagger days, I still have a few tricks up my sleeve." A smile came and went like a wave. "But Addison's move against me was inevitable. And I'm afraid it concerns you, too."

Sitting back down, she immediately refilled her glass. "Now what?"

Castor took a moment before answering, his fingers tracing the rim of his glass. "I believe that at one point, perhaps a year ago, your father made the decision to leave his company to Addison. No one wanted it more, and Harland had a soft spot for the man. But about a month ago, something changed." He looked Margo in the eye. "Your father called me, asking if I would consider a custodianship of your inheritance in the event of his death."

Her eyebrows drew together. "But he put his financial manager in charge of—"

"Not the liquid assets. The stock. In Manning."

"But . . ." She ran out of breath. The implications were too big to consider, the very idea absurd. Wasn't it? "But . . . why . . . ?"

"I don't know if Addison did something to earn Harland's distrust, or if you did something to gain his respect; but the arrangement he described to me, and to which I agreed, was that I would hold the stock and act in your interest until your eighteenth birthday—at which point you would be free to appoint a new custodian, if you chose to do so. Upon completing your education or turning twenty-one, whichever came later, the stock would revert fully to your ownership."

The silence that stretched out was absolute and deafening. Margo reached for her voice, and found it was surprisingly small. "So why did he change his mind again?"

"Margo . . . I don't believe he did." Castor's expression was pitying. "You may not be aware of this, but Clive Winchester Martin had a dark side that Addison Brand would have found

269

quite easy to exploit. I was surprised at the reading of Harland's will; but upon witnessing Brand's reaction, and Winchester's guilt-ridden descent into the bottle, I became convinced of foul play."

More dots connecting, more air squeezed from her lungs. The room closed in as Margo remembered that day at the hospital—Win releasing Dallas from his witness duties, offering Brand a ringside seat at Harland's decision to take total control of Manning out of his hands, granting his teenage daughter a guiding influence on the company.

It would have been *her* company. As chief shareholder, she'd have essentially been in charge. She didn't even know if she wanted that, if she would ever want to walk so closely in her father's foot-steps; to go from a princess to a queen. But Addison had taken the chance, the choice—her *future*—away from her.

"That is why I've had my men outside Winchester's office," Castor continued grimly. "Only a handful of people could threaten Addison's ascendancy, and a drunken, unstable attorney with a guilty secret was the most immediate danger."

"So you believe the assassin was hired by Brand."

"I've no doubt. And as he must know the role Harland envi-sioned for me, and that I had been approached about it, I'm certain that I'm next on his list." He ran his finger around the rim of his glass again. "But there's another person who could stand in his way. Who could ruin everything he's worked for, just by contesting the will." His eyes flashed, lit gold by the fire. "As the rightful heir to the Manning empire, Addison will never be truly safe until he elim-inates you, Margo. For good."

29

IN A HAZE, STRUGGLING TO HANDLE ALL THE
razor-edged puzzle pieces Reginald Castor had dumped in her
hands, Margo allowed James to escort her into a waiting car. It idled
in the drive for several long minutes while she decided where she
wanted to go. The mansion, her cave and refuge for the past weeks,
was out of the question; the Russians had followed her, had likely
seen her face, and the chances that she'd been identified to
Petrenko were high.

Finally, she gave them the safest address she could think of. The
car pulled out, winding through the Hollywood Hills, while hideous thoughts stormed her brain. *Addison Brand had killed her
father*. In their final hours together, Harland told her that he saw
her potential, recognized her leadership skills; and he'd *meant it*.
Maybe he'd always intended for Brand to succeed him as CEO, but
he'd wanted Margo to be Manning's moral compass.

She recalled the papers tucked in the assassin's waistband, and
hated herself for not grabbing them before diving out the window.
Win's final words filled her ears: *There's something I need to show
you*. Had it been the real will? Could there be more copies out there?

She'd thought that the reading of Harland's final testament had been the end of their shared story; but maybe she was wrong. Maybe their last page had yet to be recovered.

And if she had to tear Addison Brand's still-beating heart from his chest with her bare hands in order to find it, she would.

Boyle Heights was uninviting after two in the morning, and Margo's driver gave her a skeptical look when they pulled up to the curb outside a grubby stucco-and-shingle duplex. "Are you sure you want me to leave you here?"

"I'll be fine," Margo lied. As if she'd ever be fine again.

Just before she got out, the man handed over her baton; then, with a doubtful "Good night," he sped away.

Starting up the walk, still dazed by regret and anger, she almost didn't notice the hollow-eyed figure stepping down from the porch of the front unit until he was right in her path. "Hey, Blondie. You lookin' for me?"

"What? Gross." Margo recoiled. He was greasy, with bad skin and worse tattoos, exuding a smell like spoiled milk. "I'm here to see Davon."

She stepped around him, but he moved—quick as a snake—grabbing her by the arm. "That's interesting, because he's been dodging me all week, and he owes me money."

Peeling his hand off, Margo gave him a withering look. "He owes *you* money."

"Yes, you jumped-up bitch, he owes me money!" The man's eyes glowed with a feverish light she should have recognized immediately, and he seized her wrist again. "I don't like getting fucked with, and I sure as hell don't like no sass-mouth bitch talking down to me!" Jabbing a finger at her, he snarled. "You tell him he better gimme my fucking money by tomorrow, or his ass is headed to the morgue!"

"I'm going to tell you three things instead," Margo replied neatly, snatching his outthrust finger from the air. "Number one: I've had a really shitty night, and I am not in the mood." She squeezed down on the digit until she saw the pain register in his eyes. "Number two: Never touch a woman without her consent." With a sharp twist and an ugly *pop*, she dislocated his knuckle joint. "And number three: You called me a bitch. Twice."

With that, she slammed her elbow into his face. He reeled back and she released his hand, watching as he tumbled to the dusty ground. Stepping over him, she steadied her breathing and headed for Davon's door.

A VIOLIN CONCERTO HAD BEEN PLAYING, BUT WHEN HE HEARD voices in the yard, Davon turned it off. Peck had been relentless lately, hassling him about money, making threats. The fucker had even tried to break into the apartment using a key he'd copied while Georgia was on one of her benders, and if Davon hadn't gotten the locks changed—for the sixth time—it could have been ugly.

The voices stopped abruptly, and a few seconds later there was a knock at the door. Setting his jaw, Davon crept across the room, lifting a slim but heavy length of pipe from a cluttered end table. Flexing his grip, he waited. The knock came again, and then, to his surprise, a girl's voice. "Davon? Georgia? Anybody home?"

Startled, he threw open the door. "Margo? Girl, what the hell are you doing here at this time of night?"

"I'm sorry," she said, and as she stepped into the apartment, Davon was surprised again to see tears in her eyes. "I should have called first, but I didn't . . . I couldn't . . ."

She choked on the words and fell silent, shaking her head, and when Davon pulled her into his arms, she began to sob. Shutting the door, he guided her to the couch, calling out, "Hey, Georgia? We got company."

"For fuck's sake, who's here at a time like this?" his drag mother called querulously from the other end of the short hallway. A moment later, Georgia emerged, out of drag but no less flamboyant in a teal kimono and silk slippers. "It's a good thing I'm presentable at all hours, because I—" She froze, taking in the sight of Margo's quaking frame. Then, swiftly, "This looks like a job for tea."

"Chamomile, or maybe peppermint," Davon suggested. He watched until she disappeared into the tiny kitchen, until he heard water splashing into a kettle. Georgia had been sober for three straight days—a record. Maybe a miracle.

He kept his arms around Margo, murmuring in her ear— soothing phrases from a childhood frighteningly far away—until her tears subsided and her halting breaths evened out. When she straightened up again, she blew her nose. "Thanks, Davon. And . . . sorry."

"Don't apologize. Everybody falls apart." He stroked her back.

"There's just so much . . . I don't even know where to start," Margo answered miserably. The saloon doors to the kitchen swung open then, and Georgia returned.

"I made chamomile," she said, placing a tea tray on the scarred coffee table. "It's supposed to be calming. I think that's New Age bullshit, but what the hell? It can't hurt."

"Thank you," Margo said, accepting a cup. At last, her eyes seemed to take in the room around her—and the suitcases piled by the door. "Are you guys going somewhere?"

"Georgia is." Davon couldn't keep the pride and satisfaction out of his voice. "Tomorrow afternoon, thanks to the French masters, she's checking in to the Cornerstone Wellness addiction treatment facility."

"Really?" Margo turned large eyes on Georgia, who managed a weak smile of confirmation. "That's amazing! Congratulations."

"Thanks, hon." Georgia toyed nervously with a tiny, silver teaspoon, her body language radiating fear. "I don't know how I'll manage. I haven't been sober longer than a week at a stretch in about ten years, but I have to start somehow. And I guess this is how."

"You're gonna do great, Mama," Davon said confidently, willing it into the universe. He could hardly believe this day had finally come; after all the blackouts, binges, and hospital visits, money getting used up faster than it came in, Georgia was going sober. Even if they could never cash in the Petrenko jewels, Davon was getting the only thing he'd really wanted since his parents died.

"You might consider an early start." Margo jerked a thumb at the front door. "That walking bag of centipedes I met in the yard says you owe him money, and if you don't have it by tomorrow morning . . . something something morgue."

Davon squeezed his eyes shut for a moment. "I should just pay him off. We have the money now, but I can't do it. I can't reward that asshole for what he did to Georgia."

"It shouldn't be you anyway," Georgia muttered, hanging her head. "It's my debt."

"Leave it, Mama; we talked about this." Davon was resolute. To Margo, he added, "Anyway, I'm sorry you had to meet Peck. The only good thing about that son of a bitch is that he's going to die someday."

"It wasn't so bad. Kicking his ass made me feel a little better anyway."

Georgia's head snapped up, and Davon went still. "You hit Peck?"

"I gave him a short lesson on how to treat a lady," Margo said primly. "With my fists. He might have ended up in the dirt."

Instantly, Davon jumped to his feet, tension circling the room.

"Mama, put your coat on. We're leaving early. Margo, I'd appreciate a hand with those bags."

"What's happening?" Margo stood as well, confused. "You seem . . . freaked out?"

"Peck doesn't react well to violence," Davon understated. Jerking open a drawer of the end table, he snatched something out and tossed it to Margo. "Here—put these on."

"*Brass knuckles?*" She grabbed the heavy rings out of the air, incredulous. "Are you serious? Come on, you can't actually be scared of that pocket-sized creep, right?"

"Please. Give me a little credit." Davon was insulted. "Peck's a cowardly piece of shit, but he's got friends—just as mean, and a whole lot bigger—and they respond a hell of a lot faster than the LAPD in this neck of the woods."

He snatched up the pipe from where he'd discarded it, just as Georgia hustled back into the room, wearing a floor-length leopard-print coat. After a moment of thought, Margo tossed the heavy bit of jewelry back to Davon. "You keep it." With a flourish, she produced a retractable baton, flicking it out to its full length. "I'm covered."

Davon arched a brow but didn't bother to ask. There'd be time later. God willing. Grabbing one of the suitcases, he said, "Then let's move."

They were as quiet as they could be, herding out of the apartment and dragging two suitcases over the rocky ground. Peck was nowhere to be seen, but his lights were on, and music that sounded like feedback poured from his open windows. The three of them were almost to the gate when a battered truck squealed around the corner, screeching to a halt at the curb. Four men climbed out of it, rolling meaty shoulders and swinging metal bats.

Instinctively, Davon and Margo dropped their suitcases and retreated two paces, putting their backs together in a defensive formation. Over his shoulder, the boy called, "Go back inside, Georgia. Lock the door."

"Not a damn chance," she fumed in response. "I've been doing drag since the Reagan years. You think I lived this long without knowing how to bash back? Gimme that fucking pipe!"

There was no time to argue, so Davon did as he was told, and kissed his brass knuckles for luck.

THE ALTERCATION WAS SHORT AND BRUTAL. PECK'S FRIENDS had greater numbers, bigger muscles, and better weapons—but no clue what they were up against. Even four-to-two it would have been no contest; but a sober Georgia, true to her word, was a force to be reckoned with. When all four of the bat-wielding men lay at their feet, the trio stood in the moonlight, their panting breaths competing with Peck's ugly music against the winter evening. Combing her sweat-dampened hair with bejeweled fingers, Georgia grunted, "Thanks. I needed that."

They were almost giddy as they picked up the suitcases and resumed their escape.

"HOLY *SHIT*, MARGO," DAVON SAID LATER, WHEN THEY WERE camped out in a threadbare Hollywood motel room, and she'd finally relayed everything she'd experienced. They'd found the nicest of the sleaziest places off the strip, and Georgia's snoring was so loud they could hear it through the adjoining door. "This Addison dude is a fucking Bond villain!"

"And there's nothing I can do about it," she concluded with a helpless shrug. "There's no hard evidence, and whatever was used on my dad—if anything such as a 'genetically targeted toxin' even exists—it's so sophisticated that the most advanced medical laboratories in the world couldn't detect it."

"Girl, with about a week's notice, you had a machine built that duplicated a man's fingerprint." Davon flopped backward onto the bed. "You think there aren't shady scientists out there, cooking up poisonous shit all day and figuring how to make it extra?"

"So you believe me." She sounded relieved.

"Of *course* I believe you!" Davon sat up again. "My question is what the fuck are we gonna do about it? You know we have to call out the cavalry, right? Let's invade this dude's home—go through his shit, steal the evidence!"

"I wish we could." Margo stared down at her hands, electric light cutting a line across the bedspread through a slit in the curtains. "But I don't know where Brand lives. We'd need to do research, recon . . . we'd need special tech made, and the way things are going at Manning, my connection probably isn't with the company anymore. I don't even know if evidence *exists*. If Win's—" She had trouble getting the word out. "If Win's killer really has the true will, who knows where it is now? I'm sure Brand planned to destroy it."

"Lawyers make copies," Davon interjected flatly. "It has to exist somewhere."

"Maybe. But Win's office is a crime scene now, and the police will probably search his house, too. Anything valuable will be impounded long before we can get to it."

"What about what's-his-name? That thirst trap who worked for Win?"

"He is not a *thirst trap*," Margo protested, her cheeks flushing. "And he can't help us anyway. Even if he knew the contents of the original will—even if he has a draft of the original document—it doesn't prove anything! We weren't in the room when the will was amended, and the copy Win read out was signed and dated. I'd need way more than hearsay to claim it was doctored."

"So, who *was* in the room?"

"Dad, Win, and Addison Brand," Margo answered with a frustrated snort. Then she gasped. *"The cute nurse!"*

"Who?"

"There was a nurse—a second witness!" Margo swung around to face him. "I never saw her myself, but there must be some way to track her down!"

"Okay."

"You sound skeptical."

Davon winced. "It's just . . . if her signature's on a bullshit document, then Brand probably got to her, too."

"Or maybe her signature was forged."

"Anything's possible at this point," he allowed. Then, sliding his eyes toward the gap in the curtains, to where Los Angeles crackled and glowed in the darkness, he said, "The thing we gotta figure out right now is how to keep you away from Petrenko."

"There aren't a lot of places I can go," she admitted. "I could be recognized at a hotel, I burned all my bridges at Somerville when Axel's dad got arrested, and I can't even go to the Moreaus because they live too close to the mansion! Plus, Valentina knows I'm tight with them. You and Georgia were my ace in the hole."

"Our place is definitely a hole." Davon rubbed his eyes. "After tonight, though, I'm not sure any of us can go back to Boyle Heights for a while. My big, stupid plan was to ask Axel if I could stay in one of the guest rooms at the villa—"

"By which you mean *his* room, hoping Jacinta doesn't notice," Margo put in smugly.

"I didn't ask for commentary." He wrinkled his nose at her. "But what do we do with you? You can stay in shitty motel rooms forever, but sooner or later, you'll have to go back home for something." Laughing, he added, "That'll be our next big job: breaking you into your own home for clean underwear."

He was still chuckling when Margo gripped his shoulders. "Davon! You are a fucking genius."

"I've been saying."

"I'm serious." Her energy filled the room, a bar of brassy light from the window making her eyes gleam. "I'm breaking into the mansion!"

30

THE NEXT MORNING, MARGO TOOK OUT AS
much cash as she could from an ATM. Giving a chunk to Davon,
she had him book the motel room for another week. With no lobby
or restaurant, and a staff trained to forget guests' faces, it was as good
a hideout as she was going to get. She could have food delivered,
and she wouldn't have to encounter another human being unless
she wanted to. Until she managed to get herself out of the mess she
was in.

After Davon and Georgia left for Cornerstone Wellness, Margo
made an important call. She was asked a series of sharp questions
at an increasing volume, all of which she chose to ignore, and eventually received a reluctant agreement to her proposal.

To pass some time, she fantasized about feeding Addison Brand
very slowly into an active volcano, or locking him in a trunk filled
with hangry spiders. After about an hour of this, a scuffed and
battered sedan pulled into the motel courtyard. Making sure the
coast was clear, Margo darted for the car and jumped in.

"Are you sure no one followed you?" she asked, scanning the
traffic behind them. The backseat was filled with an overflowing

laundry basket the size of a small Jacuzzi, several bags of groceries, and a crate of cleaning supplies with Cyrillic labels.

"Please." Her chauffeur was insulted. "I learn to drive in Soviet Union. You think I can't spot a tail?"

"Thanks, Irina," Margo said meaningfully.

The magenta-haired housekeeper scowled, but there was concern in her eyes. "What goes on? How come you're at cheap, catbag motel and not home? How come all this sneaking around?"

"It's a really long story, and it's better if I tell you about it when we get there."

"I don't like this." Irina's knuckles were white around the steering wheel. "You're acting scared, myshka."

"I *am* scared," Margo confessed, and there was little else to say after that.

They were quiet until they reached Malibu, where Margo directed Irina past the turn-off for the mansion and instead to the deserted build site where she'd met with Vojak after the funeral. They were there for fifteen minutes, and then the sedan coasted back to the main road, up the canyon, and finally to the Mannings' front gate, where they idled.

From where she lay hidden, Margo heard the housekeeper speaking, and then a man's reply. She'd been expecting this, but still it made her blood run cold. There were people watching her house, stopping those who tried to enter; were they armed? How dangerous a mission had she asked Irina to undertake? And if the guy forced her into letting him search the vehicle . . . well, there were only so many places to hide a human in a four-door sedan, and she was in no position to attack if he found her.

The words passing back and forth were in Russian and escalated very quickly from an exchange to an enthusiastic argument—the kind that only Irina could instigate—and then the man issued what was unmistakably a command. Seconds passed, and then came a *pop* as the lid of the trunk released. Margo scrunched her eyes shut and held her breath.

The trunk was jerked open wide, and then a short silence passed. Muttering to himself, the man tossed aside books and magazines, tools and old rags, rummaging through years of accumulated detritus. Finally, grumbling loudly, he slammed the trunk shut again, barked something at Irina, and then his feet scraped against the road as he retreated.

Margo didn't breathe again until the car surged forward, until the gate had slid open and shut, and the sedan was parked in the courtyard—well out of sight from the road. Before she could move, Irina was already shouting. "That no-good punk pointed gun at me! A *gun*! At *me*!"

"I'm sorry," Margo said hastily, rising from the pile of dirty clothes in the woman's laundry basket. As hiding places went, it was better than what Joaquin endured at LAMFA, but she'd had to try very hard not to wonder just how much of what she was nestled in was used underwear. "You were amazing back there, though. You saved my ass."

Irina glared, but Margo could see satisfaction layered in her expression. "It felt good to shout again in Russian. Much more satisfying language for being angry. Now you tell me what goes on! Why am I almost killed trying to come to work?"

Margo exhaled, experiencing none of the rush she usually had when she'd just escaped a bad situation with her life. Telling this story was going to hurt. "Inside, okay?"

Standing in the kitchen, Margo revealed everything. It still sounded surreal, even in its simplest forms, and Irina was horrified. Three times the woman broke out in a litany of Russian curses, and by the end, they were both crying, holding each other. Margo wondered how many times the chasm of grief would yawn open inside her. How many times could she fall into it and survive?

"I served him food! Right here in this house!" Irina spat emphatically onto the floor. "May that mudak rot in hell!"

"He'll pay," Margo promised quietly. "You can count on it."

"And you!" Irina wheeled on her, eyes huge. "You make enemy out of *Arkady Petrenko*? Are you out of your mind? The man at the gate was part of bad-news crew—do you understand? All those tattoos mean something, myshka, and his meant *killer*. Even a man like that knows to fear Arkady Petrenko!"

"Yeah, well." The girl shifted uncomfortably. "I'm taking a crash course on fearing Arkady Petrenko now, and I'm a fast learner." It occurred to her that her housekeeper might actually be a source of information; her husband was a journalist during Petrenko's ruthless climb up Russia's post-Soviet capitalist ladder. "What can you tell me about him?"

"About Petrenko?" A shiver ran through her. "He is relentless. He has no conscience, no soul. If you took something from him, *give it back*. Give it back, and hope he gets bored trying for revenge!"

With those words hanging in the air, the woman turned to her work. It wasn't like Margo hadn't considered returning Petrenko's valuables, though. She'd held on to them in the hopes they could be sold, but now that she'd been identified, it was a different game; now those jewels represented the only possible bargaining chip she had.

The second-floor hallway was stuffy, the air thick and sour, and for the first time in weeks Margo realized how grim her life had become. Pushing into her bedroom, she encountered the depressing spectacle with fresh eyes—rumpled sheets, dishes on the floor, pajamas rank from days of continuous wear. She'd forbidden anyone, even Irina, from coming up here since Harland's death, not wanting to be disturbed in her sorrow; not able to face the prospect of anyone going through her father's things and carting away even the smallest fragment of his memory.

And now? Her lethargy and denial, her refusal to deal, might save her in the end.

Quickly and methodically, she packed a bag, putting together whatever she thought she might need for an indefinite time away. And then she got down on her knees, and reached under the bed, practically trembling with the fear of a faulty memory; terrified that she was reaching for something that wasn't there. But her fingers found an object—hard, smooth, and cool—and she pulled a cut-glass tumbler out into the light.

It was still glazed on the bottom with the remains of Brand's whiskey.

THE GROVE, AN OUTDOOR MALL ADJOINING LA'S FAMOUS Original Farmers Market at Third and Fairfax, was famous for a lot of reasons: There were chic stores and restaurants, an animated fountain, and even a trolley for tired shoppers. But what Margo loved most was the view from the top deck of the attached parking structure. From eight stories up and smack in the center of town, Los Angeles spread out in a remarkable panorama—from downtown to Westwood, and from the Valley's high passes to the glittering southward hills.

She arrived in a rented Mini Cooper. A car service had retrieved her BMW, digging it out from under a drift of parking tickets issued by the Beverly Hills police, but stowed it in a long-term garage. Driving it would be hazardous, now that Petrenko's people knew it on sight; and with them watching the mansion, she'd canceled all standing deliveries and hired—ironically enough—a private security firm to watch her front gate.

Sooner or later, Petrenko would tire of waiting for her to fall into his clutches, and he would send someone to raid the mansion.

He wouldn't find the jewels, presently under lock and key in a Pasadena bank vault, but it still felt like something she should discourage.

Parking the Mini, she hefted a carrier bag out of the back, and made her way through a grid of cars to the low wall facing north. It was midday, and even in winter, amber light fell like a veil on Los Angeles. The Hollywood sign gleamed from the hilltops, an airplane flashed in the sun as it turned toward LAX, and a woman a few feet away sighed wistfully.

"Sometimes I forget how beautiful it is here," she murmured, shielding her eyes from the glare. "Everything looks different from the ground. I guess it's a matter of perspective."

"Or maybe the farther you are from something, the fewer flaws you notice," Margo returned. Glancing over, she took in Dr. Khan's pensive expression. "I'm sorry I haven't been in touch since you came out to the mansion. How are—"

"I got fired." Nadiya gave a bitter laugh that scattered in the wind. "Addison didn't even wait for me to complete the project I was working on. I made that grand, idiotic speech, '*I won't go down without a fight*,' and then he showed me the door before I could land a single punch."

Margo smiled a little. "Well, it's time to lace up your gloves. I'm tagging you in."

"What do you mean?"

Reaching into her bag, Margo produced the tumbler. "Do you think you can analyze the contents of this glass?"

"Possibly." The woman took hold of it carefully. "I don't have a lab anymore, but I know places—and people who owe me favors. What is it? And what are you looking for?"

Margo explained, and Dr. Khan widened her eyes, examining the tumbler. Nervously, the girl asked, "Do you think you can detect it? We must have been to dozens of hospitals and clinics, and nothing ever turned up in Dad's blood samples."

"They were probably searching for the wrong things," Nadiya responded immediately. "Known drugs and toxins. If Manning is future tech, this is future biochemistry. There's no telling what it looks like on a molecular level, or how it metabolizes once it's in the body. I mean, a designer poison, engineered to such exact specifications that it only targets a single genetic profile . . . It's remarkable."

"You sound impressed."

"I am," the woman admitted with blunt candor. "It's unethical, probably illegal, and downright terrifying, but as a scientific achievement? It takes my breath away."

"It took Dad's, too." Margo was grim. "Can you do it?"

"We'll find out." Dr. Khan slipped the glass into her own bag. "This is going to sound morbid, but it would help if we had blood or tissue samples from your father, for comparison. It would help me understand the mechanics better."

"Dad was cremated." She thought for a moment. "He must have had gallons of blood drawn while we were trying to figure out what was wrong with him, though."

"Most medical facilities don't hold on to those samples indefinitely, but you might as well ask around. If he left any organs to science, he might have specified it in his will, but—"

"He didn't." Margo ran a hand through her hair. "I've read that thing so many times I could recite it in my sleep."

"Well." Dr. Khan sighed. "We do what we can with what we have. I'll take care of this as soon as I can make the arrangements, and I'll let you know what I discover."

"Thank you."

The woman laughed again, and it was not a sweet sound. "The

pleasure is all mine. Addison Brand deserves an ugly fate, and I'm happy to see him to it."

She turned and headed off across the parking deck, the sun gilding her back.

FOR THE NEXT THREE DAYS, MARGO SEARCHED FOR NINA McLeod, the nurse who'd witnessed the will. It wasn't easy; she'd quit her job at the hospital just days after Harland's death, and they had a policy against sharing contact information for former staff members—even to grieving daughters who "just wanted to say thanks."

The internet yielded a small crop of listings in the greater LA area for either Nina or N McLeod, and with what little information she had to go on, she still managed to narrow the list to three possibilities. Cranky and determined, Margo hopped in the Mini and set out to investigate.

Her first stop was a house in Sherman Oaks, where an online background-check site promised her she'd find "N McLeod," age seventy-two. That was a little older than Dallas's estimate, but not by too much. It was a tidy property, with an orange tree in the yard, and when she rang the bell, a garrulous man answered the door. His name was Nathan, he was a widower, and it took fifteen minutes to extricate herself from an ad hoc lecture about model boats.

Address number two was an apartment in Studio City, where "Nina J. McLeod" lived with about fifty-odd tropical birds. Just glancing over the woman's shoulder into the living room, Margo could see cages with brightly feathered creatures inside, and a macaw not quite the size of a pterodactyl perched on the back of a sofa. Nina J was a retired script supervisor, had never worked in a hospital, and did not appreciate being interrupted during her afternoon programming.

The last address was on the west side, near Sawtelle, and Margo drove with her fingers crossed. Pulling up outside of a modest bungalow, her heart sank when she saw the FOR RENT sign posted in the yard. Workmen came and went through an open front door, and when she addressed one of them, he surprised her by pointing her to a man in a tie—the property owner.

"Yeah, Nina was a nurse. I'm sorry you didn't track her down earlier . . . she and Jake lived here for something like twelve years. The area's rent-controlled, so I was losing a fortune on them, but they were good tenants. Left the place in great shape, considering." He gestured around, at the gutted kitchen and naked floors. "I could've left it with twelve years of wear and tear and still raised the rent five times over, but why not aim high?"

"Why not?" Margo murmured. *Aim high* was practically engraved on the Manning family crest, but she couldn't help noticing that she could have bought two Mini Coopers for less than what this man intended to charge for one rented year in his tiny bungalow.

"I thought they were pretty happy here," he went on, "but two weeks ago they told me they were leaving, just like that. And within forty-eight hours they were gone."

They hadn't left a forwarding address, he said, and he didn't know what moving service they'd used. Margo went door-to-door, talking to the neighbors, but even those who'd been friendly with the McLeods were mystified by the sudden disappearance—and no one remembered a logo on the side of the truck that departed with the couple's things.

Back in the car, Margo screamed obscenities that would have made Irina blush. It wasn't a dead end—not yet. She could start calling around to moving companies, concoct a ruse and see if she could find the one the McLeods had used and where they'd gone. If she had to, she'd hire a private detective. But she'd find Nina and shake the truth out of her.

* * *

BACK AT THE MOTEL, SHE ORDERED DELIVERY AND SPENT a few hours studying the judo throws known as the "sacrifice techniques"—so called because each one required falling with your opponent in order to use their weight and momentum against them. The yoko-wakare, the tomoe-nage, the sumi-gaeshi . . . Margo knew them by heart from years of practice; but under her current circumstances, each move served as a necessary reminder that it was possible to turn a vulnerability into a strength.

Her phone rang on the nightstand.

"Margo? It's Dr. Khan."

"Did you find something in the whiskey?"

"Yes and no. I identified several synthetic compounds—binders and reagents and a few errant proteins—and some alien organic material that's partially degraded."

"Alien?"

"Sorry—alien meaning 'unfamiliar.' Earthly, but not part of the scotch."

"Oh. But that means you found it, right?"

"I found *something*. The results are fascinating . . . I believe the proteins form the building blocks of the actual poison, catalyzed by a reagent and guided by organic matter to attack the specified target—"

"My father."

"Yes. But none of what I found is entirely conclusive."

"What the hell does that mean?"

"It means the drink was undeniably doctored—in a court of law, you could prove that Addison Brand put a foreign substance into this glass. And I believe I could demonstrate how the poison might have worked. But . . ."

"But?"

"It's all speculation. You *drank* most of this scotch, Margo, and you're fine. Until I can prove the genetic targeting—which I can't, without reconstructing the complete formula and consulting a dozen other experts—juries will see this as a fairy tale."

"Son of a bitch."

"I'm sorry. But don't give up hope. This is still progress—"

"He cannot get away with this. I can't *let* him get away with this!"

"He might have a supply somewhere, if he hasn't destroyed it yet. Maybe you can still get your hands on a complete sample."

"..."

"Margo?"

"I have to go."

31

THE FIERCE REPORT OF SPIKED HEELS AGAINST
polished marble echoed like gunshots in the Manning Tower
lobby the next afternoon. Dressed in a tweed pencil skirt and a
cream silk blouse, her hair in a neat bun and her lips the same red as
the soles of her designer shoes, Margo headed for the reception
desk. In every way possible she was dressed to kill, and struggled to
remember that she was supposed to be charming just now.

"Miss Manning!" Lloyd, the guard, blinked with surprise when
he recognized her. "You're a sight for sore eyes. To what do we owe
the pleasure of your company?"

"Hi, Lloyd." She let him give her an awkward hug. "Actually, I
was hoping to . . . well, a lot of people from the company came to
Dad's funeral, and I'm afraid I really wasn't myself. I wanted to stop
by and say a personal thank-you to a few folks; it would have meant
a lot to my father that so many people here paid their respects."

Something in the man's eyes melted. "Oh sure, of course. That's
a very high-class thing for you to do, Miss Manning. And if you
don't mind my saying so, it was quite a blow to us all when your
father passed."

"Thank you."

He stepped back to the desk, reaching for the phone. "What floor?"

"Oh, um . . ." Margo put some elbow grease into her sweet-and-doleful act. "I wanted to start on thirty-one, with HR, but . . . do you mind if it's a surprise? It would make it feel more meaningful somehow."

"I guess I can understand that." Lloyd hesitated with the phone in his hand, clearly unsure; but finally placed the receiver back into the cradle. "Well, what the hell, why not? About time everyone here had a nice surprise."

"You're the best, Lloyd," Margo said with a bright smile.

He walked her to the elevator bank, keeping up a steady stream of chatter, and guided her into an open car. Leaning inside, he swiped his card and selected the thirty-first floor. Margo bade him a friendly goodbye, but the second he turned around she pressed the button marked fifty-four.

Nadiya's suggestion had been the same as Davon's—steal evidence to incriminate Addison Brand—and Margo had been forced to reject it for the same reasons. She didn't have the luxury of time to do the necessary research, to figure out where Brand kept his supply, and under what conditions. If a supply even existed at all.

Meanwhile, Petrenko posed a looming threat, and Margo was already weary of looking over her shoulder and sleeping in a loud, shabby Hollywood motel. It was lucky that both her birds could be brought down by the same stone: If she exposed Brand, his conspiracy to arm child soldiers in a foreign conflict would be forced into the light, and then both men would get what they had coming.

When the elevator opened onto the executive floor, Margo swept right past the flustered receptionist and made a beeline for the largest corner office. She'd been inside it, of course, admired its teak wood trim and leather club chairs—admired the dazzling view northwest across the city. It was the CEO's office. Her dad's office.

Addison Brand's office.

Her rage whipped up until she was practically levitating, and she barely heard the man's administrative assistant as she stormed by the woman's desk. "Margo? Is that—wait, you can't—he's in a meeting!"

When she flung open the door, her father's killer was talking with a florid man sporting a sandy mustache. Brand glanced up in surprise at the interruption, recognition flitting into his eyes only a second before Margo grabbed him by the throat and slammed him backward across his desk.

Her father's desk.

"You son of a bitch," she snarled, her voice trembling.

"Mr. Brand!" the man's assistant cried from the doorway.

"It's all right, Donna." Addison remained utterly calm. "Please take Tom to the lounge and get him anything he needs. We'll resume our conversation when I'm done with Miss Manning."

"You'll be having it through the bars of a jail cell," Margo snapped, but the door closed on her words, Donna whisking Tom safely out of earshot.

Lightly, Brand said, "Margo, how nice of you to drop by."

"You killed my father, you piece of shit."

His features betrayed no emotion. "I notice you waited until all witnesses left the room before trotting out that little bit of slander."

"It's no slander, asshole. You poisoned him for months—right under my fucking nose! You showed up every other day like clockwork to give it to him. You watched him *suffer*. You—you . . ." she couldn't continue.

"You sound hysterical."

"*Fuck you*," Margo raged, tightening her grip. "I have proof! I took a glass of whiskey you poured from that flask of yours and had the contents analyzed. I know what you gave him, and I know exactly how it worked."

This time his face stilled, his eyes reading hers carefully. "Interesting."

"Is that all you have to say?"

"I'm wondering where you got this supposed evidence. Because I made a point to wash those glasses every—oh." Realization dawned. "The one I poured for you."

"The night before my father died."

He thought quickly—she could see it in his eyes. "Whose fingerprints will the police find on that glass?"

"Yours."

"And yours," he returned. "But not Harland's. All you've got is a claim that *you* were poisoned—but you look just fine to me. How do you expect to convince the authorities that whatever you may have found factored into Harland's death?"

"My housekeeper knew for weeks that someone was sneaking alcohol to my father." Margo bared her teeth. "I know you brought your flask to the mansion more than just once—and we both watched you pour the whiskey."

"And *I* watched you carry it up the stairs, where anything might have happened to it." Brand arched a brow. "That was weeks ago, Margo. If some kind of poison really did make its way into that glass, how do I know you didn't put it there yourself?"

She blinked. "What?"

"If anyone was systematically poisoning your father, you were in a far better position than me to do it," he went on, "and as the primary beneficiary of his estate, you had an excellent motive. Everyone knows you and Harland fought, that you resented—"

"*Fuck you!*" Margo shouted again—and in losing her composure, gave Brand his opening. With a series of swift moves, he twisted her hand free from his throat, jolted upright, and shoved her back. Stumbling over the plush carpet, she bumped against a chair, and tumbled into it.

"Now." Brand smoothed his hair and shot his cuffs. "Let me tell you a thing or two, you spoiled little brat. I know you're used to throwing your name around in this city, skipping lines and getting free things from brain-dead fashionistas, but the police don't operate on your say-so."

"You killed Win, too." Margo was embarrassed by how close to tears she suddenly was. "And I'm going to find that nurse."

"I'll be impressed if you're able to track down old Nina—and even more so if you can get her to talk. She wasn't doing so well the last time I saw her." He flashed a wolfish grin, and Margo felt sick. "In any event, you've recently come into a lot of money—"

"I already had a lot of money."

"When it comes to wealth, there is no such thing as 'enough.' And it's the first trail the police will follow." Perching on the edge of the desk, he ventured, "On that topic, what do you know about dummy corporations and money laundering?"

Margo went stiff in her chair. "I'm sorry?"

"I'll give you an example of what I'm talking about. Let's say you came into a large sum you wanted to hide from the government. You could stash it in an offshore account, maybe a tax haven in the Caribbean, where they keep fewer records and have strict privacy guarantees." He tilted his head. "By the way, didn't you go to Saint Thomas last year for some sort of vacation?" Margo was silent, and he continued, "Anyway, the point of money laundering is to take 'dirty' cash and make it 'clean,' so you can spend it openly. The bank account is registered in the name of a corporation that only exists on paper, whose only asset is a second corporation that also only exists on paper, et cetera."

"Where are you going with this?" Her voice was hoarse.

"I recently hired a forensic accountant to look into a few things," the man replied, "and he found a business called the DALM

Corporation, registered in the Cayman Islands." He looked over at Margo, who was cold to the core as her darkest secret was dragged from its hole. "The curious thing is that DALM—which is owned by an entity that's owned by an entity that's owned by another entity—only has a handful of employees. And one of them is you, Margo." She had nothing to say, so he went on, "It also employs an eighteen-year-old drag queen from Boyle Heights named Davon Stokes, a sixteen-year-old ballet student in Santa Monica named Leif Dalby, and your very own neighbor Axel Moreau."

Margo tried to speak, but nothing came out.

"What a sad story, the Moreaus. Basil was a friend, in passing, and I know the litigation surrounding his case created a great financial hardship for Jacinta and the boys." Brand fingered his necktie. "Quite a stroke of luck, then, that Axel got this amazing job with DALM. I understand he paid the tuition at Somerville for both him and his brother. And the family's property taxes, and—"

"Just get to the point," she whispered.

"When my accountant tracked DALM's finances to a bank account on Saint Croix, I told him to stop looking. But I preserved all the records, and it would be very easy for me to interest the authorities in picking up where he left off, and following the rest of the trail. Especially if questions arise about Harland's death, and your defense is that you 'have plenty of money.'" He sighed. "Poor Jacinta. I can't imagine how she would deal with her son being arrested so soon after her husband. It might even kill her."

Margo could barely breathe. "You bastard. You won't get away with this."

"The thing about that is, Margo," Brand said with a pleasant smile, "I already have." Activating the intercom on his desk, he said, "Donna, Miss Manning is ready to leave, and would like it if two of our largest guards escorted her out."

Margo had nothing to say—no snappy comeback, no brilliant counterattack, no *gotcha* loophole. He'd been ready for her. He'd been ready all along.

When the door opened and Donna reappeared with two burly, uniformed men, Brand flashed a broad smile. "Please make sure that Miss Manning leaves the building. Unfortunately, as she has no connection to the company anymore, I'm afraid I'm also going to have to insist that she not be allowed back on the premises again."

"You're a monster, Brand," Margo said, rising to her feet and heading for the door under her own power, wanting to at least claim that much dignity in defeat.

"Of course. Thanks so much for the lovely visit."

The guards took her by the elbows and led her away like a criminal.

BACK IN THE CAR, SHE CRIED—OUT OF RAGE AND IMPOTENCE— until she was exhausted. Until her body wouldn't do it anymore, and her life kept going, whether or not she cared. Being ejected from a building with her name on it was surreal, but being cornered and taunted by Addison Brand was an ugliness that would never wash clean from her memory.

For a while she listened to the sounds of Los Angeles, just breathing and wondering where she fit into it anymore. Absurdly, it was one of Brand's least offensive remarks that she couldn't stop hearing. *I know you're used to throwing your name around in this city.* The thing is, she *was*: Her name opened doors, it got people talking or it shut them up, it made things easier; but in a flash, almost everything she counted on had been taken away, and her future now depended on the mercy of silence from her father's killer.

A decision was elbowing its way to the front of her mind, and before she could face it, there was someone she wanted to see. She sent him a text, asking where he was, and the answer was cryptic: *Heading for the Colorado Street Bridge.*

She replied in punctuation: *?????*

Don't worry, nothing dire!

I need someone to talk to, she wrote.

Dots bubbled on her phone, disappeared, then reappeared.

Be on Arroyo Blvd just north of the bridge in 45 min. Leave the car running.

32

BUILT IN 1912, THE COLORADO STREET BRIDGE was a notorious span in Pasadena, stretching across LA's Arroyo Seco at a length of nearly fifteen hundred feet. It was known for its decorative arches and railings, its pendant-style streetlamps, and for the number of people who had used it as a means by which to end their lives. Margo felt something cold and tight squeezing her innards the entire drive there.

When she arrived, a black Jeep was already idling at the curb. There was nothing legal about stopping on this stretch of the boulevard, and as she opened her door and stepped out, Margo wondered what she'd been invited to attend. A guy with a ponytail, maybe twenty years old, stood by the other vehicle with an apprehensive air. When he saw Margo coming, he did a double take.

"Holy shit!" His eyes widened. "You're actually Margo fucking Manning!"

"That's my middle name," she returned, "don't wear it out."

"He said you were coming, but we all thought he was fucking with us," the guy elaborated, still staring as she approached. "Like, he told us he knew you, and we were—"

"Where is he?"

The guy pointed into the air. "Up there."

Margo turned, following the line of his arm, and gazed up at the expanse of the bridge. A barrier had been erected at street level to discourage people from making the fatal leap into the arroyo, but four individuals—two boys, two girls—had somehow made their way through it; and, with packs strapped over their shoulders, they were getting ready to jump. On the far right, Dallas Yang waved down at her.

Her heart lurching, she shouted, "YOU'RE GOING TO DIE!"

"Way to be supportive," the boy murmured, and she whirled on him.

"What is that, a hundred and fifty feet? He'll hit the ground in about three seconds!"

"He'll be fine." The guy was unconcerned. "It's a static line. There won't be any freefall."

"He could still break an ankle—or a leg, or his *spine*."

The guy shrugged. "He's done it before."

Anxiously Margo turned back to the bridge, vertigo sweeping over her as she watched the four figures tense; they were close enough to the ground that she could hear them counting down.

And then they jumped.

Four cords, clipped securely to the antisuicide barrier, went taut instantly, ripping the deployment bags clean from the jumpers' packs. Their chutes unfurled almost instantly, spreading like wings against the bright winter sky, but the fall was shockingly fast anyway, and the landing rough; Dallas hit the ground feetfirst and then rolled across the pavement.

A car sped under the bridge and came to a screeching halt as it encountered the group, horn blaring, and Dallas scrambled upright. Gathering his chute and taking off at a sprint, he shouted, "Go, go, go!"

The blond boy leaped into the Jeep, and Margo reacted instinctively, diving behind the wheel of the Mini. Dallas barely made it into the passenger seat, slamming the door shut as she pulled away from the curb and gunned the engine. "Where am I going? What the hell is happening?"

"Head for Eagle Rock," he said breathlessly. "There's an army reserve base just south of here, and they've reported us before. We have to ghost before the cops show up." She stepped on the gas, the tiny car showing amazing pickup, and as she made a sharp U-turn he added, "Thanks for the getaway."

"You know," Margo said, racing back south, "most times, when a girl texts a boy and says 'I need someone to talk to,' she doesn't mean 'please embroil me in a high-speed escape from the police.'"

"Lucky for me, I'm cute?" He turned a toothy grin her way, and Margo rolled her eyes with a smile. Dividing her attention between the road and the rearview, she slalomed through traffic and negotiated the looping turns onto the 134, grateful for the distraction.

THE ADDRESS HE GAVE LED TO AN APARTMENT BUILDING OFF York Boulevard, two stories of bleached stucco and red tile, with a fat palm tree dying in the front yard. Dallas guided Margo to the second floor, where they walked into an apartment that smelled of pot smoke and stale pizza. A deflated blow-up doll—tacked to a cardboard cutout of Han Solo—greeted them just inside the door.

"I . . . didn't know that was going to be here, I swear," Dallas said.

Margo looked around. "I'm glad I never tried to picture where you live, because I couldn't have done this place justice."

"Oh, this isn't my apartment," he said hastily. "My place is way more disgusting than this. A couple of my buddies live here, but when I told them Margo Manning wanted an audience with me . . ."

"I guess my name still opens doors in this town after all." She meant it to be a joke, but it didn't come out right.

"You look, um . . ." Dallas stopped and then laughed a little. "I don't really know what to say. I'm not sure where we left things, and I don't want to make you uncomfortable."

"It's okay. There's a lot of stuff I'm not really sure of right now, either." She kept her eyes on the floor. "I'm sorry about Win. I should have called or something, but . . ."

"No." His affable expression fell. "I should have called. First your father, and then this?" Dallas shook his head. "Things have just been so intense lately—the cops asking me all these questions because I was his intern, my mom grieving for her mentor—and I guess it hit me kinda hard, too. I mean, I just jumped off a bridge, right? How Psych 101 is that?"

"Flirting with death?"

"Feeling alive." He crossed into the narrow kitchen, opening the fridge and pulling out a bottle of beer. "You want?"

"Is there anything stronger?"

He poured them shots from a plastic jug he found in the freezer, and she shuddered when it went down. Taking the glass from her, their fingertips touching, Dallas set it in the sink. Softly, he asked, "Was that what you wanted to talk to me about? Win?"

"Yes," she said. "But there's more." Margo twisted her hands together, not wanting to say the words aloud. "Dallas . . . I'm leaving."

"Don't go yet. I know this place is a dump, but you—"

"Not the apartment. Los Angeles. And I'm not sure how long I'll be away. Maybe . . . maybe a really long time."

"Oh." His eyes fell away from her face, and he reached back into the sink, setting the shot glasses on the counter again.

"I'm going to Italy, to stay with my mom," Margo went on, babbling about the decision she'd come to in the car, while he retrieved the vodka from the freezer and poured them another round. "She probably won't be wild about the idea, but we're good at avoiding unpleasant subjects."

He handed her the shot with a sad smile. "Well, salute. Italy sounds . . . great." They drank, and he took the glass again, their hands lingering together this time. "I'm probably an asshole for thinking of myself at a time like this, but I wish you weren't going."

"I wish I wasn't going, too." And Margo burst into tears. "It's just . . . *too much*. There's just too much! My dad is gone, I can't go home, my life is crashing and burning and it feels like every choice I make blows up in my face—"

"Hey." Dallas put his arms around her, letting her cry against his chest, her head tucked beneath his chin. "Maybe getting away for a while isn't such a bad idea. They say that when you lose someone special, you need to rearrange the furniture. Makes things 'new' again, and gives you kind of a fresh start. Keeps you from being weighed down by sad memories. Maybe that's what you need—some time away to get your heart back together."

"Maybe," she mumbled, unable to explain even a tenth of what lurked behind her outburst. Unable to explain that this flight was as much to outrun Petrenko as it was to outrun grief and shame. Instead, she pressed her cheek against Dallas's chest, feeling his solid warmth, breathing him in as she regained her composure. Margo let her arms find their way around his waist, and she felt him still.

Tilting her face up, she murmured, "Do you remember what I said the other night? About knowing what I want, but not thinking it was such a good idea?"

"Yeah." His eyes were soft and warm. "I remember it pretty well."

"I've had time to think, and I've changed my mind." She moved closer, her hands climbing his back. "I'd really like you to kiss me."

Dallas emitted a nervous chuckle. "Oh boy, I, uh . . . I want to. In fact, I want to so much that I kind of need to, um—" He offered an apologetic wince, shifting his hips a little while discreetly adjusting himself. "But I think we shouldn't."

"Why not?"

"Because I remember all the other things you said, too," he answered. "Because right now, neither of us is making the best decisions. In case you forgot, I literally just jumped off a bridge."

"And if your chute hadn't opened, you'd be dead," Margo added. "And if you'd jumped a second later, that car might have hit you. If these past weeks have taught me anything, it's that sooner or later we all run out of time." She stepped back, untucking her blouse. "Safe choices are fine, but if my clock hits zero tomorrow, I don't want any regrets. I don't know how long I'll be in Italy, or what the world will look like when I come back; all I know is that we're here now, and there's no reason why we shouldn't have what we want."

"Okay, your argument is persuasive." Dallas cleared his throat as she unbuttoned her top. "Very, very persuasive."

"I like you a lot, Dallas. And if right now is all we ever get, I want to make the most of it." She slipped her blouse off her shoulders, and stood before him in her bra, pulling the pins out of her hair and letting it fall. "Are you in or are you out?"

"Fuck it," he said, yanking his shirt off over his head and flinging it into the dining nook, where it took out a pyramid of beer cans. "I'm in."

He was on her in a heartbeat, their mouths colliding, his lips plush as ripe fruit; his touch sent goose bumps racing over her arms, and one of his hands—*those hands*—slid up her neck, his fingers finding pathways through her hair. In her head, she'd imagined this scene as a sweet and romantic goodbye; but instead her heart raced, filling her with hunger for more of him, and she dug her teeth into his flesh.

They kissed in a frenzy, backing into the counter and sending the shot glasses clattering into the sink, and he managed to unclasp her bra with one hand. She pulled it off as he shoved his shorts to the floor, and then her pencil skirt tore halfway up its seams as he lifted her off her feet.

THE KITCHEN HAD BEEN A DISASTER WHEN THEY'D ARRIVED, but was in even worse shape when they finally left. Her face was flushed, and his hair was damp at the temples with sweat; her skirt was ruined, and he'd been unable to find his underwear. He declined the offer of a ride home. It felt like the right time and place for farewell.

"No regrets?" Evening was coming down on LA, the sky hazy and pink behind him as he peered at her with an earnest expression.

"No."

"I'm going to miss you." He glanced back at the apartment building, his cheeks the same rose gold as the sunset. "I wish we'd recorded that. I think I peaked in there!"

"Maybe fate will bring us back together." She tried for a smile.

"Maybe."

They reached for each other, hands linking for a moment, and then she stepped away.

No regrets.

Two days later, she returned the Mini Cooper to the rental agency at LAX and boarded a plane to Rome.

Act Four:
BITTER BUSINESS

33

Venice, Italy
One Month Later

DESPITE THE SCREECH OF GULLS, THE CHATTER of tourists, and the rumble of boats surging along the canal below her window, it was the sun that roused Margo from a sluggish, dreamless slumber. Her head throbbed and her eyes felt like they'd been taken out and put back in the wrong way. Stretching, she forced herself upright and groaned.

Daylight streamed through the arched windows she'd forgotten to shut the night before, and across the Grand Canal, a bright blue sky stretched behind a picturesque jumble of buildings in shades of gray, fawn, and rose. The water was a Disney-esque turquoise, and it filled the air with damp, giving up an earthy smell. Gentle waves lapped at weathered piers, gondolas drifted by, and springtime was just touching the breeze.

Margo slammed the wooden shutters closed, locking the sunshine out. Gulping down a painkiller with a glass of water from her bedside table, she shuffled for the door.

Ludovico Ferrara, her stepfather, was a banker based in Milan; but his company had recently purchased the top two floors of a historic Venetian palace—one of many that bordered the Grand

Canal—and had sent him to live there while he acted as supervisor to the expanding local branch. Dating back to the fifteenth century, the Palazzo Rambaldo was three stories of ornate moldings, Moorish galleries, and glossy stone floors, and it still didn't quite feel real yet.

"Good morning, sweetheart. I wondered what time we'd see you," her mother drawled from behind a copy of *La Stampa* when Margo reached the kitchen. Angela Hopwood Manning Ferrara was impeccable in pale yellow, her red hair flowing over one shoulder in an artful cascade. "There's coffee, and Vittoria made biscotti, if you're hungry."

Margo grunted, fumbling with a gleaming French press on the counter. She had planned on skipping the biscotti, out of spite, but they looked so good she took two. Flopping down on a stool across from her mother, she started to devour her breakfast.

"Had a late night, did we?" Angela's voice was a musical undertone.

"Lorenzo and Sofia had friends in from Germany, and they wanted to see Venice."

"The decent parts of this city roll up the sidewalks by midnight." Her mother gave her an arch look. "And you didn't come home until sometime after three."

"We went across the lagoon," Margo said with an air of reasonability.

"Well." Angela flipped a page of her newspaper. "Sofia is a nice girl. And even though Lorenzo is definitely cheating on her, I'm sure they kept you out of too much trouble."

Margo didn't know where to begin to answer, and decided not to try. Silence filled the kitchen, underscored by the rumble of a vaporetto cruising by outside. Margo dunked an offensively tasty biscotti in a demitasse of potent coffee and tried to remember she was supposed to be resenting this place.

"So, what are your plans for the day?" Angela asked, making an effort and pushing *La Stampa* to the side. "More time with Sofia and Lorenzo and the Germans?"

"No." The biscotti crunched between her teeth. "They're going to Padua and Verona and then Milan. They won't be back for a few days. I thought, maybe now the water's receded, I'd go sightseeing or something."

It was just her luck that she'd arrived in the middle of the Acqua Alta—Venice's regular period of flooding, when lagoon levels rose and consumed the ancient city's narrow streets. The problem was dealt with through temporary elevated walkways, but the winding alleys were far more picturesque without them.

"Oh, that reminds me!" Angela clasped her hands together. "Ludo and I are spending the day at Lake Como with friends. You're welcome to join us, but it may be rather boring."

Margo was startled, and it took her a moment to reply. "Thanks, but I'll stick with my nonplans. I figured maybe I'd treat myself to lunch or some shopping or something. And I've been here a month and I haven't even been out to the Giudecca yet."

Angela rose from her seat, placing her coffee cup in the dishwasher, tucked beneath a window overlooking a Renaissance-era courtyard. "You're not missing anything. Aside from the Redentore, there's nothing to see over there. At least the Lido has a beach."

It was fifty degrees out; why did everyone want her to go to the beach when it was freezing? "That sounds like a great idea."

"Anyway, I should get ready. We're leaving in an hour." Blowing Margo an awkward kiss, she headed for the sitting room and the stairs beyond it. "Have a nice day, sweetheart, and stay out of trouble!"

"Sure thing," the girl answered automatically. For a while after Angela had departed, Margo stared at her half-eaten biscotti, a weight pulling down in her chest. Finally, she mumbled, "Happy eighteenth birthday to me."

* * *

IT WAS A SHORT WALK FROM THE PALAZZO RAMBALDO TO Margo's favorite café on the Campo San Polo, a vast plaza ringed by colorful tenements. It spread out from the back of a Catholic church dating to the 1400s, a sturdy brick edifice with a detached campanile. In summer, the square would be thronged with tourists and elderly locals, ice cream kiosks doing a brisk trade; but in the off-season, it was peaceful.

She sat at her regular table, and her regular waitress brought her regular order—cappucino and a savory cornetto. There were a few patrons at other tables, but Margo felt like the last living person in the world. She hadn't expected a lot of fanfare, but she also hadn't expected her mother to flat-out forget that it was her birthday.

Reflexively checking her phone, she saw two missed texts from Davon and a missed call from Irina, and she hastily put the thing away. As soon as her plane had touched down in Rome, she'd sent an update to everyone, telling them where she was and why. The boys had a right to know what Addison Brand had on them, a message that was neither fun to deliver, nor received very well by the interested parties.

The truth was, she and Addison were in sort of a standoff, and she didn't think he was going to expose them. Not anytime soon anyway. That information was his ace card, and he could hold the threat of it against her forever; once he used it, there was nothing to stop her from retaliating—and even if she held fewer cards, she could still probably compel a police inquiry her father's killer wouldn't want to face.

The real problem was Petrenko. She had to assume the Russian billionaire would mention his vendetta against Margo to Brand sooner or later; and Addison was absolutely clever enough to realize that he held the names and addresses of every person on Arkady's hit list. How long would he hold on to that information? When would he decide that having Margo eliminated would be more useful than having leverage to manipulate her?

How soon would promising Arkady Petrenko the satisfaction of revenge become a negotiating tool he couldn't resist?

"Jeez, from the look on your face, I don't know if I should break into 'Happy Birthday' or a funeral dirge."

Margo's head snapped up at the unexpectedly familiar voice, and for a moment she stared in uncomprehending silence at the boy standing by her table. "*Axel?*"

He plunked down into the chair opposite her, as casually as if they'd been planning to meet, and he was just running late. "I am *desperate* for coffee. They had some on the plane, but it tasted like wastewater from a paper factory, and I was extremely not into it."

Margo continued to stare. "What are you doing here?"

"It's my best friend's birthday," he answered, signaling to the waitress. "Where else would I be?"

"How did you even know where to find me?"

"Well, ever since you stopped answering my texts and calls, I started stalking you online," he divulged conversationally. "You may be in Italy, girl, but you're still *Margo Manning*, and that MadMargo hashtag is better than an FBI satellite for tracking you down. I found like six creepy cell phone pictures of you sitting at this exact table. I came here straight from the airport." Axel ran his fingers through his dark, wavy hair. "Well, okay, not *straight* here, because I got lost for an hour. And bumped into a cute Italian boy who needed about fifteen minutes of my company."

"Venice is a labyrinth." She smiled, realizing in an instant just how much she'd missed him. The waitress made it to their table, then, and Axel ordered a caffè corretto—a potent mix of espresso and grappa. With an arched brow, Margo commented, "The best part of waking up is one-hundred-proof brandy in your cup."

"I'll have you know I'm still on California time, so it's about two a.m., hunty." He reached across the table and batted a lock of her hair. "I love this new look. Very chic—very 'international femme fatale.'"

"I'm an adult now." Margo tossed her mane extravagantly. She'd had two inches cut off, the color lightened to a champagne hue; the change had felt significant, symbolic. "You think the color's okay? Or is it too much?"

"Girl, I'm gagging," he said with approval. "And blondes have more fun, right? So more blond has to mean more fun."

"Plus gentlemen prefer us," Margo reported solemnly, even though it was starting to feel like Death was the only gentleman with a particular taste for blondes lately. After Axel's highly flammable coffee arrived, she confessed, "I've missed you."

"It hasn't showed," Axel replied, but without malice. He gave her a half smile. "So much stuff has happened since you vanished. I mean, living with the constant danger of death-by-Petrenko hovering over our heads has really shifted everyone's priorities. Kinda helped us all figure out what really matters."

"Are you trying to tell me you and Davon are back together?"

"No," he said emphatically. "No, no, no." Then, "Well, maybe we finally agreed to stop pretending that we aren't friends with benefits."

"Wow. Well, that's . . . congratulations?"

"Thanks." Axel took it sincerely. "I feel like I've unlocked a new gay achievement or something. And dating sucks, you know? Like, it's hard enough when you're femme, let alone a drag queen, *let alone* the son of the most hated man in the country."

"Well," Margo interjected, trying to determine what was called for, "I'm happy for you two."

"What else, what else . . . oh." His expression soured. "Quino and Leif are dating. Like, officially. As in boyfriends."

"They are?" Margo sat up in her chair. "That's so great!"

"No it isn't, so you can wipe that heart-eyes-emoji look off your face," Axel retorted. "It's going to screw up our whole dynamic, and I am not happy about it." With a prim little sniff, he added, "Quino's never had a boyfriend before, and let's face it: Leif is a ho."

"Talk about the pot calling the kettle promiscuous, Mr. Fifteen Minutes of Company." Margo snorted around her cornetto.

"That's different."

"No it isn't," she said pointedly. "Joaquin and Leif are both sweethearts, and unless one of them gets hurt, their relationship isn't any of our business."

Axel made a harrumphing noise but let it go. "I guess the only other news I have is Georgia. She's just about to finish up her treatment program, and we're trying to figure out what to do. They can't go back to Boyle Heights; that shithead Peck got into their apartment and trashed the place." The boy drained his beverage. "So we're apartment hunting. Everything is expensive, but thanks to the LAMFA job, D at least has enough money in the bank that his applications aren't getting rejected outright."

"That's great," Margo repeated, but somehow her happiness wouldn't quite manifest. Selfish as it might be, it was hard to hear how much better everyone else's lives had gotten, especially when her own felt so aimless for the first time. "Let me know if there's anything I can do—like, write a reference letter or something."

"That would be cool." Axel gestured at her. "So, how about you? You're living in a romantic city, filled with Italian men . . . What kind of adventures are you having?"

"Nothing special." Margo tried to sound breezy. "I've been wooed by a few boys and girls, but nothing serious." In fact, she'd had one very short fling with Sofia, the daughter of one of Ludo Ferrara's clients—who was *not* dating her friend Lorenzo, as Angela seemed to believe. They'd had fun, but Margo's heart had been else-where. Somehow, she seemed to have temporarily misplaced the organ in a shitty Eagle Rock kitchen. "Mostly, I've been trying to catch up on school. Somerville is letting me complete my coursework online so I can still graduate, but my mom had to hire a tutor because I'm so far behind."

"Is he cute?" Axel asked promptly.

"*No*, which is an outrage, and also something my mom arranged deliberately," she huffed. "How long are you here for?"

"Just tonight. Some of us have to finish school in person," he pointed out, "and Quino can't drive Mami to her doctor appointments."

"Well then, let's make the most of it," Margo declared, rising to her feet and tossing some euros down on the table. "I'm gonna show you the hell out of Venice."

34

A WARREN OF NARROW PASSAGEWAYS, TWIST-
ing among centuries-old buildings in a state of elegant decrepitude,
Venice is a challenge to navigate—even if you have a map. Lucky
for Axel, he had Margo. Following her lead, they darted down
alleyways not wide enough for them to stand side by side, scampered over canals on fairy-tale bridges, and dashed by gift shops
and cafés.

The air was redolent of gelato, warm spices, and the green stink
of algae; washing hung like prayer flags from lines strung between
tenements; and sunlight splashed across buildings colored mauve
and tan and butter yellow. Venetian boys were just as gorgeous as
the city itself, with gleaming black hair, bright teeth, and a prowl-
ing, feline sensuality. Axel was in heaven.

From the top of the famous Ponte di Rialto, he took breathtaking photos of the Grand Canal—of the jutting piers, glimmer-
ing water, and striking palazzos—before Margo dragged him
onward. They wove through the small, connected plazas on the
other side of the bridge, stopping briefly for an affogato and some
fresh-baked focaccia. Studded by tomatoes and perfumed with
rosemary, it was still warm and slippery with olive oil.

By the time they had passed the stocky, whitewashed facade of the Chiesa di San Giuliano, the streets narrowing down—crowded by tourists, lined with souvenir stands and boutiques—Axel had forgotten how tired he was.

"Through here," Margo said, and they hustled down an arched passageway and into the dazzling expanse of the Piazza San Marco. An elaborate church rose to his left, and to his right extended a vast and dramatic public square, bordered on three sides by stacked colonnades. Ahead of them rose the church's campanile, a breathtaking pile of brick and stone climbing more than three hundred feet into the air; and past that, beyond the ornate frontage of the Doge's Palace, the flashing, blue-green waters of the lagoon beckoned.

"Wow," Axel said. It was an understatement; the space was more than impressive, every angle eye-catching, and he didn't know where to start first.

As a kid, travel had been something his parents forced on him: a week in Mexico with Mami's parents; a week in Zurich, while his father tended to business; and other times it was Hong Kong, Paris, Buenos Aires . . . places he resented for their strangeness. It wasn't until it was too late, until Basil had been hauled away in handcuffs—countless privileges going with him—that Axel finally realized what he'd taken for granted.

Neither Davon nor Leif owned a passport; and Joaquin had volunteered to stay with Jacinta so Axel could make the trip. Now, standing at the rear of the Piazza San Marco, drinking in the gaudy domes of the basilica, the tower, the arcades, and the cornflower sky, he felt happy—free, for the first time in over a year.

Margo indulged his lust for photographs, trailing happily behind as he darted from one edge of the square to the next. There was a guy—college aged, dark haired, reasonably attractive—advertising skydiving lessons in heavily accented English. Dressed in a full jumpsuit, he wore a parachute on his back and waved around the heavy-duty clip of a static line at passing tourists. Margo stared at him like a long-lost relative, and Axel ached to interrogate her about it, but was afraid to break the spell of the afternoon.

From the guidebooks, he knew that St. Mark's Square was separated into two parts—the actual piazza, enclosed by the wraparound arcade, and the piazzetta, the smaller expanse that spread before the Doge's Palace and ended at the water's edge. Directly across the canal was a spit of land dominated by a pearly structure with a magnificent rotunda, and when Margo caught him admiring it, she explained, "That's the Punta della Dogana. The church is called Santa Maria della Salute—Saint Mary of Health—because it was built after a particularly gnarly outbreak of the plague. You want to see it from the inside?"

"Girl, you had me at 'the plague.'"

They saw the church, navigated more winding streets, and crossed the great, wooden expanse of the Ponte dell'Accademia with its postcard view of the Salute perched at the mouth of the canal.

The crowds grew thicker as they wended through the district of San Marco, past lavish hotels and hole-in-the-wall wine shops; past churches and campos and old wells that had been long-since sealed up. Every corner they turned presented a view worthy of a snapshot, and by the time they straggled into the district of Castello, shadows were lengthening over the city, and Axel's backpack was like a dead body draped over his shoulders.

"I hate to say it," he confessed, "but jet lag is kicking my ass and I need to sit down."

She took him to Campo Santa Maria Formosa, where another imposing church looked out on a narrow canal and a stone bridge with an iron filigree railing. The boisterous public square stretched from northeast to southwest, and the towering campanile was a weathered off-white that looked almost rosy in the late-afternoon sun. Along the embankment was an outdoor restaurant with metal mesh tables, and Margo claimed one for them. Axel sank into his chair with a groan of relief.

She ordered pasta and a bottle of champagne, and they stuffed themselves as small boats passed beneath the bridge and a group of boys shared a cigarette at the water's edge. Finally, satisfied and a little delirious from fatigue, Axel decided it was time to broach the subject he'd been working toward all day. "So . . . Venice is kind of amazing."

"Right?" Margo perked up, setting aside her champagne. "And you've barely seen anything! There's the Arsenale and the Ghetto Nuovo, and even a cemetery island—and then there's the food!" She sat back, shaking her head with disapproval. "I can't believe you're only here for one night."

"I mean, I'd love to stay, but shit keeps rolling downhill back in Malibu and I have to deal with it." He poked at the remains of his pasta. "And there's no place like home, right?"

Margo's smile flickered and faded. She reached for her champagne. "The saying I remember is, 'You can't go home again.'"

"That's not true," he said softly. She didn't answer, and he reached across the table to touch her hand. "Please come back to LA? We miss you. *I* miss you."

Clearing her throat, she took a drink. "It kinda sounds like everybody's doing awesome right now without me around to screw everything up."

"What are you—"

"You tried to talk me out of the Petrenko job, and I wouldn't listen," she finally blurted, her eyes on her plate. "Now he's after us, and it's my fault."

"I was against the Petrenko job because I was being a controlling asshole," Axel rebutted. "You and Quino both called me out on that, and you were both right. We all knew Arkady dabbled in the black market—you *told* us that—and every one of us should have seen the hazard lights. We were just too hypnotized by the money."

"It was my call," Margo tried, but he cut her off again.

"We voted. And once I stopped being a dick, it was unanimous."

"And then there's Brand," she went on, as if he hadn't spoken. "Petrenko is a loose cannon, but Addison is the one holding the fuse. All he needs is a reason to light it up."

"He doesn't need a reason!" Axel was frustrated. "Apparently, he had plenty to hold over your dad's attorney, but he killed him anyway because he got paranoid! He knows you've got shit on him, Margo, and even if he thinks he's sitting pretty, sooner or later he's going to decide that shutting you up is better than counting on you to stay quiet."

"The point is, I *don't* have shit on him!" she finally retaliated, light in her eyes. "I've got traces of a possible poison, and no way to prove where it came from; I've got a bunch of speculation from Reginald Castor, who says nothing he's got will hold up in court. And if I push him, or if I even tempt him, Brand will either expose us or hand our names to Petrenko." With a harsh laugh, she added, "I can hide, Axel, but what about Leif and Davon? What about you and Quino and Jacinta? You'd be sitting ducks."

"Is that what this is about?" Axel gestured to the church, to its backdrop of sky gone brassy and pink at the edges, to the canal and the gondolas and the people tucking up their collars against the evening chill. "You're hiding here while we all hang our asses over the line?"

"That's not fair!" Spots of color appeared in Margo's cheeks again. "I'm here because, right now, I'm the only one Petrenko knows about; I'm here because it shows Brand I'm playing ball; I'm here because LA is too full of ghosts!"

"So you're hiding," Axel summarized. It came out too fast, too cold; he was used to being honest with Margo, and unaccustomed to arguments that carried this much weight. Wearily, he exhaled. "I'm sorry. I'm punch drunk, and I'm not putting my words together right. Margo, babe . . . LA doesn't belong to Petrenko or Brand or the ghosts; it belongs to *you*. We can figure something out and kick their asses. We can help, you know? You're not alone.

"Remember how I was when we first started stealing shit in Malibu? You got me through the darkest time of my life! You're the one who built this team, and you're the one who stitched it together. We're family now, the five of us, and we don't let anyone go through anything alone." He searched her face, but it was shut down, barriers in her eyes. "Look. Leif's paid up for this year at the academy, but he's still got next year to worry about—and the summer, too, if he doesn't want to go back to East Dumptruck Corners; and Davon might have enough cash for an apartment, but rents are out of control. He'll need more. And I don't even want to get into Mami's medical bills, or what we're gonna owe in taxes next month. I don't even want to think about it. So we need you, Margo. We *need* you."

She stayed quiet, and his head was swimming, exhaustion clogging his thoughts. Tears pricked the corners of his eyes. "Margo, I miss you. Quino, Leif, Davon . . . they're family, but they're not *you*. I don't have anyone to talk to about the stuff I need to talk about—and I don't think you do, either."

Margo pulled the champagne bottle out of the ice bucket, refilling her flute, hand shaking. Her mouth turning down, her eyes sad, she said, "I'm sorry, Axel, but I'd be an idiot to start a gunfight with no ammunition, and I won't play fast and loose with other people's lives." They watched bubbles rise and break in her glass. "Maybe I am hiding, but sometimes hiding is the difference between dying and staying alive."

Her words made sense, but they were still disappointing. He'd come to Italy to convince her to return home, to mount some kind of offensive; they'd pulled off the impossible before, so why not again? Why not now, when it really counted? But for the first time since he'd known her, Margo Manning was giving up.

"I get it. I won't fight you." Rising to his feet, hoisting up his backpack, Axel struggled to make his tone light. "Anyway, if I don't get to my hostel in the next thirty minutes, I'm probably going to black out right here in the street."

"A hostel?" Margo reacted like he planned to sleep in a pile of feces. "That's stupid, Axel, my mom and stepdad have a palazzo on the canal! There are tons of rooms, and—"

"I appreciate it, but I booked a place close to the bus station on purpose. I have to be up at the ass-crack to catch my flight home." He shuffled his feet, trying not to wonder when he'd see her again. "I'm glad I came, though. Happy birthday, Margo. I love you."

He turned and started walking, not sure where he was or which direction he was headed—just desperate to get away before she could offer to walk with him. Before she could see that he was crying.

Happy birthday, Margo. I love you.

The words rang in her ears like the bells that chimed every hour in Venice, a chorus of countless churches across the constellation of ancient islands. Axel's was the fate Addison Brand had wielded against her; his safety had been a big part of the reason she'd chosen to leave . . . so why did she feel so guilty?

Was he right? Was she really just hiding, cloaking her cowardice in self-sacrifice, and hoping her mistakes wouldn't catch up with her? Maybe Brand's threats and Petrenko's fury had just been a convenient excuse to slip away from a life that had gone from sad to precarious—to avoid a challenging fight that she just might lose. As the sun slipped lower, tawny light painting the campanile, a chill breeze swept up the canal and made the boys at the water's edge shiver. Margo poured the last of the champagne into her glass.

She was so lost in her thoughts that she didn't hear footsteps approaching, didn't notice there was anyone there until she heard a deep voice: "Margo Manning? You will come with us now if you want to live."

Looking up, she saw three very large men. The jackets they wore couldn't disguise the tattoos on their hands—or the speaker's thick Russian accent. Or the guns that weighed down their pockets.

Petrenko had caught up with her after all.

35

"YOU COME WITH US NOW," THE FIRST MAN
repeated belligerently, while Margo stalled for time. He had a strip
of shiny, puckered flesh across his neck, as if he'd survived having his
throat slit, and one pocketed hand pressed a gun against the fabric
so she could see its outline. "And you will be quiet. Understand?"

"But I haven't even finished my drink yet," she protested with
calm innocence, looking them over. They were tall and bulky, and
from their body language it was clear that Scar was their leader. The
other two could be twins—dark hair, cold eyes, thin lips; but one
had a messy skull and crossbones inked on the back of his hand, and
the other wore a single earring in the shape of a dagger.

Scar reached down and boldly plucked the flute from Margo's
hand, tossing its contents out. "Now you are finished."

In Russian, he ordered the twins to grab her, and the men obe-
diently moved in. Scanning the campo in the waning, pink sunlight,
Margo thought fast; the only child of a multimillionaire, she'd been
taking self-defense classes since she was six years old, and the first
lesson was "never let them move you to a second location." They
were formidable opponents, but her chances were only going to get
worse.

The twins stepped close, one on either side, and made to haul her from her chair—but she didn't wait. Springing to her feet, Margo snatched the empty champagne bottle from the ice bucket and hammered it against Earring's skull like a club, the blow so hard she felt it up to her elbow; in the same fluid motion, she spun backward, lashing out with her right leg, slamming her foot into Crossbones's chest. Taken by surprise, the man reeled backward and stumbled off the embankment, plunging into the canal.

The outbreak of violence brought a hush over the plaza; all attention turned on Margo as she hooked her foot beneath her metal chair and launched it clumsily into the air at Scar—just as he wrestled his pistol free. It caught him in the elbow and he yelped, the gun going off, a bullet tearing into the stone at his feet. Diners screamed, evacuating their tables, and a stampede set off across the square as people fled for safety.

Weaving a little from his blow to the head, Earring had his gun out now, and came at Margo from the side. She swung the bottle at his wrist, disarming him, a sharp *crack* ringing out across Campo Santa Maria Formosa. She danced back as he took an unsteady swipe, moving to put him between her and Scar, to obscure the other man's shot.

Earring threw another punch, a haymaker, and clipped Margo in the jaw. It was a graze, but with so much force behind it that she nearly lost her footing. The ground seesawed, lights flashing, and she staggered out of range. Sucking in air, she tried to shake it off, preparing for a third advance; and when the man swung his fist again, she blocked hard, simultaneously driving a front kick into his gut.

Just as he doubled over, clearing Scar's sight line, she flung the bottle with all her strength; it streaked the short distance, smashing into the ringleader's jaw, and he pulled the trigger a second time.

The bullet caught metal and glass, but Margo was already leaping forward, spring-boarding off a chair, launching into a full rotation.

Scar recovered, bringing his gun arm up, but Margo's foot slammed into it and sent the weapon clattering to the stone pavers. As she touched the ground and straightened back up, the man threw a punch that caught her in the flank and sent her crashing into one of the abandoned tables. A steak Florentine and a massive bowl of pasta slid to the edge, water glasses toppling and spilling through the metal mesh.

Closing in, Scar pressed his advantage, and she thought fast, swinging around with the stoneware bowl and shattering it across his skull. His eyes flickered and rolled, and she rammed an elbow into his throat, dropping him—first to his knees and then flat to the ground—with an ugly gurgle.

Then an arm like an anaconda wrapped around her throat from behind, cutting off her air in an instant, and she was lifted nearly off her feet. Furiously, Earring snarled, "You fucking bitch. I teach you some manners!"

He squeezed harder, and pain shot through Margo's neck, sparkling into her jaw. Scar lay in a heap at her feet, but she could hear Crossbones dragging himself back out of the canal, and the campo was deserted—no one to hear, no one to help. She kicked hard at Earring's knee, but got his calf by mistake, and the man gave an evil laugh. Slamming his fist into her kidney, he growled in her ear as the pain nearly made her vomit.

Her vision doubled and her lungs aflame, Margo saw only one way out; thrusting a shaky hand at the vanished diner's Florentine, she came up with a sharp, serrated steak knife. Emitting a feral grunt, she drove the blade deep into the flesh of Earring's shoulder, and the man screamed piteously, releasing his grip. Gasping for air, Margo seized the narrow advantage of surprise, grabbing his head and slamming it into the edge of the metal table, dropping him to the ground.

Coughing and gagging, her vision full of stars, Margo didn't wait to confront Crossbones again. Taking off at a crooked run, she darted past the church and onto the bridge, a shot ringing out just before she plunged into the narrow safety of Calle Bande Castello—a slim corridor lined with shops and hemmed in by tall buildings, confused tourists ducking aside as she staggered past.

Her lungs ached, her lower back and right shoulder throbbing, and she struggled for air. For nearly two months Margo had been mired in depression, skipping her regular workouts in favor of comfort food and long days in bed, and her stamina was at a perilous low. Legs heavy, forehead beaded with sweat, she was already slowing down as she fought a zigzag path through the tide of nighttime revelers flooding into San Marco.

Scar and Earring were probably both down for the count, but Crossbones would be full of a vengeful rage—and ready to resort to deadly force.

Her thoughts were punctuated by two explosive reports behind her, a chorus of screams going up as tourists hit the ground. The first shot missed her by a country mile, but the second came so close Margo could practically smell the gunpowder—and then she was spinning around a corner, racing for the bridge over Rio de San Zulian, a daring and desperate plan beginning to form in her mind.

Venice was a maze of passageways with forking alleys, hairpin turns, and darkened corners, a thousand places to hide—but just as many dead ends where a man with a grudge and a gun could corner her without any witnesses. Margo didn't have the energy to outrun Crossbones, and she couldn't count on getting far enough ahead to hide somewhere he wouldn't think to look; but if she could lure him into the proper kind of trap, she just might be able to outwit him.

The crowd thickened as she reached Piazza San Marco, and Margo plunged through a rowdy stag party, the thug on her tail forced to conserve his ammunition. She ducked low, moving with the flow of foot traffic, and finally burst into the riot of the city's main public square. Buskers filled the air with music, salesmen tossed around toys that flashed with light—and she immediately found what she was looking for.

It took three hundred euros, and an argument that ate precious time while Petrenko's thug entered the piazza, but Margo got what she wanted. The crowd wasn't dense enough to hide her from Crossbones as she started across the plaza, and when she glanced over her shoulder—locking gazes with the man and seeing recognition spark in his eyes—she felt a chilly combination of satisfaction and terror as she broke into a run.

The line of people waiting to get into the soaring campanile had tripled since the afternoon, the sunset an irresistible draw for visitors, and a few of them shouted angrily as Margo barreled past them and through the door. Crossbones wasn't far behind her when she ducked the cordon, slipped into the elevator vestibule, and shoved to the front of the line as the bell rang and the doors opened. Irritable murmurs rose around her, and her hair stuck damply to her neck, but she forced a casual smile and grasped the arm of a middle-aged blonde who was just boarding the waiting car.

"I almost didn't make it!" Margo exclaimed with a rush of nervous laughter, flashing her ticket stub from earlier in the day for the benefit of the bored elevator operator. "Thanks for waiting!"

"*Vafan?*" The woman Margo had chosen for cover gave her an outraged look. "Vem som fan är du?"

"Please help," Margo returned in a frantic whisper, eyes on the restless crowd outside the elevator as Crossbones shoved his way into view. "A strange man is following me!"

His face bright with rage, his hair and clothes still wet from the canal, Crossbones kicked over one of the stanchions in the atrium, plowing clean through a group of tourists as he charged for the open elevator. The woman beside Margo gasped and wheeled on the operator. "*Shut the door! Now!*"

Flustered, the man complied, and Margo's heartbeat throbbed painfully in her jaw as the tattooed thug lunged for the closing door—a half second too late. It slid shut with a subtle *thunk*, and then the car lifted, the ground zooming away beneath them and taking the angry hit man with it. Margo was hot and cold at once under her clothes, her hands unsteady as she started preparing for the next phase of her ridiculous plan. There were two ways this could go, and she wasn't sure which of them she preferred.

If Crossbones followed her up the tower, she knew what to do; it was a risky gambit, which could go wrong more ways than it could go right and might easily end in catastrophe; but if it was a success, she'd be home free.

However, if the man stayed in the piazza—if he got over his fury and wounded pride just enough to realize that she had nowhere to go but right back down—he could simply remain in the square until the campanile closed, waiting her out. In that event, she'd have no choice but to involve the authorities, to throw her stepfather's name around and hope they took her seriously; to hope that the resulting media circus (*Mad Margo in Desperate Cry for Help!*) didn't make it even harder for her to hide once she got away. Venice was a fishbowl, and if the entire world knew to look for her there, Petrenko would have thousands of naively complicit spies on the ground every single day.

"Who was he?" The blond woman asked, cutting through Margo's thoughts, a strange expression on her face as she realized the girl was counting under her breath.

"I've never seen him before," Margo answered truthfully.

Sixteen, seventeen, eighteen . . . "He grabbed me in the piazza, and I didn't know where else to go."

"Well, someone should call the police! You should tell that man"—she pointed a blunt fingernail at the elevator operator—"and get him to do something!"

Margo nodded distantly. *Twenty-six, twenty-seven, twenty-eight . . .* The elevator was slowing, and soon it would be do-or-die. Literally. Did she want him arrested? Was that the smarter plan? Even if someone called the authorities, it was unlikely they'd arrest him; no one in the atrium had seen the fight or the chase, none of them knew he'd fired a gun at her. The police would tell him to leave the area, and he would retreat to the shadows and watch the campanile's only exit. Even if she managed to talk the entire carabinieri into giving her an armed escort back home, Crossbones could tail them to the Palazzo Rambaldo.

No. He had to enter the tower—it was the only way. She just needed to hope that his rage occluded his reason to a point where he was more eager for a quick revenge than for an anticlimactic, if cunning, victory.

"If you'd like—" the woman began, but the elevator stopped, the door opened, and Margo bolted off it before the sentence was finished.

Four to a side, sixteen arched openings looked out on the city as night closed in, the sun little more than a fiery smear on the horizon and the sky a deep purple over densely packed, cinnamon rooftops. Wind swept through the metal fencing that guarded the windows, swirling around the loggia, bringing a chill that made the sweat on Margo's neck prickle like frost.

Thirty seconds. That's how long it took for the elevator to reach the belfry, which meant she probably had less than a minute and a half—allowing for people to get off and on down below—before it returned, possibly bearing Crossbones and his gun. Steeling her nerves, she looked around. Dead center in the drafty room was a small gift shop; but just past it, behind a secured cage door, a metal staircase rose in a tight spiral to the thick shadows above.

It took three hard kicks to snap the lock, the noise explosive and dramatic, calling attention from every corner—but then she was through the door and pounding up the steps on legs weak with exertion, her three-hundred-euro escape hatch weighing her down, echoes pursuing her past the bells and up to the high ceiling.

Above the belfry and below the campanile's jade-green spire, four brick walls formed a cube surrounded by a narrow, open-air walkway. Each of the walls bore a carved relief—the lion of St. Mark facing north and south, while Justice, with her sword and golden scales, faced east and west—and substantial floodlights, bolted to the upright balusters of a stone railing, made the figures glow fiercely against the approaching darkness.

Margo burst out into the air beneath one of the sculpted figures, chest heaving, stars just beginning to poke through the sky over the lagoon. The wind was stronger up here, colder, and she shivered violently. A lifetime had passed since she'd taken in these same views with Axel that afternoon.

The elevator had doubtless reached the ground by now, and she hurried to the south railing. Music blared in the piazzetta, the brightly lit island of Isola di San Giorgio Maggiore and the Santa Maria della Salute throwing their illuminated reflections against the inky water, and Margo crouched beside a massive floodlight that glared up at a relief of St. Mark's lion. She breathed deep into her gut, time ticking down, making herself ready with a series of practiced moves and whispered prayers.

And then she heard it: A distant pounding, growing louder, feet slamming against metal as someone mounted the spiral staircase— Crossbones? A policeman? Rising, Margo peered over the railing, the stone plaza below rising and receding at the same time, and she blinked. Three hundred feet was a long way.

Just as the clanging stopped, a figure lurched into view around the corner, tall and bulky against a roiling, satin sky. She couldn't see his face, or whatever tattoos he might have on his hands, but the wind sweeping between them carried the scent of the canal, and that was good enough. Saying a quick *please* to every deity she could remember from her World Religions class, Margo leaned into the air above the piazzetta—and dropped.

Her conversation with the guy hawking skydiving lessons in the Piazza had boiled down to three matters: Yes, the chute was real; yes, it was packed properly; and yes, she could buy it. She'd carried it into the campanile, put it on in the elevator, and then snapped the clip of the static line to one of the sturdy metal arms anchoring the floodlight to the stone balusters of the railing.

Now, for one dizzying, nauseous moment, she saw her life flash before her eyes; and then the lead line snapped taut, yanking the chute free, and the fabric snapped open to catch the hurtling updraft of air. People in the square shouted, the straps pulling fiercely against Margo's flesh as her plunge slowed, but the ground still rose with alarming speed. Gunshots cracked like thunder, bullets ripping through the canvas of the chute and striking the stone below, drawing belated screams from passersby.

Margo struggled for control as she hurtled downward, rushing at the embankment. People scattered as another shot rang out, smashing into a granite column bearing up a statue of St. Theodore only yards from the water's edge. Ten feet in the air—and fifteen feet from the canal—she pulled the release, dropping hard to the ground and rolling as the chute skimmed blithely on, sailing into the lagoon and drawing more gunfire.

Bruised and breathless, Margo was on her feet in a rattled instant, sprinting east—disappearing into the scattered crowds along the waterfront, drawing curious looks as she bolted for the water taxi stand at San Zaccaria, where a vaporetto was already waiting to depart. Barging through the line with gasping cries of, *"Permesso! Permesso!"* she tumbled onto the craft, winded and shaking.

Not until it pulled away from the dock, engines throbbing as they churned through the water toward the Arsenale and beyond, did Margo finally begin to sob—with relief, with terror, and with something that felt almost like joy.

By the time the boat reached Sant'Elena, she had regained her composure enough to make a call.

Groggy and unhappy, Axel answered on the fifth ring of her third try. "What. The. Fuck?"

"You were right." Margo's voice was hoarse but determined. "I'm coming back to LA. These assholes want to fight, and now so do I."

Los Angeles, California
Three weeks later

THE STREETS OFF LAUREL CANYON TWISTED

into the hills, a tangle of threads cast over the craggy mountain-side, shockingly steep in some places and prone to blind corners. Speeding along Willow Glen, the headlamp of a matte-black Zero DSR motorcycle carved a tunnel through the stygian, late-night darkness. The rider, dressed in black leather and a gleaming helmet, watched carefully as the beam picked out trees, telephone poles, and the occasional car tucked against the downslope side of the road.

Screened by jasmine, manzanita, and cypress, with foundations well below street level, many of the grand homes were nearly invisible at night; but the rider's GPS pinged when the bike reached a wide metal gate—behind which a pale, geodesic dome stood like a lonely igloo in the Southern California moonlight. Bringing the Zero to a stop, swinging a long leg over the seat and removing her helmet, Margo Manning shook out her champagne-blond hair and buzzed the metal call box beside the short driveway.

Since her return from Europe, she'd been staying at the villa with Davon, Georgia, and the Moreaus. When she'd escaped his grasp in Italy, Petrenko had ordered his men to resume their watch of the mansion in Malibu, and now she could only come and go from the canyon under cover of darkness, hidden in the backseat of the Challenger or rendered anonymous by helmet and leathers on Axel's borrowed motorcycle.

It suited her fine. She had few advantages to press, and surprise was the cheapest to come by.

A voice came through the call box speaker. "Yes?"

"It's me," she said, looking into the security camera mounted overhead.

There was no response, but with a buzz and a click, the gate rolled aside, and Margo steered the Zero onto the terrace. Parking the bike, she reached the dome just as its security door opened to reveal James—Reginald Castor's hulking, broken-toothed manservant.

"Long time, no see," Margo greeted him awkwardly. He just stared, his face stony and expressionless, and she cleared her throat. "Not long *enough* no see, but—"

"Did anyone follow you?" James interrupted curtly, eyes on the gate. A gentle wind stroked the hills, making leaves chatter softly, but otherwise the neighborhood was silent.

"No, and I'm insulted by the question." Margo put some frost into her voice. "I mean, sure, the last time we met was because a bunch of mafia guys followed me, and then *you* guys followed me—"

"Inside," James snapped with a short gesture. Shutting her mouth, she stepped past him and into the dome. Just beyond the doorway, a staircase plunged down into the body of the house, and Margo descended with care, watching as honeyed light touched the plush carpets, African art, and priceless antiques she remembered from her previous visit.

Castor, seated exactly where she'd seen him last, was waiting for her. A fire still danced in the hearth, opera music still floated in the air, but this time it was a bottle of sherry and two tiny glasses that sat on the tray between the two wing chairs. With a regal nod, the man gestured to the empty seat. "Margo, so nice of you to come. Did you have any trouble finding the house?"

There was a smug twinkle in his eye, which Margo graciously chose to ignore. Castor was unlisted, and he'd refused her calls for an entire week. It wasn't until she'd managed to plant a device on his car—one she knew he'd find immediately—that he finally accepted she wasn't going to give up.

He filled both glasses. "I hope you had a nice time in Italy. From what I hear, your exit was characteristically dramatic."

"Everything I do is dramatic, Reginald," she answered crisply, "including getting snatched off the street and taken against my will to hilltop mansions."

"And here you are again, like a bad penny." He sniffed the sherry and then slurped some into his mouth, making a rather disgusting noise as he aerated it on his tongue.

Margo narrowed her eyes as she picked up the other glass, seized with the urge to fling its contents into his face. "I feel like you're trying to piss me off, and I don't like it. I went to Italy because I thought it was the best way to keep myself alive, but three men tried to kill me anyway, so I came back. If I'm going to have a short life of looking over my shoulder, I'd rather live it on my own terms."

His smirk dissolved. "Should I assume I'm being recruited to help turn the tables on your enemies?"

"I know this isn't your fight," Margo began restlessly, "but the information you gave me about Brand and Petrenko's dealings is the closest thing I've got to a weapon right now." The sherry was redolent of hazelnuts and citrus; dense, tangy, and sweet on her tongue. She fought the urge to fan herself. "You told me the communiqués you found were incomplete, but I'm betting there's more. I don't think you told me everything you knew."

"Suppose that's true." The man didn't even blink. "If I kept something from you—even after, as you say, 'taking you against your will to my hilltop mansion' so we could speak on the matter—why would I consider sharing it now?"

"Lots of reasons." She'd had plenty of time to consider. "You're former intelligence; you had a career built on stockpiling information and using it as currency." Taking another sip of sherry, Margo tried not to groan out loud. Holy shit, it was good. "I'm a teenager, a socialite . . . not a great risk, on paper."

"To be honest," Castor said bluntly, "I assumed you'd be dead by now."

"You don't trust people, by occupation, and if you were planning a move of your own, there's not a chance in hell you'd share valuable information with someone like me. You told me just enough to see what I'd do with it, and I failed the test."

"You were grieving—"

"I'm *still* grieving." She set her glass down with a *click*. "Addison Brand killed my father. Dad and I didn't always get along, but I'll move heaven and earth to see that Brand gets what's coming to him."

"Justice?"

"Fuck justice. I want revenge."

"You know," Castor said contemplatively, "if you're trying to convince me not to see you as an impulsive risk—"

"If you had a strong move, you'd have made it." Margo's assessment was direct. "But you're not as invested in this as I am. You won't gamble what you can't afford to lose on an uncertain hand." She showed him her palms, fingers wiggling. "I've got no hand, Castor, no cards—but I've got nothing to lose, either." Slugging back the rest of her sherry, she met his gaze. "So give me what you've got. Maybe I can use it. If I fail, you're no worse off than you are now, and if I succeed . . . things improve for both of us."

"You might have a point." Castor crossed his legs, staring

thoughtfully into the fire. "You're right, of course. I found more than I shared—a chain of emails between Brand and Petrenko discussing how to get those guns into the hands of General Tembo's rebels—"

"And that wasn't enough ammo for you?" Just like that, Margo forgot she was trying to sweet-talk the man. "All this time, you've been sitting on clear evidence of an arms deal?"

Calmly, Castor replied, "I've been sitting on evidence that any good lawyer—and they would have the very best—would be able to exclude from the record with hardly any effort at all." He shifted in his chair. "Contrary to what you might think, Margo, I'm not indifferent about this; I did endeavor to collect the proof necessary for decisive action."

"Such as?"

"Did you know that a copy of your father's will—his real, original will—survives?"

She sat up straight in her chair. "How? Where?"

"When your father's attorney was killed, his files were ransacked, and everything with a capacity for electronic storage was taken from the office." Castor poured more sherry into their glasses. "What the police have kept quiet is that, on the same night, burglars broke into Winchester's home with an identical objective." He pushed the glass her way, amber wine and delicate bevels catching the firelight. "Addison destroyed it all, naturally, but not before every bit of information was uploaded to his private server."

"But why?" Margo frowned. "If the whole point was to eliminate all traces of the will, why copy it? Why save it? He could have dissolved those drives in acid or thrown them off the boat to Catalina or something!"

"You're asking why Addison Brand would want the private files of an attorney to some of LA's most powerful citizens?" Castor cocked a brow. "It will take the man months to itemize all the valuable secrets he now has at his fingertips." With a shrug, he added, "In any event, he did eliminate every trace of the real will once he had the data copied over."

"Can we stop playing rhetorical keep-away?" Margo demanded impatiently. "You said there's still a copy of it, so tell me where!"

"On a server at Manning." Castor's eyes were hooded and shrewd, a hint of a smile playing at the corners of his mouth. "Addison did his best, but email is quite tricky. Once you've sent a file, it's not in your computer anymore—or in the computer of the now-deceased client who was the intended recipient."

Margo's mouth fell open. "You mean—"

"I mean that even by deleting Winchester's outbox and having your father's account scrubbed, he still didn't wholly erase their communication. In the weeks before Harland died, he and his attorney exchanged many emails hammering out the details of his legacy." Fingering the cuffs of his shirt, Castor smiled. "Any file sent through a Manning email address is backed up on a company server; and if you're an ex-intelligence officer who has come to suspect something is rotten in the state of Denmark, maybe you find that server and clone its contents."

Margo didn't know whether to hug him or shove him through one of the floor-to-ceiling windows that looked out on his pool and magnificent view. "So you have evidence of an arms deal *and* a tampered will . . . what were you waiting for? A signed confession?"

"In a manner of speaking, yes. At the risk of sounding like a broken record, the emails won't prove that your father didn't change his mind at the last minute. It's still circumstantial, which isn't good enough when the stakes are this high."

"Damn it, I came to you for help." Margo slammed her glass down again, hard enough to send an echo ringing through the spacious room. "You keep baiting me and then telling me what you've got is useless; if you can't help me, just fucking say so!"

"My apologies," the man said with a contrite smile. "It's rare that I have company, and sometimes I like to make the most of it."

"I am literally going to take this glass of delicious sherry and make you eat every last shard of it if you don't get to the fucking point right now," Margo said as politely as she possibly could.

"I told you I used to work counterintelligence. Well, the second the will was read and I smelled a rat, I'm afraid I decided a little espionage was called for," the man revealed smugly. "I bugged Addison's office, and there are recordings of him more or less admitting to having the will forged. Additionally, there *is* still an existing sample of the poison he used to kill Harland, secured in his office safe, along with some bearer's bonds and assorted blackmail material." He swirled his drink, eyes glinting. "And last, I created an echo for his email account, so every message he has sent or received since your father died has been copied to a hidden location."

His tone was smug, but not triumphant, and Margo shifted her jaw. "But?"

"That location is one of Manning's servers." He swallowed the last of his sherry and set the glass aside. "I saved the recordings there, as well, and protected it with my own private firewall. Without my access key, it would be easier for Addison to bicycle to Mars than hack into it." Then his tone became humble for the first time. "All this happened very quickly, Margo—finding his files, transferring data, setting up my relays—but before I could do anything more than glance at it, he detected the intrusion and shut me out.

"He can't prove it was me, but he suspects, and under the guise of new security protocols, he's had my clearance at Manning revoked. Now I need permission and an escort to enter the building, even for board meetings." Castor looked disgusted. "He won't let me out of his sight when I'm on the premises. He knows about the hack, but I don't think he knows his emails are being doubled. Not yet, anyway."

"Are you in danger?" It seemed like the polite thing to ask.

"Three attempts have been made on my life so far," the man answered proudly. "I'd forgotten what it feels like to have someone out there wanting me dead. They've been subtle, nothing overt—so far—but Addison is definitely in the mood for blood."

"Too bad for him." Margo tried to sip her sherry, but it was just too fucking good. Sucking it down, she relegated the glass to the tray again. "I'm keeping mine."

"It won't be easy," Castor said, amused. "You're no more welcome there than I am, and Manning has one of the best security systems in the world. To gain access to what I've hidden in the servers, you won't be able to do it remotely; even with my codes, you'll still need direct access to the mainframe—which means access to the building, which means top-flight gear and a skilled and unquestionably loyal team at your disposal."

Margo settled back into the cushions of her wing chair, reaching for the bottle of sherry to pour one last glass, trying not to sound too smug. "Piece of cake."

37

THREE DAYS LATER, AT SEVEN IN THE MORNING,
Margo's calves burned as she rounded a trail on the north side of
Mount Lee. The city of Burbank cut a neat diagonal across the valley below, with the emerald swath of Forest Lawn Cemetery hugging the base of the slope. It was a clear day, and she paused to drink
from her water bottle. She'd trained hard to get her strength and
stamina back after returning from Venice, and she'd hiked up from
Beachwood Canyon at a grueling pace.

Pushing on, she reached the last switchback, curving around
the summit, and emerged on the south side—where a chain-link
fence was all that stood between her and one of LA's most iconic
landmarks. Impressive even from behind, the letters of the
Hollywood sign staggered in an uneven row just beneath the ridge-
line. The trail continued on, climbing to a radio tower on one side
and a small overlook on the other, where Margo dropped onto a narrow bench and felt her heart thud in her chest.

From this vantage point, she could see all nine of the bone-
white letters; she could see the glittering reservoir of Lake
Hollywood, the dark dome of Griffith Observatory, the dense

greenery clinging to the hillsides—tumbling all the way down to where the city flattened out in a sea of concrete, asphalt, and steel.

Far off, gleaming in the morning light, she could just make out the thunderbolt *M* on the side of the Manning Tower, rising up from Bunker Hill.

Within ten minutes, she heard feet scuffing the path below, and then Dr. Nadiya Khan ascended to the overlook. Dressed in leggings and a track jacket, the woman was barely winded, and she flashed Margo a genuine smile. "The prodigal daughter returns."

"I got tired of people trying to kill me and figured I might as well come home."

Taking a seat beside Margo, the woman stretched out her legs. "I'm glad for it. I hated to see you give up, and I hate to see a villain prevail."

"He might *still* prevail," the girl pointed out unhappily. "I already tried to fight him once, and it didn't go so well. And this time the battle is a little more . . . uphill."

Dr. Khan gave a slow nod. "I did manage to piece together a working model of that poison. Explaining the genetic targeting still requires conjecture I can't fully wrap my head around, but I can convincingly show how the compound could have caused your father's symptoms and general decline."

Margo toyed with her water bottle. "Dr. Khan—"

"Please call me Nadiya," the woman interrupted. "I believe we're past formalities at this point."

"Nadiya," Margo corrected herself, enjoying the feeling of it. She'd looked up to Dr. Khan ever since the woman came to work for Manning—had been impressed by her focus, confidence, and intellect; being on a first-name basis felt like leveling up somehow. "It turns out that complete samples of the poison still exist. I even know where they are."

"You do?" The woman straightened up, eyes flickering; but her excitement evaporated instantly when Margo told her they were in Brand's private safe, and she huffed a defeated sigh. "They might as well be in a stateroom on the lower decks of the *Titanic*, then. Unless you're planning to somehow con Addison into handing them over."

"No, my plan is nowhere near that good." Margo watched a hawk float and then dive. "Grifting isn't my strong suit. I'm better at the direct approach."

Dr. Khan frowned sharply. "You're not considering a break-in at Manning." When the girl didn't respond, Nadiya exclaimed, "Margo, it would be certain death!"

"I have a plan," Margo insisted, but she squirmed a little as she said it.

"That's why you called me, isn't it? You're planning a suicide mission and you need tech for it." The woman pinched the bridge of her nose. "Margo, you have no idea how much things have changed since you left. Addison hasn't been dragging his heels—he's purged the company of anyone who won't swear fealty to him, he's clamped down on the flow of information between departments, and he has half of R&D working on secret projects even the new lab director doesn't know about!" Struggling for a more level tone, she continued, "He's become paranoid, convinced he's surrounded by spies and traitors. The entire executive floor was cleared out, save for his own office, and he has a private firm guarding it around the clock!"

Margo took a moment to absorb all this, and then attempted a smile. "That definitely sucks, but . . . I don't really have a choice." She turned her gaze to the distant skyscrapers of downtown, shining like knives in the morning sun. "The poison isn't the only thing I need that won't come to me. I *have* to go in. And if I don't . . . well, there's already a price on my head, and I'm not going to be able to dodge the men looking to collect it forever."

"Margo . . ." Dr. Khan looked at her imploringly. If there was some additional argument she wanted to make, she failed to find the words. After a moment of silence, she sighed. "The kind of op tech you'd need . . . I don't have many resources these days. There's a little I can do on my own, and favors I can call in, but I don't have unfettered access to a lab anymore. If you need more experimental gear—"

"These friends who owe you favors," Margo cut in. "Do any of them still work at Manning?"

Dr. Khan narrowed her eyes. "A few. But they'd be reluctant to do anything that could cost them their jobs. And they don't have the authority to commission prototypes."

"That's fine. Almost everything on my list is already in the lab vault." And there, at the top of Mount Lee, with a hawk making lazy figure eights above the Hollywood sign, Margo detailed her plan. When she was finished, Nadiya was silent, and the girl pressed, "At most, I'd need you—or someone—to make a couple of minor tweaks to the existing hardware, but otherwise it's all stuff we've used before."

The scientist shifted. "You make it sound so easy."

"I know it won't be."

"It could work, though. If the stars align."

"There are still some crucial kinks to iron out before this is even a possibility," Margo acknowledged.

Nadiya laughed, a bright tinkling sound. "If anyone can pull it off, Margo, it's you."

"You think?" The girl glanced up.

"Look at everything you've pulled off so far." Dr. Khan gestured around, her hands taking in all of LA County. "You shouldn't doubt yourself, you know. Your father had a habit of making everyone feel like a failure so they'd forever struggle to do better; but you deserve to be proud of yourself—to *believe* in yourself. Don't let men or tabloids or even your father's ghost make you question your greatness." Tucking her hands into the pockets of her jacket, Nadiya Khan inclined her head. "I believe in you. And I'll do what I can to get what you've asked for. If I accomplish nothing else in my life, bringing Addison Brand to his knees will be a worthy epitaph."

"I'm so glad," Margo said, letting out a sound that was somewhere between laughter and relief. "If you couldn't help me, plan B was to put on a fake mustache and pass myself off as the new janitor." As they stood to part ways, Margo slipped her sunglasses off and handed them over. "I almost forgot. These shorted out when I, uh . . . took an emergency dip in the pool on our last job. I meant to get them to you right away, but then Dad was hospitalized, and life went a little haywire. Do you think you can fix them?"

"Probably," the woman said with a smile. She tucked them into her pocket. "I'm glad you're back, Margo."

Feeling lighthearted for the first time in a while, the girl grinned. "Me too."

IT HAD BEEN ALMOST TWO YEARS SINCE THE LAST TIME COMing home after school was something Joaquin actually looked forward to. With so many people staying at the villa—filling its empty rooms with music and conversation, chasing away the ugly pall of loss and anger that had smothered their family—it was finally a happy place again. Even if Margo and Axel bickered all the time like an old married couple. And Axel and Davon. And Davon and Georgia.

There were like twenty rooms in the house, and the six of them couldn't stay out of one another's way. It was kind of great.

And then there was Leif. Kissing him that very first time had been like finding out that Hogwarts was real, and Joaquin could go there any time he wanted. Whenever their lips touched, he fell into this dream world where time didn't exist, where no amount of contact was close enough, long enough, or deep enough. For the first few weeks, they'd made out for hours—until they were breathless, their mouths pink and swollen.

Now that they were official, they didn't have to hide from Axel anymore; but Leif didn't have a car and Joaquin couldn't drive, so their time alone was still unjustly rare, and their kisses were hungrier and more aggressive as a result. *Ugh*, just thinking about their tongues pressing together made him hard.

"Why are you sitting like that?" Axel's sour, suspicious question was like a bucket of ice water down Joaquin's pants, and the boy scowled, trying to make it less obvious that he was concealing an erection.

"Why do you care?" Not the most elegant comeback, but he was sick of Axel's sharp-eyed stares and intrusive questions whenever his thoughts wandered to Leif Time.

"Girls, you're harshing my buzz," Davon murmured from the other side of the table, eyes fixed on the pages of a salacious romance novel. Jacinta had a whole library of them, and Davon was determined to read every single one. *Mama, I am sweating to these oldies*, he'd exclaimed once when Axel caught him fanning himself over some steamy bodice-ripper about a horny duchess.

"Axel, leave your brother alone." Perched on a stool by the counter, her dark hair tied back, Jacinta fixed him with an imperious glare. For a moment it was just like old times.

They were all in the kitchen—Joaquin and Axel, Davon and Georgia, Margo, and even Mami—cooking, reading, and/or fantasizing about sex things while they waited for Leif to arrive. The brothers' double share of the LAMFA money had meant more than just keeping the lights on; they'd been able to enroll Jacinta in an experimental treatment program at Cedars-Sinai that was having an incredible effect.

She wasn't cured. They knew that. They'd been warned repeatedly that a complete reversal of her health problems was probably impossible . . . but her good days had gone from once a fortnight to two or three a week, which was more than any of them had dared to hope for.

Tonight, feeling up to it for the first time in years, Jacinta was making her green chile tamales. The air was fragrant with cumin, sharpened by the tang of the peppers, and Bobby Capó played softly on the speakers. Margo, who had recently parachuted out of a three-hundred-foot church tower, was struggling to frost a tres leches cake; Georgia, resplendent in a salmon kimono, grated a block of cheese the size of a toaster while chattering about shows she did in Mexico City in her twenties; and even though Axel was being an asshole, everything finally felt a little bit right with the world.

Then the doorbell rang, and Joaquin's stomach did a flip as he jumped from his chair. "I'll get it!"

Leif stood on the doorstep, blond hair in its usual, adorable disarray, fitted jeans hugging his obscenely muscled thighs—those *thighs*, for fuck's sake—and when their eyes met, they both grinned stupidly. Shyly, Joaquin managed, "Hi."

"Screw the tamales, you look good enough to eat." Leif grabbed a fistful of the boy's shirt, dragging him in for a kiss. Their tongues slipped together exactly the way they had in Joaquin's imagination, and suddenly his briefs were a noose around his dick.

"IS THAT LEIF?" Axel shouted theatrically from the other room, ruining the moment.

"To be continued," Leif whispered in Joaquin's ear, and goose bumps tightened the skin between his shoulder blades while they walked together for the kitchen.

Dinner was boisterous, but by the end, Jacinta was flagging and excused herself for an early night; Georgia graciously announced that she would take care of the dishes and shooed the teenagers outside. A scrim of clouds obscured the night sky above the covered pool, and the air was thick with an ocean scent as they settled around a dusty patio table.

Without ceremony, Margo uncapped a cardboard tube and withdrew a series of diagrams. They were blueprints for Manning Tower, specs for the alarm and camera systems, and information about the servers and computer mainframe. She spread them out and added everything she'd learned regarding the changes made under Brand's direction.

Finally, she revealed her plan, step by meticulous step. It was bold and risky, and depended upon certain factors that weren't guaranteed just yet; but they were used to danger by now, and Joaquin felt a swell of excitement in his chest as he thought about the important role that was slotted for him. *It could work.*

Davon, unsurprisingly, zeroed in on only one specific detail. "So, when you say 'real drag,' do you mean we get to wear heels? Like, *actual* heels, and not those Spice Girl boots you always make us stomp around in?"

"Yes, Davon," Margo said patiently. "I mean heels, dresses, good wigs—the works. Just, you know, remember to keep the dial at, like, six instead of eleven. No fetish gear, no sequins, no feathers."

"You're only saying that because you haven't seen my sexy mermaid-angel look."

"And hopefully she never will," Axel interjected dryly. "I've got kind of an important question. Margo, babe, what you've got in mind is daring as fuck, and if we hit every mark dead-on, we're golden, but . . ."

"I know." Margo rolled up the schematics with a glum expression.

Axel said it anyway. "We don't have enough people."

"I know," Margo repeated. "I've thought about it a dozen different ways, tossed around the variables, but this is the only way it can work." Looking around at each of them, she stated, "We'll need a sixth team member to pull this off."

After a moment, Davon began haltingly, "Georgia is sober now—"

"No." Margo cut him off flat. "She kicked ass in that Boyle Heights throw-down, but she's fifty-whatever and just out of rehab. She's not ready."

"What about Castor?" Axel chewed his lip. "He's a former spy, right? And he wants Brand taken down, too. Maybe he's got somebody. That Frankenstein butler."

"*James?*" Margo shuddered at the thought of a long evening with Castor's pallid, affectless manservant. "We can't trust Castor, not fully. He's still running his own game, and he wants to come out on top whether we pass or fail. Anyone he gave us would be working for him alone."

"So who, then?" Davon asked, a little impatiently. "Who's left?"

Margo took her time resealing the cardboard tube, eyes anywhere but on those of the boys, until she finally stated, "I have someone in mind."

38

THE SANTA MONICA PIER WAS A TWENTY-

four-hour nightmare, clogged with tourists drawn by its carousel, roller coaster, and arcades, with amateur photographers capturing every sunny angle of the arching coastline. Two days after the summit at the villa, Margo pushed through the crowd to the pier's end, leaning against a railing that overlooked the ceaseless waves of the Pacific.

Gulls shrieked and music blared, but she was only there a few minutes before the person she was waiting for sidled up to her, muttering under his breath, "It's the strangest thing. A while back, this girl I know told me she was moving to Italy, maybe forever."

"What a sad story," Margo commented.

"It was," he agreed. "And then today I get this message: *Meet me at the end of the Santa Monica Pier at three p.m. I'll be wearing gold.*" Dallas Yang turned a shrewd eye on her. "I don't know why, but I figured that meant, like, a gold evening gown or something."

Margo cocked her head. "Why would I wear an evening gown at three in the afternoon?"

"I don't know! Why are you dressed like C-3PO?"

Margo looked down at her attire. Aware that she was heading

to one of LA's most heavily touristed destinations, she'd disguised herself as a living statue—a street performer who stood motionless, clad head to toe in clothing sprayed with metallic paint, only moving to give a bow or salute when rewarded with a tip. At the moment, she wore a gold bodysuit, gold boots and gloves, a golden helmet, and her skin was slathered with brassy greasepaint.

"This is what everybody is wearing in Europe these days," she said innocently. "I'm just upholding my reputation as a trendsetter."

Shaking his head, Dallas laughed. "Oh, man. I've missed you, Margo."

"I've missed you, too." They gazed at each other, and she drank in his presence for the first time in two months—the angles of his jaw, his constellation of freckles, the subtle curves of lean muscle that filled out his chest and upper arms—and her nerve endings came alive. Water slapped against the pilings below, and children shouted, but she could still hear her skirt splitting as he lifted her off her feet in Eagle Rock.

"So," he finally began, "at the risk of stating the obvious: You're back! And . . . you're dressed like a robot from outer space. Is there some backstory I should know about?"

"Yeah, there is . . . there's a lot you should know about." Margo exhaled.

She started with the basics: the truth about Harland's death; what really happened to Win; her first conversation with Reginald Castor, and the disastrous confrontation with Brand; and, finally, the actual flight for her life in Venice that convinced her to stop running. When she concluded, Dallas had a hand over his mouth, eyes wide, and she couldn't tell if he was shocked—or if he was afraid she'd completely lost her mind.

"Actually, it was your whole flirting-with-death routine, jumping off that bridge in Pasadena, that gave me the idea for how to escape," she prattled on, nerves taking over her mouth. "And if you don't believe me, I've got a scar I can show you from when I tucked and rolled after hitting the ground." He still didn't say anything, and she swallowed. "You don't believe me, do you?"

"No—I mean, yes, Margo. Yeah. I believe you." Dallas pushed his fingers through his hair, eyebrows tented. "It explains a lot. The way Win fell apart after your dad died? I proofread the original will, and when it came out totally different at the reading, I was . . . you know, *shook*." He gazed out at the scalloped coastline, fading to a blue haze in the distance. "I'm sorry I couldn't tell you. Win wouldn't answer any of my questions, and he warned me that if I said anything to you he would report me to my advisor *and* the Bar Association, and make sure my legal career was over before I even finished undergrad."

Margo didn't quite know how to respond. She'd suspected as much, and had struggled with the impulse to be angry at him for not casting all that aside in the name of what was right and just; but the truth was that even if he had spoken up, it wouldn't have helped. "You couldn't have proven anything anyway. And because both Win and this Nina McLeod are gone now, there's no one to say that Dad didn't want those changes after all."

"Still, I just . . . It's so fucked up." Dallas gave her a stricken look. "I'm sorry, Margo. And I'm sorry you've had to face this on your own. Addison Brand is even worse than I gave him credit for." He picked uncomfortably at the railing. "I don't understand the part about the Russian mob, though. What's their connection to Manning?"

"That's an even longer story." Squaring her shoulders, Margo readied herself to reveal secrets that would put everyone she cared about in jeopardy. Despite having the boys' approval, she'd tried to come up with a new strategy that wouldn't depend on Dallas; she believed that she could trust him—but what if she was wrong? What if the whole truth was more than he could handle?

But there were no other options. For reasons, and for *reasons*, it had to be Dallas.

"I have a plan," she finally said, "to bring Addison down and challenge the will. But in order to make it work, I'll need your help."

"Anything." His answer was immediate. "Whatever you need, I'm with you."

She almost smiled. "Don't be too hasty. I'm not talking about a lawsuit. My idea's a lot more stupid and dangerous than that, so . . . don't agree until you know what you're agreeing to."

"Margo." He slid his hand along the railing until his fingers closed over hers. "Anything."

A current zipped between them, one that tightened Margo's stomach and filled her with tingling memories. His touch made the past two months collapse into nothing; but did he feel the same? They'd never defined their terms, and he'd had no reason to expect her to come back. What if he was already seeing someone else?

"Win was practically a part of my family," Dallas went on. "If Brand killed him, and I can help bring that motherfucker to justice, count me in. No matter what."

Nodding, looking him square in the eye, she said, "I'm breaking into Manning and stealing the proof that he murdered my dad."

He stared at her for a beat. "That's . . . You're joking, right?"

"No joke." Calmly, she explained about the contents of Brand's safe.

"Margo . . ." Dallas struggled. "There must be a zillion security precautions in place there! Even if you still have your father's keys or whatever—"

"I don't," she stated. "From what I've been told, Brand rescinded Dad's security clearance the minute he died, so none of his cards and codes work anymore."

"Okay, so it's even worse than I thought." Dallas sucked in a breath. "What's the play, then? Disguise yourself as a janitor and try to sneak past the guards?" He was joking, but the way Margo laughed seemed to alarm him. "You're acting so blasé about this, Margo. I don't think you know what you're up against!"

"Dallas, I'm acting blasé because I know *precisely* what I'm up against." Steeling herself, she came out with it. "A while ago, you asked me who I am when the cameras aren't on. Well . . . this is it. This is who I am. My friends and I . . . we're thieves."

He stared for a long moment, fighting an uncertain chuckle, waiting for the punch line. Producing her phone, she then drew up articles that had been written about their past jobs: LAMFA, the Chinese consulate, the MGM Grand—one by one, she walked him through every break-in, explaining how each heist was executed, adding precise details the reports had left out.

"I don't understand," Dallas stammered when she was finished, no longer laughing; now he looked frightened, and a chilly thread of apprehension traveled her spine. "You really . . . you *did* all this?"

"I was bored and looking for a way to rebel." Margo's hands were slick inside her tinted gloves. "At first it was just about breaking the rules and feeling like a badass, which is embarrassingly typical, but then . . . well, we had actual reasons to keep going. And it was exciting. And we're *good*." From her pocket, she pulled out an earring—rubies set in solid gold. "I took this from a secured case in a locked room in a fortified fucking *castle* the night my dad was hospitalized. I've studied judo, jujitsu, krav maga, capoeira, and mixed martial arts; I can fire a crossbow, hold my breath for over ninety seconds, and parachute out of tall buildings. And I make a killer red velvet cake." She said the last part with a nervous laugh, watching Dallas's eyes unfocus. When he didn't say anything, she nodded. "You think I made all this up, don't you?"

His eyes snapped to hers, like he was seeing her for the first time. "No. I actually think I believe you. Which is sorta scary." Gazing at the earring, he said, "A castle?"

Without getting into specifics, she described the Topanga Canyon adventure. "It's the reason I'm in disguise. The guy identified me, and now he wants my head on a plate."

"Wow." Dallas's expression was unreadable, his eyes taking her in from head to toe. "You really are full of surprises. And, you know, trouble. Apparently."

Margo felt a little sick. "If this is too much for you, I get it. I wouldn't be bringing my trouble to your door if the situation weren't desperate—and I'm sorry for dumping all this on you and asking you to help me go after Brand. If you've changed your mind, and you need to walk away from me, I get it; but I need you, Dallas. And I really hope you're still in."

"Are you kidding?" He grinned exuberantly, an intensity crackling in his bright brown eyes. "All the risky shit I've done since Win died—jumping off bridges and out of planes—made me realize how bored I am when I'm not about to die. I don't think I'm a normal person, Margo, and you have no idea what it's like to know a girl this sexy, this smart, who's into even more life-threatening shit than me. You bet your ass I'm still in."

Margo laughed, the sound bubbling up on a wave of relief. "Jeez, if I'd known the way to your heart was through your adrenal glands, I'd have told you about this stuff a lot sooner. Most guys aren't really amped to date kick-boxing cat burglars."

The dimples appeared in his cheeks. "I really want to kiss you, Margo Manning."

She grabbed him by his T-shirt and pulled, and he fell into her. Their mouths met, his thumbs on the pulse points below her ears while she felt his heart thumping against her palm, even through her glove—and despite the fact that Dallas was blocking her light, Margo could feel the sun on her face.

When they split apart, still gazing at each other, Margo giggled again. "You've, uh . . . got a little something on your face . . ."

With a lazy smile, Dallas scrubbed gold paint off his mouth with the back of his hand. "So when do we get started?"

"As soon as possible. I know I look fabulous in this outfit, but I want to get the target off my back so I can wear my own clothes again. If my plan works, it'll bring down the guy who's after me as well."

"Where do I come in?"

"We'll talk full details later, but there are a few things you can do right away." Some vacationers crowded the railing, snapping photographs, and Margo stepped closer. In low murmurs, she described what she had in mind. "Do you understand what I'm saying? Can you pull that off?"

"Yeah, for sure." He smiled, his cheeks flushed. "You've got no idea how long I've been waiting for a challenge like this."

She chuckled again, uneasy. "See, now I feel like *you're* the one who's being a little too blasé."

"Not blasé," he promised smugly. "I just know I'm good under pressure."

It was a statement that rang true enough; skydiving wasn't exactly the sport of a guy prone to panic or self-doubt. "Thank you, Dallas. I don't think I can even begin to tell you how much this means to me."

"You don't have to thank me. I've spent months trying to play lawyer, and now I feel like I'm finally doing something I'm cut out for." Gazing at the sparkling ocean, waves breaking into pearly froth, Dallas shielded his eyes. "Just be careful, okay? I've already lost you twice; I don't want to go through it again."

"Neither do I." Margo drew back, wishing she could stay a little longer. "You be careful, too."

Turning, she slipped into the throng of tourists that flocked the pier, head down as she pushed toward the ramp leading to the street.

The ball was rolling; Dallas was on board, the plan was in motion—and it was going to work. She could feel it.

THE GOLD HELMET GLEAMED UNTIL IT WAS SWALLOWED BY the crowd, and Dallas gripped the railing, watching her disappear. A pensive line formed between his eyebrows. Her story had been outlandish, but not so hard to believe—in fact, for reasons he'd kept to himself, he'd almost been expecting it. Pulling out his phone, he dialed a number.

The call was answered on the first ring. "You certainly took your time getting in touch."

"She just left, like, thirty seconds ago," Dallas returned, already irritated.

"My sources tell me she's been in the US for over three weeks now. You expect me to believe that this is the first time she's made contact?"

"You might be surprised to hear this, but I don't care what you believe." Dallas's voice was ice-cold. "You said you'd pay for information about Margo, but let's be clear: I don't *owe* you shit. If you're going to talk to me like one of your flunkies, I formally invite you to go fuck yourself."

"Such language." Addison Brand gave a smarmy chuckle, his breath puffing through the speaker. "You need to relax, Mr. Yang. And you also need to remember that what I offered to pay for was not 'information about Margo,' but specifically—"

"I remember the offer," Dallas stated, "vividly. You said you expected her to plan some kind of move against you . . . and you were right. She just asked me to help her."

"I see." The man was quiet for a moment. "What did you say?"

"What do you think? I said yes."

"So duplicitous." Brand sounded almost pleased.

"Not necessarily. There are lots of reasons to back her horse; I want to know how many reasons you're willing to give me not to."

Brand snorted, pressing his mouth against the receiver. "Listen to me, you chiseling little shit: We already discussed this, and you know exactly what the amount is."

"I know what it was then," Dallas replied, "but inflation is a bitch."

There was a long silence, and then Brand came back. "I'm not paying you a dime until I know your intel is worth something."

"And I'm not delivering shit until I've seen enough untraceable currency with my own two eyes to convince me you're playing ball." Dallas switched hands with his phone. "No shady bank transfers, no suitcases full of dye and explosives . . . I'll bring my own bag, you'll give me clean currency, and I'll tell you what you need to know."

There was another, lengthier pause. Then, "Fine. It's a deal. Come by my office tomorrow."

When he hung up, Dallas tucked his phone away and stared off at the shoreline, his jaw tense and his eyes trained on the gulls spiraling over the bluffs.

Trying not to think too hard about what he'd just done.

39

THE VALLEY ALWAYS SEEMED TO BE TEN DEGREES
hotter than the rest of Los Angeles, and the next afternoon was no
exception. It was April, and temperatures were already nudging
ninety in Van Nuys; by the height of summer it was going to be
cooler in the earth's core than on its surface—at least in any neighborhood Davon and Georgia could afford.

They'd already looked at three listings that day, one in Sun
Valley and two in Reseda—the twenty-sixth, twenty-seventh, and
twenty-eighth apartments they'd seen in total—and it was beginning to feel hopeless. Rents rose by the hour, and even with the
remaining money from the LAMFA job, many places were still out
of their long-term price range. And then there were the application
fees they had to turn over for the privilege of having their credit
scores rejected by faceless rental corporations; after their tenth such
wasted expense, they'd become a lot less enthusiastic about the
search.

When their last dismal visit concluded, Davon announced that
they were done for the day. To cheer them up, instead of returning
straight to Malibu, he drove to the Japanese Garden in Woodley

Park. Six and a half acres of carefully manicured greenery, stone pathways, and man-made pools, it sounded like exactly the kind of peace and serenity that would clear their minds.

What he'd failed to take into account was the water reclamation plant that made the site possible; expansive, retro-futuristic, and industrial, it sat like an abandoned UFO on one side of the garden, its glass-paned frontage visible from everywhere but inside the bathroom. The gummy stench of algae clung to the air, ducks and egrets defecated on the trails, and Davon struggled to sound chipper as he cooed over the budding cherry trees.

Georgia was uncharacteristically silent, her expression drawn, and eventually Davon ran out of things to say. When they came upon a model teahouse, with a spacious interior of bamboo floors and paper screens, they sat and looked out at plants flowering around a gray-green pond.

Davon was just about to ask if something was wrong when Georgia spoke. "I want to come back to Tuck/Marry/Kill, Davon. I need to be working."

"I don't know, Mama." He eyed his drag mother unhappily, wishing he could cancel the conversation. "Are you sure that's such a good idea?"

"You mean, is it a good idea for a recovering addict to work in a bar? Probably not." She snorted a laugh. "But as hard as sobriety is, not performing is worse. I know you're nervous about me relapsing, but I can handle it. I'm okay."

"No offense, girl, but I've heard those words before." Davon couldn't quite meet her eyes. "And we got a lot going on here. Let's take care of our housing crisis before we focus on jobs, you know?"

"If I started working again, we'd look better on those applications."

"That's true. But if you *did* relapse . . . Mama, you can't ride this roller coaster forever. It was kind of a miracle that we were able to make Cornerstone happen. Next time, if there is a next time . . ." He trailed off, squirming a little.

Georgia took a moment before speaking, her voice controlled. "Davon, I've been fucked up on booze and pills for most of my life, and getting my head clear for the first time in about thirty-odd years helped me face some things I've been avoiding." She plucked a little nervously at her collar. "Drugs are an easy escape from stuff that's hard, or scary, or confusing, you know? Whenever something tipped me into the red, I could always disappear into my downers." She crossed her ankles, then uncrossed them again. "These past two months, I haven't had my escape hatch to jump through. When confusing shit came up, I had to deal with it, and . . . and I accepted something that I need to share."

Davon looked over at her and realized she was trembling. Placing his hand over hers, he squeezed. "Mama, you can tell me anything, you know that. I love you, you messed-up bitch."

Georgia started to laugh, and a tear slipped out of her eye. Swiping it away, she smiled bravely. "Drag saved my life, you know? I hated the world and everything in it, and I hated myself until I found Georgia Vermont. The first time I beat my face and put on a pair of heels, I saw God, and I'm not kidding. When I'm onstage, I'm *alive*, Davon. That's the only time I feel like myself, like I fit my skin." Taking a shuddering breath, she paused, shifted, and then blurted, "I'm not a man. Not a man in a dress, or a man who just prefers lady pronouns, or any other kind of man at all. I'm just not."

"Okay," Davon answered, relieved to his very core that the confession had nothing to do with cancer. Absorbing this information wouldn't be a huge challenge, all things considered. Lots of trans girls found themselves in the drag community. "So, you're a woman. That's great! I'm glad you told me. I mean, this a good thing. Listen, on the way home, maybe we should pick up a cake and have them write 'It's a Girl' on—"

"I don't think I'm a woman, either," Georgia interrupted, and Davon shut up, because this was a twist he hadn't expected. His drag mother watched her feet. "I should say, I *know* I'm not a woman. Not exactly. I guess I feel more like one than a man, but most of the time . . . most times I'm somewhere in between? The only thing I've never felt like at all is someone called 'Stanley Darga.'"

"Okay," Davon repeated, nodding. "Well, fine. Because you're Georgia Vermont, and you're too fabulous to be contained by anything as boring as a gender binary. We'll get that cake and have it say 'It's Georgia' with a big old exclamation point, because fuck it, let's celebrate!"

"Davon, I'm being serious," Georgia murmured uncomfortably.

"So am I!" He took her hands and met her eyes. "This is a big deal, Mama! You're sober and figuring shit out; you are Georgia Vermont, Somewhere in Between; you're my fucking hero, don't you know that?" With a heartfelt smile, he said, "You're my person, and I only get one of you. So sue me if I want to make a thing out of it."

"Do you really mean that?"

"Of course I mean it! I'm sorry if I'm doing a bad job of saying what it is I want to say. I just love you, and I support you, and I'm happy as fuck that things are finally falling into place." Davon got to his feet. "And I won't push you into anything that makes you uncomfortable, only it seems to me that we *could* be eating cake in Malibu right now, but instead we're roasting alive in motherfucking Van Nuys."

"I'm lucky I met you, Davon." Georgia wiped her eyes as she stood up. "I meant what I said before, though. I'll always be an addict, but I'm done trying to escape. I need Tuck/Marry/Kill. I need to be doing drag again."

Davon tossed his hands out. "Well, shit, you don't need my permission. I'll worry about you, but I'd worry about you anyway." With his arm linked through hers, they started down the path to the garden's entrance. "Truth is, the show's just not the same without Georgia Vermont."

"Of course it's not," she stated indignantly. "What's this 'not the same' bullshit? It's my fucking show! What have you done with it?"

Davon patted her hand, his smile hardening in place. "It's great to have you back."

SALMON-HUED CURTAINS UNDULATED IN THE SALTY BREEZE, filtering the light and glazing the walls in rich, decadent warmth. The room was large, but bare as a monk's cell, and every squeal of the bedsprings echoed like a falcon's cry.

"Shit, we really need to stop," Leif panted, trying to stifle an inappropriate laugh. "There's no way your mom can't hear us. The *Valley* can probably hear us!"

"My mom's asleep on the other side of the house." Joaquin was breathless, his lips rosy and swollen, and he dug his long, slim fingers deeper into his boyfriend's hair. "We could blow up a tank in here and she wouldn't know." Primly, he added, "And anyway, we're not even naked."

He was right, technically; they were still in their underwear. Their legs tangled together, their chests pressed so close Leif could feel the boy's heartbeat against his own, they were making the absolute most of their time together.

The countdown was already on to the break-in at Manning. Best-case scenario: They all got a new lease on life; worst-case: Well . . . in the event of the worst-case, Leif wanted to make sure he got as much Joaquin Time as possible beforehand.

Leaning back in, he nipped his boyfriend's chest and collarbone, kissed his way up the steady pulse in the boy's neck, and growled when their mouths met again. With a grunt, Leif hoisted Joaquin's knees higher, so their bodies would fit together a little tighter—so he could eliminate just a little more space between them.

Soft music played, his blood hot and close to the surface, and when Joaquin's hand slipped down along his back—reaching the waistband of his underwear before stopping—Leif expelled an agonized breath. "You can keep going. If you want to."

After a moment, the hand dipped farther, finding the curve of ballet-hardened muscle with a cautious squeeze. Leif growled again, sinking his teeth into Joaquin's bottom lip, and the boy flinched, pulling his hand back.

Shoving himself up, Leif blinked with concern. "Sorry—was that too much? Did I hurt you?"

"No, it felt good, I just . . ." Joaquin swallowed. "I liked it. I just . . . I mean . . ."

"What is it?" Leif eased into a sitting position. Dust motes drifted in the ginger light, and Joaquin's face was flushed, his eyes on the wall. "Did I do something wrong?"

"No, I just . . ." His boyfriend hesitated. "I'm not sure how far I want to go. What I'm ready for, I mean. And I wanted to say something, before . . ."

"Yeah, that's okay," Leif cut him off with a reassuring smile, stroking Joaquin's leg a little. "I didn't mean to—I don't have any expectations, or whatever, you know? I just like being with you."

"I know." The boy still wouldn't meet his eyes. "But you're used to dating guys with more experience than me. I mean, *you've* had more experience than me. I mean . . ." He covered his face and groaned. "Leif, you're the first person I've even kissed, okay?"

"I am?" Leif asked, both surprised and somehow aroused by the revelation.

"I kissed a girl in the eighth grade, on a dare," Joaquin amended miserably, "and we both thought it was gross. And then Dad got arrested, and after that . . . I mean, the only people who talk to me at all are these scary foreign exchange girls, and all they're interested in are my eyelashes, for some reason."

"Your eyelashes are really pretty," Leif pointed out.

Joaquin groaned again but uncovered his face. "This is the most I've ever done. With anybody. And . . . I think I want to go slow?"

"Okay. Slow is okay."

"Really?" Joaquin struggled up onto his elbows, the muscles in his stomach flexing, the rich sunlight gleaming on his swollen lips. "Because I know you're used to more, and I don't want you to be frustrated, or—"

"I'm not." Leif looked him in the eye. "Look, I think about it, maybe a lot—and it would be great; but that's not the reason I'm with you. And there's no pressure, or whatever." Rubbing his thumb in a circle over his boyfriend's knee, he hitched a shoulder. "My experiences with other guys were about those relationships. Or about me."

Coming to LA from his stifling hometown had been like emerging from a cave and feeling the sun for the first time; Leif couldn't get enough. He wanted to bathe in it, to roll around in it as much as possible. Safe from his parents and Pastor James, he'd finally been able to free himself, and he'd gone through sort of a slutty phase. He'd made good choices and bad ones, and only a handful he actually regretted—like hooking up with his "straight" roommate—but what he felt for Joaquin went beyond self-exploration or horniness.

"I'm with you because you're cute and funny, and you make that adorable noise when I tickle you," he explained softly. "I'm with you because you make me feel good. Because you make me happy. And I can wait until you're ready. It's worth it."

"I make you happy?" One corner of Joaquin's sulky mouth turned upward, and the room got even warmer. He was so beautiful, with his dark eyes and long lashes and coy smile; how had nobody kissed him before?

Two days earlier, on the phone with his parents, Leif had

opened his mouth to tell them he was gay—and instead, another lie popped out. Temporarily freed from the weight of needing their money, and with another perilous job on the horizon, he'd felt reckless and ready; but he hadn't been able to go through with it.

At sixteen, even with his tuition settled for the year, he still needed their permission to stay at the academy; at any time, if they chose, they could simply call the registrar's office and have him unenrolled. With his secret out, he'd be shunned and scorned back home, mocked by the creative bullies and assaulted by the uncreative ones. He knew how to fight now, thank God, but he would never go back there. Never. Not if he could help it.

"*You won't win every fight,*" Margo told him during his first training session, just after he'd been recruited, "*but the key to success isn't dominating every single battle; sometimes it's retreating—living to fight another day when the odds are better. Find your strengths, learn your weaknesses, pick your battles.*"

So he was picking his battles. He'd walk this tightrope for two more years, until all he had to fear was rejection, and then try again. In the meantime, he'd invented a girlfriend.

Part of him was ashamed for lying; but another, greater part of him was so relieved at keeping them away from a joyfulness they would surely obliterate, that it made him break out in a cold sweat. Gazing down at his boyfriend, his heart full, Leif managed, "Yeah. You make me really happy."

"Good. Because you make me happy, too." Joaquin reached up, pulling Leif closer. "And just because I'm not ready to do *everything* doesn't mean I'm not ready to do *anything.*"

Leif hesitated. They were so close together he could feel Joaquin's breath against his lips. "Um. What does that mean?"

"I could tell you," his boyfriend answered, his hand sliding down Leif's back again, "or I could show you."

His fingers moved underneath the waistband of Leif's underwear this time, skin slipping across skin—and when their mouths met, Joaquin was the one who growled.

His plastic chair was uncomfortable, and the overhead fluorescents cast everything in a harsh, pitiless light. The room had a strange smell, too, a mix of bleach and body odor, and Axel's stomach revolted against it. A lifetime had passed since an armed guard led him into this windowless cement box, and for the millionth time, he asked himself what the hell he was doing—cursed himself for not backing out while he still could.

He'd had to make an appointment for this, spend long nights dreading it in advance, and make the drive out with his nerves rattling together like coins in a pouch. It was more than an hour from Malibu to Terminal Island, the federal penitentiary where Basil Moreau had been ordered to fulfil his debt to society, and Axel had talked himself out of turning back at least once every minute of it.

It was all Davon's fault, with his constant prodding and quiet *suit yourself* shrugs. He'd planted the seed of this idea, and now its roots had grown so robust they were cracking through the pavement of Axel's thoughts. *You obviously have a lot to say to him, and it might do some good to let it out.* Finally, caught in a vulnerable, tequila-fueled delirium, he'd let his friend with benefits talk him into it.

It was a sick joke that his father was confined so close to home. The man had spent the last of the Moreaus' savings on a high-priced lawyer, who'd convincingly sold the judge on Terminal Island. Wringing pathos from Jacinta's chronic illness and the boys' ages, the attorney had begged the court to show mercy on Basil's family— to not punish them by placing the man somewhere they'd never get to see him.

The last time Axel had set eyes on his father was at the sentencing, where Basil Moreau had sobbed over his own fate and given not a single thought to what would happen to his wife and sons. If the judge had asked for the family's input, Axel would have suggested stranding his dad on the Bikini Atoll—or maybe Neptune—somewhere far enough away that they had a chance at forgetting he ever existed.

Now, nearly two years later, Axel fidgeted in an unstable chair, staring at his hands, waiting for the man he hated most in the world. His fingernails were varnished a bright red—Liesl Von Tramp's color—and he dug them into the flesh of his palms, trying to leach some strength from his alter ego.

Drag wasn't a disguise or an illusion; it was armor. When he stepped onstage, Axel became someone fierce and untouchable, a force of nature that gave no fucks and couldn't be bothered. He brought hecklers to their knees, read homophobes until they needed the Da Vinci Code to piece their dignity back together, and faced the worst with a smart remark and a tongue pop. Liesl was both shield and weapon, the only refuge he'd had from these ugly years. To capture at least a little of her magic, he'd painted his nails—and contoured his eyebrows, because he wasn't an animal—but now, staring into an abyss that stared right back, it suddenly wasn't enough.

An abrupt *click* shattered the peace in the room, a metal door swinging open, and Axel's heart spiraled up his throat as a burly guard entered with a tall, slim figure in a prison jumpsuit. He'd lost some weight, along with most of the color from his hair, but otherwise Basil Moreau looked remarkably the same: the dark eyes, the square chin, the healthy tan. Unaccountably, Axel began to shake.

"No touching," the guard reminded them as Basil sat down.

"Axel. Wow." A bright grin lit his father's face, one so familiar it made the boy's chest ache. "You look— You're a man now. You must have grown six inches since the last time I saw you."

"Three." Axel's voice was all wrong, a tune played on an unfamiliar instrument. "I've only grown three inches."

"Three." Basil had his hands on the table. They were veined and strong, the nails neatly trimmed, and Axel frowned. "I think about you all the time, Axel. All the guys here are sick of my stories by now—right, Fields?" This question was for the guard, apparently, who mumbled a reply. "How's your mother? I've been worried about her."

"Mami's okay." The words came out automatically, his brain sluggish, trapped in a strange bubble. "We got her into an experimental treatment program. It's helping."

"That's great." Basil's smile spread wider. "Maybe she can come visit soon, too. You don't know how much I've missed you guys. Tell your mom and Quino that I—"

And that's when the bubble popped. "I didn't come here to take your fucking messages!" Basil fell silent, his expression shuttering, and Axel dug his neon-red fingernails into his palms until the skin began to split. "Is that all you have to say? 'How's your mom? Tell her blah-blah-blah?'" Rage burned his stomach, made his vision sparkle. "Do you have any idea what we've been through? What we're *going* through because of you?"

"Axel—"

"Stop saying my name! You don't deserve to say it!" His eyes filled and his throat closed, choking his words. "How could you do it? How could you?"

"Axel, I— You . . ." Basil trailed off, shaking his head. "I don't have an excuse. I made a terrible mistake, and I—"

"No." Axel swiped at his tears with unsteady hands. "A 'mistake' is when you type your address wrong, or wave to a stranger at the mall. It's not when you spend an entire fucking *decade* stealing money from everybody you know, and leave your family behind to pay the price!" Breathing hard, he struggled for control. He couldn't fall apart until he got this out. "Do you even care what's happening to us? You're down here making friends and keeping up your tan, while we're hiding in the dark from the enemies you made! We still get death threats taped to the gate every other week. Did you know that?"

"No. I didn't," Basil answered, subdued.

"Of course you didn't." Scorn rubbed his throat raw. "You ruined us. You ruined *everything*, and all you have to say is, 'tell your mom I miss her'? What about *sorry*? What about, 'Sorry for the anchor I tied around your necks and the ocean of liquefied shit I dumped you into before I went off to Club Fed'?"

When he finished, his words rang off the concrete walls, deadly arrows driving back and forth. Basil was quiet for a moment, his lips pale. "Is that what you came to hear? That I'm sorry? Because I am, Axel. I don't have any self-defense to offer. I stole because it was easy—because there were things I wanted, and I had clients with money they would never miss." He turned his hands over in a helpless shrug. "But you have to know that I never meant for you and Quino and your mother to get caught up in it. Never."

"Nobody ever means to get caught," Axel retorted bitterly.

"No. You're right." The man sagged, pulled down by unseen hands. "I was selfish. I didn't think about anything but what I wanted and how I could get it."

"Don't you dare agree with me." The surrender in his father's voice was almost more than Axel could stand. "We are *not* on the same side!"

"But you're right." Basil spoke softly. "If I hadn't gotten arrested, I'd probably still be doing it—because it was working, and because . . . because I was greedy." He was quiet for a long moment, the room breathing bleach and sweat, thickening the air. "I never gave a thought to the consequences of what I was doing until it was too late to make things right again. But I would do anything to change what's happened, Axel. I would."

"Yeah, no shit." Axel tried to sound hurtful, but he could barely breathe. His vision was loose and wet, his throat knotting around every syllable as he battled his tears.

"I would." His father turned his hands over again, his palms as bare as the regret in his expression. "I've had nothing but time to think about what I've lost, and what I did to deserve losing it; and out of everything they took—the cars, the yacht, the properties, even my freedom—all I really miss is you." There was no guile in Basil's tone, no silver edge to his tongue. "You, your brother, your mom . . . you guys are what mattered, and I know I can't make up for what I did. But I'm sorry, Axel. I'm really and truly sorry."

Axel could barely keep his chin steady. His mouth opened and shut, working to produce the three words he'd come all the way from Malibu to say. He'd meant for them to be cold and strong, but when he finally got them out, they were soft and broken.

"I hate you."

"I know." Basil nodded, his eyes filming over, his lips twitching down. "I know. But I love you, Axel. I love you so much."

The boy's fingers released, Liesl's bright red support slipping away, and he buried his face in his hands. A sob wrenched his body, and then he was weeping openly, tears slipping over his palms and trailing down his wrists. Rough and high-pitched, his muffled reply was barely audible.

"I love you, too."

The executive floor at Manning was a carpeted graveyard—a honeycomb of abandoned cubicles drenched in silence, set against a backdrop of windows gazing out at the San Gabriel Mountains. Five men, as large as the one who'd escorted Dallas up on the elevator, lounged restlessly in what had once been the office space of the CEO's administrative assistant. Seated in swivel chairs or leaning against flimsy workstation walls, they glared at the boy with theatrical mistrust as he was squired to Addison Brand's door.

After some complicated call-and-response, the door unlatched, and Dallas entered Brand's sanctum sanctorum. It was a throne room usurped, and the air was laced with the stale reek of paranoia. Pale and edgy, seated behind his desk in a high-backed ergonomic chair, Addison greeted the boy with a rictus grin. "So. Tell me about Margo."

"Money first," Dallas replied coolly, slamming a metal briefcase down on the desktop and popping it open to reveal a hungry interior. "You promised me untraceable currency, and I want to see it before I give you what I have. I'm not getting screwed here."

Brand laughed, a sound like ice being chipped off a gravestone. "This isn't some frat house poker game, Mr. Yang. One word from me, and those men will gladly smash a window and throw you fifty-four stories down onto Grand Avenue. We're not negotiating."

"Your call, I guess." Dallas swallowed, channeling his inner James Bond. "But forty-five minutes from now, a video message I made explaining the nature of this meeting will pop up all over the internet, and it might be inconvenient for you if I'm too dead to say it was a joke." Pointedly, he crossed to one of the windows and leaned against the glass with a toothy smile. "Anyway, I'm not scared of heights—or death, either, really. So pay me or kill me, but if you pick Door Number Two you'll find out what Margo's planning the hard way."

"For fuck's sake." Brand rolled his eyes with a disgusted grunt. "The problem with your generation is that you watch too many superhero movies, where every self-destructive gesture has an accompanying swell of dramatic music." Shoving to his feet, he turned to an oil painting hung behind his desk in a thick, silver frame.

Swinging it open like a door, he revealed the metal face of a safe with an electronic keypad. "I've no intention of dishonoring our agreement. But you only get paid if I think the information is worthwhile."

As he reached up to enter the safe's access code, Brand angled his body to block Dallas's view of his fingers. He had it opened and closed in a matter of seconds, producing a bulging envelope with one hand as he swung the painting back into place with the other.

He gave Dallas enough time to confirm that the package contained genuine bearer's bonds in the amount they'd agreed upon, and then took them back, holding them ransom while he waited to be impressed. Seated again, the boy grinned. "She's planning a three-pronged attack. I don't know all the details yet, but I can give you the basics."

"And?"

"The first step involves Nina McLeod, the nurse—"

"I know who you mean," Brand cut him off impatiently, "and I also know there isn't a chance in hell of Margo finding Ms. McLeod, or compelling her testimony against me. If this is all—"

"That's not entirely true." It was Dallas's turn to interrupt, and he savored the taste of the silence that followed. "Maybe she can't find the woman, but words are easy. A sworn affidavit bearing McLeod's signature, confessing to her role in covering up Harland Manning's will, could be damning, for instance—and Margo knows a former legal intern who could forge just such a document *and* who has access to the woman's signature."

Brand flexed his hand until the ligaments popped. "It'll never hold up in court."

"Doesn't have to." Dallas shrugged. "Margo only needs it to be seen. In two weeks, when copies arrive at all the media outlets, they'll be everywhere overnight; and even if the document is fake, the accusation is true, and lots of people will start talking. Margo's a celebrity, don't forget. A bereaved daughter who can cry on cue is prime-time gold."

"Parlor tricks." Brand waved a dismissive hand—but his fingers twitched.

"The night before the affidavit goes live, she plans to break into Manning—"

"*Here?* Is she out of her mind?" Brand actually laughed. "It's ludicrous! She'll get shot trying to enter the lobby. Honestly, she'd be doing me a favor!"

"You shouldn't underestimate her," Dallas warned calmly. "If she wants to get in, she will. But she doesn't even need to take anything for the play to be a success—that's what so brilliant about it."

"What does that mean?"

Keeping his eyes on the man, Dallas replied, "Someone told her there was evidence here, in the building, linking you to Harland's death."

Brand huffed, snatching a ballpoint pen off his desk. "Who? Who said such a thing?"

"She hasn't told me—yet—but the point is, she thinks this person was lying. She's convinced the evidence exists, but that you've got it at home." He grinned when some of the color drained out of Addison Brand's face. "So: step three. With you rattled and against the ropes, focused on the Manning break-in and the media circus over the affidavit, she strikes where you live, gets what she really wants . . . and buries you with it."

"No, no, no." Brand shook his head compulsively. "She'll never get into my home. It's almost as protected as . . . as . . ."

"As Arkady Petrenko's castle?" His tone was innocent, but the question connected like a slap to the face. Brand's jaw clenched, his knuckles going white where he gripped the pen, and Dallas leaned across the desk to pluck the envelope of bearer's bonds from the man's distracted grasp. "Anyway, I better take my money and go before those video messages start uploading. Pleasure doing business!"

Brand sat quietly as the boy stashed the envelope in his briefcase and started for the door, but then found his voice at last. "Mr. Yang. I don't care how it happens, but Margo Manning doesn't survive the break-in here at Manning. Is that understood?"

"Sure," Dallas replied, looking back with an easy smile. "And I hope *you* understand that I don't actually work for your ass. You paid me for services rendered, and if you want more, you better have another offer. I'll wait to hear from you."

Exiting the office, he slammed the door on Addison Brand's brooding silence and started for the elevator, the briefcase handle biting into his fingers.

40

THE GROUND DIPPED AND THEN ROSE, A WAVE covered in blossoming chaparral, the petals like sunshine in a children's picture book. Point Dume—a high bluff kissed by salt air, with a vista encompassing nearly all of Malibu—was one of Margo's favorite spots. She'd picked it for this rendezvous because, in case things went poorly, she wanted an excuse to see it one last time.

Following a trail through the flowers, she ascended to the dusty clearing at the summit, and drank in the cool morning breeze. To one side, the ocean pushed against the crescent of Dume Cove, foam rolling over shaded sand; to the other, the golden ribbon of Zuma Beach snaked up the coastline; and dead ahead, the Pacific stretched out to the horizon, an endless ream of shining blue silk.

Two families were already there, snapping selfies against the shoreline, and Margo ducked past them in her dun-colored wig—crossing to where Nadiya Khan already stood at the edge of the bluff. A large beach bag at her feet, the woman kept her eyes on the water even as she murmured a surreptitious hello.

"It's my first time up here," Nadiya remarked. "The view is beautiful."

"You should see it at sunset."

"I'll come back." Dr. Khan fell quiet as a child scampered past them with a shout, and then gestured to her oversized bag. "I almost can't believe it, but I managed to get everything you asked for."

"I'm impressed," Margo said, filled with a purifying relief, "but not surprised."

"You should know, the key card is low-level access, and only works for the parking deck. All other parts of the building require security clearance, and entries are recorded and identified by the system—meaning a cloned or borrowed card would incriminate the owner." She gave the girl a look. "There were no volunteers."

Margo nodded slowly, fighting the urge to dig into the bag and examine the goodies. They were quiet a moment, watching surfers rise and fall with the waves. "What's the latest on the refugees?"

A smile lit Dr. Khan's features, and she glanced over. "We've saved nearly a hundred people in the past few months. The money you provided paid for a lot of new futures."

"I'm glad."

"Me too." Her smile faded gradually. "It never feels like enough, though, does it? Money buys things, but not peace. Not empathy or human kindness."

Just like that, Margo felt every bruise she'd gotten while battling Win's assassin, her gut-punched breathlessness over the Malawi arms deal, and the steady throb of Addison Brand's carotid artery beneath her itchy fingers. "Do you really believe in human kindness?"

"Of course." Dr. Khan regarded her with surprise. "I see it every day in the people who risk their lives for the refugees, in those who give to the homeless, in children who are selfless because they haven't been taught selfishness yet . . ." Her cheeks flushed. "Perhaps I'm oversimplifying. But I believe everyone is capable of charity. My faith demands it."

"I wish . . ." Margo struggled for words. "I wish I shared your conviction."

They watched the horizon for a while longer, and then Margo picked up Dr. Khan's bag and started down from the bluff.

FOUR DAYS LATER, FRIDAY EVENING, MARGO AND THE BOYS gathered in the abandoned dining room at the villa; the sun slowly bled out over the purple-black ocean outside, while the air around them was so charged they could almost hear it hum. Once Nadiya's contributions had been inventoried, Margo revealed a few party favors of her own.

"I wish we had a little more time to practice with this stuff," Axel remarked wistfully, inspecting an item he would soon have to use. "And maybe more of these things. Is this really all you were able to get? Because—"

"On short notice? Yeah, that's it." She didn't mean to be brusque, but she was on edge, worry sinking its teeth into her gut. Too many things could go wrong, even with their numbers bumped up to six. Supposedly up to six, anyway—Dallas still hadn't arrived yet. "When you're paying cash for untraceable weaponry, sometimes you just get what you get."

Margo resumed pacing, rerunning the strategy in her head, time slipping away while they waited—and then, finally, there came the hollow *click* of the front door, Dallas's voice resounding through the cavernous shell of the villa, "Uh, hello? Anybody home?"

"Back here," Margo called out, more relieved than she cared to admit. She hadn't realized it until that moment, but she'd been afraid he wouldn't show. "Follow the light."

His footsteps thumped closer, and the boys all turned to the door, watching like spaniels awaiting the mailman until Dallas appeared. "Uh, hi! Sorry I'm late."

He sketched a wave with one of his broad hands, flashing a sheepish grin. Leif stared, Axel smoothed his hair reflexively, and Davon made a squeaking sound in the back of his throat. Grinning smugly, Margo announced, "Boys, this is Dallas. Dallas, these are the boys. Leif, Joaquin, Axel, and—"

"*Dibs*," Davon announced immediately. "I call dibs!"

Axel whirled on him. "Excuse you, sis, I saw him first! He was at the funeral—"

"Excuse you both, but you can't call dibs on a *person*," Margo interrupted, appalled. "Especially not using my dad's funeral to do it!" When they were suitably chastened, she added, "Besides, *I* saw him first."

"Spoilsport," Davon grumbled, giving Dallas a coy smile anyway.

With the team fully assembled for the first time, Margo walked them through the plan again. They were only going to get one shot at this, and they couldn't afford to be lazy about it. When she was sure every step was memorized, she looked each one of them in the eye. "Unless anyone has questions, I guess that's it. Time to suit up."

No hands were raised; and then, as the boys left the room, tossing interested looks back at their new teammate, Dallas turned an amused smile on Margo. "What about you? Don't you usually 'suit up'?"

"Not this time," she answered. She'd considered doing her Miss Anthropy drag, but ultimately decided against it. The building they were breaking into had her name on it, and she intended to go in as herself. Gesturing to the canvas bag over Dallas's shoulder, she asked, "You bring me anything?"

"Only what you asked for. You want to see it now? Or—"

"Gimme." She wiggled her fingers eagerly.

"I did a pretty excellent job, if I must say." Dallas went on without a trace of modesty, producing a tablet computer from the bag. "I think you'll be pleased."

The screen came alive, showing the first frame of a paused video: Addison Brand, seated behind his desk—Harland's desk—scowling into the lens. Margo pressed play.

"*You promised me untraceable currency, and I want to see it before I give you what I have. I'm not getting screwed here,*" Dallas's voice sounded through the tablet's speaker, coming from behind the camera.

"*This isn't some frat house poker game, Mr. Yang,*" Brand replied with a laugh. The high-def image was crystal clear, and Margo's pulse picked up.

"This is good." She zoomed in, the details staying crisp and precise. "The quality is fantastic. But did you—"

"Skip ahead," Dallas advised softly, his breath against her ear, and goose bumps pebbled the back of her neck. He reached around her and tracked forward until Brand rose from his chair, turning to the painting on the wall. Margo held her breath as he revealed the safe.

"*I've no intention of dishonoring our agreement,*" Brand was saying, "*but you only get paid if I think the information is worthwhile.*"

"Dallas, he's blocking the camera!"

"Watch."

On-screen, Brand glanced over his shoulder and then moved to block Dallas's sight line from the window—and in so doing, cleared the sight line of the tiny camera that had been hidden inside the boy's briefcase. Margo nearly gasped as she watched Addison tap out his private code on the safe's keypad, each stroke captured perfectly. Replaying it again in slow-motion, she memorized the combination.

"I did good?" Nervousness underscored Dallas's question, and Margo looked up at him with the moon in her eyes.

"You did amazing." Unable to resist, she pressed her lips to his, tasting the fresh mint of toothpaste on his breath.

"You were right about the poison samples," he said when they broke apart. "You can see it all over his face. How'd you know Castor was lying about them being at the office?"

"He has a tell." She allowed herself to gloat, just a little. "I knew he was holding back in our first little tête-à-tête, so I watched him closely the second time. When he lies, he swirls his drink."

"I'm impressed, but . . ." Dallas wrinkled his nose. "If he was lying about the poison, how do you know he wasn't lying about everything?"

"I don't. Not for certain. But I have a sense for people . . . I don't know how to explain." She shook her head. "Castor's an egotist, and withholding a key piece of information in order to maintain his power position—something he could use later as leverage—would be irresistible to him. He was bragging when he told me how he secured the hidden computer data, but he gave away the location of the poison for nothing, and it made me suspicious."

"And Brand?" Dallas pressed. "What if the poison *wasn't* at his home? Or what if it was, and he keeps it there? What if he moved it to a bank or something?"

"No chance. Addison is too paranoid to let something that valuable outside of his immediate control. He's not Petrenko, and his home can't compete with corporate security; he'll pick the place where he can guarantee the strongest safeguards, and that's Manning."

"You've really thought about this."

"I've thought about nothing else." Scooping up a bag from where it rested beside the door, she said, "By the way, I have something for you, too."

Dallas made a face when he saw what it was. "Is this really necessary?"

"If you still want to come with us, it is."

"Of course I'm coming, I just . . . is everybody getting one, or—"

"Just you." Off his disappointed look, she added, "It's your first job. You've never faced what we're about to face, and I don't know what your strengths and weaknesses are yet. I'm sorry if this feels like training wheels, or like I'm doubting you, but it eliminates a variable I can't predict, and . . . I have a thing about that."

"You're the boss," he acknowledged. Then, carefully, "You know Brand's going to be ready. I told him you were planning to strike next week, but he won't drag his feet."

"No he won't." Margo squeezed her fists until her knuckles popped. "I still have connections, and I know how much he's escalated security since you met. It tells me he's definitely moved the evidence there, anyway."

"And it's now or never?"

"It'll only get harder." She glanced at the time. "Speaking of which, we should head out before Friday night traffic throws our whole schedule off."

They climbed the stairs, following voices and laughter to a large bathroom with wide mirrors and bright lights. There, four boys stood, stripped to the waist, their faces half-painted and their hair pinned beneath stocking caps. Music played as they applied their makeup, but you could barely hear it over the quips and comebacks, over a camaraderie as sharp as knives and tighter than a fist. Margo watched them with a pang of jealousy; she led the team, but she would always be an outsider to this secret sisterhood.

"We're taking off," she finally said, and a hush fell over the group. The boys looked up at her, their eyes dramatic—but still understated, *thank God*—and she projected a confident smile. "You guys know the drill."

Axel nodded back—solemn, determined. "See you on the other side."

* * *

THEY TOOK LAS VIRGENES TO THE 101, AND THEN HEADED east along the Valley, Dallas's SUV as quiet as a tomb. In the dark silence, Margo sent up a silent prayer, asking a creator with whom she wasn't wholly familiar to let her father know what she intended to do that night. She hadn't even visited Harland's grave, for fear of Petrenko's men staking it out.

What if they failed? What if she couldn't read people as well as she thought? *When he lies, he swirls his drink.* Reginald Castor wasn't LA's only egotist.

But her "sense for people" wasn't all magic and guesswork, either. Years of observing Harland taught her how to read intentions and body language; her martial arts training had honed an instinct for identifying weaknesses and strengths; and seeing her mother rise, confident, from a bad marriage had taught Margo to trust herself.

She was right. Her plan would work.

The SUV stopped suddenly, and she glanced up with a jolt, realizing they'd reached their destination. An aviation tower, slung with lights, rose behind a low building in front of them, and a tiny jet lifted noisily into the twinkling sky. To their right, blades churning with a rhythmic thud, a helicopter waited on a stretch of tarmac—the pilot a friend of Dallas's from all the time he spent jumping out of airplanes.

"This is it, you know." Margo's mouth was dry. "This isn't your fight, and you've already helped more than I could ever repay. I won't hold it against you if you back out."

"Margo—"

"No, listen, please. It's the point of no return, right? The boys and I are on a hit list, and this is our way off it; it's my responsibility to get us off it, since I got us on it in the first place." Then, with the coppery tang of vengeance in her throat, she added, "I also owe a debt to Addison Brand. But you don't owe anybody anything, and if you want to wish me well and leave—"

"Margo. I'm not going anywhere." Dallas gripped the steering wheel. "I . . . there's a million reasons I could walk away, but I haven't felt this alive in ages, and it's a feeling I've missed." He looked over at her. "And then there's you. I've never dated anyone that makes me feel the way you do—who makes me feel like it's okay to not be 'normal.'"

Margo leaned forward. "Are we dating?"

He laughed out loud. "I hope so. I mean, that's what I'd like, if you're into it." Reaching across, Dallas ran his fingers through her loose blond hair. "Seems like our timing is always screwed up, and bad shit keeps getting in the way, but . . . Eagle Rock wasn't enough for me. Not even close." Grinning crookedly, he said, "I'm doing this for you, but it's for me, too. I'm doing it because I can't imagine *not* doing it. I'm all in, Margo Manning. No matter what. Let's go snatch victory from the jaws of defeat."

The helicopter beat its steady rhythm, lights flashing from the aviation tower, and Margo looked up at the boy she was falling for. "You've got a deal, Dallas Yang."

They hurried across the tarmac to the helicopter, ducking when they neared the blades, and clambered aboard. Strapping in as the aircraft lurched into the sky, they watched the Valley fall away—a river of lights that flowed between black velvet hills.

41

VIVALDI'S STRINGS FILLED THE CAR, PLASTERING over a tense silence as Davon drove the boys toward Bunker Hill. He'd boosted a low-profile sedan, something forgettable, swapping its plate for one with lots of sevens on it. He wasn't superstitious, but the number was supposed to be lucky, and it sure as hell couldn't hurt.

Tonight they'd eschewed their Technicolor manes for wigs in natural colors. Davon's lace-front was black and wavy; Axel's was a fall of loose curls in chestnut brown; Joaquin's was an auburn cascade trailing past his shoulders; and Leif's was ash blond, sleek and severe. The skirts and dresses they wore were business casual, and from a distance, they looked like four boring office workers.

Which, of course, was the entire point.

On Grand Avenue, Davon slowed, turning in at the entrance of the Manning Tower parking garage, and stopped beside an electronic reader. Lowering the window, he swiped the key card Margo had gotten from her op-tech genius. The gate grumbled open, and they drove down a ramp into the bilious, golden embrace of underground safety lights.

* * *

JUST AS THE GATE WAS SLIDING SHUT AGAIN, A DARK HELICOPTER thudded across the dome of night sky over Bunker Hill. It made a lazy circle, the bright streets dizzyingly far below, before finally hovering some five hundred feet above the landing pad that crowned the Manning spire.

Quickly, Margo and Dallas checked the straps on their parachutes, donned their goggles and helmets, and stepped to the helicopter's open door. The landing pad seemed ridiculously small, but there was no time to linger or second-guess; with their static lines clipped into place, they exchanged a brief nod—and then jumped into the air.

Margo's chute snapped open, the harness biting into her groin and underarms, and she gripped the controls that would guide her descent. The helicopter pulled away, its drone fading and vanishing, swallowed by the roaring updraft of wind. Below, the rooftop closed in, rushing at her with astonishing speed—and when she touched down, the impact drove the air from her lungs. Pulling the cutaway handle to release the canopy as a precaution, she just managed to reel it in before it blew off into the night.

Dallas landed a few seconds later, his chute collapsing behind him, and they convened before a square metal structure that rose up from the flat surface of the roof. Removing his goggles, the boy grinned, eyes aglow. "Ready to crash the party?"

"I'm Margo Manning," she returned, tossing her blond hair with exaggerated insouciance. "I'm always ready to party." Activating her comm, she announced, "Miss Anthropy and guest in place. Liesl, Dior, Electra, Anita: What's your twenty?"

After a moment, Axel's voice came back. *"In place and approaching the elevators. All systems are go, Miss A."*

From her utility pack, Margo pulled out a small black box—a miniature EMP, identical to the one they'd used on the LAMFA job—and turned to a heavy door set into the metal structure before them. Guarded by an electronic locking mechanism, it opened onto a staircase leading into the building. Fixing the micro-charge in place, she activated it and pulled Dallas a few feet away.

There came a dry *pop* and the crackle of dying energy, and then silence. Stepping forward, Margo tested the door, and it opened without resistance. Through her comm, she said, "Ready, set, go."

THE PARKING DECK WAS A GRIM, OIL-STAINED MAZE OF CON-crete and sulfurous lighting, and the clatter of high heels echoed like rain on a tin roof as the boys headed for the elevator to the lobby. Set in an alcove that glowed beneath a strip of fluorescent bulbs, two sets of double doors bore a painted P1—Parking, first level. A bubble of black plastic bulged from the ceiling, betraying a surveillance camera, and Axel licked his painted lips. "Game faces on, girls."

Heads down, they began to laugh and gesture as they came within range of the camera, their steps languid. Upstairs, there were three armed guards in the lobby—two more than usual, after hours—and, having received an alert when the gate to the parking deck opened, all of them would be watching the surveillance feed from the garage. The monitor would show four women, tipsy from drinks after work, returning to the office.

Davon pushed the call button and the doors opened. Their charade continued for the short ride up—a pantomime of conversation performed for an electronic eye—while Axel slipped both hands into his shoulder bag. His blood quickened, his breathing slowed, and he found his center. He was the only one getting off when they reached the lobby, and if he failed in the task before him, the game was over; the other boys would retreat and escape, while Margo and Dallas recalled their helicopter. As for himself...

Joaquin's eyes were on him, he realized, nervous behind an

artfully subtle cut-crease effect; and Axel forced a confident smile that was almost genuine.

The car slowed, the bell dinged, the doors slid apart . . . and time slowed.

Axel stepped off the elevator, swinging two guns free from his shoulder bag as he strode into the lobby. One guard had already been on his way to intercept them, with a second just behind, the third remaining seated at the reception desk before a bank of security monitors—and a button that would activate Manning's silent alarm.

Surprise dawned on the faces of the two guards closing in, the whites of their eyes showing as they noticed the weapons; but Axel fired before they could react. Tranquilizer darts streaked across the lobby, one hitting the second guard just beneath his hip and the other plunging into the seated man's shoulder as he tried to twist away.

The pistols could only hold one dart at a time, and with the first guard already snapping open the holster at his hip, there was no chance to reload; tossing his weapons to the floor, Axel lunged forward, slamming his forehead into the bridge of the man's nose. The guard staggered back, eyes rolling, and the boy launched an outside crescent kick that sent him crashing to the floor. Quickly, then, he removed a third dart from his purse and plunged it into his dazed opponent's backside, letting the drug drain into his bloodstream.

Four seconds after the elevator bell had rung, all three guards lay sprawled on the floor, and Axel stood over them, his breath a soft shush that filled the marble atrium.

The fifty-fifth floor, at the very top of the sky-scraper, commanded the building's most stunning views. For this reason, it was reserved for conference rooms and exhibition space, where both investors and journalists could be dazzled by LA's sun-soaked sprawl.

Now, the sun down and the rooms vacant, the floor was sepulchral as Margo and Dallas emerged from the stairwell by the elevator bank. The carpeting underfoot absorbed sound like a black hole, their footsteps silent as they made their way to an unlocked conference room. The nighttime city filled the wall of windows behind the elongated table like a cyclorama of fairy lights in the darkness.

Margo was eyeing a large vent in the wall when her comm came to life, Davon's voice crisp and professional. *"Lobby secured. Phase One complete."*

"We're on fifty-five," Margo replied softly. "We'll check back soon."

They wasted no time unscrewing the grate, slipping on rubber knee and elbow pads, and climbing into the metal shaft that channeled fresh air between the floors. The breeze sweeping up from below lifted Margo's hair, chilling the sweat on her neck and making her shiver.

IN FULL VIEW OF THE STREET, THE LOBBY HAD BEEN AN unavoidably high-risk place to take down three guards; and no matter how quickly Axel had managed it, Joaquin knew that they were as good as fucked if anyone passing by had seen it happen. His heart beat so hard he could feel it in the roof of his mouth as they hustled the unconscious men into a supply closet—stripping off their uniform shirts, cuffing them, and taping their mouths shut.

Leif disassembled the firearms, emptying their bullets into the trash and tossing the slides, barrels, and other parts into a mail chute. Slipping on one of the guard's shirts, a peaked cap resting atop his glossy black wig, Davon took a seat behind the console.

From the street, he'd look like the guard on duty: bored and waiting for the night shift to end. Into his comm, he reported, "Lobby secured. Phase One complete."

Dressed in another guard's shirt and hat, Axel swept the chestnut curls out of his face and held up the downed man's key card. Before he'd give it to Joaquin, however, he made the boy meet his eyes. "Are you ready?"

"I can do this," Joaquin replied tightly, annoyance sparking to life in his gut—but Axel surprised him with an honest smile.

"I know you can do it," his brother said. "I asked if you were *ready*."

"I am," Joaquin promised. "And Leif's got my back. We'll be fine."

"I know. I know." Axel still wouldn't relinquish the card. "I just . . ." He cleared his throat, and—to Joaquin's surprise—his eyes started to fill. "I want you to know how proud I am of—"

"Ohmygosh, Axel." Joaquin's throat closed, pressure building immediately behind his own eyes. "Are you kidding me? Don't do this right now."

"I have to." His brother sucked in a shaky breath and swept a tear from his false eyelashes. "Whatever happens tonight, I need you to know that I'm proud of you. I'm lucky to have you as my brother—and my drag sister, too. I know I've been a shit, and I'm sorry. When this is over . . ." He took another deep breath. "I'll help you unenroll from Somerville. I know you hate it there, and you deserve to go where you want to."

"Seriously?" Joaquin stared, suddenly grateful for the deadly peril they were in. "In that case, fuck it." He snatched the plastic card from his brother's hand. "Let's see them *try* to kill me. I made it through two years at Somerville—dodging bullets will be a cakewalk."

"Be careful," Axel called after him as the boy scurried for the elevators that accessed the rest of the tower. "I love you!"

"STOP EMBARRASSING ME!" Joaquin shouted over his shoulder. He jumped onto the first open car, Leif beside him, swiping the key card and pressing the button marked forty. Just before the doors closed, though, Joaquin called back, "I love you, too!"

The elevator shut, jolted, and surged upward. As his stomach dropped, he reached for Leif's hand. Their fingers laced together, Joaquin closed his eyes and smiled.

THE REVERSE SCREWDRIVER MADE QUICK WORK OF THE VENT one floor down, and even though the burn had barely started in her thighs and shoulders, Margo still breathed a sigh of relief as she climbed out of the shaft. They were fifty-four stories above the ground, and the column plunged straight down for at least a hundred feet before it bent again.

She found herself in an abandoned corner office on the executive floor, stripped clean of its furnishings. The fixtures were dusty, the carpet indented where a desk once stood, and a faint, woodsy aroma still lingered in the air. A pair of booted feet swung through the vent then, and Dallas slid into view, dropping to the ground.

"That was kinda fun," he remarked, peeling off his rubber pads. "Like rock climbing, but without the rocks. I still say you should have let me go first, though. I'm a lot bigger, and if I'd slipped, I could have landed on top of you."

"Who says having you on top of me isn't part of tonight's plan?" Margo parried with an innocent smile.

An animal glimmer flashed in Dallas's eyes, and she could have sworn actual sparks climbed up her arms when he took a step closer. Adrenaline pumping, their senses were heightened and the usual magnetism that drew them together had been dosed with electricity. The danger was intoxicating, and with some difficulty, Margo took a step back.

After a long moment, Dallas turned and took in the room. "Where are we?"

"This used to be Brand's office." She looked around the barren space, not even a scrap of paper left behind. Where had it all gone? Harland's office had seemed practically unchanged when she'd confronted Addison there two months earlier. It was as if the man had cast off his old skin and tried to step right into her father's.

A strip of light showed under the door to the hallway, and Margo crossed the room, pressing her ear to the jamb. Voices, male and overlapping, reached her from somewhere outside. Knuckles flexing, she spoke into her comm again. "Okay. Begin Phase Two."

Behind a locked, steel-reinforced door on level forty, in a room kept at a frosty temperature around the clock, were the servers that supported the computer network for Manning Tower. The beating heart of a hand-built empire, it housed a universe of sensitive information, and Addison Brand had been determined to protect it. While beefing up other security protocols, he had also hired an extra armed guard to watch the server room after hours, just one more added precaution against an expected break-in.

That night, lost down an internet rabbit hole of conspiracy theories about the death of James Forrestal, the US Secretary of Defense who mysteriously fell from the sixteenth story of a naval hospital in 1949, the new guard almost believed he was hallucinating when he heard the sharp *ding* of an elevator arriving at his floor.

The padded walls and acoustic ceiling tiles gobbled ambient noise with frightening efficiency, so the chime of a bell was more than startling. Half the lights were off, shadows plying their trade against vacant workstations along one side of the extensive corridor that stretched from the server room to the elevator alcove—

where a thin slice of light spilled into the hallway, as if one of the bays stood open.

"Hello?" the guard called after a long period of unsettling silence. "Anybody there?"

No answer returned, but the light remained; and when the quiet stretched out like taffy, growing stickier and refusing to break, he stood. "Hello?"

The silence only got louder, and nerves tickled the back of his neck. Finally, he slid the pistol from his holster and began creeping down the hall, wondering if he should be calling for backup— wondering if he'd ever live down calling for backup because no one answered him when he said "hello."

Reaching the elevator bank, his eyes went wide.

Sprawled across the floor was the body of a young woman, lying half in and half out of an open elevator. Dressed in a charcoal skirt and lavender blouse, her ash-blond hair was a thick tangle obscuring her face.

Dropping to one knee, the guard put his hand on her arm. "Miss? Miss! What happened? Are you okay?"

When the body sprang suddenly to life under his touch, he was caught completely by surprise.

THE ADVANTAGE TO ACOUSTIC TILES IS THAT THEY'RE EASILY lifted out of place; the disadvantage, beyond just how ugly they are, is that they're also precariously insubstantial.

The second the elevator door opened, Leif boosted Joaquin up, allowing the trained acrobat to dislodge one of the fiberglass and vinyl squares and hoist himself into the dusty space above the ceiling grid. Despite his light weight and slim build, the boy still had to cling to metal and PVC pipes that zigzagged around the lighting fixtures to keep from plummeting through the flimsy tiles to the hallway below.

He could hear the guard calling out as he inched along, could picture his boyfriend on the ground in the alcove, waiting for a man with a gun to come find him. It made Joaquin's stomach twist into an ice-cold pretzel, but he kept pushing forward. Access to the server room required a level of security clearance they couldn't duplicate, so their only hope of getting in was for Joaquin to bypass the door entirely and drop in from the ceiling.

And he would. If his sweaty grip on the pipes didn't give out before he got there.

"Miss? Miss! What happened? Are you okay?"

Vaulting into action, Leif flipped over, legs swinging. Drawing on a decade of ballet and eighteen months of interdisciplinary martial arts training, he snatched at the guard's gun hand while simultaneously wrapping his thighs around the man's neck. Nothing strengthens your quads and adductors like endless hours of barre, pliés, and pirouettes—and simply by flexing his muscles he had the man's oxygen supply cut off immediately.

Eyes bulging, the guard fumbled for control of his weapon, but Leif had the safety blocked with his thumb; bucking and squirming, the man struggled to breathe, eyes growing glassy and unfocused as his scrabbling fingers slowly lost their strength.

Leif didn't want to go too far. In an ideal world, he'd have a dart pistol to play with; but Margo had only been able to obtain three, and they were needed elsewhere. So instead, he waited until the second the guard's eyes rolled back, his body slumping into unconsciousness, and then released his hold on the man's neck.

"Server guard is down," he reported into his comm, zip-tying the man's wrists and ankles together. The guy was breathing deeply, face slack and limbs heavy, and Leif carefully stripped his weapon down and scattered the parts around the fortieth floor.

He was just finishing when a deafening wail split the air.

THE SECOND HE KNEW THE GUARD WAS OUT OF COMMISSION, Joaquin abandoned the concept of stealth entirely and began slithering through the ductwork as fast as he could. By the time he reached a spot above the server room, he was sweaty and breathless, his green dress ruined. His arms aching from the journey, he carefully lifted one of the ceiling tiles and peered into the room below. A gust of blessedly cold air rushed up to greet him, and he almost groaned with relief.

"*I see you,*" Davon cooed into his ear. "*Nice work, Anita Stiffwon.*"

Leaning down through the opening, Joaquin scanned the room—the rows of hulking processors, great boxes of metal that hummed and blinked—until he found the surveillance camera, and gave it a little wave. And then he froze. Past the camera, mounted to the wall and flashing a lazy, red light, was a small, square panel. It was half light switch, half bike reflector, and all bad news. Hissing into his comm, Joaquin forced out, "Motion sensors."

"*What?*"

"There are motion sensors in the server room!" Now that he'd spotted the one, he quickly found two more. "How come nobody mentioned this?"

The line was silent for a moment, and then Margo's voice returned. "*I didn't know. They might be new, or . . . well, Castor's the only one who could have warned me, and he's clearly got his own agenda.*"

"*So what now?*" It was Axel. "*Do we abort?*"

"No." Joaquin surprised himself with his determination. "We'll never get another shot at this. Dior, is this anything you can control from down there?"

"*Sorry, girl, but I have access to the cameras and that's it.*"

There was a longer silence, and then Margo spoke. "*We knew there was a chance we'd trip over one of Brand's security measures, and we knew this would be a tight window.*" She sighed. "*I can't be objective about this. It's up to you guys if—*"

"I'm going in," Joaquin decided—and before anyone could change his mind, he swung his legs through the gap in the ceiling and dropped to the floor.

Before he even touched down, the alarm started to howl.

42

THE ALERT WASN'T CONFINED TO THE FORTIETH
floor; sirens whooped on the executive level as well, and the cohort of armed men outside Brand's office at the other end of the hall raised their voices to compete with it.

"Shit!" Margo exclaimed under her breath. "*Shit.*"

"*Hey, Miss Anthropy?*" Davon's words came through her earpiece. "*The outside line is blowing up down here, and your pals on fifty-four are demanding an explanation over the shared frequency. What's the play?*"

"Don't answer," she replied immediately. "Stay by the monitors as long as you can, but be ready. The windows down there are bullet-proof, and when the cops get here they'll establish a perimeter first, so we still have some time."

"*I . . .*" Davon exhaled. "*Not my favorite thing to hear, but okay. Roger all that.*"

"Margo, are you sure?" Dallas arched a worried eyebrow. "You could tell the police it's a false alarm, and, like . . . trick the guards into heading for the wrong floor or something. It could buy us some extra time."

She shook her head. "That's not the police on the outside line, it's an off-site monitoring service; *they'll* notify the cops, and unless Davon or Axel can produce the current password out of thin air, nothing they say over the phone will stop that from happening." Margo jerked a thumb at the door. "As for the rented guerillas out there, we'd get two minutes, tops, before they realized they'd been tricked. There are six guards up here and three sweepers making rounds throughout the building; that's more than enough to cover forty *and* fifty-four, while more armed dudes go guns-blazing into the lobby."

And if they regained control of the monitors, all of them would be sitting ducks.

"Our best chance is for Dior and Liesl to go defense, and you and me to go offense," she stated, loading the third dart pistol. "You up for that?"

Cracking his knuckles, Dallas answered with a wolfish grin. "I'm feeling pretty offensive tonight. Let's rock and roll."

"Would you *please* stop pacing?" Seated before the security monitors, Davon spoke through clenched jaws, his expression studiously casual while he fitted a pair of brass knuckles onto one fist. "You are wearing me out, girl!"

"Oh, I'm sorry. Turns out shrieking sirens aren't great for my anxiety!" Axel replied tartly. He'd been stomping nervous laps since the alarms began, and over Davon's shoulder, he could see action unfolding on the tiny screens—his little brother searching for the right server, Leif dragging the body of an unconscious guard, armed men in different parts of the building barking into their radios. "I just wish we were *doing* something, you know? Besides waiting around for ex-military dudes to come down here and open fire, I mean."

"We *are* doing something." Davon gestured at the matrix of camera feeds. "We're the all-seeing eye!"

Axel couldn't resist a glance through the massive windows fronting Grand Avenue, at the traffic that swept past—waiting for police lights to come paint the street red and blue. They weren't even remotely "all-seeing," and Axel's stomach twisted into knots that would have confounded a sailor as he thought of all the ways things could still go wrong.

Shutting his eyes, he blew out some air. He was trying to be more positive. If he'd gained nothing else from his visit to Terminal Island, he'd at least realized that where he'd thought clinging to anger had strengthened him, it had done the opposite. His new goal was to reject negativity. But still. "I just wish we were fucking shit up! You know how much I hate sitting around and doing nothing."

"Would you stop saying that?" Davon shot him an indignant glare. "Whenever some dumbass in a movie says, 'I wish things were more exciting,' all the shit hits the fan!"

As if on cue, the walkie-talkie resting on the console sparked to life, a tinny voice echoing through the atrium. "*Sweeper team: Lobby's not answering their radio, and we can't raise Espinosa on level forty, either. Two of you need to head downstairs, and one of you better check those servers. Guns out, boys; expect trouble.*"

With a withering look, Davon crossed his arms. "Happy now?"

"You know something?" Axel perked up as he pulled Margo's retractable baton from his shoulder bag, extending it with a flick. "I kind of am."

His king-sized mattress was from Hästens, and was without question the most comfortable thing he'd ever laid down on. It had been ridiculously expensive, but every time he brought someone home he could brag about the horsehair stuffing, hand stitching, and the Swedish royals who refused to sleep on anything else. It made the one-hundred-and-sixty-thousand-dollar price tag worth it.

But for all that, Addison Brand hadn't slept peacefully in more than a month. It turned out that once you started poking at your choices and checking for sore spots, you found them everywhere. And the pain was horribly addictive.

At the time, allowing Margo Manning to fuck off to Italy had seemed a wise move. Harland's death was still making headlines, and if she'd died so soon afterward, it would have invited sensationalism. There'd have been news specials, books, maybe a TV movie. But she was just another airhead socialite, and he had her cornered—or so he'd believed.

Now he couldn't stop thinking he should've had her killed after all, drowned her in a canal or arranged a deadly mugging—or simply handed her over to that bloodthirsty maniac, Petrenko. Now he'd waited too long. She was back in town, planning a coordinated move against him, and for the first time in his life he felt vulnerable.

Once more, Addison cursed himself for pouring that glass of whiskey. He'd been so giddy about Harland's collapse, so proud of himself for the plan that was finally paying off, that he'd gotten cocky. He'd fed Margo the same poison that killed her father because it pleased his sense of perversity, and now he was paying for it.

When the Yang kid told him Margo knew the remaining samples of the toxin were in his home, he'd nearly choked. Someone was feeding her information, and until he knew for certain how much had been said—and by whom—he was caught in a wretched spiral of self-recrimination. She had to die.

Repeatedly, he had considered destroying the poison, but always balked. The day was approaching when all of Harland's people would be purged from the company and only loyalists would remain; when scientists he trusted could analyze the toxin, determine how the genetic targeting worked, and re-create it—for the highest bidder.

The electronic chime of a phone call pierced the thin membrane of his restless, fitful sleep, and he jolted upright. Instantly he knew. It was a full week early, and yet without even glancing at the display, he knew who was calling and why.

"Yes?"

"Mr. Brand? This is Kelly, from Sloane Security and—"

"*I know who it is.* What's happened?"

"An alarm has been activated at Manning. My computers show a motion sensor was tripped roughly two minutes ago, and several guards cannot be reached over the radio. The police have been notified, but—"

"I'll be there as soon as I can."

"Mr. Brand—sir, I would strongly advise against your heading to the scene until we have more information. We still don't know—"

He terminated the call abruptly, ignoring Kelly's words, and heaved a few deep breaths. *Margo.* Of course. Of course that surf-rat Yang kid had lied to him. *Of course.*

Dropping to the floor, he pulled a box out from beneath his expensive bed and popped it open. He wanted to be there when the police learned Margo Manning was the burglar. He would be Johnny-on-the-spot with a dazed tale of her violent and grief-fueled visit to his office—maybe embellishing it a little with some off-the-wall threats and accusations. And he would deliver it tearfully, while standing over her dead body.

From the box, he withdrew his nickel-plated Luger and made sure it was loaded. Then his gaze drifted to the window, through which he had a clear view of the Manning Tower. While that pretentious dullard Harland had insisted on living in Malibu,

Addison had taken a penthouse apartment in a building in the heart of downtown, minutes from the office. If he hurried, he might even beat the police.

Tonight, Mad Margo had a date with Death.

BACK AGAINST THE WALL, MARGO LOOKED DALLAS IN THE eye. "Ready? We only get one try, so I hope you've got a strong arm."

He grinned. "Remember how long I held you up while we were in that kitchen—"

"Let's not talk about the kitchen," Margo interrupted hastily, warmth once again flooding the pit of her stomach. "I can't afford to be distracted right now."

"Oh? Thinking about our little *liaison* distracts you?" He pronounced "liaison" with an exaggerated and deliberately terrible French accent, and Margo had to clap a hand over her mouth to keep from guffawing out loud. "You know, I've been working out since then, and I bet I have even more stamina—"

"Stop, I'm begging you," she gasped through her fingers. "Let's focus on getting not-killed first, and then maybe later we can talk about how much stamina you have."

"Okay." He sighed a little, examining the pair of black plastic cylinders he held in his hands. "But I'm telling you, it's a lot. Like when your favorite song comes on in the club, but it's a remix, and the intro goes on for like thirty minutes before they get to hook? That's me. I'm the extended dance remix of boning."

Margo had to put both hands over her mouth this time. "Why . . . *why* . . . is this . . . turning me on?"

"Because girls like when guys talk dirty?" Dallas swiveled his hips. "I'm so good at boning they gave me an honorary degree in forensic archaeology. I'm so good they call me Napoleon *Bone*-aplenty. And I hope you don't like boneless chicken wings, because—"

This time she put her fingers over his lips, her shoulders shaking with silent laughter. When she could breathe again, she said, "I'm so good that scientists measure bone density on a scale of Margos."

And then they were kissing, giggling into each other's mouths while the alarms squalled, and it was totally inappropriate—and very perfect. Finally, forcing herself to stop, she murmured, "Get those grenades ready to fly, Napoleon, because it's go time." Into her comm, she announced, "Dior, we're about to move. What's it look like out there?"

Davon's voice came back a moment later. "*Six men, armed like Robocop, but right now they're huddled up in the outer office, so the coast is as clear as it's gonna get. I'd hang out and watch, but . . . we're about to have company.*"

"Go. And watch your backs, okay?" Turning to Dallas, she said, "Now."

When the door opened, she dove out headfirst, somersaulting across the hallway to take cover behind a wall on the opposite side. Dallas followed, and together they crouched beneath a metal fuse box, listening carefully. Voices floated in the distance, strangled by the alarm, and they waited a sweaty eternity to find out if they'd been spotted.

When no footsteps came pounding down the hallway, Dallas slipped out from their hiding spot. Peering around the corner, heart thumping at the base of her throat, Margo watched him prance up the corridor, his footsteps obscured by the siren. She could see the entrance to the outer office, where Harland's assistant used to sit—where Brand's men were even now debating their strategy for handling the intruders.

Hunkering behind an upholstered partition that had once been someone's workspace wall—before Addison Brand had the executive floor emptied out—Dallas activated the cylinders in his hands.

Rising up, he hurled them through the air, end over end across the abandoned cubicles, until they landed in the assistant's office.

A shout came up from the guards, and Margo ducked back, yanking open the fuse box to reveal the breakers that controlled the power for the floor. As the cylinders detonated, with an ear-popping *bang* and a coruscation of fierce light that rippled across darkened windows, she slipped her night vision sunglasses into place. The explosives were stun grenades, nonlethal incendiaries designed to cause temporary blindness and auditory distortion—to render the private security team disoriented for just long enough.

Flicking her optoelectronic filters on, Margo snapped the breakers shut, plunging the fifty-fourth floor into darkness.

For some unknown and frustrating reason, the computer servers were identified with nonsequential serial numbers, and it took Joaquin forever to find the one he needed. By the time he plugged his portable touch screen and storage drive into the right ports, urgently entering commands, even the chilly air wasn't enough to stave off his nervous sweat.

It was almost impossible to comprehend the vastness of the data stored on the Manning mainframe. Stashed in one tiny corner of the mind-boggling network were the tiny ones and zeroes that would unveil Brand's secrets and Petrenko's complicity. Two birds with one stone—and all they had to do was get out of the building alive.

With no time to search for individual files, Joaquin instructed the system to copy all of Castor's data to his portable drive. As the request was processed, voices chattered in his earpiece—Margo and Dallas preparing to launch their assault, while Davon and Axel readied for an invasion of the lobby—and he flexed his hands compulsively. A window popped up on his screen, and the boy's heart plummeted into his stomach.

Files transferring. Time remaining: 5 minutes.

Five minutes. With an involuntary twitch, Joaquin turned to the windows, LA's bright lights making a mockery of nighttime. The police would have been notified by now, and they wouldn't waste time. They could reach the building before the transfer was complete—and then the media would begin to arrive.

Looking back at the touch screen, Joaquin tightened his hands into trembling fists, anxiety needling its way up his veins and boring straight into his heart.

THE GUARD WHO BURST FROM THE STAIRWELL ONTO THE fortieth floor was named Calfo. Breathing hard, gun already out, his face was sweaty from climbing the steps at a near sprint. The elevator alcove was empty, and from it he could see a small reception desk and the partitions of cubicles on either side. The floor was a hive of cramped workstations, and one of the few overhead fluorescents that remained lit after hours was flickering.

Calfo had trained to use his weapon, but he'd never actually exchanged fire before, and didn't know how he felt about it; he'd chosen private security work because it sounded exciting and the money was good. Now, rushing headlong into a potentially dangerous situation with no backup, he was starting to wonder if the money was good *enough*.

Steadying his gun, he took a deep breath and jumped clear from the alcove.

One-two, he checked both directions, looking down the barrel of his weapon, but there was no movement—anywhere. No one cowered behind the reception desk, and the cubicles he could see had nothing in them but shadows. At the far end of the carpeted corridor, however, just outside the server room, a shape lay motionless on the floor.

A shape dressed in a uniform exactly like his own.

"Espinosa is down!" Calfo barked hoarsely into his radio. "I repeat: Espinosa is down, and I don't see the intruder!"

There was no answer, and after a confused moment of waiting, the man swallowed a lump in his throat and started down the hallway. Espinosa's body was contorted awkwardly—face to the wall, legs bent, hands twisted behind him like they'd been tied—and whenever Calfo passed an open cubicle, he thrust his gun into it, just in case.

When he reached the bend in the hall where Espinosa lay—just before the door marked SERVER ROOM—he checked carefully around the corner, to find that stretch of corridor empty as well. Apart from the unmoving body at his feet, Calfo was completely alone. Holstering his weapon, he got to his knees, and reached for the fallen guard's pulse.

To his shock, the body came alive under his touch, flipping over. Espinosa's peaked cap fell off, revealing a cascade of ash-blond hair, and the face that looked up at Calfo was one he'd never seen before—strikingly beautiful and elaborately made up. With bright blue eyes and a perky smile, the person who was definitely *not* Espinosa trilled, "Surprise!"

Before Calfo could get his fingers back on his gun, a pair of muscular thighs clamped tightly around his neck, and his wrist was pinned in an iron grip. His head throbbed as the pressure built, panic stoking his oxygen-starved lungs, and he stared in helpless wonder at the exaggerated beauty of his assailant.

As his brain fogged over, just before he lost consciousness, Not-Espinosa said, "Sorry about this. No hard feelings."

THE TWO MEN DISPATCHED TO THE LOBBY—REED AND Barnett—reached the ground floor just as Calfo was succumbing to Leif's sleeper hold. They'd run down more than twenty stories, and when they burst out through the door at the back of the eleva-

410

tor alcove, they were winded and on edge. The lobby was dark, illuminated only by light cast in from the street outside, long shadows stretching over marble tile and potted plants.

Their ragged breaths echoing in the still air, Reed and Barnett slowly eased into the open with their weapons drawn. To the right, the lobby extended and turned a corner, where additional doors opened onto an adjoining plaza with a food court and some shopping; to the left, it stretched into the waiting area, where the reception desk sat empty. Even from where they stood, they could see that all the security monitors had been switched off, their screens black.

"You check over there while I get the monitors back on," Reed decided.

Barnett balked. "Shouldn't we check over there together? I mean . . . where *is* everybody?"

"If we split up, we cover twice as much ground and make it harder for them to escape." Reed started for the desk. "Backup's coming, and they're probably not even down here anymore anyway. Don't be such a pussy."

Barnett finally conceded, moving reluctantly for the opposite end of the atrium just as Reed reached the console. The shadows loomed more heavily by the desk, movement beyond the towering windows tickling his peripheral vision, unnerving him. His hands were jumpy as he searched for the power switch and flipped it on.

Lights blinked to life, and the grid of screens went from black to deep gray before populating one by one with feed from all over the building—empty corridors and vacant workstations, the inside of an elevator, a lonely break room. Then the feed for the lobby came up, and to his amusement, Reed saw himself on one of the monitors, leaning over the desk, his face lit by the grouped screens . . . the darkness behind him shifting and changing as something took shape: a face with a great mass of curly hair and a pair of sunglasses.

Gasping, Reed spun around, raising his gun—but he was too slow. The woman was already swinging something at him, and it cracked against his wrist before he could aim. He yelped, the weapon jumping from his fingers, and he stumbled back into the desk. The woman advanced, her lips generous and bright red, her expression implacable, and Reed opened his mouth to shout.

With breathtaking speed, she spun, slamming a foot into his chest with so much force it lifted him clean off the ground. Emitting a gurgled yelp, Reed flipped backward over the desk and crashed hard to the stone floor, the air driven from his lungs.

Woozy and racked with pain, he struggled to right himself, to get up while he still could; but his body resisted, his lungs throbbing, and by the time he managed to sit up, he was facing the business end of a dart pistol.

"Night-night," the woman said. And she pulled the trigger.

BARNETT HAD ALREADY ROUNDED THE CORNER, BEGINNING his unhappy check of each darkened hiding spot on the north side of the building, when his partner's surprised gasp resounded through the glass and stone lobby. Reversing course, he hurried back, clearing the turn just in time to see Reed flip over the console and land with a loud smack. Through the dense shadows, he could just make out a figure with curly hair and dark glasses circling the desk, aiming a gun at his colleague.

"Night-night," the woman intoned, voice echoing.

Barnett shouted, but he was too late; the woman was already pulling the trigger, the weapon making a strange *thwack*, Reed jerking and falling to the floor. The assassin spun toward Barnett, but not before he was able to get his firearm trained on her. "*Drop it! Drop the gun!*"

The woman hesitated, but complied, casting it away with a loud clatter. Barnett began to close the space between them—a long journey that he took with careful steps, in case this killer had any surprises in store.

"Get down! Hands behind your head!" He ordered. Breathing hard, he was trying to remember takedown protocol as he passed one of the stone-paneled support columns; and with his attention laser-focused on the curly-haired assassin, Barnett was taken completely by surprise when a second figure lunged out from behind the pillar.

A Black woman in a blue dress slammed her foot into the back of his knee, dropping him to the floor. With a sharp cry, Barnett pulled the trigger by accident, the explosion booming through the lobby like a rocket launch, the bullet punching the safety glass of the windows. His attacker drove a fist adorned with gleaming brass into the tendon above his elbow, and the fire that burst through his nerve endings stole all the feeling from his arm.

The gun dropped from his unresponsive right hand, and Barnett scrabbled desperately for it with his left; but he had no time. There was a *click*, followed by the high whine of electricity, and he barely registered the woman's stun gun before its metal teeth touched his neck. His body lit up with an agonizing *snap*—and then everything went dark.

43

DISORIENTED BY THE FLASHBANGS, BRAND'S small, private army was less of a threat—but by no means incapacitated. Men spilled into the corridor, stumbling crookedly and falling to the carpet, weapons out as they shouted to one another. For now, they were holding their fire, not knowing who or what they might hit—but soon they'd start to panic.

And there was always the chance that one or more of them might have managed to take cover before the grenades detonated.

Three guards were in the hallway, and Margo sighted them through her optoelectronic lenses, their eyes rendered shiny and inhuman by the night vision filter. Kneeling, she took aim with her dart gun and opened fire. The first two shots were bull's-eyes—the men panicking when they felt the impact, then quickly slumping over as the concentrated sedative took effect—but the third dart missed, and she fumbled to reload.

She hit the target on her second try, but an uncomfortable sensation squirmed beneath her skin. With limited time and resources, Dr. Khan only had been able to produce a small quantity of the fast-acting anesthetic Margo needed, and her supply of darts was crucially limited. There were still three men left, and she could only afford one more error.

Loading the pistol with a precious fifth dart, she crept down the corridor with Dallas at her heels. The last guard was resisting the drug, his fingers moving sluggishly on his gun, and adrenaline drove skewers through Margo's chest when he found the trigger. Signaling to Dallas, she stopped cold, precious seconds escaping until the man went limp at last, succumbing to sleep. Finally, they completed their advance, and she pressed her back to the wall for a moment, letting her heart slow; then she signaled to Dallas again, and ducked through the doorway to the outer office.

The first thing she saw was the barrel of a gun—aimed at her face—and she barely managed to lunge back in time to avoid the bullet that tore a grapefruit-sized hole in the partition behind her. Diving to the floor, Margo and Dallas rolled into the thick shadows of the corridor, breathing hard. At least one man had escaped the effects of the stun grenade.

Frantically, the pair debated strategy with a series of rapid hand signals, until—with a sharp nod—Dallas lifted a gun from one of the unconscious guards. Angling it around the doorway, he squeezed off three ear-splitting shots at the windows, bullets smashing through the panes, orbital fractures creating webs of moonlight in the glass.

The guards in the outer office hit the floor, instinctively ducking live fire; while, simultaneously, Margo took aim through the massive hole in the partition, finding the gunman and putting a tranquilizer dart into his leg.

Dallas fired two more bullets into the ceiling as Margo scuttled back into the room, taking out the two remaining men and then disarming them.

Wind whistled through holes in the glass, harmonizing with

the alarm, and fifty-four stories down they could see the flashing red-white-blue parade of cop cars streaming their way. They were just starting for the office door when they heard footsteps in the corridor, and when two figures dashed into sight through the doorway, Margo had her last dart loaded and ready to fire before she realized who it was.

"Don't shoot!" Axel threw his hands up. "We're just burglars!"

"Burglars who didn't announce themselves over the comm," Margo clarified with a disgruntled huff, lowering her weapon.

"Sorry about that," Davon said contritely. His lipstick was smeared, and Margo had a feeling the pair of them had been distracted on the ride up from the ground floor. "Good news is, the lobby guards are down and I disconnected the feed to the monitors. Bad news is, I didn't have a chance to disable the elevators."

"It's okay." Margo dug the electronic picklock from her pack and headed for Brand's office door. "We're all running a little behind."

Axel's eyes bulged. "You haven't gotten in there yet?"

Before Margo could respond, more footsteps sounded in the corridor, and then Leif and Joaquin appeared. They were breathless, eyes bright, their clothes disheveled—and like the other two boys, didn't seem remotely aware of how much they'd smeared their lipstick while getting it on in the elevator.

"I have it!" Joaquin declared proudly, brandishing the external hard drive. "I copied everything and did a spot check. There are *tons* of files on here, but we got all of it!"

"Good work." Margo beamed at him before turning back to the keyhole, the mechanized pick working the tumblers. "Head for the roof. Our ride's coming back in a few minutes, and we need to be ready to go the second it touches down."

It was an order, and with four precise nods, the boys vanished into the hall, heading for the elevator bank. Seconds later, the lock released with a *click*, and the door opened.

To his grit-toothed glee, Addison *did* manage to beat the police to the tower—but only just. They were one block behind him, sirens keening as they raced for Bunker Hill, and a feeling of power suffused him as drivers cleared his path. He wondered what the cops thought of his glossy Porsche going ninety, ninety-five miles per hour, expanding the gap between them.

All he needed was a few precious seconds to reach Manning first—to get inside before a cordon was set up. He needed to find Margo before anyone else.

His tires hugged the pavement like a lover as he shrieked onto Grand, and he decelerated to a sudden but graceful stop before the card reader to the underground garage. When the gate opened, he sped through, the metal clanging back into place only a half second before the first police cruisers streamed into view behind him.

The office was exactly as she remembered: the neat desk and cushy chairs, the bar cart with its fancy crystal glasses—and, on the wall behind Brand's ergonomic chair, the oil painting in its hinged frame. Fingers itching with anticipation, Margo swung it open, revealing the hidden safe and its electronic keypad.

And just like that, her excitement curdled into something cold, disbelief wrapping around her throat. Turning, eyes wide, she barely managed to say, "Dallas."

He looked from her to the safe, registering what she'd seen, and the color drained from his face. "That wasn't there before. There's no . . . it wasn't there!"

Beside the electronic keypad, wired into the locking mechanism, was a small sensor plate. A fingerprint scanner. Brand had added a secondary security mechanism in the past week, and Margo had no plan for getting around it.

For a moment, the room spun, the feelings inside her too intense for her body to contain. Rage, despair, and self-recrimination pulled her into three pieces, and she staggered a few steps backward. With a shout of fury she spun around, sweeping her arms across Brand's desktop and hurling its contents to the floor; next she launched the man's overpriced, ergonomic chair—her *father's* chair—at the windows; and then turned to the bar cart, with its fragile, expensive, and very smashable crystal cups.

"*Margo!*" Dallas rushed forward, grabbing her shoulders. "Stop—I, I know this sucks, but we've accomplished so much already. We got everything off the server, which should be enough proof—"

"It's not!" she shouted furiously. "We don't even *know* what's on the server! I have no idea how much of Castor's story I can believe; all I know is that without the actual toxin, I've got nothing but a fairy tale." Even if one of Brand's emails showed the man bragging outright about killing Harland with a genetically targeted poison, all he'd have to do is challenge the court to prove that such a substance existed. No one could. "I need to get into that safe!"

"You can't." He was gentle, but firm, trying to meet her eyes. "It's over."

But she was still looking at the bar cart. "It's not." Facing him at last, she said, "According to my estimate, we still have roughly four minutes before helicopters start to arrive. Head to the roof, but give me that much time."

Dallas blinked. "Are you kidding?"

"Not even a little. I think . . . I think I have a plan."

"Margo—"

"I'm serious," she said adamantly. "Four minutes. If I can't pull it off in that window, I'll give up. I promise. But you have to let me try."

"Then I'm staying with you."

"No. You're not." Margo gave him a grateful look. "Dallas, I can't tell you how much it means to me that you've been by my side throughout all this—that you tricked Brand, that you jumped out of a fucking helicopter with me . . . but the original plan had you out of danger by now, and that's where I want you; I told you before that this is my fight, and you have to let me make this call."

He still hesitated, looking miserable. "This is one of those situations where you're the boss and I have to do what you say even if I hate it, isn't it?"

"Yes." She nodded, but not without sympathy. "I'm afraid so."

"Okay." He fought a smile onto his face. "For the record? I hate it. But I'll see you on the roof." Reluctantly, he turned and started out the office door. Just before he vanished into the shadows, he called over his shoulder, "Four minutes or I'm coming back for you!"

"No you're not!" she shouted, but he was already gone.

She turned back to the bar cart. Two glasses stood separate from the others, their insides coated with a thin film of sticky amber residue. One showed traces of lipstick, and the other didn't, but both were smudged all over with fingerprints. Her brain clicking like the tumblers in Brand's lock, Margo reached out with gloved and greedy hands.

THE POLICE WASTED NO TIME BLOCKING OFF GRAND AVENUE, cruisers arriving every few seconds. Some idiot was already shouting through a megaphone, his voice distorted and jarring as it bounced down the parking ramp and reverberated off the concrete walls. Addison set his teeth, skulking through the shadows, avoiding the elevators—visible from the street—and hurrying for the stairs instead.

He didn't think he'd been seen, and he'd long since shut off his phone, putting himself out of reach of the security service, the cops, and the media. Everything he'd worked for hung in the balance. He would find Margo, he would kill her, and then maybe he would check his voice mail.

When the elevator opened, Margo stepped out into a sterile, half-lit waiting room, a space that felt bleak and haunted. Past the small reception desk, a sturdy gray door bore a familiar placard: AUTHORIZED PERSONNEL ONLY BEYOND THIS POINT.

The lab.

She knew what she needed to get into Brand's safe. The problem was that, assuming the items even existed, they would be inside the laboratory.

From her burner phone, she sent Manning's former chief scientist a text: *Supposing one were at the reception desk, how would one bypass the security protocols and force open the door to the lab? Asking for a friend.*

Moments later, a response came back. *Tell your friend there's an emergency fail-safe. Pull the fire alarm beside the door, then access a program on the computer titled COVENANT. When prompted, enter "countdown" and the door will unlock after fifteen seconds.*

Dots bubbled, an additional message coming in. *Unless everything has been changed. Then I don't know.*

Margo rolled her eyes, nerves frayed; but she booted up the computer, pulled the alarm, and then opened Covenant. When a blank window appeared with a blinking cursor, she typed "countdown" and hit the enter key. Fifteen seconds later, when the door clicked open and the room did *not* fill with poisoned gas, she breathed out a sigh of relief.

Precious minutes passed while she was inside. It took time to locate carbon powder and a fast-setting polymer spray to solidify the ghostly ridges and whorls on the tumbler with Addison's fingerprints; to find tape to lift them cleanly from the glass, solid and intact.

Nadiya's duplicator would have done the job six times faster; but when she at last walked out of the lab, her temples damp and her nerves sparking, Margo had a perfect copy of Addison Brand's thumbprint.

THE HELICOPTER WAS DEAFENING AS IT SETTLED ONTO THE roof of Manning Tower, hurling a furious wind in every direction; and as the other boys tried quite literally to keep their wigs on, Dallas had his eye pinned to the door through which he and Margo had first entered the building earlier that night.

On the ground, the skyscraper was now surrounded by police vehicles, their lights licking hungrily at the windows. It had been more than four minutes. *Where was she?*

The helicopter evened out and Joaquin scurried for it, followed by Leif and then Axel, skirts dancing in the swirling gusts. Davon hung back, his dark eyes filled with the same trepidation Dallas felt in his gut. "Come on, Prince Charming. Our pumpkin's waiting."

"Margo isn't here yet," Dallas stated the obvious.

"I know." Davon's expression was sad as he stepped backward, inching toward their one and only chance at escape. "But that's not the point."

Sometimes, stating the obvious sucked.

REACHING THE DOOR AT THE TOP OF THE STAIRS, ADDISON froze. Through the small, square window, past the lobby, he could see cop cars and policemen in the street outside, their lights splashing garishly against the stone of the atrium. Even as he stood there, another cruiser pulled up—and another, and another. A break-in on Bunker Hill and thirteen unresponsive guards was an event they'd decided to take seriously.

Addison hesitated, shifting his jaw. Unless he wanted to climb endless flights of stairs, he had to take the elevator; and to do it he'd have to enter the alcove in full view of the entire LAPD. Well, fuck it. The only thing that mattered was eliminating Margo without witnesses; he was rich enough now that the cops would believe what he told them to.

The Luger a dead weight in his coat pocket, he shoved the door open, ignoring the response from outside. Officers at the front doors pounded on the bulletproof glass, wide-eyed and barking orders. He didn't even glance in their direction. Jabbing the call button, a grin spread across his face when the bell resounded with an immediate and cheerful *ding*.

LOST IN THOUGHT, MENTALLY REHEARSING HER NEXT MOVES, Margo was taken by surprise when the elevator up from the lab came to a stop with a crisp tone of the bell. The second the doors opened, she lunged out onto the fifty-fourth floor, and sprinted for Brand's office.

The addition of a biometric sensor to the safe's locking mechanism meant all bets were off; even if the reproduced fingerprint actually worked, there was no guarantee the code hadn't been changed, but Margo was ready to believe. She'd done her homework, and she'd recognized the number sequence Brand had chosen—it was the day he started working for Manning. She had his dossier committed to memory, a wealth of significant dates, and she was sure she could do it.

The safe opened on the fifth try, and her pulse tripped like a snare drum as she drew out a small metal case. The lock broke easily, and when she lifted the lid, she found five glass vials full of a clear, colorless solution. Margo's throat closed. This was the substance that killed her father; Brand had ordered it, paid for it, administered it systematically for months—all while she sat by in ignorance.

She took only one of the samples. Leaving the rest was a difficult decision, knowing Brand would eliminate all traces of what remained when he realized she'd gotten to it; but she only needed enough for Nadiya to understand how it worked, to connect it incontrovertibly to the substance found in Brand's whiskey. If he really planned to implicate her in her father's murder, she couldn't risk being caught with the entire supply, when she had no legally acceptable explanation for how she came by it.

She'd have to rely on the fingerprints on the vial, and the communiqués she hoped Castor had been honest about, to chisel Brand's guilt into stone. Returning the case to the safe, she activated her comm. "I'm on my way."

Turning, she rushed out of the office—and stopped short the second she passed through the doorway. Her feet turned to lead and her heart stuttered when, for the second time that night, she found herself staring down the barrel of a gun.

"Good evening, Margo," Addison Brand said, his voice cool, the orbital fractures in the window panes casting spidery, moonlit shadows over his pale skin. "You know, I thought I was very clear during our last encounter that you were no longer welcome in the building."

"I don't like it when assholes tell me what to do," she replied, but the room didn't feel big enough for both her and the gun. "My father could've told you that. But you killed him."

Brand rolled his eyes, bored by the complaint. "Harland should've sent you to a military boarding school. You're just another example of his misguided sympathies, bringing nothing but disgrace and humiliation to the Manning name."

Fire streaked through Margo's veins, stealing the oxygen from her blood. "What the fuck do you even know about the Manning name?"

"*I am the Manning name!*" Addison roared, his eyes flaring. "This is *my* empire now, you smart-mouthed little tramp! Your father was an anchor holding this company to a past that no longer exists, and he battled against every rational move to expand our profits, our influence, our *dominance*! All his silly lines in the sand, throwing good money after bad and jeopardizing our success for the sake of his fossilized principles—"

"You mean like in Malawi?" Margo interjected, hands clammy on the straps of her pack. "Because instead of helping destabilize a sovereign nation and arm *child soldiers*, he wanted to do the right thing?"

"The 'right thing'?" Brand scoffed as if she'd referenced the tooth fairy. "Those mines in Malawi employed hundreds of people, did you know that? Thousands depended on the income from those jobs, but the government got greedy and interfered." He shook his head. "They've all been out of work for months. Manning's productivity has dipped, our costs have risen, and now we have to cut jobs to maintain our profits; and the same is true for a dozen other corporations that rely on the output of those sites! You have no idea how many lives hang in the balance because of Harland's overpriced altruism."

"People are *dying* over there, you sick fuck!" Margo stared at him in disbelief. "All those families? They're in the middle of a war now, thanks to you. You designed a military weapon meant for children, and you're trying to talk to me about lives in the balance?" She wanted to hit him in the face. With a car. "You are literally a war criminal, Addison Brand. You're exploiting the entire population of an economically depressed country so you can increase your profit margins, but you have the gall to lecture me about greed?"

He didn't seem moved by her speech; if anything, his eyes only grew colder and more determined. After a beat, he asked, "Where's the Yang boy?"

"He's gone already." It was sort of truthful. "Sorry."

"I'll deal with him later, then." Brand's tone was ugly. "What's in your bag? What did you take from my office?"

"Nothing," Margo answered reflexively, but her tone was a dead giveaway.

"Hand it over."

"No."

Brand thrust the gun forward, closing another inch or two of precious space between her and the bullets inside. "I'll shoot you if you don't."

"If I know you at all, you're going to shoot me anyway," she countered, her mouth so dry she was surprised her tongue didn't catch fire.

He actually grinned, his teeth pearly and sharp, his hand steady on the Luger's grip. "You *are* going to die tonight, Margo. But if you cooperate with me, it doesn't have to happen right this very second."

It wasn't much of a proposition, but she knew better than to bargain, and way better than to refuse on principle; the satisfaction wouldn't follow her into her subsequently early grave. Freeing her pack—briefly considering the possibility of throwing it at him or over the partition—she tossed it with a *thump* at his feet. There was no sense in attempting some half-cocked Hail Mary; if he even flinched, her head would burst like a piñata.

Crouching down, Brand kept the gun on her while he dug through her things. He turned up the sunglasses, the spent EMP, and the dart pistol. At last he found the poison, drawing the vial free with a nasty grin and tucking it into the safety of his pocket.

Getting to his feet, he leveled the gun with her forehead—and the universe spun like a tornado, tearing Margo's nervous system to shreds as she prepared to blink out of existence.

Her lungs compressed and her eyes slid shut, and Addison Brand said, "All right, let's take a short walk."

THE CONFERENCE THAT TOOK PLACE INSIDE THE HELICOPTER, between four drag queens and a former legal intern, was tense.

"We have to go!"

"We're not leaving without her."

"We're already off schedule, and every second we stay here brings all six of us that much closer to fucked!"

"*Double penetration* fucked! The cops, the media—when they get their birds in the air, they don't even need to catch us; all they need is a picture of our serial numbers and it's game over!"

"She's on her way!"

"*Is* she? I didn't want to be the one, but . . . she should've been here by now."

"We *have* to go—those are her orders. It's what Margo wants!"

"Yeah, well, Margo isn't here."

"I know. It sucks. But if anyone can beat the odds, it's her."

"And if she can't?"

The response was silence.

THE PHRASE "A SHORT WALK" HAD CONJURED A HOPEFUL fantasy in Margo's mind of a rooftop execution. The trip up would give her more chances to turn the tables, and if by some miracle the helicopter was still there, it would be six against one.

But their journey ended at the elevator bank, a rectangular alcove stifled by shadows, the only light coming from a small square window in the door to the staircase. The building was serviced by six lifts, three on one side and three on the other, and Margo's stomach rolled when she saw one set of doors gaping open to expose a pitch-black void.

"Here we are," Brand announced cheerfully. "I was thinking a nice fall down an elevator shaft would be nice. The car for this one is in one of the subbasements, which will give you a few extra seconds to stay alive. I am capable of generosity, after all."

Margo had trouble with her words. "It would be easier just to shoot me."

"Easier, yes. And also harder to explain, and full of possible future unpleasantness if you've put contingencies into place in the event you don't make it out of here—I know how your mind works." His breath was hot and rank against her cheek. "You'd prefer if I shot you, and I would prefer if you had a nice, clean accident. But make no mistake: I could empty my gun into you and still get away with it. Courts love to give guys like me the benefit of the doubt. At least if you do it my way, you go with some dignity."

"That's it?" Margo tried to sound scornful, but scorn was hard to manage with a gun pressed to the base of her skull. "That's your plan? An *accident*? At least if you shoot me you can claim it was self-defense. No jury on this planet will believe that I somehow snuck into the building unseen, took out thirteen men, and then 'accidentally' stepped into a randomly open elevator shaft and fell to my death!"

"To be honest, I'm not looking for constructive criticism." He gave her a hard shove that propelled her almost a foot closer to the elevator's gaping maw. "Jump down that shaft or I'll shoot you in the head."

Margo stared at the black pit that yawned before her, a cold sweat spreading under her clothes, her throat clogged by her heartbeat. It seemed impossible. She'd cheated death so many times in eighteen years that she'd almost believed Death had given up; but now? Two choices and no options: the frying pan or the fire. There was no zip line to safety, no parachute to break her fall.

Now was the time to surprise Addison with a precise kick, to show him what the Manning name *truly* meant—but he was too far away for that. It would be convenient for him if she died with no trace of his involvement, but his eyes had betrayed just how much he was hoping for an excuse to pull the trigger. If Margo so much as shifted her weight wrong, he would shoot; and if she didn't die instantly, the impact might just send her hurtling into the shaft all the same.

She took a step forward, struggling to believe there was still a chance—that maybe she could grab the elevator cable on the way down without it ripping the flesh clean off her hands—and that's when she heard the faint clatter of noise in the stairwell. A shadow passed across the small window, the door crashed open . . . and time split into fragments, a rapid-fire set of images like playing cards being slapped down one atop the other.

Dallas, teeth bared, his leather jacket slicked with gold from the lighted staircase as he lunged into view; Brand, pivoting sharply, surprised and fearful, his finger closing instinctively on the trigger; the deafening report of the gun in the narrow alcove, like lightning striking her eardrums; Dallas flying backward, slamming into the wall beside the door, the impact fissuring the plaster; and then his body sliding limply to the ground.

A howl escaped Margo's lungs, and she finally delivered that precise kick just as Brand was turning back to face her. Her boot caught his gun hand, knocking the weapon free and sending it into the dark. Before he could think to react, she slammed a fist into his jaw, a satisfying pain rocketing up the length of her arm.

Advancing as he reeled, she swung again—but he blocked, retaliating with a hard blow to her stomach that stole her air and left her dazed. Grabbing a handful of her loose blond waves, he pulled hard and forced her head back, stepping close enough that she could feel his spittle against her face as he snarled, "I should've known you were lying about being alone in the building. Now, let's get you into that fucking shaft before the police finally decide to do their jobs."

He started marching her across the floor, pain lighting up her scalp as she fought for some kind of leverage, struggling against the deadly plunge behind her—six hundred feet of greedy darkness, ready to swallow her alive—but her spine was twisted and she couldn't find purchase with her feet. Finally, so close to the edge of the pit that warm air breathed up her back, Margo's fingers found Brand's collar, and she gripped it as tightly as she could.

Hurling herself to the floor, she pulled him with her, bracing a foot against his pelvis at the same time and kicking upward as hard as she could. It was a judo throw—the tomoe-nage—one of the sacrifice techniques she'd studied months ago in that filthy Hollywood motel. His own momentum working against him, Addison Brand had no defense when his body inverted, his legs and hips swinging up into the air. Flipping over Margo's head, he sailed past her, screaming, into the hollow elevator shaft.

She only saw the man's eyes for a moment, realization dawning with a naked display of bright horror before the darkness snatched him and dragged him down, his voice flooding the alcove with a shrieking, terrified echo. Even after the sickening *crunch-clang* of meat against metal far below, his cry survived him—ringing up the empty column to underscore the sound of his grisly death—while Margo lay on the floor of the elevator bank and gasped through her tears.

CURTAIN CALL

MAY COULD BE AN UGLY MONTH IN LOS ANGELES, temperatures spiking before the notorious lull of the June gloom; but the air-conditioning on the top floor of Manning Tower worked just fine, and the windows of the room where Margo was about to hold her first-ever press conference were thankfully tinted.

Standing behind a podium that bristled with microphones, looking out at orderly rows of journalists waiting to hear her speak, Margo struggled to believe that only six weeks had passed since she'd struggled up the stairs past this very floor, desperate for her last chance to escape.

She'd wept openly upon finding the helicopter still waiting when she reached the roof, its blades whipping the night air. Dangerous lights burned on the horizon, the LAPD and the media closing in on Bunker Hill with their own aircraft, and they took off with a nauseating lurch that left her sweaty and shaking in her seat. Arms encircled her—Axel, Joaquin, Leif, Davon—but no one spoke until after they'd landed again, at an anonymous airfield in San Bernardino County where a stolen truck was waiting to take them home.

"I'd like to thank everyone for coming," Margo began, and the microphones shrieked. Her hands shook a little, so she tightened them on her note cards. She was wearing four-inch heels, a short black dress and tailored jacket, her eyelashes false and her hair bleached platinum. *Drag is armor, girl,* Axel had insisted over her objections as he more or less styled her by force, *and you need all the armor you can get.* Clearing her throat, she channeled Miss Anthropy and started again. "Thank you all for coming. I know everyone here is aware—because you've been reporting on it for a month and a half now—that Manning is going through . . . you know, kind of a rough patch." There was some awkward giggling from the gallery, and Margo began to relax. "I'd like to start things off by saying that the company is working in full compliance with the ongoing federal investigation into Addison Brand's crimes, and that we are eager to earn back the public's trust."

Beyond just the news-at-eleven bonanza spurred by Brand's gruesome death and the dramatic infiltration of Manning Tower by a group of daring, still-unidentified women, the morning after the break-in brought a new shock: In the night, a secret informant had sent digital files to every media service in Southern California— as well as the FBI, the LAPD, and the State Attorney General— containing documents, photos, and email chains that spelled out a diabolical conspiracy on behalf of Addison Brand and other parties to commit an impressive array of criminal acts.

"No one was more horrified than me to learn the truth behind my father's death," Margo continued, making eye contact with the reporters in the front row. They still called her Mad Margo; they still labeled her a socialite and a party girl. She was looking forward to shattering their low expectations. "I never anticipated taking a role in the family business this young, and I'm aware of the popular skepticism about my influence over the future of Manning. I'm also aware that our stocks have been jeopardized by recent events, by the revelations of Brand's felonies and the involvement of Arkady

Petrenko—a man with whom this company has collaborated for years on important international projects."

The prurient sensationalism of Petrenko's involvement had proven irresistible to the media; a foreign national with untold wealth and a habit for making enemies, notorious for his rumored ties to organized crime, his name added star power to the ugly scandal. He had been apprehended by federal agents while trying to flee the country, and every day the news reports dug a little deeper into his sordid past.

"I'd like to thank the shareholders who have stood by Manning through this difficult time while we recover and forge ahead in the direction my father truly saw for his legacy." Glancing aside, she blinked a few tears from her eyes, fighting the urge to wipe them away. Axel had put so much makeup on her, she'd end up smearing it all over her face and look like the Hamburglar in the press photos. "He should be here now. I stand in his place because his life was unfairly cut short, taken from him by two men he trusted."

In the immediate aftermath of the break-in, the outrageous conspiracy to arm the rebel uprising in Malawi dominated the airwaves. It was a diplomatic disaster, a crisis of international proportions, and the media had tweezed apart every detail it could for maximum exposure. Then, just as they began to run out of fresh material, another astonishing story emerged: the murder of Harland Manning and the substitution of an artificial will allowing Addison Brand to seize total control of the company.

In another mysterious twist, ten days after Petrenko was arrested, two small packages were delivered—one to Interpol and one to the FBI—containing matching items: a pair of Czarist-era ruby earrings, which had gone missing from a Soviet vault in 1932. The Russian government immediately claimed them as property of the State, and was now demanding the extradition of Arkady

Petrenko, whose fingerprints were the only ones found on the stolen jewelry.

Overnight, Petrenko's attitude toward the feds had gone from obstreperous to cooperative, realizing that he was far better off serving life in an American penitentiary than facing whatever fate awaited him back home. As for his daughter, Valentina had vanished altogether from the public eye, hiding out in Topanga Canyon to weather the storm. There was no way to tell how much information Arkady had shared with his family, and so Margo was privately keeping tabs on the girl and her mother, just in case. She didn't want any ugly surprises.

Meanwhile, an official search had begun for Nina McLeod, although odds were slim to none that the missing nurse would turn up alive—if she ever turned up at all. Brand had been confident enough to boast that Margo, even with all of her considerable resources, would likely never find the woman. So far, his prediction held true.

Taking a breath, Margo flipped her index cards. "The last time I spoke to Addison Brand, he told me that my father had been an anchor holding Manning in the past. I don't agree. But times do change, and companies must change with them, seeking bolder, younger, and more forward-thinking leadership." Agitated murmurs spread through the crowd, and she waited them out before continuing. "For that reason, I have asked Manning's former chief scientist, Dr. Nadiya Khan, to act as custodian of my controlling interest in the company stock until I have completed my education—per my father's final wishes. I am delighted to say that she accepted, and as her first act as chairman of the board, she has confirmed Reginald Castor as acting CEO while a permanent replacement is sought."

Convincing Nadiya to accept the responsibility had been harder than Margo expected. As a scientist, the woman far preferred the lab to the boardroom, and argued like a skilled lawyer that she belonged downstairs. *Put me back in the lab*, she'd demanded, *and let Castor be chairman like your father wanted!* But Margo couldn't trust Castor, not fully, and after much clashing of wills, she convinced Nadiya to accept the position at least until they could find a more suitable candidate, together.

"I'm going to cede the floor now to Dr. Khan and Mr. Castor, both of whom have a few words to say," Margo concluded briskly, stacking her note cards together. From a chair in the back row, a familiar figure stood and moved silently for the exit, meeting Margo's gaze a second before vanishing into the hall.

With a quick thank-you, she left the room, hired security escorting her all the way to the elevator bank. One bay remained out of order, and she tried not to shudder as she boarded one of the working cars and rode it down to the lobby.

He was waiting for her, as she knew he would be, leaning against one of the hefty support pillars. A smile spread across his stupidly gorgeous face as she crossed over to him, and when he wrapped his arms around her, she breathed in his scent for one long moment before pressing her lips to his.

"Ow," he said into her mouth, when her hands became a little aggressive, pawing at the muscles under his shirt.

"Aw, poor baby." Margo gave him a sympathetic frown. "Are you still sore?"

"Am I still *sore?*" Dallas blinked with mock affront. "I got *shot* in the *chest!*"

"I remember that. I was there when it happened," she pointed out. "But that was, like, six weeks ago. Haven't you healed yet?"

Dallas narrowed his eyes. "This is about sex, isn't it? You're mad because the doctor said I should avoid strenuous activity, and that means we can't bone."

"Your mouth did write a whole lot of boning checks that your ass has so far refused to cash," she acknowledged, "but mostly I'm just sorry for you that it still hurts."

"Yeah. Turns out that cracking your ribs in, like, sixty places at once kinda sucks."

Margo gave him a smart look. "Bet you're glad I made you wear the training wheels now, aren't you?"

Dallas shook his head. "You are the only person I know who would refer to bulletproof body armor as 'training wheels.'"

Her one condition for his joining the team had been that he wear a Kevlar vest the night they broke into the tower. Knowing that the two of them would be advancing on at least six armed men, down a long and narrow corridor with no decent cover, she wanted to do everything possible to increase their odds. The only reason she hadn't worn body armor as well was because it was difficult to obtain untraceably.

"If you hadn't been wearing it, you'd be dead right now," Margo reminded him. "And if you'd done what I'd told you, you wouldn't have been shot in the first place."

"And if I hadn't gotten shot, *you* would be dead right now," he countered smugly. "So everything worked out."

What sucked is that he was right, and she couldn't argue back. If he hadn't come through the door exactly when he had, drawing Brand's fire, Margo never would have managed to turn the tables. She still sometimes woke up at night in a cold sweat, heart pounding from a familiar nightmare: the bullet or the drop. Which would she have picked in the end?

"You are the only person I know who could get shot in the chest and call it 'everything working out,'" Margo retorted, but in a second she was kissing him again, his hands hot and firm on her waist.

"So, Margo Manning." His breath was soft against her bottom lip. "You just saved the world, avenged your father, and reclaimed your birthright. What are you going to do next?"

"Well. Starbucks has this new Frappuccino I've been afraid to try," she murmured back, earning a laugh.

Truthfully, she wasn't sure how to answer. She still had a lot of work to do with her tutor to finish her graduation requirements, and she'd decided to take a gap year once she'd earned her diploma. Even with Brand dead and Petrenko behind bars, she wasn't fully out of the woods. There was no reason to assume the Russian billionaire had relinquished his private vendetta, and so—for a time, anyway—it made sense not to commit herself to an easily tracked schedule. Even under lock and key, the man could find a way to get to her.

"Honest answer?" Taking Dallas's hands, she stated, "I'm going to graduate, I'm going to spend some time with this cute guy I like, and I'm going to get to know a little bit more about Margo Manning. Starting with a volunteer stint at a certain clinic that doesn't technically exist."

When Margo finally reached his side that night in the tower, Dallas's skin had been ashen, his breathing labored, and she'd all but dragged him to the roof of Manning Tower. He'd lost consciousness in the helicopter, and it was clear he needed immediate medical help; but an emergency room would ask questions they couldn't answer, and so there was only one person Margo could count on.

Irina had been furious, frantic, and delighted to be called into action. Through her connections at the underground clinic, she managed to get Dallas through the back door at a small hospital, where he was examined and treated—his injuries officially attributed to "collision with the steering wheel" during a single-car accident.

That made it twice that Irina and her clinic had come through when Margo needed help the most, and she wanted to repay their goodwill. Washing instruments and helping schedule appointments, or whatever she was asked to do, seemed like very little in return.

"I definitely like that part about spending time with a cute guy," Dallas told her, wiggling his eyebrows a moment before freezing. "Wait. You are talking about me, right?"

"Obviously, you narcissist. I mean, I do spend a lot of time with other cute guys, but none of them are into me." She gave a helpless shrug. Then her phone buzzed, and she straightened up, giving him a quick kiss on the lips. "But before I do any of that stuff, I'm going on a short vacation, and I do believe my ride is outside."

"Wait, you're leaving for a vacation *now*?" he protested as she started for the lobby doors. "What am I supposed to do while you're gone?"

"Recuperate!" She flashed him a brilliant smile. "I expect a full subscription to *Bone Appétit* magazine when I get back."

"But when will that be? And where are you going?"

Pushing the door open, sunlight streaming around her, she offered a coy response. "I'll send you a postcard."

Blowing him a kiss, she turned and scampered down the shallow steps in front of Manning Tower, to a long, black limousine that waited at the curb. As soon she was inside, nestled into the leather cushions, the driver took off and pulled into traffic.

The tinted windows were no match for the fierce sunlight beating on the glass. Margo squinted against the glare until a hand reached across from the bench seat opposite her, offering a pair of dark glasses. "Here you go, girl."

Margo slipped them on, sighing with relief. "Thanks."

Another hand reached out. "Champagne?"

"Don't mind if I do." She accepted the flute with a smile.

Yet another hand. "And here's your giant fucking bag. Thing weighs as much as I do."

"Don't be a bitch," Margo replied good-naturedly. "It's heavy for a reason." She looked across at the four people sharing her limo— Joaquin, Leif, Davon, and Axel—and felt the current in the air. "There's a few million dollars worth of Russian jewels in there."

With her father dead and her mother half a world away, Margo had finally realized something obvious: These four boys were her family. As were Irina, Georgia, and Jacinta. She didn't know what she'd do without any of them. On impulse, she'd asked all of them to move into the mansion with her, and was giving them time to decide. It was a bold and weird idea, but somehow she knew it could work.

"We're still trying to move that shit?" Davon arched a brow from behind his own sunglasses, gesturing at Margo's heavy bag. "Didn't we decide it was too hot to handle?"

"That was before Petrenko was in custody, and before I found a crooked jeweler in Geneva and fences in Paris and Málaga who can sell off at least some of the merchandise." She took a sip of champagne, the bubbles tickling her nose. "We'll keep some of it in loose stones, of course. Better than currency."

"What the hell does *that* mean?" Axel frowned.

Simultaneously, Leif perked up. "We're going to Europe?"

"We're going to Europe," Margo confirmed, "and what it means is that we'll have to obtain certain things while we're over there, and cash won't always be the best collateral."

"That's not an answer," Davon pointed out, "and you told us all to bring our 'drag stuff' on this little getaway, so I'm waiting for the other stiletto to drop here."

Margo turned to her window—watching people pass on the sidewalk, sunlight bouncing off high windows. "You're right. I'm planning another job. This one's also personal, so if you just want to hang out in Europe for a couple weeks and then bail—"

"Please!" Joaquin interrupted. "You know we're all in. Just tell us what the target is."

Her chest swelled. Of course they were in. They were family: Anita Stiffwon, Electra Shoxx, Dior Galore, Liesl von Tramp, and Miss Anthropy.

"Somewhere in an offshore laboratory there's a scientist who took money to design the poison that killed my father." She lifted her champagne, watching as sunlight turned the bubbles into fireworks. "I want revenge."

ACKNOWLEDGMENTS

In November of 2016, my editor at Feiwel and Friends, the incomparable Liz Szabla, replied to one of my emails with the following sentence: "I just peeked at the WIP doc and saw 'jewel-thieving drag queens'—I might be all in based on that phrase alone!!" If it weren't for her enthusiasm and willingness to take a chance, this book wouldn't be in your hands. Thank you, Liz, from the bottom of my fabulous, kickboxing heart, for wanting this story as badly as I wanted to write it.

I would truly be up a creek without a paddle if it were not for the perpetually steady hand and patient guidance of my agent, the magnificent Rosemary Stimola! You keep making my dreams come true, and I know exactly how lucky I am because of it—thank you. And on the subject of dreams coming true, I could not ask for a better publisher than Jean Feiwel. Every time we meet, you make me feel like family, and I hope the experience is mutual. Thanks for everything, and especially for letting me shout "I'm a three-times published author!" when I'm throwing my weight around.

There is no greater team than #TeamMacmillan, and every day the folks who work there prove it. Brittany Pearlman keeps me organized (and entertained!), and no one can talk me down from the ledge like Molly Ellis; Ashley Woodfolk is as brilliant at marketing as she is at writing; and Kim Waymer, Mandy Veloso,

Allison Verost, and Jon Yaged make the winds blow that fill these sails. I'm lip-syncing a heartfelt ballad of gratitude to you all!

I gathered inspiration from a lot of places for this novel: heist comedies like *The Pink Panther* (1963) and *How to Steal a Million* (1966); cheeky, candy-colored action flicks like *Modesty Blaise* (1966) and *Charlie's Angels* (2000); and Alfred Hitchcock's final film, *Family Plot* (1976), in which Karen Black robs a jewelry store in high drag. I revealed none of this when I turned in my pages, and yet Rich Deas—senior creative director for Macmillan Children's Publishing Group—reached *right into my very soul* and pulled out the vibrant, mod/pop influences that made this story, and put them on its cover. No one can convince me that he is not a wizard. Rich, thank you *times infinity* for your breathtaking work.

2017 and 2018 were, and I cannot put too fine a point on this, extremely difficult years in which to write, and I want to thank everyone who helped me get through them. Celeste Pewter: I can hardly begin to express the appreciation you deserve for the incredible and important work you do. You've helped me stay focused and balanced, and reminded me I can still make a difference, even when things are ugly. My profound thanks to you and the entire Road to 2018 crew.

To the Real Housewives of YA—Adam Sass, Kevin Savoie, and Phil Stamper: Where would I be without you bitches? I'm glad I'll never know. Thank you for listening, for advice and comfort, for laughing every time I use that react of the old lady at the computer, and for being my friends. It's energizing to be part of a foursome so boring I become the Samantha by default!!

In the past two years, I've given a lot of digital real estate over to talking up civic engagement to my followers. Your elected officials draw a salary to serve your interests, so call yr reps and tell them what your interests are! Do it every day! And here, dear reader, is where I thank everyone who has done exactly that these past two years—but especially: Jennzah Cresswell, Jonathan Goldhirsch, Emily Howald, Emery Lord, Maureen Meadows, Alex Rich, Anna Wetherholt, and Carmen from YA Wednesdays. Keep fighting the good fight!

To Tapani Salminen and Erkki Mäkelä: You two are our family in Finland, and I need to thank you once again for your boundless generosity and unqualified friendship. I wrote the first half of this book in the apartment on Hämeentie, an aerie that gave me respite from a pretty remarkable amount of stress. Suurkiitokset!

Endless thanks to Kristin Cast, Cale Dietrich, Karen M. McManus, and Kara Thomas for their support and friendship; thanks to Mitali Perkins, Jennifer Mathieu, and Anna-Marie McLemore for an idyllic Fierce Reads tour; and my everlasting gratitude to book-world superheroes Dahlia Adler, Jennifer Gaska, Eric Smith, Nena Boling-Smith (and Langston and Agent Auggie!), Erin Stein, Rachel Strolle, Katie Stutz, Danielle Stull-Meisner, Shelly Zevlever, and Kelly and Christy from BookCrushin. You guys have all helped make this past year a little bit better. (And Rachel—you helped me figure out an aspect of Margo's identity that had been eluding me, and I am super grateful!! ♥)

A shout-out is called for to Ian Carlos Crawford, who is a good friend, who cohosts an amazing podcast (check out *Slayerfest98!*) and who has offered to do a Thing for me. Even if it doesn't pan out, you have still earned a lifetime supply of band candy!

My friends have been my safety net this year. Grant and Kasey Myers: We had so much fun with you guys in the Valley in 2017, and we miss you; Gwen Mesco and Afsheen Family: No thanks in the world can encompass our gratitude for helping us escape to Northridge from our own private hell for a while; Natalie Furlett: You opened your home on a moment's notice so I could fly across the country and search for apartments—and look where we are now! Angela Parrish: I MISS YOUR SILLY FACE. Angela Hopwood

Manning Ferrara didn't turn out to be quite the Janice Dickinson I envisioned when I set out to write this book, but I hope you're not disappointed!

To my family, from coast to coast, from sea to shining sea—and then across those seas and clear on till Europe: I love you guys!!

In the summer of 2017, a fire broke out at Grenfell Tower in North Kensington, West London. In the tragic aftermath, agent Molly Ker Hawn and author Harriet Reuter Hapgood arranged a charitable auction—Authors for Grenfell—that raised over £180,000 for the survivors. (Thanks to them for this incredible initiative!) The item I submitted was "have a character named after you in Caleb Roehrig's third novel!" and the winner of that bid was Ryan Labay! Ryan, that contribution helped make a difference in someone's life, and I'm grateful that both of us played a part in it. I'm sorry your namesake turned out to be kind of a jerk, though!

Uldis: I'm writing this seven years to the day after we stood in an apple orchard on an island in Lake Champlain and took a great big step together. It amazes me when I think of how many adventures we've had since then, and how many more await us in the future. Condragulations, you are the winner of this book's challenge! Es tevi mīlu, Ulditi.

Thank you for reading this FEIWEL AND FRIENDS book.
The Friends who made

DEATH prefers BLONDES

possible are:

Jean Feiwel
PUBLISHER

Liz Szabla
ASSOCIATE PUBLISHER

Rich Deas
SENIOR CREATIVE DIRECTOR

Holly West
EDITOR

Anna Roberto
EDITOR

Kat Brzozowski
EDITOR

Val Otarod
ASSOCIATE EDITOR

Alexei Esikoff
SENIOR MANAGING EDITOR

Kim Waymer
SENIOR PRODUCTION MANAGER

Anna Poon
ASSISTANT EDITOR

Emily Settle
ASSISTANT EDITOR

Mandy Veloso
PRODUCTION EDITOR

Follow us on Facebook or visit us online at mackids.com.

OUR BOOKS ARE FRIENDS FOR LIFE